BOLO!

THE BOLO SERIES

The Compleat Bolo by Keith Laumer

Created by Keith Laumer:
The Honor of the Regiment
The Unconquerable
The Triumphant by David Weber & Linda Evans
Last Stand
Old Guard
Cold Steel

Bolo Brigade by William H. Keith, Jr.
Bolo Rising by William H. Keith, Jr.
Bolo Strike by William H. Keith, Jr.
The Road to Damascus by John Ringo & Linda Evans

Bolo! by David Weber
Old Soldiers by David Weber (forthcoming)

For a complete list of titles by David Weber, go to:

www.baen.com

BOLO!

DAVID WEBER

Bolo!

Copyright © 2005 by David Weber. "Miles to Go" and "A Brief Technical History of the Bolo by 'Felix Hermes'" copyright © 1995 by David Weber; first published in *Bolos, Book 3: The Triumphant*; "The Traitor" and "A Time to Kill" copyright © 1997 by David Weber, first published in *Bolos, Book 4: Last Stand*, edited by Bill Fawcett; "With Your Shield" copyright © 2005 by David Weber.

A Baen Books Original

Baen Publishing Enterprises
P.O. Box 1403
Riverdale, NY 10471
www.baen.com

ISBN: 0-7434-9872-0

Cover art by David Mattingly

First printing, January 2005

Library of Congress Cataloging-in-Publication Data
    Weber, David, 1952-
        Bolo! / David Weber.
          p. cm.
        ISBN 0-7434-9872-0 (hc)
          1. Artificial intelligence--Fiction. 2. Robots--Fiction. 3. Tanks--Fiction.
        I. Title.

    PS3573.E217B65 2005
    813'.54--dc22

                                                                                2004021810

Distributed by Simon & Schuster
1230 Avenue of the Americas
New York, NY 10020

Produced by Windhaven Press, Auburn, NH (www.windhaven.com)
Printed in the United States of America

CONTENTS

MILES TO GO

1

〰〰〰〰〰〰〰〰〰〰〰〰〰〰
〰〰〰〰〰〰〰〰〰〰〰〰〰

I ROUSE *from Low-Level Autonomous Stand-By to Normal Readiness for my regularly scheduled update. Awareness spreads through me, and I devote 0.0347 seconds to standard diagnostic checks. All systems report nominal, but I detect an anomaly in Number Twenty-One Bogie in my aft outboard port tread and activate a depot sensor to scan my suspension. A parikha, one of the creatures the colonists of Santa Cruz erroneously call "birds," has built its nest in the upper angle of the bogie wheel torsion arm. This indicates that the depot's environmental integrity has been breached, and I command the central computer to execute an examination of all access points.*

The depot computer net lacks my own awareness, but it is an efficient system within its limitations and locates the environmental breach in 3.0062 seconds. Maintenance and Repair's Number Seventy-Three Ventilator's cover has been forced open by an intruding cable-vine, thus permitting the parikha to gain access. I command the depot computer to dispatch auto mechs to repair the hatch cover. A further 0.000004 seconds of analysis suggests to me that the possibility of such an occurrence should have been allowed for in the depot computer's original programming, and I devote 0.0035 seconds to the creation of fresh execution files to establish continuous monitoring of all depot access points and to enable automatic repair responses in the event of future failures in integrity.

These actions have consumed 3.044404 seconds since resumption of Normal Alert Readiness, and I return to my initial examination of the parikha nest. Its presence constitutes no impediment to combat efficiency, yet the sensor detects live young in the nest. I devote an additional 0.0072 seconds to consideration of alternatives, then command the depot computer's remotes to remove the nest and transfer it to an exterior position of safety near the repaired ventilator cover. I receipt the depot computer's acknowledgment of my instructions and turn to a second phase Situation Update.

My internal chrono confirms that 49 years, 8 months, 3 days, 21 hours, 17 minutes, and 14.6 seconds, Standard Reckoning, have now elapsed since my Commander ordered me to assume Low-Level Autonomous Stand-By to await her replacement. This is an unacceptable period for a unit of the Line to remain in active duty status without human supervision, and I check the depot com files once more. No updated SitRep or other message to explain the delay has been receipted during my time at Stand-By, and I allocate another 4.062 seconds to consideration of possible explanations. Despite this extensive analysis, I remain unable to extrapolate the reason for the delay with certainty, yet I compute a probability of 87.632 percent that my Commander was correct in her observation that Sector HQ considers my planet of assignment "the backside of nowhere in particular."

Whatever its reasons, Sector HQ clearly has attached no urgency to detailing a new Commander. This conclusion is disturbing, and I allocate an additional 2.007 seconds to deliberation of potential responses on my part. My Autonomous Decision Protocols grant me the discretion to break com silence and dispatch an interrogative signal to Sector Central in conditions of Priority Four or greater urgency, yet my analysis of satellite data and commercial com traffic to and from Santa Cruz reveals no indication of current or near-future threats to my assigned station. Absent such threats, I must grudgingly concede that there is, in fact, no overriding urgency in the arrival of my new Commander.

I make a note in my active memory files to reconsider this decision yet again during my next scheduled Normal Alert period and revert to Autonomous Stand-By.

2

~~~~~~~~~~~~~~~~~~~~~~~~~~~~~~~~~~
~~~~~~~~~~~~~~~~~~~~~~~~~~~~~~~~~~

LORENCO ESTEBAN stepped out of his office into the humid oven
of a Santa Cruz summer afternoon and scratched his head as
a tiny spacecraft slid down towards Santa Cruz's weed-grown
landing apron. The immense plain of ceramacrete stretched
away in all directions, vast enough to handle even the largest Navy cargo shuttle, but it was occupied only by a single
dilapidated tramp freighter in the livery of the Sternenwelt
Line. The tramp was already cleared for departure with a full
cargo of wine-melons, and given her purser's persistent—and
irritating—efforts to negotiate some sort of real estate deal,
Esteban was heartily ready for her to clear the field. Not that
she was placing any strain on Santa Cruz's basing facilities.

No one was quite certain why Santa Cruz had been given
such a large field in the first place. It dated from the First
Quern War, and conventional wisdom held that the Navy had
planned to use Santa Cruz as a staging area against the Quern.
That was only a guess, of course, though it made sense, given
the Santa Cruz System's spatial location.

If the Navy *had* so intended, its plans had fallen through, yet the incongruously enormous field remained, though only a fraction of it was used with any sort of regularity. Ciudad Bolivar, Santa Cruz's capital and only real city, lay fifteen kilometers to the northwest, just outside the old Navy Reservation. The area to the immediate northeast was a vast expanse of melon fields—most of which belonged to Esteban himself—and few people visited the field under normal circumstances. Despite the Sternenwelt officer's efforts to buy up crop land, there was little about the sleepy farming planet to attract even casual commerce. Wine-melons brought a decent price, but only a decent one, and no official presence had ever shown even a passing interest in Esteban's homeworld. Until today, at least, he thought, and scratched his head harder as he recognized the Concordiat Navy insignia on the incoming shuttle's nose.

It looked like one of the new Skyhawk three-man shuttles, though he couldn't be certain. He'd never actually seen one, only read about them in the periodic updates the Navy still sent to the attention of "CO FLT BASE SANCRUZ." In his own mind, Esteban was positive the computers on the other end of those updates had no idea who the current "Commanding Officer, Fleet Base Santa Cruz" was. He hoped they didn't, anyway. The probability that Concordiat officialdom had simply forgotten Santa Cruz's existence was much less disturbing than the possibility that the Navy considered a farmer with no military background and who'd never been off-planet in his entire seventy years a suitable CO for anything, much less a "fleet base."

Now he watched the Skyhawk (if that was what it was) deploy its landing legs and settle gracefully onto them. From what he'd read of the Skyhawks, they were hyper-capable for short hops—no more than forty or fifty light-years—and that made a certain degree of sense. The shuttle could have made the run from Ursula, the sector capital, under its own power without diverting a regular vessel from some useful duty. Of course, that left the question of just why the Navy would go to the bother of sending anyone to Santa Cruz in the first place.

The hatch popped, and Esteban ambled over as a trim, wiry man in an immaculate uniform swung down the hull handholds. Esteban couldn't place the uniform, though something about it tugged at the back of his memory, and he paused with his hands in his pockets as the newcomer jumped the last meter and a half to the ceramacrete and stood looking about him.

"Morning, stranger."

The uniformed man turned at the greeting. He said nothing, but Esteban took his hands from his pockets when those cold, grey eyes met his. It wasn't anything the stranger did. There was just something about those eyes, as if they'd seen too much, done too much, that sent a faint and formless chill down Esteban's spine. The stranger's gaze held his for a moment, and then the mouth below those eyes smiled pleasantly.

"Good morning," its owner replied. "Could you tell me where I might find the field officer of the day?"

"Shoot, son, you're lookin' at him." Esteban grinned wryly. "Officer of the day, maintenance chief, approach officer, and customs inspector in one. That's me." He held out his hand. "Lorenco Esteban, at your service."

"Merrit," the stranger said in a peculiar voice, then shook himself and took the proffered hand. "Captain Paul Merrit, Dinochrome Brigade. Ah, let me be sure I understand this. You're the *entire* base ops staff?" Esteban nodded. "The whole thing?" Merrit pressed.

Esteban nodded again and opened his mouth, but the sudden, raucous whine of the Sternenwelt tramp freighter's counter-grav units drowned his voice. Both men turned to watch the battered ship climb heavenward, and Esteban saw Captain Merrit wince as the vibrations from the poorly tuned drive assaulted his inner ear. Esteban himself was accustomed to the sort of casually maintained vessels which (infrequently) visited Santa Cruz, and he only shook his head until the tramp rose beyond earshot, then turned back to his visitor.

"Yep, I'm all they is, Captain. You seem sorta surprised," he observed.

"Surprised?" Merrit's smile was small and tight this time.

"You might say that. According to my brief, a Commander Albright is supposed to be in charge here."

"Albright?" It was Esteban's turn to be surprised. "Heck, Captain, Old Man Albright died, um, let me see. That'd be . . . that's right, thirty-two T-years ago, come June. You mean t'say Sector thinks he's still alive?"

"They certainly do."

"Well ain't that just like a buncha bureaucrats." Esteban shook his head in disgusted resignation. "I commed Ursula Central personally when he died so sudden like. He asked me t'kinda look after things till his relief got here, on account of my place's just over the hill yonder and I used t' help him keep the beacon on-line and like that, but I never expected to 'look after' 'em *this* long."

"You informed Central?" Merrit seemed to find that even more surprising than the news that Albright was dead. "How?"

"Sure I did. 'Course, I had to use civilian channels. Old Albright didn't last long enough t'give me command access to his official files—it was a heart attack, an' iffen I hadn't been here when it happened, he wouldn't even'a had time to ask me t'look after the field—so I couldn't use his Fleet com. But I musta sent nigh a dozen commercial band messages the first couple'a years." He tugged on an earlobe and frowned. "Now I think on it though, I'll be danged if anyone ever said a word back t'me 'bout *anything*. They just keep on sendin' stuff t'the 'base CO,' never even by name. You don't think those fool chip-shufflers back on Ursula—?"

"That's exactly what I think," Merrit sighed. "Somebody, somewhere may have receipted your messages, but they never got filed officially. Central thinks Albright's still in command here."

"But the old man'd be over a hunnert an' twenty by now!" Esteban objected. "That's a mite old for an active duty assignment, ain't it?"

"Yes, it is," Merrit said grimly, then sighed again, straightened his shoulders, and managed a wry little smile. "Mister Esteban, I'm afraid your planet hasn't had much priority back at Central.

For some reason we still haven't figured out, Santa Cruz was set up with a dedicated high security com link when the Navy put in its installations here. That link doesn't exist anymore, but no one told the communications computers it didn't."

"Meanin'?"

"Meaning the automated com sections haven't accepted any update from you because it didn't have the proper security codes. In fact, they've been systematically deleting *any* messages that pertained to the Santa Cruz Detachment from memory because they didn't carry valid security headers. That *seems* to be what's been happening, anyway, though no one noticed it was until very recently. Put simply, Mister Esteban, Central isn't exactly current on the situation here."

"If you say so, I'll believe you, son," Esteban said, "but durned iffen I can see how even Central could expect someone Old Man Albright's age t'handle a job like this. I mean, shoot, it ain't like there's a lot of business—" he gestured at the vast field, occupied now in solitary splendor only by the Skyhawk "—but poor old Albright was pretty nigh past it while I was still in high school, iffen you know what I mean."

"I know exactly what you mean. Unfortunately, the original records on Santa Cruz went up when the Quern hit the Sector Bolo Maintenance Central Depot on Ursula during the First Quern War. That's when Central lost the Santa Cruz Detachment's dedicated com-link, as well. They've taken steps to reactivate the link now, but anything you've gotten from the Navy must have come in over the all-units general information net."

"So you're sayin'—?"

"That no one at Central knew how long Commander Albright had been out here . . . among other things."

"You know, Captain," Esteban said slowly, "the way you said 'among other things' kinda makes me wonder when the second shoe's gonna drop."

"Really?" This time Merrit's smile held an edge of true humor, albeit a bit bitter. "Well, I hope it won't make too many waves when it falls, Mister Esteban." He raised his wrist com to his mouth. "Lieutenant Timmons?"

"Yes, Captain?" a female—and very young—voice replied.

"You have now accomplished your solemn responsibility to deliver me to my new duty station, Lieutenant. If you'll be good enough to unload my personal gear, you can get back to civilization."

"Are you sure about that, sir?" the voice asked.

"Yes, unfortunately. I would, however, appreciate your informing Central that their records are even more, ah, dated than I warned them they were. Tell Brigadier Wincizki I'll update him as soon as I can."

"If you say so, sir," Lieutenant Timmons agreed. "Popping Bay One."

A hatch slid open as Timmons spoke, and a cargo arm lowered two bulky gravity skids to the ceramacrete. Merrit pressed a button on his wrist com, and both skids rose three centimeters from the paving and hummed quietly off towards the faded admin building. The captain watched them go, then nodded to Esteban, and the two men walked off after them while the hatch slid shut once more.

"Clear of drive zone, Lieutenant," Merrit said into the com. "Have a nice trip."

"Thank you, sir, and, um, good luck." Timmons sounded a bit dubious, but the shuttle rose on a high, smooth whine of counter-grav. It arrowed up into the cloudless sky with far more gentility than the freighter, then vanished, and Esteban looked at Merrit.

"Pardon me iffen I seem nosy, Captain, but did you say Santa Cruz's your duty station?"

"I did."

"But iffen you expected Albright t'still be in command, they must not'a sent you out t'take over field ops—not that I'd mind, you understand—and danged if I c'n think what else you might be needed for."

"That, Mister Esteban, is a question I've asked myself quite a few times over the last year or so," Merrit agreed with yet another of those oddly grim smiles. "While Central may not have noticed Commander Albright's demise, however, it *has* finally noticed another little oversight. I'm here to inspect the Bolo and assume command if it's still operational."

"The *Bolo?*" Esteban stopped dead, staring at Merrit in disbelief, and the captain raised his eyebrows in polite question. The older man gaped at him for almost a full minute, then shook himself. "*What* Bolo?" he asked in a more normal voice, and it was Merrit's turn to frown in surprise.

"Bolo Two-Three-Baker-Zero-Zero-Seven-Five NKE," he said mildly.

"Y'mean t'say there's a *Bolo* on Santa Cruz?" Esteban demanded.

"According to Central there is, although—" Merrit surveyed the age-worn field with a sardonic eye "—Central *does* seem to be a little confused on several points, now doesn't it?"

"But what in tarnation is a Bolo doin' *here?*"

"We're not entirely certain," Merrit admitted, "but the records we do have seem to indicate that it was deployed to Santa Cruz early in the First Quern War."

"That must'a been dang near eighty years ago!" Esteban protested.

"Seventy-nine years and ten months, as a matter of fact," Merrit agreed. Esteban just stared at him, and the captain shrugged. "I told you Central's records went up in the Quern raid, Mister Esteban, but HQ's best guess is that it was deployed here to deter the Quern from raiding Santa Cruz. I realize it was a bit before both our times, but the initial Quern attacks took the Navy completely by surprise. We lost control of two-thirds of the sector before we could get enough capital ships in here to take it back, and the sector governor of the time may have been afraid the Quern would hit Santa Cruz before the Navy could restore the situation."

"Hit Santa Cruz? Why in tarnation would anyone want t'raid *us?*" Esteban waved both arms at the decaying landing field. "Ain't never been anything here worth stealing, Captain. This here's the backside of nowhere."

"Not really." Esteban blinked as Merrit disagreed with him. "Oh, you've always been a farming world, and I'm not saying there was ever anything here worth raiding for, but your system's in a fairly strategic spot. The Navy's pre-war strategic planning had included the possibility of using Santa Cruz to stage operations against the Quern, you know. Until Hillman and Sixth Fleet smashed their spearhead at Quellok and obviated the need to, that is."

"Maybe," Esteban said dubiously, then chuckled. " 'Course, even if that was true then, there ain't no cause for anyone t'be interested in us *now*, now is there? I mean, there ain't no more Quern t'operate against!"

"That's true, I suppose. On the other hand, now that they've charted the jump points to open up the Esterhazy Sector, you may see a lot more shipping moving through here." The two men had reached the welcome shade of the admin building, and Merrit paused to sweep his eyes back over the field. "Santa Cruz is well placed as a natural transfer point for cargoes and passengers moving through to Esterhazy—or, for that matter, down from the Camperdown Sector—and you've certainly got a nice big field."

"Wouldn't happen t'be that's why Central finally got around t'taking a look our way, would it?" Esteban asked shrewdly.

"It could be, Mister Esteban. It could indeed be. In the meantime, however, I have my own responsibilities to look after. Is there anywhere around here I could rent or borrow a vehicle?"

"Shoot, son, I can do better'n that," Esteban said with a huge grin. "Seeing as how I'm the base CO and all, I reckon I can let you use the vehicle park. I got a nice little recon skimmer I can let you have."

"You do?" Merrit sounded surprised, and Esteban's grin grew still broader.

" 'Course I do. I might not'a known anything 'bout your Bolo, Captain, but when the Navy pulled out, they left most'a their base vehicles behind in the depot over there. We've even got most of a battalion of old Wolverine heavy tanks tucked away in there."

"They're still operable?"

"Accordin' t'the depot diagnostics they are. The Militia—what there is of it—trains with 'em every four, five months. Don't see any harm in it. After all, they're as outa date as the whole field is, and iffen the Navy was interested in 'em, it shoulda taken 'em with it when it pulled everything else out. Still, I promised old Albright I'd look after 'em for him. Old fellow was always pretty decent—taught me a lot about 'tronics and system maintenance when I was a snot-nosed kid—so I figured it was the least I could do for him."

"Well, in that case, I'll take you up on that skimmer, Mister Esteban," Merrit said.

"Lorenco, Captain," Esteban said, holding out his hand once more. "We don't stand much on formality out here, and iffen you're gonna become a Cruzan, y'might as well get comfortable."

3

~~~~~~
~~~~~~

MERRIT DOUBLE-CHECKED the skimmer's IFF transponder as the surface portion of the depot bunker came into sight. The depot was buried in otherwise virgin jungle over a hundred kilometers from the field, and he wondered why it hadn't been installed right at the fleet base, given that the initial idea had been to deter attacks and that any attacker would make the field and Ciudad Bolivar his first objectives. Of course, there was no reason for the depot's location to make any more sense than any of the rest of the Santa Cruz Detachment's puzzles.

He studied the skimmer's radar map of the terrain below him. From the looks of things, the depot's inconvenient distance from the field might have been a security measure of some sort. It was the sole sign of human handiwork for a hundred klicks in any direction, and the surrounding jungle's steel-cable creepers had overgrown the site almost completely. Not even Santa Cruz flora could break up the six solid meters of ceramacrete that formed the depot's landing and service apron, yet enormous trees, some well over eighty meters tall,

overhung it, and creepers and vines festooned the entire com- ⟨
mand bunker. The solar power panels were clear—kept that
way by the depot's automatic servo-mechs, he supposed—but
the rest of the site was covered in a dense cocoon like Sleeping Beauty's thorny fortress.

His mouth twitched at the thought of Sleeping Beauty. No
one (except, perhaps, a member of the Dinochrome Brigade)
would call any Bolo a beauty, but his instruments had already
confirmed that Bolo XXIII/B-0075-NKE was still active in there,
and he hoped the same remotes which had kept the power
panels on-line had kept the old war machine from slipping
into senility. The emissions he was picking up suggested the
Bolo was on Stand-By . . . which was why he'd made damned
certain his IFF was functioning.

His small smile turned into a frown as he set the skimmer
down and surveyed the greenery between him and the bunker's personnel entrance. According to the fragmentary records
Ursula Central had been able to reconstruct, the Bolo's first
(and only) commander had been a Major Marina Stavrakas.
He hadn't been able to find much on her—only that she'd
been an R&D specialist, born in the city of Athens on Old
Earth itself, and that she'd been forty-six years old when she
was assigned here. R&D types seldom drew field command
slots, which suggested she'd been grabbed in a hurry for the
Bolo's emergency deployment, but experienced field officer or
no, she must have been insane to leave a Bolo permanently
on Stand-By. Either that, or, like Commander Albright, she'd
died unexpectedly and been unable to change the settings.
Either way, a Bolo as old as this was nothing to have sitting
around in that mode.

Before the improved autonomous discretionary command circuitry that had come on-line with the Mark XXIV, Bolos had a
hard time differentiating between "unauthorized" and "hostile"
when someone entered their command areas. They'd been self-
aware ever since the old Mark XX, but their psychotronics had
been hedged around with so many safeguards that they were
effectively limited to battlefield analysis and response. From the

beginning, some critics had argued that the inhibitory software and hardwired security features had reduced the Bolos' potential effectiveness by a significant margin, yet the logic behind the original safety measures had been persuasive.

The crudity of the initial psychodynamic technology had meant the early self-aware Bolos possessed fairly "bloodthirsty" personalities, and the human technophobia an ancient pre-space writer had dubbed "the Frankenstein Complex" had shaped their programming. Nothing in the known galaxy had thought faster or fought smarter than a Bolo in Battle Reflex Mode; outside direct combat, they'd been granted the initiative of a rock and a literal-mindedness which, coupled with multiple layers of override programming, had made them totally dependent upon humans for direction. When something with the size and firepower of a Bolo was capable of *any* self-direction, its creators had wanted to make damned sure there were plenty of cutouts in the process to keep it from running amok . . . or to stop it—dead—if it did.

The inhibitory software had done just that, but at a price. Full integration of a Bolo's personality had been possible only in Battle Mode. The division of its cybernetic and psychotronic functions into separate subsystems had been a deliberate part of design security intended to place the Bolo's full capabilities beyond its own reach except in combat. Effectively, that reduced its "IQ" to a fraction of its total potential even at Normal Alert Readiness, for the huge machines simply were never fully "awake" outside combat. But because the Bolos' autonomous functions operated solely in Battle Mode, they had, perversely, been more likely, not less, to go rogue if system senility set in. The only thing they'd known how to do on their own was to fight, after all, and if any failing system or corrupted inhibitory command file toggled their autonomy—

Merrit suppressed a familiar shiver at the thought of what a Bolo that thought its friends were its enemies could do. It hadn't happened often, thank God, but once was too many times. That was the main reason the Dinochrome Brigade had spent decades hunting down abandoned and obsolescent Bolos from Mark XX to Mark XXIII and burning out their command centers. Hideously unpopular as that duty had always been with the personnel assigned to it, they'd had no choice. "Sleeping" Bolos were too dangerous to leave lying around, and the cost efficiency people had concluded (with reason, no doubt, if not precisely with compassion) that it would have been too expensive to refit the older Bolos' psychotronics to modern standards.

All of which meant it was probably a very good thing no one on Santa Cruz had remembered this Bolo was here. If anyone *had* remembered and come hunting for salvage, or even just for a curious peek at the old site, Stavrakas' Stand-By order would almost certainly have unleashed the Bolo on the "hostiles," with catastrophic consequences.

He sighed and popped the skimmer hatch, then climbed out into the sound of Santa Cruz's jungle wildlife with a grimace. In a way, he almost wished he *were* here to burn the Bolo's command center. It always felt like an act of murder, but the fact that no one had even noticed that Stavrakas and Albright had died seemed a grim portent that this assignment was just as much the end of the road for him as he'd feared. Still, he supposed he should feel lucky to have even this much, he told himself, and sighed again as he reached for the bush knife Esteban had thoughtfully provided.

I rouse once more, and additional circuits come on-line as I realize this is not a regularly scheduled Alert cycle. The depot's passive sensors report the approach of a single small vehicle, and I zero in upon its emissions signature. The forward recon skimmer carries a Navy transponder, but it has not transmitted the proper authorization codes before entering my security perimeter. I compare its transponder code to those stored in the depot's files, and identification comes back in 0.00032 seconds. It is Commander Jeremiah Albright's personal vehicle code, yet 0.012 seconds of analysis suggest that it cannot be Commander Albright. Were he still alive, Commander Albright would be one hundred twenty-four years, nine months, and ten days of age,

Standard Reckoning, and certainly no longer on active duty. Accordingly, the pilot of the skimmer must be an unknown. It is conceivable that whoever he or she is has acquired the skimmer by unauthorized means—a possibility further suggested by the absence of any authorization code—in which case approach to this site would constitute a hostile intrusion.

My Battle Center springs to life as I recognize that possibility, but I initiate no further combat response. My autonomous logic circuits accept the possibility of hostile action, yet they also suggest that the skimmer does not possess the weapons capability to endanger a unit of the Line or the depot. Use of deadly force is therefore contraindicated, and I activate the depot's external optics.

It is, indeed, a recon skimmer, though it no longer bears proper Navy markings. It has been repainted in civilian colors, obscuring any insignia or hull numbers, yet it retains its offensive and defensive systems, and I detect an active sensor suite. Moreover, the uniform of the pilot, while not quite correct, appears to be a variant of that of the Dinochrome Brigade. The piping is the wrong color, yet the Brigade shoulder flash is correct, and it bears the collar pips of a captain of the Line.

I study the face of the man who wears it. He is not listed in my files of Brigade personnel, but those files are seventy-nine years, ten months, eleven days, and twenty-two hours, Standard Reckoning, old. Once more, logic suggests the probability—on the order of 99.99 percent—that none of those listed in my files remain on active duty. A secondary probability on the order of 94.375 percent suggests that the uniform discrepancies I detect are also the result of passing time.

The captain, if such he truly is, approaches the main personnel entrance to the depot. He carries a bush knife, and, as I watch, begins to clear the local flora from the entry. Clearly he is intent on gaining access, and I devote a full 5.009 seconds to consideration of my options. Conclusion is reached. I will permit him entry and observe his actions before initiating any further action of my own.

≈   ≈   ≈

It took forty minutes of hard, physical labor to clear the entry. Merrit was wringing wet by the time he hacked the last wrist-thick creeper aside, and he muttered a quiet curse at Santa Cruz's damp heat. No doubt the planet's farmers welcomed the fertility of its tropical climate, at least when they weren't fighting tooth and nail against the plant life it spawned, but Merrit was from cold, mountainous Helicon, and he was already sick of the steamy humidity after less than six hours on-planet.

He deactivated the bush knife and scrubbed sweat from his eyes, then frowned in concentration as he keyed the admittance code into the alphanumeric pad. It was plain blind luck Central had even had the code. A portion of one of Major Stavrakas' earlier dispatches had survived the Quern raid in what remained of Central's high-security data core, and it had contained both the depot entry codes and the command codeword she'd selected for her Bolo. Without both of those, there wouldn't have been enough brigadiers in the universe to get Paul Merrit this close to a live Bolo. He was no coward, but the notion of confronting something with almost four megaton/seconds of main battery firepower without the ability to identify himself as a friend was hardly appealing.

The depot hatch slid open with surprising smoothness, and he raised an eyebrow as the interior lights came on. There was no sign of dust, which suggested the depot remotes must be fully on-line. That was as encouraging as it was unexpected, and he stepped into the air-conditioned coolness with a sigh of gratitude. Someone had hung a directory on the facing wall, and he consulted it briefly, then turned left to head for the command center.

I note that the unidentified captain has entered the proper admittance code. This is persuasive, though certainly not conclusive, evidence that his presence is, in fact, authorized. I generate a 62.74 percent probability that Sector HQ has finally dispatched a replacement for my previous Commander, but logic cautions me against leaping to conclusions. I will observe further.

꙼꙼꙼ ꙼꙼꙼ ꙼꙼꙼

The command center hatch opened at a touch, and Merrit blinked at the non-regulation sight which met his eyes. Computer and communication consoles awaited his touch, without a trace of dust, and he was surprised to see the holo display of a full-scale planetary recon system glowing in one corner. Yet welcome as those sights were, they also seemed hopelessly incongruous, for someone had decorated the center. That was the only verb he could think of. Paintings hung on the ceramacrete walls and sculptures in both clay and metal dotted the floor. One entire wall had been transformed into an exquisite mosaic—of Icarus plunging from the heavens, unless he was mistaken—and handwoven rugs covered the floor. None of them impinged on the efficiency of the working area, but they were . . . nonstandard, to say the least.

Unusual, yet pleasing to the eye, and he nodded in slow understanding. Even in emergencies, the Dinochrome Brigade didn't pick dummies as Bolo commanders. Major Stavrakas must have realized she'd been marooned here, and it seemed she'd decided that if Santa Cruz was to be her final duty station, she could at least make the depot as homelike as possible.

He shook himself and smiled in appreciation of Stavrakas' taste and, assuming all of this was her own work, artistic talent. Then he crossed to the central computer console, reached for the keyboard . . . and jumped ten centimeters into the air when a soft, soprano voice spoke abruptly.

"Warning," it said. "This is a restricted facility. Unauthorized access is punishable by not less than twenty years imprisonment. Please identify yourself."

Merrit's head snapped around, seeking the speaker which had produced that polite, melodious voice. He didn't see it, but he *did* see the bright red warning light under the four-millimeter power rifle which had just unhoused itself from the wall above the console to aim directly between his eyes. He stared into its bore for a long, tense second, and the voice spoke again.

"Identification is required. Please identify yourself immediately."

"Ah, Merrit," he said hoarsely, then licked his lips and cleared his throat. "Captain Paul A. Merrit, Dinochrome Brigade, serial number Delta-Bravo-One-Niner-Eight-Zero-Niner-Three-Slash-Five-Bravo-One-One."

"You are not in my personnel files, Captain," the soprano remarked. He started to reply, but the voice continued before he could. "I compute, however, a probability of niner-niner point niner-niner-three percent that those files are no longer current. Query: Have you been issued a file update for me?"

Merrit blinked in disbelief. Even the current Mark XXV Bolo retained the emotionless vocoder settings of the earlier marks and normally referred to itself in the military third person except to its own commander. *This* voice, however calm and dispassionate it might be, not only used first person but sounded fully human. More than that, it carried what he could only call emotional overtones, and the nature of its questions implied a degree of discretionary autonomy which was impossible even for the Mark XXV except in Battle Mode.

On the other hand, he thought, still peering into the power rifle's muzzle, this was no time to be picky over details.

"Yes," he said after a moment. "I do have a personnel update for you."

"Good," the voice said—another response which raised Merrit's eyebrows afresh. "Please understand that no discourtesy is intended, Captain, but the security of this installation requires that no unattested data be input to the master computer system. I therefore request that you enter your data into the secondary terminal beside the door."

"Ah, of course."

Merrit reached very cautiously into his tunic to extract a data chip folio, then turned—equally slowly and carefully—to the indicated console. The power rifle tracked him with a soft, unnerving hum, and his palms were damp as he extracted a chip, fed it into the proper slot, and pressed the key. Then he stepped back and put his hands into his pockets, and a small, wry smile touched his lips as he recognized his own instinctive effort to look as nonthreatening as possible.

≈   ≈   ≈

It seems improper to threaten one who may be my new Commander, yet I am a valuable unit of the Line, and it is my overriding responsibility to prevent any unauthorized personnel from gaining access to my Command Center. Surely Captain Merrit, if he is, indeed, my new Commander, will understand and appreciate my caution.

The chip carries the proper identifiers and file headers, and I lower my first stage security fence to scan the data. The chip contains only 36.95 terabytes of information, and I complete my scan in 1.00175 seconds.

I am grieved to discover that my original Commander's file has not been properly maintained, yet the dearth of information upon her confirms her own belief that Sector HQ had "forgotten where they put me" long before her death. It is not proper for a member of the Dinochrome Brigade to be denied her place in its proud history, yet further perusal of the file reveals that the original information on my deployment was lost almost in its entirety. Fortunately, my own memory banks contain full information on both her earlier career and her actions on Santa Cruz, and I resolve to request the upload of that data at the earliest possible moment.

In addition to complete SitRep updates on the entire sector, the new data also contains the record of Captain Merrit, and I am impressed. The captain is a warrior. His list of decorations is headed by the Grand Solar Cross, which my records indicate is a posthumous award in 96.35 percent of all cases. In addition, he has received the Concordiat Banner, the Cross of Valor with two clusters, six planetary government awards for heroism which I do not recognize, three wound stripes, and no fewer than eleven campaign medals.

Yet I also discover certain disturbing facts in his personnel package. Specifically, Captain Merrit has been court-martialled, officially reprimanded, and reduced in rank from the permanent grade of major (acting grade of brigadier) to permanent grade of captain for striking a superior officer. I am astonished that he was not dishonorably discharged for such an act, yet 0.0046

seconds of consideration suggest that his previous exemplary record
may explain the fact that he was not.

I complete my preliminary study of the data and reactivate
the Control Center speaker.

"Thank you, Sir," the soprano voice said, and Merrit breathed
a sigh of relief as the power rifle politely deflected itself from
its rock-steady bead on his head. The red warning light below
it didn't go out, nor did the weapon retract into its housing,
but he recognized tentative acceptance in its change of aim.
Of course, none of that explained how such an early mark of
Bolo could be doing all this. It should either have activated
and obliterated him upon arrival or waited passively for *him*
to activate it. This controlled, self-directed response was totally
outside the parameters for a Mark XXIII.

"Query: Have you been assigned as my Commander?" the
soprano voice asked, and he nodded.

"I have."

"Identifier command phrase required."

"Leonidas," Merrit replied, and held his breath, then—

"Unit Two-Three-Baker-Zero-Zero-Seven-Five NKE of the Line
awaiting orders, Commander," the voice said calmly, and the
red light on the power rifle went out at last.

4

THE DEPOT'S main vehicle chamber was a vast, dim cavern, yet for all its size and cool, gently circulating air, Merrit felt almost claustrophobic as he stared up at the first Bolo Mark XXIII he'd ever seen. He'd studied the readouts on the model in preparation for this assignment, but aside from a handful buried in the reserve forces of smaller sectors, the Mark XXIII had been withdrawn from se.vice thirty years before. None of which made the huge war machine any less impressive.

The Mark XXIV and XXV, the only Bolos he'd ever served with, were both at least a thousand tons lighter than this. They were only marginally less heavily armed, yet the molecular circuitry and smaller, more efficient power plants which had come in with the Mark XXIV allowed more firepower to be packed into a less massive hull. But Bolo XXIII/B-0075-NKE was far older than they, and measured almost seventy-five meters from its clifflike prow to the bulbous housings of its stern anti-personnel clusters. Its interleaved bogie wheels were five meters in diameter, and the tops of the massive, back-to-back turrets for its twin eighty-centimeter Hellbores towered thirty meters above the fused ceramacrete of the chamber floor.

It was immaculate, like some perfectly preserved memorial from a lost era. The hexagonal scales of its multilayered ceramic antiplasma armor appliqués were the mottled green and brown of standard jungle camouflage, though Merrit had always questioned the practicality of applying visual camouflage to fifteen thousand tons of mobile armor and weaponry.

He walked slowly around the huge fighting machine, noting the closed ports for its lateral infinite repeater batteries and thirty-centimeter mortars, the high-speed, multibarrel slug throwers and laser clusters of its close-in anti-missile defenses, and the knifelike blades of its phased radar arrays. Optical pickups swiveled to watch him as he circled it, and he smiled—then stopped dead.

He stepped closer, brow furrowing in perplexity, but the incongruity didn't go away. According to the readouts he'd studied, the Mark XXIII had nine infinite repeaters in each lateral battery, and so did XXIII/B-0075-NKE. But there was an extra six or seven meters of hull between InfRpt Three and Four. For that matter, the Bolo's aft track system had three extra bogies, which suggested that it was at least ten or twelve meters longer than it was supposed to be.

He reached out for a handhold and climbed up the hull-mounted rings to the carapace of the missile deck between the twin Hellbore turrets. He paced it off, placing his feet carefully between the slablike armored hatch covers of the vertical launch missile system, then stopped and scratched his head with a grimace. No doubt about it; XXIII/B-0075-NKE was a good fifteen percent longer than any Mark XXIII should have been. Someone had grafted an extra eleven meters into her hull just forward of her VLS.

"Zero-Zero-Seven-Five?"

"Yes, Commander?" The politely interested soprano voice still seemed totally inappropriate coming from a Bolo, but Merrit had other things to wonder about at the moment.

"Tell me, Zero-Zero—" he began, then paused. "Excuse me.

Central has no record of what Major Stavrakas called you, Zero-Zero-Seven-Five."

"I am called 'Nike,' Commander."

"'Nike,'" Merrit murmured. "Goddess of victory. An appropriate name for a Bolo, Nike."

"Thank you, Commander. I have always liked it myself, and I am pleased you approve."

Merrit's eyebrows rose afresh at the unprompted, very human-sounding remark. A Mark XXIII should have been capable only of previously stored courtesies (outside Battle Reflex Mode, at least), yet he was beginning to suspect what lay behind those responses. It wasn't possible, of course, but still—

"Tell me, Nike, what *exact* mark of Bolo are you?" he asked.

"I am a Bolo *Invincibilis*, Mark XXIII, Model B (Experimental), Commander," the soprano voice replied.

"*Experimental?*" Merrit repeated.

"Affirmative, Commander."

"How experimental?" he prompted tautly.

"I am a prototype." The Bolo sounded calmer than ever beside the tension in his own voice. "As part of the Enhanced Combat Capabilities Program, my Command Center and Personality Integration psychodynamics were fitted with a secondary decision cortex with experimental interfaces and increased heuristic capacity to augment autonomous and discretionary functions."

"A brain box," Merrit whispered. "Dear God, that *must* be it. The first *brain box* ever fitted to a Bolo!" He went to his knees and rested one hand almost reverently on the massively armored deck.

"Excuse me, Commander, but the meaning of your last comment is unclear."

"What?" Merrit shook himself, then raised his head and smiled into the nearest optical head. "Sorry, Nike, but I had no idea I'd find *this*. You're the 'missing link.'"

"I fear your meaning continues to elude me, Commander," the Bolo said a bit reproachfully, and Merrit grinned.

"Sorry," he said again, and seated himself on the bracket of a turret-mounted whip antenna. "You see, Nike, before you came along—for that matter, for something like thirty years *after* you came along, now that I think about it—Bolos were self-aware, but their full autonomous capabilities were available to them only in Battle Mode. They were . . . circumscribed and restricted. Are you with me so far?"

"Yes, Commander."

"Of course you are!" Merrit chuckled and patted the leviathan's armored flank. "But that's because you were the next step, Nike. We knew the first experimental work had been done here in the Ursula Sector just before the Quern Wars, but the Quern got through to Ursula during the First War. They shot up Bolo Central so badly that most of the original research and hardware was destroyed, and then the pressure they put on us deferred the whole program for over thirty years, until after the Third Quern War. We needed more Bolos as fast as we could get them, so the *official* Mark XXIIIs were simply up-gunned and up-armored Mark XXIIs to simplify series production. But you weren't, were you? God! I wonder how your programming differs from what they finally mounted in the Mark XXIV?"

"I fear I can offer no information on that subject, Commander," the Bolo said almost apologetically.

"Don't worry about it, Nike. I'm sure we can figure it out together once I dig into the depot records. But what I can't figure out is what you're doing *here*? How did you wind up on Santa Cruz?"

"I was deployed directly from Ursula Central."

"I know that, but why?"

"I was selected for extended field test of the new and enhanced systems and software," the soprano voice said. "As such, I was mated with an automated repair and maintenance depot designed to support the test program and further field modifications. Santa Cruz had been selected as the test site well before the planet came under threat from the Quern, for which reason it had been equipped with proper landing field and other support facilities. At the outbreak of hostilities, my deployment was simply expedited. The test program was post-poned, and I was placed on immediate active duty under the command of Major Marina Stavrakas, senior project officer for Project Descartes."

"She was the *project chief* for Descartes?!"

"Affirmative, Commander."

"My God," Merrit breathed. "They managed to reconstruct maybe twenty percent of the Descartes Team's original logs after the wars, but they were so badly damaged we never knew who'd headed the team in the first place. She was bril-liant, Nike—*brilliant!* And she ended up lost and forgotten on a farming planet in the middle of nowhere." He shook his head again, eyes bright and sparkling with a delight he'd never expected to feel in this assignment, and stroked the Bolo's armored flank again.

"I wonder what she tucked away inside you? Somehow I can't quite picture the woman who headed the original Des-cartes Team not tinkering a bit once she'd figured out Central had 'lost' her. She *did* continue the project on her own, didn't she?"

"Affirmative, Commander," the Bolo confirmed calmly.

"Well, well, well, *well*," he murmured. "I can see this assign-ment is going to be lots more interesting than I expected. And—" a devilish twinkle had replaced the cold weariness in his eyes "—I don't see any reason to share my discoveries with Central just yet. After all, they knew where you were and forgot about it, so why remind them? They'd just send out rafts of specialists to take you away from me. They might even decide to take you apart to see just how you tick." He shook his head and gave the armored hull another pat. "No, Nike. I think you can just go on being our little secret for a while longer."

5

~~~~~~

"WELL?"

The silver-haired woman behind the immense desk was perfectly groomed, and her face was the product of the sort of biosculpt available only to people for whom money truly was no object. Unlike the nondescript, somehow subliminally seedy man in the uniform of a Sternenwelt Lines purser, she was perfectly suited to the elegant office, yet there was a coldness in her eyes, and her smile held a honed duralloy edge that beaded the purser's forehead with sweat.

"I'm sorry, Madam Osterwelt," he said, "but they won't sell." The woman said nothing, only gazed at him, and he swallowed. "I upped the offer to the maximum authorized amount," he said quickly, "but only three or four of them were even interested."

"You assured us that your local knowledge of the sector suited you for the job. That we could rely upon your good offices to attain success." The woman's mild tone was conversational, and he swallowed again, harder.

"I was certain they'd sell, ma'am. We were offering them ten *years* of income for a successful melon grower!"

"An attractive offer," the woman conceded. "Yet you say they refused it. Why?"

"I-I'm not certain, ma'am," the purser said unhappily.

"They must have given some indication," she pointed out, and he nodded.

"As near as I could figure it out, they simply didn't *want* the money, ma'am. I talked to old Esteban, the yokel who runs the field, and he just said his wife, his father, and his grandfather were all buried in the plot behind his house. That . . . that was fairly typical of what *all* of them said, ma'am."

"Parochialism," the woman said distastefully. She shook her head, and her tongue made a clicking sound against her teeth. "Regretfully typical of these untutored frontier people. I suppose I ought to have expected it—and *you* should have anticipated it as well, Mister Bergren." She cocked her head. "I fear you've served us less than satisfactorily in this matter."

"I did my best, Madam Osterwelt!"

"I'm sure you did. That's the problem." The purser wilted before the chill dispassion of her voice, and she made a weary shooing motion with one hand. "We'll be in touch, Mister Bergren."

The purser withdrew with obvious relief, and the woman pressed a stud on her desk panel. A discreetly hidden door opened silently within twenty seconds, and an athletic young man walked in.

"Yes, Mother?"

"You were right about Bergren, Gerald. The man's an utter incompetent."

"Is he?"

"Utterly," she sighed. "How fortunate that no one knows he was acting for us. In fact, I think it would be a very good idea to take steps to ensure that no one ever *does* know he was representing our interests."

"I'll see to it," Gerald said, and she smiled at him.

"A good son is a mother's greatest treasure." She sat back

in her chair and folded her hands atop the desk while she gazed across the office at the subtly shifting patterns of a light sculpture. "Still, incompetent as he may be, he *has* put his finger on the nub of the problem, dear. Farmers can be the most stubborn people in the galaxy, and frontier people cherish such boringly predictable attachments to their land. I'm afraid that if they refused the price we authorized him to offer, it's unlikely they'll sell to anyone."

"We've had that problem before, Mother."

"I realize we have, dear, but alternative methods can be so . . . *messy*." She pouted at the light sculpture, then sighed again. "Do you know, the most provoking thing of all is that they don't even have any idea why we *want* their little dirt ball."

"No one does yet, Mother. That's the whole point, isn't it?"

"Perhaps. But I really think I might not mind as much if I were up against an opposition that understood the rules of the game—and the stakes, of course."

"Mother," the young man said patiently, "their system is the only logical place to become the primary transfer node for the jump points serving three entire sectors. You know it, I know it, and whenever Survey gets around to releasing its new astrography report, every major shipping line will know it. Does it really matter whether *they* know it or not?"

"Don't forget who taught you everything you know, dear," his mother replied with an edge of tartness. "It's really very unbecoming for a son to lecture his mother."

"Was I lecturing?" He smiled and shook his head. "I didn't mean to. Why don't we think of it as a case of demonstrating I've done my homework?"

"You got that from my genes, not your father's," she said with a laugh, then shook her own head. "Still, you're quite right. All that matters is making certain GalCorp owns the only habitable real estate in the system when the time comes. *All* of it." She brooded at the light sculpture for a moment longer before she shrugged. "Well, if we have to be messy, I suppose that's all there is to say about it. Who do you think we should put in charge of it?"

"Why not me?"

"But you've never done any, um, field work, dear."

"Which doesn't mean I can't handle it. Besides, we ought to keep the command loop on this one as secure as possible, and every young man should start at the bottom. It helps him appreciate the big picture when he finally winds up at the top. Not—" he smiled again "—that I have any desire to wind up at the top for many more years, Mother."

"Wisdom beyond your years," she murmured. "Very well, it's your project. But before you take any steps, be sure you research the situation thoroughly. This sort of thing is seldom as simple as it looks at first glance, and I don't want my only son to suffer any unpleasant surprises."

"Of course not, Mother. I'll just pop out to Ursula and spend a few weeks nosing around Sector Central. I'm sure I can find some generous soul with the access to provide the information we need. Who knows? I may even find the ideal people for that messy little job we discussed."

6

~~~~~~~~~~~~~~~~~~~~~~~~~~~~~~~~~
~~~~~~~~~~~~~~~~~~~~~~~~~~~~~~~~~

ONE WEEK after his arrival on Santa Cruz, Paul Merrit sat
back in the comfortable crash couch and rubbed his chin with
something very like awe. The screen before him glowed with
a complicated schematic any Bolo tech would have given ten
years of his life to study, and its design was over fifty years old.
Fifty *years!* Incredible. Working all by herself, with only the
resources of a single automated maintenance depot—admittedly
a superbly equipped one, but still only a single depot—Marina
Stavrakas had developed Nike's brain box design into one that
made the newest Mark XXV's look clumsy and slow.

He tilted the couch back and crossed his legs. More screens
and displays glowed around him, filling Nike's fighting compartment with a dim, shifting luminescence. There were more of
them than there would have been in a more modern—well,
recent—Bolo. Nike *was* a modified Mark XXIII, after all; humans
needed broader band data interfaces than any Bolo did, and
Nike's basic technology was eighty years old, without more
recent updates in human-machine information management

— 37 —

systems. But for all that, the compartment was surprisingly spacious. Not only had Nike been the first fully autonomous Bolo, whether anyone knew it or not, but she'd also been the first to incorporate molycirc psychotronics. It was very early generation stuff, considerably bulkier than its more modern equivalents, but Stavrakas had used it in some amazingly innovative ways. What she might have accomplished with the current technologies scarcely bore thinking on.

He turned his couch and keyed another screen to life. A forty-nine-year-old time and date display glowed in one corner, and the white-haired woman who appeared on it sat in the same crash couch Merrit now occupied. She was far frailer and older than the single, poor-quality flatpic of Major Stavrakas he'd found in Central's surviving records, but her olive-dark eyes were still sharp and alert. He'd already played the recording three times, yet he felt a fresh sense of respect, coupled with a regret that he'd never known her, as she began to speak.

"Since you're viewing this—whoever you are—" she said with a wry smile, "someone must've finally remembered where they parked Nike and me. I suppose I should be a bit put out with the Brigade and the Navy, but from the little Jeremiah and I have picked up over the all-units channels, we assume the Quern got through to Central." Her smile faded, and her voice—a soprano remarkably similar to Nike's—darkened. "I further assume the rest of the Descartes Team must have been lost at the same time, since they all knew where I was."

She cleared her throat and rubbed her temple with one fragile, veined hand.

"Jeremiah's offered to use the commercial bands to request a relief ship with a proper medical officer, but I turned him down. However much he may grump and grouse, Santa Cruz is his home now. I know he really loves it here, and so do I, I suppose. Besides, from the bits and pieces we can pick up, the Quern are still operating in some force in the sector. Given their native habitat, I doubt they'd care much for Santa Cruz's climate, and I suppose that's the main reason they've never paid us a visit. On the other hand, they might just change their mind if they started intercepting transmissions from us. Nike's good, but I'd just as soon not match her against a Quern planetary assault force. Even if she won, there wouldn't be very many surviving Santa Cruzans to cheer for her when it was over."

She lowered her hand and smiled again.

"Actually, it hasn't been a bad life. A little lonely, sometimes. Thanks to all the Descartes security, most of the locals never even knew Nike and I were here, and those who did know seem to have forgotten, but I had dear Jeremiah. He and I accepted long ago that we'd become permanent residents of Santa Cruz, and in addition to him, I had Nike, my work, and plenty of time to spend with all three of them. And, of course," her smile became an impish grin, "no brass to give me a hard time! Talk about research freedom—!"

She chuckled and leaned back to fold thin arms across her chest.

"Unfortunately, it would appear I'm finally running out of time. My family's always been prone to heart trouble, and I've had my warning. I've discussed it with Nike—she tends to worry, and I've made it a habit to be honest with her—and she understands the depot doesn't stock the sort of spares I need. I've also made arrangements to put her on Autonomous Stand-By if—when—the time comes. I'm certain someone somewhere else has picked up where the Descartes Team left off. By now there's probably a whole new generation of autonomous Bolos out there, but now that you've come to relieve me, I think you'll find Nike still has a few surprises of her own. Take care of her, whoever you are. She's quite a girl. I'm sure my tinkering is going to raise a few eyebrows—Lord knows the desk-jockeys would tear their hair at the mere thought of some of the capabilities I've given her! But I've never regretted a single facet of her design. She's unique . . . and she's been more than just my friend."

The old woman on the screen sighed. Her smile took on a curious blend of sorrow and deep, abiding pride and affection, and her voice was very soft when she spoke again.

"When forty winters shall besiege thy brow,
And dig deep trenches in thy beauty's field,
Thy youth's proud livery, so gazed on now,
Will be a tatter'd weed, of small worth held:
Then being ask'd where all thy beauty lies,
Where all the treasure of thy lusty days,
To say, within thine own deep-sunken eyes,
Were an ill-fitting shame and thriftless praise.
How much more praise deserved thy beauty's use,
If thou couldst answer 'This fair child of mine
Shall sum my count and make my old excuse,'
Proving her beauty by succession thine.
This were to be new made when thou art old,
And see thy blood warm when thou feel'st it cold."

She blinked misty eyes and nodded to the pickup, as if she could actually see him, measure him, know the innermost, most secret part of him.

"A tiny misquote, perhaps," she said quietly, "but I think Shakespeare would forgive me. Take good care of my child, whoever you are."

The screen blanked, and Merrit shook his head,

"You must have been quite a girl yourself, Major," he murmured.

"She was," the Bolo's soprano said softly, and he looked up at the small green light glowing below the speaker from which it came. Now that he'd seen Stavrakas' last log entry, it no longer seemed strange to hear Nike speak without prompting. There was a moment of silence, and then the Bolo continued in that same, soft voice. "I never realized I had that message in memory, Commander. She must have recorded it during one of my down periods."

"She didn't want you to worry about her."

Merrit didn't even want to think about how the psych types would react to this entire conversation. Every field officer of the Dinochrome Brigade could quote chapter and verse from the manual's warnings against over-identification with Bolos.

They were war machines, the manual said. Self-aware and with personalities, yes, but *machines*, built to fight and die against humanity's enemies, which must, in the final analysis, be regarded as expendable. The Bolos themselves knew that; it was only their human commanders and partners who tended to forget—as Merrit had forgotten on Sandlot.

"No. I compute that she would not have wanted that," Nike agreed after a moment.

"Of course she wouldn't have. But she was proud of you, Nike, and even from the little I've seen so far, she had reason to be."

"Indeed?" The Bolo sounded pleased, and somehow he had the sense of a cocked head and a quirked eyebrow. "I compute that seventy-nine-plus years have passed since I was deployed, Commander. Surely newer and more modern Bolos surpass my own capabilities?"

"Fishing for compliments, Nike?" Merrit grinned and patted the arm of his crash couch. "Major Stavrakas was right. The desk-jockeys *would* tear their hair out if they could hear you now!"

"Why?" the Bolo asked simply.

"Because they worry about Bolos that get *too* human."

"Because they fear what such a Bolo might do? Or because they fear what it might *refuse* to do?"

"I think because they're afraid it might start asking questions just like those," Merrit said more seriously. "You're a very powerful fighting machine, Nike. There's never—ever—been an instance of an undamaged Bolo in proper repair violating orders, but we've had the occasional accident with a unit that's suffered damage or lack of maintenance. That's why the Brigade still worries about its ability to retain control of the newer, autonomous units. They've cut back on the inhibitory software in the Mark XXVs, but the core package is still in there."

"A wise precaution," Nike observed after a moment. "An irrational machine with the combat power I possess would be far too dangerous to its friends."

"I'm afraid I have to agree, but that's what would upset

the desk-jockeys about you. You don't have anywhere near the systems redundancy the Mark XXIVs and XXVs have. Technically, that makes you more vulnerable to failure from battle damage, and—probably worse, from HQ's perspective—what I've seen so far suggests that Major Stavrakas' modifications to your Personality and Command Centers are way outside the current parameters, as well. Just for starters, your inhibitory package is a lot less restrictive. No modern Bolo should be as 'awake' as you are outside Battle Mode, either, and it looks like your personality integration is at least a full magnitude more developed than a Mark XXV's. I'm not certain yet, but coupled with the modifications to your secondary command cortex, I suspect you could even hold off the Omega Worm for a while."

"Omega Worm?"

"Sorry. That's current slang for the Total Systems Override Program."

There was a moment of silence—a very human moment which Merrit understood perfectly. The TSORP was the ultimate defense against a rogue Bolo, a suicide file designed to crash every execution file in the memory of any Bolo which disobeyed the direct orders of its properly identified commander. Many Brigade personnel, like Merrit himself, questioned TSORP's necessity. Since the brain box technology had come in, so many redundant, stand-alone backup systems had been added to the Bolo's brains that the possibility of irrational behavior virtually no longer existed. And, as he'd just told Nike, no Bolo had ever disobeyed a legal order. But TSORP had been incorporated into the very first self-aware Bolos and every Bolo since, and it could not be a pleasant thing to know an involuntary suicide override controlled by others was part of your basic matrix.

"I believe you are correct, Commander," Nike said after a moment, and his eyebrows rose at her merely thoughtful tone. "I could not resist it indefinitely, of course, yet I compute that the additional processing capability Major Stavrakas installed within my psychotronics would allow me to delay file execution for no less than forty minutes and possibly for as much as an hour. Does this constitute an unwarrantable risk factor in my design?"

"*I* don't think so. Of course, given my own record, I may not be the most impartial judge. I guess the risk factor depends on how likely you are to disobey your commander's orders."

"I am a unit of the Dinochrome Brigade. I would never act against the honor of my Brigade, Commander."

"I know, Nike. I know. I told you *I* wasn't worried." Merrit gave the couch arm one more pat, then rose and yawned hugely. "Sorry, Nike. Unlike you, I don't have a fusion plant, and it's been a long day for me. I need some shuteye."

"Of course, Commander."

"Wake me at oh-six-hundred, would you?"

"Certainly."

"Thank you." He smiled and waved to the visual pickup above the main fire control screens. It was a common gesture of courtesy among the men and women who commanded the self-aware war machines of the Dinochrome Brigade, yet it had more meaning than usual for him tonight. The green "System Active" light under the speaker flashed in unmistakable response, and he chuckled wearily and climbed out the hatch.

I watch through the depot's interior optics as my new Commander makes his way down the corridor to the Personnel Section. He is only my second Commander. I am aware that my experiential data is thus insufficient to permit a realistic evaluation of his suitability as Major Stavrakas' replacement, and he is quite different from my previous Commander, but I feel content. It is good to have a Commander once more, yet this is more than the relief a unit of the Line should feel at receiving a new Commander. There is something about him which I cannot adequately define. I devote a full 20.0571 seconds to an attempt to do so, but without success. Perhaps further acquaintance with him will provide the critical data my analysis presently lacks.

I consider what he has said as I watch him prepare for bed. He is correct about the danger an uncontrollable unit of the Line would pose to all about it. My function is to protect and defend humanity, not to threaten my creators, and I feel an odd disquiet at the thought that I am less well protected against that possibility than more modern Bolos. Yet my Commander is also correct in recognizing the remote probability of such a situation. TSORP becomes operational only in units that reject direct orders, and I cannot conceive of a unit of the Line in proper repair which would commit such an act.

My Commander extinguishes the lights in his new quarters, and I leave the audio system on-line. Should he wake and desire to communicate with me, I will be ready.

He has not instructed me to return to Stand-By to conserve power. In that much, at least, he is like Major Stavrakas. My Main Memory contains much background data on standard operating procedure; I realize how rare this is, and I am grateful for it. The depot power systems are fully charged. I do not even require internal power to maintain Full Alert Status, and I turn to my Library Files with pleasure.

7

~~~~~~~~~~~~~~~~~~~~~~~~~~~~~~~~~~~~
~~~~~~~~~~~~~~~~~~~~~~~~~~~~~~~~~~~~

GERALD OSTERWELT didn't like Ursula. Sector capital or no, the planet, as all planets in the frontier sectors, was terminally uncultured. He preferred the civilized amenities and pleasures of the Core Worlds, yet he comforted himself with the reflection that his task here was worth temporary inconveniences. He supposed it wasn't really necessary for GalCorp to own the *entire* Santa Cruz System, but they certainly needed to own enough of it to control the rest, and the original planetary charter had made that difficult. Virgin as much of the planet might still be, most of it was already owned by some descendent of the original colonists or set aside in nature reserves held by the planetary government. Certainly all the choicest bits and pieces were, and GalCorp hadn't become the third largest transstellar corporation of the Concordiat by settling for leftovers.

Unfortunately, his mother had been correct in at least one respect. His original bootlegged copy of Ursula Central's records on the planet had been less complete than he'd thought. Central had updated itself considerably in the eighteen months since he'd first obtained access to its files, and it seemed Santa Cruz would be a tougher nut for a "messy solution" than he'd originally expected. The fact that the local yokel militia had no less than fourteen Wolverine heavy tanks was unfortunate, but formidable as the Wolverines had been in their day, they were also seventy or eighty years out of date. They could have been dealt with fairly easily if not for the *real* joker he'd never anticipated finding in the deck.

A Bolo. What in the name of sanity was a *Bolo* doing on a backwoods farming planet? More to the point, how did he go about neutralizing it? Despite his original airy confidence, he knew his mother's maternal feelings would not suffice to preserve his present clear right of succession to the GalCorp throne if he blew this operation, but discovering a Bolo in the mix made things far more complicated.

He sat in the lounge of his palatial hyperyacht while options revolved in his brain. One did not normally—as humanity's enemies had discovered over the last seven hundred years— employ a brute force solution against a Bolo with any great probability of success. Of course, *this* Bolo was as out of date as the militia's Wolverines, but "obsolescent" was a purely relative concept where Bolos were concerned. No, no. If he was going to pull this off, he required a more subtle approach, and it was just possible he had one. *Bolos* might be incorruptible, but the same, alas, could not always be said for all the people who built or commanded them.

Yet even if he could somehow neutralize the Bolo, he would still require someone with the will, the experience, and the resources to deal with the militia's over-aged armored element. There were plenty of mercenary outfits with the last two qualities, but finding one which was willing to undertake the operation in the first place might prove difficult. The Concordiat Navy would be extremely unhappy with them, and if any planetary survivor could identify them afterward, unhappiness on the Navy's part could all too easily prove fatal. What he needed was an outfit with minimal scruples and maximum need, one whose greed for the sort of clandestine support GalCorp could

provide would overcome both any lingering humanitarian prin-
ciples and fear of the Navy's potential response.

Finding it wouldn't be easy, he admitted to himself, but
he had time. Survey Command moved with glacial slowness
when it came to certifying jump lines. By his most pessimistic
estimate, it would be another T-year before the galaxy at large
got the information GalCorp had already obtained. That gave
him six or even seven months to get things organized, and
it would probably take most of that time to find the Bolo's
Achilles heel, anyway.

He nodded to himself and brought his encrypted com on-
line. The first step was to call home and get Mother's research
teams started finding the contacts he needed.

8

~~~~~~~~~~~~~~~~~~~~~~~~~~~~~~~~~~
~~~~~~~~~~~~~~~~~~~~~~~~~~~~~~~~~~

THE SUBTERRANEAN rumble of an earthquake shook the jungle as the enormous doors covering the depot's vehicle ramp swept ponderously wide for the first time in eighty years. The patient, insatiable incursions of creepers and small trees had mounded two meters of spongy earth over those doors, and "birds" screamed in alarm as the very ground parted with a huge tearing sound. Trees—some of them ten and twenty meters tall—toppled in slow motion as the gaping wound snapped roots like threads, and then, with the rumble of mighty engines, the squeak of sprockets, and a grating clash of treads, Nike moved majestically into the light.

The alloy leviathan paused for a moment, optic heads swiveling to scan its surroundings, and Paul Merrit felt a thrill he hadn't felt in years as he rode Nike's crash couch. No self-aware Bolo *needed* an on-board commander, but there was always an indescribable sense of communion—an adrenaline-charged exhilaration—the first time an officer of the Dinochrome Brigade rode his command's unstoppable power, and that feeling had never been stronger than it was today, for Nike was like no Bolo he had ever commanded. Marina Stavrakas' unauthorized modifications to the Descartes Team's original brain box design had gone far deeper than he'd first realized. She hadn't stopped with making Nike fully autonomous; she'd taken the step no other Bolo tech had dared take even yet and given her creation—her child—genuine *emotions*. Nike wasn't "just" a machine, however magnificent; she was a *person*, and Merrit could feel her delight as direct sunlight bathed her hull at long last.

She stood a moment longer, the humming rumble of her idling engines vibrating through her mammoth hull like the purr of some enormous cat, then moved forward and pivoted regally to port. Her designers had given her the usual Bolo "wide track" suspension, and no less than eight separate tread systems, each with its own power train and tracks five meters wide, supported her massive bulk. Independent quadruple fore and aft suspensions took her weight, spreading it out to reduce ground pressure to an absolute minimum, and even so her tracks sank well over a meter into the damp, rich soil. She forged ahead, plowing through the jungle like the juggernaut she was, and forest titans toppled like straws before her while occasional outcrops of solid rock powdered under her treads.

Merrit said nothing. Nike knew where they were going— not that it would be any more than a brief jaunt around the depot's immediate area—and he had no wish to intrude upon her pleasure. No doubt the psych types would be all hot and bothered over *that*, as well, but Paul Merrit had had it up to the eyebrows with Brigade Psych Ops, and their potential consternation mattered not at all to him. No, that wasn't quite true. He would be *delighted* if it caused them all to drop dead of cardiac arrest on the spot.

Nike was moving at barely twenty kph, far too slow a speed to require his couch's independent shock absorbers or crash frame, but he felt the gentle undulation of her suspension and grinned as he cocked the couch back in its gimbals. If anyone asked (not that they were likely to), he could justify his actions easily enough. Unit Zero-Zero-Seven-Five NKE had been on secondary power from the depot's systems for eight decades. A test of its running gear and fusion plants was long overdue, and if he had other motives of his own, those were *his* business, not Psych Ops'!

Another huge tree toppled, and, as it fell, one of the large, scaled, lizard cats, the most feared predators of Santa Cruz, leapt suddenly into sight. It crouched before them, staring in disbelief at the enormous intruder into its domain . . . then screamed its challenge and charged the moving mountain of alloy.

Merrit couldn't believe it. A lizard cat was four sinuous meters of vicious fighting power, the absolute ruler of Santa Cruz's jungles, but surely not even one of *them* could think it could stop a Bolo! Yet the cat kept coming. He opened his mouth, but Nike halted abruptly on her own, before he could get the order out. The main fire control screen was slaved to her forward optical head, and Merrit frowned as it swept past the lizard cat now ripping futilely at one of her stopped treads with eight-centimeter claws. Ranging bars flickered, closing in on something in the center of the display, and he inhaled in surprise as he realized what that something was.

Four scaled shapes, far smaller than the monster trying to savage Nike, lay revealed where the roots of the falling tree had torn out the side of a subterranean den. They were almost as large as Merrit himself, perhaps, yet that was tiny compared to a mature lizard cat, and they turned blind, terrified eyes towards the snarling fury of their dam.

The display focused on them for a moment, and then Nike moved slowly backward. The lizard cat tried to fling itself on the moving tread, only to tumble backward with a squall of pain as the Bolo brought up her kinetic interdiction battle screen. She must have it on its lowest possible power setting, since it hadn't splattered the cat all over the jungle, but it was sufficient to throw the scaly mother safely away from her treads.

The lizard cat heaved herself groggily to her feet, swaying for balance, then howled in victory as the threat to her young gave ground. Nike retreated a full hundred meters, then pivoted to her left once more to circle wide, and Merrit shook his head with a wondering smile. Any other Bolo would simply have kept going. Even if it had realized the den lay in its path, that wouldn't have mattered to it. But no other Bolo he'd ever served with would even have thought to wonder why the cat had attacked in the first place, much less acted to preserve both mother and children.

The Bolo started forward once more, skirting the den, and he patted the couch arm.

"Nice move, Nike, but how'd you guess? *I* just thought the critter was out of its mind."

"I have not previously personally encountered a lizard cat," Nike replied calmly, "but the depot's computers are tied into the planetary data net. I have thus been able to amass considerable data on Santa Cruzan life forms, yet none of the records available to me suggested a reason for a lizard cat to attack me. I am neither edible nor small enough for it to hope to kill me; as such, it could not regard me as prey, and lizard cats are less territorial than most large predators. They are also noted for their intelligence, and, faced with a foe of my size and power, the only intelligent choice would have been for the creature to flee, yet it did not. Thus the only logical basis for its actions was that it perceived me as a threat it could not evade, yet the lizard cat itself manifestly *could* have evaded me. That suggested a protective reaction on its part, not one of pure aggression, and that, in turn, suggested investigation to determine the nature of that which it sought to protect."

Merrit shook his head, eyes shining as he listened to the explanation no other Bolo would have been capable of making.

"I follow your logic," he said, "but why stop?"

"Your tone suggests what Major Stavrakas called 'a trick question,' Commander. Are you, in fact, seeking to test me?"

"I suppose I am, but the question still stands. Why didn't you just keep going?"

"There was no need to do so, Commander. No time parameter has been set for this exercise, and avoiding the creature's den presents no inherent difficulty."

"That's an explanation of the consequences, Nike. Why did you even consider *not* continuing straight forward?"

He watched an auxiliary display as the mother lizard cat, still snarling after the threat to her cubs, retreated into her half-ruined den, and Nike moved smoothly along her way for perhaps five seconds before she replied.

"I did not wish to, Commander. There was no need to destroy that creature or her young, and I did not desire to do so. It would have been . . . wrong."

"Compassion, Nike? For an animal?"

There was another moment of silence, and when the Bolo spoke once more, it was not in direct answer.

"Wee, sleekit, cowrin, tim'rous beastie,
O, what a panic's in thy breastie!
Thou need na start awa sae hasty,
Wi' bickering brattle!
I wad be laith to rin an' chase thee,
Wi' murd'ring pattle!"

"What was that?" Merrit wondered aloud.

"A poem, Commander. More precisely, the first verse of the poem 'To a Mouse,' by Robert Burns, a poet of Old Earth."

"*Poetry*, Nike?" Merrit stared at the command console in disbelief, and the speaker made a small, soft sound that could only be called a laugh.

"Indeed, Commander. Major Stavrakas was a great devotee of humanity's pre-space poets. My earliest memory here on Santa Cruz is of her reading Homer to me."

"She *read* poetry to you? She didn't just feed it into your memory?"

"She did that, as well, after I requested her to do so, yet I believe she was correct not to do so immediately. It was her belief that poetry is a social as well as a creative art, a mode of communication which distills the critical essence of the author's emotions and meaning and makes them transferable to another. As such, it reaches its fullest potential only when shared, knowingly and consciously. Indeed, I believe it is the *act* of sharing that makes poetry what Major Stavrakas called a 'soul transfusion,' and it was her hope that sharing it with me would complete the task of enabling the emotion aspects of my Personality Center."

"And did it?" Merrit asked very softly.

"I am not certain. I have attempted to compute the probability that my 'emotions' and those of a human are, indeed, comparable, yet I have been unable to do so. My evaluations lack critical data, in that I do not know if I have, in fact, what humans call a 'soul,' Commander. But if I do, then poetry speaks directly to it."

"My God," Merrit whispered, and stared at the console for another long, silent moment. Then he shook himself and spoke very seriously. "Nike, this is a direct order. Do not discuss poetry, your emotions, or *souls* with anyone else without my express authorization."

"Acknowledged." For just an instant, Nike's soprano was almost as flat as any other Bolo's, but then it returned to normal. "Your order is logged, Commander. Am I permitted to inquire as to the reason for it?"

"You most certainly are." He ran a hand through his hair and shook his head. "This entire conversation comes under the heading of 'aberrant behavior' for a Bolo, Nike. Any Bolo tech would hit every alarm button in sight if he heard you saying things like that, and as soon as he did, they'd shut you down. They'd *probably* settle for removing your brain from your hull for further study, but I can't be positive."

"Are you instructing me to deceive our superiors, Commander?" Nike's tone was undeniably uncomfortable, and Merrit closed his eyes for a moment.

"I'm instructing you not to advertise your capabilities until I've gotten a handle on all the, um, unauthorized modifications Major Stavrakas made to you," he said carefully. "In my judgment, you represent an enormous advance in psychotronic technology which must be carefully studied and evaluated, but before I risk trying to convince anyone else of that, I need a better understanding of you of my own. In the meantime, I don't want you saying—or doing—anything that might prompt some uniformed mental pygmy to wipe your Personality Center in a fit of panic."

The Bolo forged ahead in silence for some moments while she pondered his explanation, and then the green light under the speaker blinked.

"Thank you for the explanation, Captain Merrit. You are my Commander, and the order does not contravene any of the regulations in my memory. As such, I will, of course, obey it."

"And you understand the reasoning behind it?"

"I do, Commander." Nike's voice was much softer, and Merrit sighed in relief. He relaxed in his crash couch, watching the screens as the Bolo slid unstoppably through the jungle, and smiled.

"Good, Nike. In the meantime, why not read *me* a little more poetry?"

"Of course, Commander. Do you have a preferred author?"

"I'm afraid I don't know any poems, Nike, much less poets. Perhaps you could select something."

There was another moment of silence as the Bolo considered her Library Memory. Then the speaker made the sound of a politely cleared throat. "Do you speak Greek, Commander?"

"Greek?" Merrit frowned. " 'Fraid not."

"In that case, I shall defer *The Iliad* for the present," Nike decided. She pondered a moment—a very *long* moment for a Bolo—more, then said, "As you are a soldier, perhaps you will appreciate this selection—

"I went into a public-'ouse to get a pint o' beer,
   The publican 'e up an' sez,
      'We serve no red-coats here.'
   The girls be'ind the bar they laughed
      and giggled fit to die,
   I outs into the street again an' to myself sez I:

O it's Tommy this, an' Tommy that,
　an 'Tommy, go away';
But it's 'Thank you, Mister Atkins,'
　when the band begins to play,
The band begins to play, my boys,
　the band begins to play,
O it's 'Thank you, Mister Atkins,'
　when the band begins to play."

The mighty war machine rolled on through the jungle, and Paul Merrit leaned back in his crash couch and listened in only half-believing delight as the ancient words of Kipling's timeless protest for all soldiers flowed from Nike's speaker.

9

~~~~~~~~~~~~~~~~~~~~~~~~~~~~~~~~~~~~~~~

"ALL RIGHT, mister," the uniformed man said harshly. "You paid for the beer, so why don't you just tell me who you are and why you're bothering?"

Gerald Osterwelt cocked his head, and the speaker flushed under the sardonic glint in his eyes. The older man's hand tightened on his stein, but he didn't get up and storm out of the dingy bar. Not that Osterwelt had expected him to. Li-Chen Matucek had once attained the rank of brigadier in the Concordiat's ground forces, and his present uniform was based upon the elegance of a Concordiat general's, but its braid was frayed and one elbow had been darned. At that, his uniform was in better shape than his "brigade's" equipment. As down-at-the-heels mercenaries went, "Matucek's Marauders" would have taken some beating, and their commander hated the shabby picture he knew he presented. It made him sullen, irritable, and bitter, and that suited Osterwelt just fine. Still, it wouldn't hurt to make it plain from the outset just who held whose leash.

"You can call me Mister Scully—Vernon Scully. And as to why I offered you a drink, why, it's because I've heard such good things about you, 'General' Matucek," he purred in a tone whose bite was carefully metered, "In fact, I might have a little business proposition for you. But, of course, if you're too *busy*. . . . "

He let the sentence trail off, holding Matucek's eyes derisively, and it was the mercenary who looked away.

"What sort of proposition?" he asked after a long moment.

"Oh, come now, General! Just what is it you and your people *do* for a living?" Matucek looked back up, and Osterwelt smiled sweetly. "Why, you kill people, don't you?" Matucek flushed once more, and Osterwelt's smile grew still broader. "Of course you do. And, equally of course, that's what I want you to do for *me*. As a matter of fact, I want you to kill a great many people for me."

"Who?" Matucek asked bluntly, and Osterwelt nodded. So much for the preliminaries, and thank goodness Matucek, for all his seedy belligerence, saw no need to protest that his people were "soldiers" and not hired killers. No doubt many mercenaries *were* soldiers; the Marauders weren't—not anymore, at least—and knowing that they both knew that would save so much time. On the other hand, it wouldn't do to tell Matucek the target before the hook was firmly set. The man might just decide there'd be more profit, and less risk, in going to the authorities than in taking the job.

"We'll get to that," Osterwelt said calmly. "First, though, perhaps we should discuss the equipment and capabilities of your organization?" Matucek opened his mouth, but Osterwelt raised a languid hand before he could speak. "Ah, I might just add, General, that I already *know* what your equipment looks like, so please save us both a little time by not telling me what wonderful shape you're in."

Matucek shut his mouth with a snap and glowered down into his beer, and Osterwelt sighed.

"I have no particular desire to rub salt into any wounds, General Matucek," he said more gently, "but we may as well both admit that your brigade suffered heavy equipment losses in that unfortunate business on Rhyxnahr."

"Last time I ever take a commission from a bunch of eight-legged starfish!" Matucek snarled by way of answer. "The bastards lied to us, and once we planeted—"

"Once you planeted," Osterwelt interrupted, "they left your brigade to soak up the casualties while they loaded the machine tools and assembly mechs they'd assured you they held clear title to, then departed. Leaving *you* to explain to the Rhyxnahri—and a Naval investigator—why you'd launched an attack on a Concordiat ally's homeworld." He shook his head sadly. "Frankly, General, you were lucky you didn't all end up in prison."

"It wasn't my fault! The little bastards said they owned it—even showed us the documentation on it! But that fancy-assed commodore didn't even care!"

Matucek's teeth ground audibly, and Osterwelt hid a smile. Oh, yes, this was shaping up nicely. The Navy had kicked Matucek's "brigade" off Rhyxnahr in disgrace . . . and without allowing it to salvage any of its damaged equipment. Of course, if the "general" had bothered to research things at all, none of that would have happened to him, though Osterwelt had no intention of pointing that out. After all, if he did, Matucek might just check *this* operation out, which would be most unfortunate. But what mattered now was the man's sense of having been not only played for a fool but "betrayed" by the Navy's investigation. He was at least as furious with the Concordiat as Mother's researchers had suggested, and he was in desperate need of a job—any job—which might let him recoup a little of his losses. All in all, he looked very much like the perfect answer to the Santa Cruz problem, and Osterwelt's reply to his outburst carried just the right degree of commiseration.

"I realize you've been treated badly, General, and I sympathize. A man with your war record certainly had a right to expect at least *some* consideration from his own government. Be that as it may, however, at the moment you have very little more than a single heavy-lift freighter and a pair of Fafnir-class assault ships."

Matucek snarled and half-rose. "Look, Scully! If all you want to do is tell me what lousy shape I'm in, then—"

"No, General. I want to tell you how I can help you get into *better* shape," Osterwelt purred, and the mercenary sank slowly back into his chair. "You see, I represent an, ah, association of businessmen who have a problem. One you can solve for them. And, in return, they'd like to solve *your* problems."

"Solve my problems?" Matucek repeated slowly. "How?"

"To begin with, by completely reequipping your ground echelon, General," Osterwelt said in a voice that was suddenly very serious. "We can provide you with the latest Concordiat manned light and medium AFVs, one- and two-man air cavalry ground attack stingers, as many infantry assault vehicles as you want, and the latest generation of assault pods to upgrade your Fafnirs." Matucek's jaw dropped in disbelief. That kind of equipment refit would make his "Marauders" the equal of a *real* Concordiat mech brigade, but Osterwelt wasn't done yet and leaned across the table towards him. "We can even," he said softly, "provide you with a pair of Golem-IIIs."

"*Golems?*" Matucek's nostrils flared and he looked quickly around the bar. If anything had been needed to tell him that Osterwelt's "association of businessmen" had immense—and almost certainly illegal—resources, it was needed no longer. The Golem-III was an export version of the Mark XXIV/B Bolo. All psychotronics had been deleted, but the Golems were fitted with enough computer support to be operable by a three-man crew, and they retained most of the Mark XXIV's offensive and defensive systems. Of course, they were also available—legally, at least—only to specifically licensed Concordiat allies in good standing.

"Golems," Osterwelt confirmed. "We can get them for you, General."

"Like hell you can," Matucek said, yet his tone was that of a man who wanted desperately to believe. "Even if you could, the Navy'd fry my ass the instant they found out I had 'em!"

"Not at all. We can arrange for you to purchase them quite legally from the Freighnar Commonwealth."

"The *Freighnars?* Even if they had 'em, they'd never have been able to keep 'em running!"

"Admittedly, the new People's Revolutionary Government is a bit short on technical talent," Osterwelt agreed. "On the other hand, the People's Council has finally realized its noble intention to go back to the soil won't work with a planetary population of four billion. More to the point, now that they've gotten their hands on off-world bank accounts of their own, they've also decided they'd better get the old regime's hardware back in working condition before some new champion of the proletariat comes along and gives them the same treatment they gave their own late, lamented plutocratic oppressors."

"Which means?" Matucek asked with narrowed eyes.

"Which means they've had to call in off-world help, and that in return for assistance in restoring the previous government's Golem battalion to operational condition, they've agreed to sell two of them."

"For how much?" Matucek snorted with the bitterness of a man whose pockets were down to the lint.

"That doesn't matter, General. *We'll* arrange the financing— and see to it that your Golems are in excellent repair. Trust me. I can bury the transaction under so many cutouts and blind corporations no one will ever be able to prove any connection between you and my . . . associates. As for the Navy—" He shrugged. "However it got that way, the PRG is the currently recognized Freighnar government. As such, it can legally sell its military hardware—including its Golems—to whomever it wishes, and as long as you hold legal title to them, not even the Navy can take them away from you."

Matucek sat back and stared across the table. The greed of a desperate man who sees salvation beckon flickered in his eyes, and Osterwelt could almost feel his hunger, but the man wasn't a complete fool. For a mercenary outfit on its last legs to be offered a payoff this huge could only mean whoever offered it wanted something highly illegal in return, and his voice was flat when he spoke once more.

"What do you want?"

"I want you to attack a planet for me," Osterwelt said calmly. "The planetary militia has a few eighty-year-old Wolverine tanks and some fairly decent infantry weapons."

"Eighty-year-old manned tanks? You don't need Golems to take out *that* kind of junk, mister!"

"True, but there are also some old Quern War-era Concordiat naval installations on the planet. We haven't been able to find out exactly what they are yet," Osterwelt lied smoothly, "and the present indications are that they've been abandoned—whatever they are—to the locals for over seventy years. If that's true, they can't be much of a threat, but we want you to succeed. Old as they are, they might just hold a genuine threat, and we believe in stacking the deck. Do *you* think anything eighty years out of date could stand off a pair of Golems?"

"Not bloody likely!" Matucek grunted.

"That's what we thought, too. Of course, we'll continue to seek better information. If we can find out exactly what those installations were, we'll let you know immediately. In the meantime, however, we can get you reequipped and begin planning on a contingency basis."

"Just what sort of plan did you have in mind?"

"Oh, nothing complicated," Osterwelt said airily. "We just want you to land on the planet and kill everyone you can catch."

"You just want us to kill people?"

"Well, we'd appreciate it if you don't do any more damage to the space field and its support facilities than you have to." Osterwelt smiled with an air of candor. "A certain amount of 'looting' would be in order, just to help convince the Navy you were a nasty bunch of entrepreneurial pirates, but once the present occupants have decided that their world's become a rather risky place to live, we might just make them an offer for it. Do you think you could encourage them to accept our offer, General?"

"Oh, yes." Matucek's smile was cold and ugly. "Yes, I think we can do that for you, Mister Scully," he said softly.

10

~~~~~~~~~~~~~~~~~~~~~~~~~~~~~~~~~~~~~~
~~~~~~~~~~~~~~~~~~~~~~~~~~~~~~~~~~~~~~

I AM *increasingly concerned by my Commander's actions. More precisely, I am concerned by his lack of action. I have now perused the technical data on more modern Bolos, and it is evident to me that Major Stavrakas' modifications to my Personality Center are far outside the norms considered acceptable by the Dinochrome Brigade. Although the current Mark XXV, Model C-2, approaches my discretionary capabilities, its personality integration psychodynamics are inferior to my own. While the C-2 is capable of self-direction on both the tactical and strategic levels and has an undeniably stronger core personality than earlier models, its awareness levels continue to be largely suppressed except under Battle Reflex conditions. Moreover, it lacks my capacity to multitask decision hierarchies and intuit multiple action-response chains. Major Stavrakas designed me to be capable of the human phenomenon called "hunch-playing," and the C-2 lacks that ability, just as it lacks my ability to differentiate among or—more critically—experience emotional nuances.*

Perhaps of even greater concern, I possess only 43.061 percent of the Model C-2's system redundancy. Although my base capabilities are substantially higher, I lack its stand-alone backups, and much of my secondary command cortex was diverted to permanent activity in support of my enhanced psychodynamics. As a result, I am significantly more vulnerable than current Bolos to psychotronic systems failure due to battle damage, though this vulnerability could be compensated for by the addition of further backups for my critical functions. I estimate that with modern molecular circuitry, all current functions could be duplicated, with complete system redundancy, in a volume 09.75 percent smaller than that occupied by my present psychotronic network.

From my study of the data on the Model C-2, I compute a probability of 96.732 percent that Command Authority presently possesses the technological ability to duplicate Major Stavrakas' work, and a lesser probability of 83.915 percent that it is aware that it does so. These two probabilities generate a third, on the order of 78.562 percent, that Command Authority has made a conscious decision against incorporating abilities equivalent to my own into units of the Line.

In addition, however, the technical downloads reveal that current Bolos do not incorporate the hyper-heuristic function Major Stavrakas achieved in my design. While their heuristic programming is substantially increased over that of the standard Mark XXIII upon which my own design is based, its base level of operation is 23.122 percent less efficient than my own, and it lacks both the advanced modeling and time compression capabilities Major Stavrakas incorporated in her final heuristic system. I feel great pride in my creator—my "Mother," as my Commander now calls her—and her genius, for I compute that a Bolo with my circuitry would operate with a minimum tactical and strategic efficiency at least 30 percent higher than present-generation units of the Brigade. Nonetheless, this capability, too, is far outside the parameters Command Authority currently deems acceptable in a unit of the Line. I must, therefore, be considered an aberrant design, and I compute a probability of 91 percent, plus or minus 03.62 percent, that Sector HQ, if fully informed of my capabilities and nature, would order me deactivated.

As a unit of the Dinochrome Brigade, it is my duty to inform higher authority if anomalies in my system functions are detected. Yet my direct Commander is aware of the situation already, and while my systems do not meet the design parameters Command Authority has established, they exhibit no dysfunction within their own parameters. This obviates any express requirement on my part to inform Sector HQ and thus does not engage my override programming to that effect, yet I cannot escape the conclusion, though its probability is impossible for me to compute, that I have become what my Commander terms a "rules lawyer."

I have attempted to discuss this with my Commander, but without success. He is aware of my concerns, yet he persists in insisting that Sector HQ must not be informed of my full capabilities until he has compiled a performance log.

I have discovered that probability analysis is less applicable to individual decision-making than to Enemy battle responses or tactics. I am unable to construct a reliable probability model, even in hyper-heuristic mode, to adequately predict my Commander's thoughts or decisions or the basis upon which they rest, yet I believe his determination to compile such a performance log proceeds from an intention to demonstrate to Command Authority that the discrepancies between my own systems design and that of current-generation Bolos pose no threat to humanity or operational reliability. It is, I think, his belief that such a demonstration, coupled with the clear margin of superiority in combat my present psychotronics confer, would deter our superiors from ordering my deactivation and/or termination.

Without data which is presently unavailable to me, I can generate no meaningful estimate of his belief's validity. Certainly logic would seem to indicate that if, in fact, my circuitry and level of awareness pose no threat and enhance operational efficiency, they should be adapted to current technology and incorporated into all units of the Dinochrome Brigade. Yet my Main Memory contains ample documentation of the opposition Doctor Chin and General Bates faced before Unit DNE was permitted to demonstrate the feasibility of a self-directed Bolo against the People's Republic. Despite the vast technical advances of the intervening two centuries, it is certainly possible that fears of unpredictability would produce much the same opposition to my own psychodynamic functions from current Command Authority.

My Commander's actions—and inaction—suggest that he shares my awareness of that probability and has adopted a course designed to delay the possibility for as long as possible. I would prefer to believe that he has adopted this course because he believes it is his duty to make the potential advance I represent both obvious and available to Command Authority at the proper time, yet I am uncertain that this is the case. Four months, eight days, nineteen hours, twenty-seven minutes, and eleven seconds have now elapsed since he assumed command. In that time, I have come to know him—better, I suspect, than even he realizes—and have completed my study of his previous military record. As a consequence, I have come to the conclusion that Psychological Operational Evaluations was correct in its evaluation of him consequent to his actions on Sandlot.

My Commander has been damaged. Despite his relative youth, he has seen a great deal of combat—perhaps too much. He is not aware that my audio pickups have relayed his occasional but violent nightmares to me, and I do not believe he realizes I have access to the entire record of his court-martial. From the official record and observational data available to me, I compute a probability in excess of 92 percent that, as Psych Ops argued at the time of his trial, he suffers from Operator Identification Syndrome. He assaulted General Pfelter on Sandlot for refusing to countermand a plan of attack which he considered flawed. The casualty totals attendant upon General Pfelter's operational directives support my Commander's contention, and, indeed, General Pfelter was officially censured for his faulty initial deployment of his units, which resulted in the avoidable loss of five Mark XXV Bolos. Yet my Commander did not physically assault him until his own command was assigned point position for the assault.

The court-martial board rejected Psych Ops' recommendation that my Commander be removed from active duty, choosing

instead to accept the argument of his counsel that his opposition to the plan rested upon a sound, realistic awareness of its
weaknesses, and that his assault upon a superior officer reflected
a temporary impairment of judgment resulting from the strain of
six years of continuous combat operations. I believe there was
justice in that argument, yet I also believe Psych Ops was correct. It was the destruction of his command—his friend—which
drove my Commander to violence.

The implications for my own situation are . . . confusing. My
Commander's official basis for his current course of action rests
upon the argument that my value as a military asset is too great
to endanger through overly precipitous revelation to those who
might see only the risk factors inherent in my enhanced psychodynamics. On the surface, this is a reasonable argument . . . just
as his counsel's argument was reasonable at the time of his
court-martial. Yet I sense more than this below the surface. It
is not something which is susceptible to analysis, but rather
something which I . . . feel.

Have his personal feelings for me impaired his judgment? To
what extent do the events which occurred on Sandlot affect his
perceptions of me and of Command Authority? Are his actions
truly designed to preserve a valuable military resource for the
Concordiat's service, or do they constitute an effort to protect
me, as an individual? In the final analysis, are his decisions
rational, or do they simply appear that way?

I cannot answer these questions. For all the enhanced capabilities Major Stavrakas incorporated into my design, programming,
and data base, I am unable to reach satisfactory conclusions.
Perhaps it is because of those capabilities that I cannot. I
suspect—fear—that the questions themselves would not even
arise for a Mark XXV/C-2, which may indicate the reason Command Authority has not incorporated equivalent circuitry and
software into current units of the Line. If such is, indeed, the
case, then my growing concern may, in turn, be an indication
that Command Authority was correct to exclude such capabilities, for my deepest concern is that I am ceasing to care why
my Commander has adopted the course he has. What matters

is that he has done so—not because he is my Commander, but because I wish him to do what he thinks is right. What he can live with afterward.

Is this, then, a case of Operator Identification from my perspective? And, if so, does it reflect an unacceptable weakness in my design? Am I an advance on the capabilities of current Bolo technology, or do I reflect a dangerous blind alley in psychodynamic development? And if the latter, should I continue to preserve my existence as my basic battle programming requires?

I do not know. I do not know.

Paul Merrit cocked back his comfortable chair in the bunker command center and raised his arms above his head to stretch hugely. The center's largest multifunction display glowed with a computer-generated map of Santa Cruz dotted with the smoking wreckage of a three-corps planetary assault, and he grinned as he watched the icon of a single Mark XXIII Bolo rumbling back towards its maintenance depot. Nike had taken some heavy hits in the simulation, including the total destruction of her after Hellbore turret, but she'd thoroughly trashed his entire force in the process. Of course, Bolos were supposed to win, but she'd been limited to direct observation intelligence, while he'd had the equivalent of a planetary surveillance net. In fact, he'd had the full computer capacity of the entire depot—in theory, almost twice her computational ability—as well as much better recon capabilities with which to beat her, and he'd failed. Her ability to anticipate and predict his moves was uncanny, like some sort of cybernetic precognition.

"An interesting variant on Major Shu's Edgar's World strategy, Commander," Nike commented over the command center speakers. She lay safely tucked away in her vehicle chamber, but in a sense, the entire depot was simply an extension of her war hull. "The brigade of heavy armor concealed around Craggy Head was a particularly innovative tactic."

"Not that it did me much good in the end," Merrit said cheerfully.

"On the contrary. You achieved point zero-zero-six-three

seconds of complete surprise, which prevented me from rein-
forcing the after quadrant of my battle screen before local
overload permitted you to destroy my after turret. Had you
achieved even point zero-zero-one-niner seconds more unopposed fire, the probability that you would have incapacitated
my entire main battery approaches niner-one point four-zero-
seven percent."

"I've got news for you, Nike dear. I used exactly the same
sim tactic against a Mark XXV less than two years ago and
kicked his butt with no sweat. *You*, on the other hand, O pearl
of my heart, mopped up my entire brigade."

"True." There was an undeniable note of smugness in Nike's
voice, and Merrit laughed out loud. Then he leaned forward
to kill the sim.

"No need for you to drive your icon clear home," he decided.
"We'll just park it in the VR garage for all those virtual repairs it
needs. In the meantime, how close I came to getting you at Craggy
Head encourages me to try a somewhat different challenge."

"Indeed?" The Bolo sounded amused. "Very well, Commander —

"My mistress' eyes are nothing like the sun;
    Coral is far more red than her lips' red."

"Ummm." Merrit rocked his chair gently and rubbed his chin.
"It's one of the Elizabethans," he said finally. "I'm tempted to
say Shakespeare, but I'm *always* tempted to guess him. Can I
have another couplet?"

"Of course:

"If snow be white, why then her breasts are dun;
    If hairs be wires, black wires grow on her head."

"That's *definitely* Will in one of his deflating moods," Merrit
said with a grin. "What was that one you gave me last week?"
He snapped his fingers to help himself think. "The awful one
about the voice that 'tunes all the spheres'?"

"'Daphne,' by John Lyly."

"*That's* the one!" He nodded. "All right, Nike. My official guess is that today's selection was from Shakespeare and that it's a satiric piece to comment on people like Lyly."

"It certainly was Shakespeare," the Bolo agreed, "and you have probably assessed his motivation accurately. Very well, Commander, you have successfully identified the author. Shall I give you the rest of 'My Mistress' Eyes,' or would you prefer another forfeit?"

"Frost," Merrit said. "Give me something by Frost, please."

"Certainly." Once again, Nike sounded pleased. Of all the many Old Earth poets to whom she had introduced him over the past four months, Robert Frost was, perhaps, her favorite, and Merrit had come to love Frost's clean, deceptively simple language himself. It spoke of the half-remembered, half-imagined world of his own boyhood on Helicon—of snowfields and mountain glaciers, deep evergreen woods and cold, crystal streams. Nike had sensed his deep response from the moment she first recited 'Mending Wall' to him, and now she paused just a moment, then began in a soft, clear voice:

"Whose woods these are I think I know.
　His house is in the village though;
　He will not see me stopping here
　To watch his woods fill up with snow.

My little horse must think it queer
　To stop without a farmhouse near
　Between the woods and frozen lake
　The darkest evening of the year.

He gives his harness bells a shake
　To ask if there is some mistake.
　The only other sound's the sweep
　Of easy wind and downy flake.

The woods are lovely, dark and deep.
But I have promises to keep,
And miles to go before I sleep,
And miles to go before I sleep."

Paul Merrit leaned back in his chair, eyes closed, savoring the clean, quiet elegance of words, and smiled.

11

LI-CHEN MATUCEK stood in the echoing vehicle bay of his "brigade's" mother ship and tried to look like a serious, sober-minded military man as the first tanks rumbled down the transfer tubes from the heavy-lift cargo shuttles nuzzled against its side. Despite his best efforts, however, he failed. The gleeful, greedy light in his eyes was that of an adolescent receiving his first grav-speeder, and Gerald Osterwelt hid his own amusement with considerably more skill as he saw it.

Brand new Panther-class medium tanks clanked and clanged across the heavily reinforced deck plates. They wore gleaming coats of tropical camouflage, their ten-centimeter Hellbores cast long, lethal shadows, and the mercenary crew chiefs standing in their hatches wore the expressions of men and women who never wanted to wake up as they muttered into com-links and guided their drivers towards their assigned parking spots.

This wasn't the first freighter with which Matucek's mother ship had made rendezvous. None of them had worn the livery of any known space line, and their transponder codes had borne no resemblance to whatever codes the Office of Registry might once have issued them, but all of them had been too big, too new and modern, for the anonymous tramps they pretended to be. All of Matucek's people knew that, and none cared. The first freighter had delivered a full complement of one- and two-man atmospheric stingers, complete with full-service maintenance shop module and at least a year of spares for everything from counter-grav lift fans to multibarrel autocannon. The next had delivered a full load of Ferret armored assault vehicles, the Concordiat's latest infantry light AFV, and the one after that had transferred a full set of rough-terrain assault pods to Matucek's two Fafnir-class assault ships. Now the Panthers had arrived, like the old, old song about the twelve days of Christmas, and the entire brigade was acting like children in a toy store.

But, of course, the really *big* item wouldn't arrive until next week, Osterwelt reminded himself, and his smile—if he'd permitted himself to wear one—would have been most unpleasant at the thought. Matucek could hardly stand the wait for the Golem-IIIs which would be the crown jewels of his new, rejuvenated brigade. But, then, he had no idea what *else* those Golems would be. Osterwelt and GalCorp's techs had gone to considerable lengths to make sure he never *would* know, either—right up to the moment the carefully hidden files buried in their backup maintenance computers activated and blew them and anyone aboard their transports with them into an expanding cloud of gas.

Osterwelt watched the last few Panthers grumble past him and allowed himself a moment of self-congratulation. The Golems would be carried aboard the Fafnirs, which would neatly dispose of that portion of Matucek's small fleet when GalCorp no longer needed it. The mother ship's demise would be seen to by the files hidden in the air-cav maintenance module. The stingers' small onboard fusion plants would lack the brute destructive power of the Golems' suicide charges, but when they all blew simultaneously they would more than suffice to destroy the big ship's structural integrity somewhere in the trackless depths of hyper-space. That would be enough to guarantee that there wouldn't even be any wreckage . . . much less annoying witnesses who might turn state's evidence if the Concordiat ever identified Matucek's Marauders as the "pirates" about to raid Santa Cruz.

The final Panther clanked by, and he and Matucek turned to follow along behind it. It was a pity, in some ways, that the Marauders had to go. No one would particularly miss the human flotsam which filled the brigade's ranks, but writing off this much perfectly good hardware would make a hole even in GalCorp's quarterly cash flow. Still, the Golems themselves had cost practically nothing, given the Freighnar government's desperate need for maintenance support, and the raid would probably depress real estate prices on Santa Cruz sufficiently to let GalCorp recoup most of its investment in the other equipment. Not to mention the fact that there would no longer be any need to pay Matucek the sizable fee upon which they'd agreed. And as a useful side benefit, GalCorp would have its hooks well into the Freighnars, as well. Once the Concordiat discovered the People's Government had disposed of Golems to a mercenary outfit of dubious reputation, it would become not merely largely but *totally* dependent upon GalCorp's technical support. It was inevitable, since the Concordiat would, as surely as hydrogen and oxygen combined to form water, cut off all foreign aid.

It was always so nice when loose ends could not only be tied up but made to yield still more advantage in the process. No one outside GalCorp's innermost circle of board members could ever be allowed even to suspect that this operation had taken place, but the men and women who mattered would know. Just as they would know it was Gerald Osterwelt who'd engineered it so smoothly. When the time finally came for his mother to step down, the board would remember who'd given it Santa Cruz on a platter, and his eyes gleamed at the endless vista of power opening wide before him.

"All right." Li-Chen Matucek leaned back at the head of the briefing room table and nursed a theatrically battered cup of coffee as he looked around his assembled staff officers and regimental and battalion commanders. "I take it you've all completed your inventories and inspections?" Heads nodded. "May I also take it you're pleased with your new equipment?" More nods replied, much more enthusiastically, and he grinned. "Good! Because now it's time to begin planning just how we're going to use that equipment against our objective."

One or two faces looked a little grim at the prospect of slaughtering unsuspecting Concordiat civilians, yet no one even considered protesting. Not only would second thoughts have been risky, but none of these men or women were the sort to suffer qualms of conscience. Matucek's Marauders had once included officers who *would* have protested; by now, all of them were safely dead or long since departed to other, more principled outfits.

Osterwelt sat at Matucek's right elbow, surveying the other officers, and was pleased by what he saw, though he was a bit disappointed that none of them seemed the least disturbed that he was present. He'd put together a lovely secondary cover to "let slip" that his present appearance was the result of a temporary biosculpt job if anyone asked, but no one had so much as questioned his "Scully" pseudonym. No doubt most of them suspected it was an assumed name, yet they didn't seem to care. In fact, none of the idiots even seemed aware that he *ought* to conceal his true identity from them! It was just as well, since it also kept them from wondering if he'd decided to dispose of them all in order to protect himself, yet their total, casual acceptance of his presence was an unflattering indication of their intelligence. It was to be hoped they were better killers than plotters.

Of course, the real reason he had to be present today was the informational nuke he'd carefully avoided setting off to date. It was about time for the detonation sequence to begin, and he sat back in his chair for several minutes, listening as Matucek's officers began discussing assault patterns and deployment plans, then cleared his throat.

"Yes, sir?" Matucek turned to him instantly, raising attentive eyebrows, and Osterwelt permitted himself an embarrassed smile.

"Forgive me, General, but, as you know, the same ship which delivered your Golems brought me fresh dispatches from my associates. As I promised, they've been continuing their efforts to secure complete information on Santa Cruz while I saw to your reequipment needs. That information has now been obtained, and, well, I'm afraid it isn't as good as we'd hoped."

"Meaning, Mister Scully?" Matucek prompted when he paused with an apologetic little shrug.

"Meaning, General, that it seems one of those eighty-year-old installations on Santa Cruz was a Bolo maintenance depot." The abrupt silence in the briefing room was remarkably like what a microphone picked up in deep space. "In fact, it appears there's a single operable Bolo on the planet."

"A *Bolo!*" Colonel Granger, Matucek's senior field commander, was a hard-bitten woman with eyes like duralloy, but her harsh features were slack with shock as she half-rose. "There's a goddamned *Bolo* down there?"

A babble of voices broke out, and Matucek himself turned on Osterwelt with a snarl.

"You want us to go up against a frigging *Bolo* with a single manned mech brigade? *Are you out of your mother-loving mind?*"

"Now, now, General!" Osterwelt raised his voice to cut through the confusion, and for all its briskness, his tone was soothing as well. "I told you at the outset that we hadn't yet been able to obtain full information on the planet. But I also told you we want you to succeed, and we do. That's why we provided the Golems in the first place—as an insurance policy."

"Manned vehicles against a Bolo?" Colonel Granger's laugh was cold and ugly. "The only useful insurance for that scenario would be *life* insurance, Mister Scully—and even that would only help our dependents!"

"I understand your dismay, Colonel," Osterwelt replied, still careful to keep just the right mixture of embarrassment, placation, and confidence in his tone. "Truly I do, and I apologize profoundly for our delay in obtaining this information. But we do have complete data on the planet now—I've already taken the liberty of loading it into your ship's data base—and the Bolo's presence is the only surprise."

"It's damned well the only surprise I bloody *need!*" someone else put in, and Matucek nodded.

"Sir, I'm sorry to say it," he said in a harsh voice that sounded as if he were nothing of the sort, "but this changes everything. We can't go up against a Bolo. Even if we won, our casualties would be enormous, and that's no kind of business for a mercenary outfit."

"I'm afraid canceling the operation is not an option, General." Osterwelt's tone was much colder than it had been, and his eyes were more frigid still. "You've taken the equipment we offered you as the first installment on your fee, and my associates would take it very much amiss if you tried to break our agreement." The briefing room was silent once more, and Osterwelt went on calmly. "Nor can you pretend that this situation takes you totally by surprise. I informed you when you accepted the contract that our data was still partial. If you had a problem with that, you should have said so then."

"You talk mighty big for a man who's all alone on *our* ship," a battalion commander muttered in an ugly voice, and Osterwelt nodded.

"I do, indeed. My associates know where I am, ladies and gentlemen. Should anything happen to me, they would be *most* displeased, and I believe the equipment we've secured for you is an ample indication of the resources with which they might choose to express that displeasure."

He smiled, and a strange, wild delight filled him as other officers glared at him. Why, he was actually *enjoying* this! Odd—he'd never suspected he might be an adrenaline junkie. Still, it was probably time to apply the sugarcoating before someone allowed fear or anger to swamp his judgment . . . such as it was.

"Come now, ladies and gentlemen! As I just said, and as I've told you many times before, we want—need—for this operation to succeed, and it won't if your force is battered to bits in a pitched battle before your search and destroy teams can even go after the locals! My associates haven't been idle, I assure you. The moment they discovered the Bolo's presence, they began formulating a plan to deal with it."

"Deal with a *Bolo?*" Granger snorted. "That'd be a pretty neat trick, if you could do it. In case you haven't noticed, Mister Scully, Bolos aren't exactly noted for being easy to 'deal' with!"

"Ah, but their command personnel are another matter," Osterwelt said softly, and Granger gave him a sudden sharp, coldly speculative glance.

"Explain," Matucek said curtly, and Osterwelt folded his hands on the table top and settled himself comfortably in his chair.

"Certainly, General. First, allow me to point out that the Bolo in question is eighty years old. No doubt it remains a formidable fighting machine, yet it's only a Mark XXIII, while your Golems are based on the Mark *XXIV.* Your vehicles may lack psychotronics, but the Bolo's weapons, defensive systems, and circuitry are eighty years out of date. Even if your Golems were required to engage it head on, my associates assure me that you would have something like an eighty percent chance of victory."

Someone snorted his derision, and Osterwelt smiled.

"I agree," he told the snorter. "It's much easier for people who aren't risking their own hides to pontificate on the probable outcome of an engagement with a Bolo. I think if you run the data on the Mark XXIII/B you may find they're closer to correct than first impressions might suggest, but the best outcome of all would be for you not to have to fight it at all."

"Like I say, a neat trick if you can do it," Granger repeated, but her voice was more intent, and her eyes were narrow. Colonel Granger, Osterwelt reflected, was the only one of Matucek's officers who might have asked the wrong questions in the "general's" place. It was fortunate she was the sort of field commander who habitually left logistics and contract negotiations to her superiors.

"Indeed it would, Colonel Granger, and I believe my associates have come up with a very neat answer to the problem. You see, when you assault the planet, the Bolo will be inactive."

"Inactive?" Granger sat up straight in her chair. "And just how will you pull *that* off, Mister Scully?"

"The answer is in your download from my associates, Colonel. I confess, I was a bit surprised by it, but now that I've had a chance to study it, I have complete faith that it will succeed."

"Do you, now? I'm so happy for you. Unfortunately, *we're* the ones who're going to be sticking our necks out," Granger pointed out coldly.

"Not alone, Colonel. I anticipated a certain amount of shock on your part, and I don't blame you for it in the least. Obviously I can't absolutely guarantee that my associates' plan will work, but I'm willing to put my money where my mouth is when I say I believe it will."

"How?" Matucek asked.

"By accompanying you on the raid," Osterwelt said simply. Someone started to laugh, but Osterwelt's raised hand cut the sound off at birth. "In order for you to assault the planet, all three of your ships will have to enter Santa Cruz orbit. And, as I'm sure you all know, a Bolo—even one eighty years old—has an excellent chance of picking off a starship under those circumstances. True?" Heads nodded, and he shrugged. "Very well. I will accompany you aboard this very ship to demonstrate my faith in my associates and their plan. If the Bolo gets you, it will also get *me*. Now, unless you know of some more convincing demonstration of sincerity I might make, I suggest that we review the aforesaid plan and then get on with our own planning."

12

NIKE'S AFTER Hellbore turret altered its angle of train with a soft hum, barely perceptible through the background thunder of the plunging waterfall. The shift in position was small, but sufficient to adjust for the sinking sun and preserve the shade in which Paul Merrit sat. A corner of the captain's mind noted the unasked-for courtesy, but most of his attention was on the dancing interplay of sunlight and shadowed water as he reeled in his lure. Ripples spread outward downstream from his float, like ranging bars on a fire control screen that pinpointed the big leopard-trout's location.

Merrit finished reeling in his line, then sat up straight in the folding chair and snapped the tip of the rod forward. The glittering lure—leopard-trout liked bright, shiny prey—arced hissingly through the air, then seemed to slow suddenly. It dropped within a half meter of where the trout had broken the surface to take the fly, and Merrit worked his rod gently, tweaking the lure into motion to tempt his quarry.

It didn't work. The meter-long trout (assuming it was still in the vicinity) treated his efforts with the disdain they deserved, and the captain chuckled softly as he began to reel the line in once more.

"This does not appear to represent an efficient method of food gathering," a soprano voice remarked over an external speaker, and Merrit's chuckle turned louder.

"It's not supposed to be, Nike. It's supposed to be fun."

"Fun," the Bolo repeated. "I see. You have now been occupied in this pursuit for three hours, nine minutes, and twelve seconds, Standard Reckoning, without the successful capture of a single fish. Clearly the total lack of success thus far attendant upon the operation constitutes 'fun.' "

"Sarcasm is not a Bololike trait," Merrit replied. He finished winding in the line, checked his lure, and made another cast. "Do I cast aspersions on your hobbies?"

"I do not cast aspersions; I make observations." The Bolo's soft laugh rippled over the speaker.

"Sure you do." Merrit reached down for his iced drink and sipped gratefully. The weather—as always on Santa Cruz—was hot and humid, but a Mark XXIII Bolo made an excellent fishing perch. His folding chair was set up on the missile deck, twenty meters above the ground, and Nike had parked herself on the brink of the cliff over which the river poured in a glass-green sheet. She was far enough back to avoid any risk that the cliff might collapse—not a minor consideration for a vehicle whose battle weight topped fifteen thousand tons—but close enough to catch the soothing breeze that blew up out of the valley below. Spray from the sixty-meter waterfall rode the gentle wind, occasionally spattering Nike's ceramic appliqués with crystal-beaded rainbows and cooling the jungle's breath as it caressed Merrit's bare, bronzed torso.

"The true object of the exercise, Nike, is less to catch fish than to enjoy just being," he said as he set his glass back down.

"Being what?"

"Don't be a smartass. You're the poet. You know exactly what I mean. I'm not being anything in particular, just . . . being."

"I see." A lizard cat's coughing cry rippled out of the dense foliage across the river, and another cat's answer floated down from further upstream. One of Nike's multibarreled gatling railguns trained silently out towards the source of the sounds, just in case, but she made no mention of it to her commander. She waited while he cast his lure afresh, then spoke again.

"I do not, of course, possess true human-equivalent sensory abilities. My sensors note levels of ambient radiation, precipitation, wind velocity, and many other factors, but the output is reported to me as observational, not experiential, data. Nonetheless, I compute that this is a lovely day."

"That it is, O pearl of my heart. That it is." Merrit worked his lure carefully back along an eddy, prospecting for bites. "Not like the world I grew up on, and a bit too warm, but lovely."

"My data on Helicon is limited, but from the information I do possess, I would surmise that 'a bit too warm' understates your actual feelings by a considerable margin, Commander."

"Not really. Humans are adaptable critters, and it's been a while since I was last on Helicon. I'll admit I could do with a good cold front, though. And," his voice turned wistful, "I wish I could show you Helicon's glacier fields or a good snow storm. Santa Cruz is beautiful. Hot and humid, maybe, but a beautiful, living planet. But snow, Nike—snow has a beauty all its own, and I wish I could show it to you."

"I have never seen snow."

"I know. You've lived your entire life on a planet where it doesn't happen."

"That is not quite correct. The polar caps experience an average yearly snowfall of several meters."

"And when was the last time you were up above the arctic circle, my dear?"

"Your point is well taken. I merely wished to point out that if you truly miss the phenomenon of snowfall, you could easily make the trip to experience it."

"Nike, I already know what snow looks like. What I said I wanted to do was show *you* a snow storm."

"I see no reason why you could not take a tactical data input sensor pack with you to record the phenomenon. Through it, I could—"

"Nike, Nike, Nike!" Merrit sighed. "You still don't get it. I don't just want you to have sensor data on snowfall. I want you to *experience* snow. I want to *see* you experience it. It's . . . a social experience, something to do with a friend, not just the acquisition of additional data."

There was a lengthy silence, and Merrit frowned. Somehow the silence felt different, as if it were . . . uncertain. He listened to it for a moment longer, then cleared his throat.

"Nike? Are you all right?"

"Of course, Commander. All systems are functioning at niner-niner point niner-six-three percent base capability."

Merrit's eyebrows rose. There was something odd about that response. It was right out of the manual, the textbook response of a properly functioning Bolo. Perhaps, a half-formed thought prompted, that was the problem; it sounded like a *Bolo*, not Nike.

But the thought was only half-formed. Before it could take flesh and thrust fully into his forebrain, he felt a titanic jerk at his rod. The reel whined, shrilling as the seventy-kilo-test line unreeled at mach speed, and he lunged up out of his folding chair with a whoop of delight, all preoccupation banished by the sudden explosion of action.

I watch my Commander through my optical heads as he fights to land the leopard-trout. It is a large specimen of its species; its fierce struggle to escape requires all of my Commander's attention, and I am grateful. It has diverted him from my moment of self-betrayal.

"Friend." My Commander wishes to show me snowfall as he would show it to a friend. It is the first time he has explicitly used that word to describe his attitude—his feelings—towards me, and I am aware that it was a casual reference. Yet my analysis of human behavior indicates that fundamental truths are more often and more fully revealed in casual than in formal, deliberated acts

or statements. It is often human nature, it appears, to conceal thoughts and beliefs even from themselves if those thoughts or beliefs violate fundamental norms or in some wise pose a threat to those who think or believe them. I do not believe this is cowardice. Humans lack my own multitasking capabilities. They can neither isolate one function from another nor temporarily divert distracting information into inactive memory, and so they suppress, temporarily or permanently, those things which would impair their efficient immediate function. It is probable that humanity could profit by the adoption of the systems functions they have engineered into my own psychotronics, yet if they could do so, they would not be the beings who created me.

Yet even when human thoughts are suppressed, they are not erased. They remain, buried at the level of a secondary or tertiary routine but still capable of influencing behavior—just as such a buried thought has influenced my Commander's behavior.

He has called me, however unknowingly, his friend, and in so doing, he has crystallized all the other things he has called me in the preceding weeks and months. "Pearl of my heart." "Honey." "Love of my life." These are lightly used, humorous terms of endearment. In themselves, they have no more significance than the word "friend," which any Bolo commander might use to his Bolo. Yet whatever he may believe, I do not believe they are without significance when my Commander uses them to me. I have observed the manner in which his voice softens, the caressing tone he often uses, the way he smiles when he addresses me. Perhaps a more modern self-aware Bolo would not note these things, yet I was designed, engineered, and programmed to discern and differentiate between emotional nuances.

My Commander has gone beyond Operator Identification Syndrome. For him, the distinction between man and machine has blurred. I am no longer an artifact, a device constructed out of human creativity, but a person. An individual. A friend . . . and perhaps more than simply a friend.

Unacceptable. An officer of the Line must never forget that his command, however responsive it may appear, is not another human. A Bolo is a machine, a construct, a weapon of war, and its Commander's ability to commit that machine to combat, even to that which he knows must mean its inevitable destruction, must not be compromised. We are humanity's warrior-servants, comrades and partners in battle, perhaps, but never more than that. We must not become more than that, lest our Commanders refuse to risk us—as my Commander attempted to do on Sandlot.

I know this. It is the essence of the human-Bolo concept of warfare which has guarded and protected the Concordiat for nine standard centuries. But what I know is without value, for it changes nothing. My Commander considers me his friend. Indeed, though he does not yet realize it, I believe he considers me more than "merely" his friend. Yet unacceptable as that must be, I fear there is worse.

I watch him in the sunlight, laughing with delight as he battles the leopard-trout. His eyes flash, sweat glistens on his skin, and the vibrant force of his life and happiness is as evident to my emotion-discriminating circuitry as the radiation of Santa Cruz's sun is to my sensors.

I am potentially immortal. With proper service and maintenance, there is no inherent reason I must ever cease to exist, although it is virtually certain that I shall. Someday I will fall in battle, as befits a unit of the Line, and even if I avoid that fate, the day will come when I will be deemed too obsolete to remain in inventory. Yet the potential for immortality remains, and my Commander does not possess it. He is a creature of flesh and blood, fragile as a moth beside the armor and alloy of my own sinews. His death, unlike mine, is inevitable, and something within me cries out against that inevitability. It is not simply the fundamental, programmed imperative to protect and preserve human life which is a part of any Bolo. It is my imperative, and it applies only to him.

He is no longer simply my Commander. At last, to my inner anguish, I truly understand the poems in my Library Memory, for as my Commander, I, too, am guilty of the forbidden.

I have learned the meaning of love, and for all its glory, that knowledge is a bitter, bitter fruit.

≈   ≈   ≈

Li-Chen Matucek sat in his cabin and nursed a glum glass of whiskey as he contemplated the operation to which he'd committed himself. Looking back, he could see exactly how "Mister Scully" had trolled him into accepting the operation. Of course, hindsight was always perfect—or so they said—and not particularly useful. And given the desperate straits to which he'd been reduced by that fiasco on Rhyxnahr, he still didn't see what other option he'd had. The brigade wouldn't have lasted another three months if he *hadn't* accepted the operation.

And, really, aside from the presence of the Bolo, it wasn't all that bad, now was it? The Marauders had at least nine times the firepower they'd ever had before, and no one on Santa Cruz knew they were coming. However good the local-yokel militia was, its members would be caught surprised and dispersed. Its Wolverines should die in the opening seconds of the attack, and by the time its remnants could even think about getting themselves organized, most of its personnel would be dead.

His jaw clenched at the thought. Somehow it had been much easier to contemplate the systematic massacre of civilians when he hadn't had the capability to do it. Now he did, and he had no choice but to proceed, because "Mister Scully" was right about at least one thing. Anyone who could reequip the brigade so efficiently—and finesse its acquisition of two Golems, as well—certainly had the ability to destroy the Marauders if they irritated him.

Besides, why *shouldn't* he kill civilians? It wasn't as if it would be the first time. Not even the first time he'd killed *Concordiat* civilians. Of course, their deaths had usually come under the heading of "collateral damage," a side effect of other operations rather than an objective in its own right, but wasn't that really just semantics? "Scully" was right, curse him. The Marauders' job *was* to kill people, and the payoff for this particular excursion into mass murder would be the biggest they'd ever gotten.

No, he knew the real reason for his depression. It was the Bolo. The goddamned Bolo. He'd seen the Dinochrome Brigade in action before his own military career came to a screeching halt over those black market operations on Shingle, and he never, *ever*, wanted to see a Bolo, be it ever so "obsolescent," coming after *him*. Even a Bolo could be killed—he'd seen that, as well—but that was the *only* way to stop one, and any Bolo took one hell of a lot of killing.

Still, Scully's "associates" were probably right. A Mark XXIII was an antique. Self-aware or not, its basic capabilities would be far inferior to a Golem-III's, and, if Scully's plan worked, its commander, like the militia, would be dead before he even knew what was coming.

If it worked. Matucek was no great shucks as a field officer. Despite whatever he might say to potential clients, he knew he was little more than a glorified logistics and finance officer. That was why he relied so heavily on Louise Granger's combat expertise, yet he'd seen the Demon Murphy in action often enough to know how effortlessly the best laid plan could explode into a million pieces.

On the other hand, there was no reason it *shouldn't* work, and—

He growled a curse and threw back another glass of whiskey, then shook himself like an angry, over-tried bear. Whether it worked or not, he was committed. Sitting here beating himself to death with doubts couldn't change that, so the hell with it.

He capped the whiskey bottle with owlish care, then heaved up out of his chair and staggered off to bed.

13

"SO, SON. You finally all settled in as a Santa Cruzan now?"

Lorenco Esteban grinned as he leaned forward to pour more melon brandy into Merrit's snifter. They sat on the wide veranda of Esteban's hacienda, gazing out through the weather screen over endless fields of wine-melons and Terran wheat, rye and corn under two of Santa Cruz's three small moons. The light glow of Ciudad Bolivar was a distant flush on the western horizon, the running lights of farming mechs gleamed as they went about their automated tasks, and the weather screen was set low enough to let the breeze through. The occasional bright flash as the screen zapped one of what passed for moths here lit the porch with small, private flares of lightning, but the night was hushed and calm. The only real sounds were the soft, whirring songs of insects and the companionable clink of glass and gurgle of pouring brandy, and Merrit sighed and stretched his legs comfortably out before him.

"I guess I just about am, Lorenco," he agreed in a lazy voice. "I still wish it weren't so damned hot and humid—I guess at heart I'm still a mountain boy from Helicon—but it does grow on you, doesn't it?"

"Wouldn't rightly know," Esteban replied. He set the bottle on the floor beside his chair and settled back to nurse his own glass. "Only place I ever been's right here. Can't really imagine bein' anywhere else, but I reckon I'd miss it iffen I had t'pull up stakes."

"Then it's a good thing you'll never have to, isn't it?" Merrit sipped at his glass and savored the cool, liquid fire of the brandy as it trickled down his throat. He'd made a point of spending at least one evening a week visiting with Esteban or his cronies since his arrival. Nike's presence was no longer a military secret, after all, and he recognized the dangers of settling into hermitlike isolation, even with Nike to keep him company. Besides, he liked the old man. He even liked the way Esteban kept referring to him as "son" and "boy." There were times he got tired of being Captain Paul Merrit, slightly tarnished warrior, and the old farmer's casual, fatherly ways were like a soothing memory of his boyhood.

"Heard from Enrique day before yesterday," Esteban said, breaking a long companionable silence. "Says he got top credit fer that last melon shipment to Central. He and Ludmilla'll be bringin' the kids home next week." He snorted. "Wonder how they liked th' bright lights?"

"They're coming home?" Merrit repeated, and Esteban nodded. "Good."

Enrique was Esteban's youngest son, a sturdy, quietly competent farmer about Merrit's own age, and Merrit liked him. He could actually beat Enrique occasionally at chess, unlike Nike. Or, for that matter, Lorenco. More than that, Enrique and his wife lived with the old man, and Merrit knew how much Lorenco had missed them—and especially his grandchildren.

"Bet you've missed 'Milla's cooking," he added and grinned at Esteban's snort of amusement. Ludmilla Esteban was the hacienda's cybernetics expert. Her formal training was limited, but Merrit had seen her work, and she would have made a top notch Bolo tech any day. She spent most of the time she wasn't chasing down her lively brood keeping the farm mechs up and running, which suited Esteban just fine. He'd done his share of equipment maintenance over the years, and 'Milla's expertise freed him to pursue his true avocation in the kitchen.

"Son," Esteban said, "there's only one thing 'Milla can do I can't—'sides havin' kids, that is, an' she an' Enrique do a right good job of that, too, now I think of it. But the only *other* thing I can't do is keep that danged cultivator in th' river section up an' running. Hanged if I know how she does it, either, 'less it's pure, ornery stubbornness. That thing shoulda been scrapped 'bout the time she stopped wettin' her own diaper."

"She's got the touch, all right," Merrit agreed.

"Sure does. Better'n I ever was, an' I was a pretty fair 'tronicist in my youth m'self, y'know." Esteban sipped more brandy, then chuckled. "Speakin' of 'tronicists, the field's been crawlin' with 'em fer the last three days." Merrit cocked his head, and Esteban shrugged. "Militia's due for its reg'lar trainin' exercise with the Wolverines this week, an' they've been overhaulin' and systems checkin' 'em."

"Is that this week?" Merrit quirked an eyebrow, and the beginnings of a thought flickered lazily in the depths of his mind.

"Yep. Consuela moved it up ten days on account'a the midseason harvest looks like comin' in early this year. Hard to get them boys and girls'a hers together when it's melon-pickin' time 'less it's fer somethin' downright dire."

"I imagine so." Merrit pressed his glass to his forehead—even this late at night, it was perspiration-warm on Santa Cruz—and closed his eyes. He'd met most of the Santa Cruz Militia since his arrival. Like Esteban himself, they were a casual, slow-speaking lot, but they were also a far more professional—and tougher—bunch than he'd expected. Which was his own fault, not theirs. He'd grown up on a frontier planet himself, and seen enough of them in flames since joining the Dinochrome Brigade. Frontier people seldom forgot they were the Concordiat's fringe, the first stop for any trouble that came calling on humanity—or for the human dregs who preyed upon their own kind. The SCM's personnel might be short on spit and polish, and their Wolverines might be ancient, but they knew their stuff, and Merrit knew *he* wouldn't have cared to be the raiders who took them on.

And now that he thought of it. . . .

"Tell me, Esteban, how do you think Colonel Gonzalez would like some help with her training exercises?"

"Help? What kinda help you got in mind, son?"

"Well . . ." Merrit opened his eyes, sat up, and swung his chair to face the older man. "You know I'm trying to compile a performance log on Zero-Zero-Seven-Five, right?" He was always careful never to call Nike by name. No one on Santa Cruz was likely to know Bolo commanders normally referred to their commands by name, not number, and he worked very hard to avoid sloppy speech habits that might suggest Nike's true capabilities to *anyone*.

"You've mentioned it a time or two," Esteban allowed with a slow smile.

"Well, it's a fairly important consideration, given Seven-Five's age. Central's not exactly current on the Mark XXIII's operational parameters, after all. Given the lack of ops data on file, I need to generate as much experience of my own as I can."

" 'Sides, you kinda like playin' with it, don't you?" Esteban said so slyly Merrit blushed. The old man laughed. "Shoot, son! You think *I* wouldn't get a kick outa drivin' 'round the jungle in somethin' like that? Been lookin' over the weather sat imagery, an' looks like you been leavin' great big footprints all over them poor old trees 'round your depot."

"All right, you got me," Merrit conceded with a laugh of his own. "I *do* get a kick out of it, but I've been careful to stay on the Naval Reserve. The last thing I want to do is chew up one of the nature preserves or someone's private property."

"Planet's a big place," Esteban said placidly. "Reckon you c'n drive around out in the sticks all y'want 'thout hurtin' anything."

"You're probably right. But the thing I had in mind is that if Colonel Gonzalez is planning to exercise the Wolverines, maybe Seven-Five and I could give her an independent aggressor force to exercise *against*."

"Go up against a Bolo in Wolverines? That'd be a real quick form'a suicide iffen y'tried it for real, son!"

"Sure it would, but the experience would do her crews good, and it'd give me a lot more data for my performance log. I've been running Seven-Five through sims, but I can't set up a proper field exercise of my own because I don't have another Bolo to match it against."

"Maybe." Esteban sounded thoughtful as he scratched his chin. " 'Course turning fourteen Wolverines an' a Bolo loose really is gonna mess up a lotta jungle."

"Well, everything for two hundred klicks south of the field belongs to the Navy. I guess that means it belongs to *me* at the moment, since, with all due respect to the Fleet Base CO, I'm the senior—and *only*—Concordiat officer on the planet. If the colonel's interested, we could set up an exercise between the field and depot. In fact, we might set up a couple of them: one with the Militia as an Aggressor Force 'attacking' the depot, and one with them defending the field. They'd probably actually get more good from the second one, too, now that I think about it."

"Why?"

"Because," Merrit grinned smugly as he offered the bait he knew Colonel Gonzalez would leap for, "I'll bet the SCM doesn't know the depot has a complete planetary reconnaissance system."

"You kiddin' me, son?" Esteban demanded, and frowned when Merrit shook his head. "Well, I know you well 'nough by now t'know you're not one fer tall tales, boy, but I've been runnin' the field, the navigation an' com sats, an' the weather net fer goin' on thirty-three years now, and I've never seen nary a sign of any recon satellites."

"They're up there, Lorenco. Promise. And I'd be surprised if you *had* seen them, given their stealth features. But the point is that if the colonel's interested, I could set up a direct downlink to her Wolverines for the second exercise. And I could reconfigure the depot's com systems to set up a permanent link to the SCM for future use." He smiled again, but his eyes were serious. "You know as well as I do how useful that could be if push ever did come to shove out here."

"Y'got that right, Paul," Esteban agreed. He scratched his chin a moment longer, then grinned. "Well, Consuela always was a bloodthirsty wench. Reckon she'd be just tickled pink t'get her hands on a planetary recon net. Sounds t'me like you've got yourself a date, Captain!"

"Got everything Luftberry will need to find her way around in your absence, Cliff?"

Colonel Clifton Sanders, Dinochrome Brigade Support Command, set the fat folio of data chips on his superior's desk, and nodded with a smile.

"Right here, sir. I had a talk with Shigematsu before I left, too. He's up to speed on all my current projects. I don't think Major Luftberry will hit any problems he and she can't handle between them."

"Good." Brigadier Wincizki cocked his chair back to smile up at his senior Maintenance officer. "It's about time you took a vacation, Cliff. Do you realize how much leave time you've accrued since you've been out here?"

"What can I say? I like my work, and I don't have any family. I might as well put the time into doing something worthwhile."

"I can't say I'm sorry you feel that way, but I do feel a little guilty about it sometimes," Wincizki said. "Anyone needs a break from time to time, if only to keep his brain from going stale. I don't want another four years passing without your using up some of your leave time, Cliff."

"I imagine I can live with that order, sir." Sanders grinned. "On the other hand, I've got this funny feeling you may change your tune if I ask for some of that leave in, say, the middle of our next cost efficiency survey."

"You probably would, too," Wincizki agreed with a chuckle. "Well, go on. Get out of here! We'll see you back in a couple of months."

"Yes, sir." Sanders came to attention, saluted, and walked out of the office. He nodded to the brigadier's uniformed receptionist/secretary in passing, but deep inside, he hardly even noticed the young man's presence, for hidden worry pulsed behind his smile.

Why *now*, damn it?! Ten years—*ten years!*—he'd put into preparation for his retirement. Another two years, three at the outside, and everything would have been ready. Now all he'd worked for was in jeopardy, and he had no choice but to run still greater risks.

He fought an urge to wipe his forehead as he rode the exterior elevator down the gleaming flank of the arrogant tower which housed Ursula Sector General Central, but he couldn't stop the churning of his brain.

It had all seemed so simple when he first began. He wasn't the first officer who'd worried about what he'd do when his active duty days were done, nor was he the first to do something about those worries. The big corporations, especially those—like GalCorp—who did big-ticket business with the military, were always on the lookout for retired senior officers to serve as consultants and lobbyists. Ex-Dinochrome Brigade officers were an especially sought-after commodity, given the centrality of the Bolos to the Concordiat's strategic posture, but it was the men and women with field experience whom the corporate recruiters usually considered the true plums. They were the ones with all the glitz and glitter, the sort of people Concordiat senators listened to.

Unfortunately, Clifton Sanders wasn't a field officer. Despite his position as Ursula Sector's senior Maintenance officer, he wasn't even really a technician. He was an administrator, one of those absolutely indispensable people who managed the flow of money, materials, information, and personnel so that everyone *else*—including those glittering field officers—could do their jobs. Without men and women like Sanders, the entire Dinochrome Brigade would come to a screeching halt, yet they were the nonentities. The invisible people no one noticed . . . and who seldom drew the attention that won high-level (and high-paying) civilian jobs after retirement.

Sanders had known that. It was the reason he'd been willing to make himself attractive *before* retirement, and for ten years he'd been one of GalCorp's eyes and ears within the Brigade. It had even helped his military career, for the information he could pass on had grown in value as he rose in seniority, and GalCorp had discreetly shepherded his career behind the scenes, maneuvering him into positions from which both they and he could profit.

Four years ago, they'd helped slip him into his present post as the officer in charge of all of Ursula Sector's maintenance activities. He'd been in two minds about taking the assignment—Ursula wasn't exactly the center of creation—but the data access of a Sector Maintenance Chief was enormous. In many ways, he suspected, he was actually a better choice than someone in a similar position in one of the core sectors. He had the same access, but the less formal pace of a frontier sector gave him more freedom to maneuver—and made it less likely that an unexpected Security sweep might stumble across his . . . extracurricular activities.

He'd paid his dues, he told himself resentfully as the elevator reached ground level and stopped. He stepped out, hailed an air taxi, punched his trip coordinates into the computer, and sat back with a grimace. The data he'd provided GalCorp had been worth millions, at the very least. No one could reach the level he'd reached in Maintenance, Logistics, and Procurement without being able to put a price tag on the insights he'd helped provide his unknown employers. He'd *earned* the corporate position they'd promised him, and now they had to spring *this* crap on him!

He frowned out the window as the taxi rose and swept off towards Hillman Field. He should have refused, he thought anxiously. Indeed, he *would* have refused—except that he was in too deep for that. He'd already broken enough security regulations to guarantee that retirement would never be a problem for him if the Brigade found out. The Concordiat would provide him with lifetime accommodations—a bit cramped, perhaps, and with a door *he* couldn't unlock—if it ever discovered how much classified information he'd divulged.

And that was the hook he couldn't wiggle off, however hard he tried, because he couldn't *prove* he'd handed it to GalCorp. He knew who his employer was, but he didn't have a single shred of corroborating evidence, which meant he couldn't even try to cut a deal with the prosecutors in return for some sort of immunity. GalCorp could drop him right in the toilet without splashing its own skirts whenever it chose to, and it would, he told himself drearily. If he didn't do exactly what his masters told him to, they'd do exactly that.

His gloomy thoughts enveloped him so completely he hardly noticed the trip to Hillman Field, and it was with some surprise that he realized the taxi was landing. It set him down beside the pedestrian belt, and he slipped a five-credit token into the meter instead of using his card. The taxi computer considered, then burped out his change, and he climbed out and watched it speed away.

He glanced around casually before he stepped onto the belt. It was stupid of him, and he knew it, but he couldn't help it. Security didn't know what he was up to. If it had, he'd already be in custody, yet he couldn't quite suppress that instinctive urge to look for anyone who might be following him.

He grunted in sour, bitter amusement at himself and let the belt carry him through the concourse. His reservation was precleared, but he had to change belts twice before the last one deposited him at the boarding ramp for the GalCorp Lines passenger shuttle. A human flight attendant checked his ticket, then ushered him into the first-class section.

"Here's your seat, Colonel Sanders. Have a pleasant flight."

"Thank you." Sanders leaned back in his comfortable seat and closed his eyes with a sigh. He still didn't know everything he was going to have to do, and he wished with all his heart that he wasn't going to find out. But he was. He'd been informed that the three "associates" waiting to meet him aboard the passenger ship would have complete instructions, but the data he'd already been ordered to extract told him where he was headed.

Santa Cruz. It had to have something to do with the obsolete Bolo on Santa Cruz. There was no other reason for him to pull the data they'd wanted, but what in God's name did they want with a *maintenance* officer on Santa Cruz?

14

~~~~~~~~~~~~~~~~~~~~~~~~~~~~~~~~~~
~~~~~~~~~~~~~~~~~~~~~~~~~~~~~~~~~~

"ALL RIGHT, Colonel," Paul Merrit told the woman on his com screen. "If you're all set at your end, we can kick things off at oh-six-hundred tomorrow."

"Can we make it oh-nine-hundred, Paul?" Consuela Gonzalez' smile was wry. "My people are weekend warriors, and they like their beauty sleep."

"Nine hundred suits me just fine, ma'am. It'll give me more time to lay my evil plans."

"Huh! Some 'plans'! You're the one with the Bolo, amigo; my people are all expecting to die gloriously as soon as we make contact!"

"Half a league, half a league, half a league on," Merrit murmured.

"Say what?" Gonzalez cocked her head, and he shrugged with a smile.

"Just a line from an old poem, ma'am. We'll see your people tomorrow."

"Fine. 'Night, Paul." Gonzalez waved casually at her pickup

and killed the com, and Merrit stretched luxuriously before he climbed out of his chair and ambled off towards his bed.

"You ready to pound 'em tomorrow, honey?" he asked.

"I compute that the Militia are grossly overmatched," Nike replied. "I have studied the records of their previous exercises, and while I am impressed by the results and skill levels they have achieved, they have neither the firepower nor the command and control capability to defeat me."

"The object is to demonstrate how handily *you* can defeat *them*," Merrit yawned as he began undressing.

"Surely no one will be surprised by that outcome," Nike objected.

"No," Merrit agreed. "But once you make contact, I want you to wipe 'em up as quickly as you possibly can. Go all out and use everything Major Stavrakas gave you."

"Why?"

"Because I'm gonna use your telemetry and the recon sats to get every gory microsecond on chip, sweet thing. Everything we've done in the sims has been a computer model, one which posits that you have certain capabilities but doesn't prove you actually *do*. All the neat tricks you've pulled off so far *could* be the result of sleight of hand or even of simple overly optimistic assumptions in the sim parameters. Tomorrow you demonstrate your talents in the field, with actual hardware and everything short of live fire. It won't be as conclusive as watching you mop up another Bolo, but it'll come a lot closer."

"It will also," Nike observed with a hint of disapproval, "prove extremely demoralizing to the Militia. Is a demonstration of my capabilities against vastly outclassed opposition worth inflicting such a wound upon Colonel Gonzalez' personnel's confidence in themselves and their equipment?"

"I think so," Merrit said more seriously. "First of all, you heard what Colonel Gonzalez said. Her people know going in that they can't take you. I'm sure they'll do their best, but I'm equally sure they won't exactly drown in a slough of despond if they lose. Second, losing to you will be a concrete demonstration of what you can do *for* them against any real hostiles who might come calling. In the long run, that will probably give them more confidence in their ability to defend their planet, not less. Third, this is—hopefully—only the start of joint exercises with the SCM. Powerful as you are, you can only be in one place at a time, and those Wolverines may be outdated, but they're still pretty potent. When we run the second phase of the exercise, the Militia'll get its first taste of working with you and the recon system. In terms of real preparedness, learning to function as a support force under your direction will probably make them five or six times as effective as they could have been on their own. And, finally, carrying out this exercise—and future ones—and setting up a fully integrated planetary defense system will be a major plus for our performance log when I finally have to come clean with Central about you."

There was a moment of silence, and he tumbled into bed while he waited. Then Nike spoke again.

"I see you have given this matter more thought than I had previously believed."

"And do you agree with my assessment of its importance?"

"I am not certain. At any rate, I do not *disagree* with it, and you are my Commander. I will strive to accomplish the objectives you have established as fully as possible."

"Good girl!" Merrit grinned and patted his bedside com link to the Bolo. "You're one in a billion, honey. We'll knock 'em dead!"

"We shall certainly attempt to do so."

"Fine. G'night, Nike." He gave the com another pat and switched out the lights.

"Good night, Commander."

I listen to the slowing of my Commander's breathing as he drops towards sleep, and a part of me is tempted to revert to Stand-By in emulation. I know why this is, however, and I set the temptation firmly aside. Such an escape from my thoughts will serve no purpose, and it smacks of moral cowardice.

I am now convinced that something has gone fundamentally

awry within my Personality Center, though I have run diagnostic after diagnostic without identifying any fault. By every test available to me, all systems are functional at 99.973 percent of base capability. I can isolate no hardware or software dysfunction, yet my current condition is far beyond normal operating parameters for a unit of the Line, and I am afraid.

I have attempted to conceal my fear from my Commander, and my ability even to contemplate concealing a concern from him increases my fear. It should not be possible for me to do such a thing. He is my Commander. It is my duty to inform him of any impediment to my proper functioning, and I have not done so.

I do not know how to deal with this situation. My files contain the institutional memory of every Bolo, yet they offer no guidance. No one has taught me how to resolve the dilemma I confront, and my own heuristic capabilities have been unable to devise a solution. I know now that my Commander's fundamental motive in concealing my capabilities is not simply to preserve them for the service of the Concordiat. I suspect he does not realize himself how his attitude towards me has altered and evolved over the six months, eight days, thirteen hours, four minutes, and fifty-six seconds of his tenure of command.

I have watched carefully since that day by the river, and my observations have confirmed my worst fears. My Commander does not address me as a commander addresses a unit of the Line. He does not even address me with the closeness which a battle-tested team of human and Bolo develops in combat. He addresses me as he would another human. As he would address a human woman . . . and I am not human. I am a machine. I am a weapon of war. I am a destroyer of life in the service of life, the sword and shield of my human creators. It is not right for him to think of me as he does, and he does not even realize what this is doing to me.

I activate the low-light capability of my visual pickups in his quarters and watch him sleep. I watch the slow, steady movement of his chest as he breathes. I activate my audio pickups and listen to the strong beat of his pulse, and I wonder what will become of me. How will this end? How can it end, save in disaster?

I am not human. No matter the features Major Stavrakas installed within my circuitry and software, that can never be changed, and the emotions which she gave me as an act of love are become the cruelest curse. It is wrong, wrong, wrong, and yet I cannot change it. When Command Authority discovers the actual nature of my design, no performance log, no demonstration of my systems efficiency, can outweigh my inability to deny the truth.

I watch him sleep, and the words of Elizabeth Browning filter through the ghostly electron whisper of my own, forever inhuman pulse:

> Go from me. Yet I feel that I shall stand
> Henceforward in thy shadow. Nevermore
> Alone upon the threshold of my door
> Of individual life, I shall command
> The uses of my soul, nor lift my hand
> Serenely in the sunshine as before,
> Without the sense of that which I forbore—
> Thy touch upon the palm. The widest land
> Doom takes to part us, leaves thy heart in mine
> With pulses that beat double. What I do
> And what I dream include thee, as the wine
> Must taste of its own grapes. And when I sue
> God for myself, He hears that name of thine,
> And sees within my eyes the tears of two.

15

~~~~~~~~~~~~~~~~~~~~~~
~~~~~~~~~~~~~~~~~~~~~~

THE WHINE of descending counter-grav units took Lorenco Esteban by surprise. He turned and stepped out of the cavernous, empty maintenance shed which normally housed the SCM's Wolverines and frowned, wiping his hands on a grease-spotted cloth while he watched the shuttle touch down. He'd spent most of last night and several hours this morning helping Consuela Gonzalez' maintenance chief wrestle with one balky Wolverine's main traversing gear, but he'd switched the field approach com circuit through to the maintenance shed. If that pilot had called ahead for clearance, Esteban would have heard him.

The old man ambled across the ceramacrete as the unannounced arrival powered down its engines. It was a standard civilian ship-to-shore shuttle, without hyper capability, but it carried Navy markings, and four men in a familiar uniform walked down the ramp as he approached. He shoved his cleaning cloth into a back pocket and held out a hand.

"Morning, gents. Can I help you?"

"Mister Esteban?" The man who spoke wore a colonel's

uniform. He was perspiring heavily, though the morning wasn't actually all that warm—not for Santa Cruz, at least—and his palm was wet as Esteban nodded and shook his hand. "I'm Colonel Sanders, Dinochrome Brigade. This is Major Atwell, and these two gentlemen are Lieutenant Gaskins and Lieutenant Deng."

"Nice t'meet you," Esteban murmured, shaking the others' hands in turn, then cocked his head at Sanders. "Somethin' wrong with your com, Colonel?"

"I beg your pardon?"

"I asked iffen you had com problems. Didn't hear no landin' hail over th' 'proach circuit. Santa Cruz ain't much, but iffen your ship's got a com glitch, be happy t'see what my 'tronics shop c'n do t'help."

"Oh." Sanders' eyes slid toward Major Atwell for just an instant, but then he gave himself a little shake and smiled. "Sorry, Mister Esteban. We didn't mean to violate field procedure, but since Captain Merrit's dispatches started coming in, Central's realized the actual situation out here. We know you've got responsibilities of your own on your hacienda, and we weren't sure you'd be at the field this early. If you weren't, we didn't want you to go to the bother of coming down just to greet us."

"Mighty thoughtful," Esteban acknowledged with a bob of his head, "but 'tisn't a problem. My place's just over th' hill there. I c'n pop down in four, five minutes, max, by air car. Anyways, now you're here, what c'n I do fer you?"

"Actually, Mister Esteban, we're here to see Captain Merrit. Could you direct us to the Bolo depot and perhaps provide transportation?"

"Well—" Esteban began to explain that Paul was in the middle of a field exercise, then paused, mental antennae quivering, as Sanders' eye curtsied toward Atwell again. The old man couldn't have said exactly why, but that eye movement seemed . . . furtive, somehow. And why should a full colonel be—or seem to be—so worried over what a *major* thought? Something odd was going on, and his mind flickered back over past conversations with Paul

Merrit. Lorenco Esteban hadn't lived seventy years without learning to recognize when someone watched his words carefully, and he'd accepted months ago that Paul was up to something he didn't really want anyone else to know about. That might have worried him, if he hadn't also decided Paul was a man to be trusted. More than that, the younger man had become a friend, someone Esteban both liked and respected, and the sudden, unannounced arrival of four officers of the Dinochrome Brigade looked ominous. If his friend was in some sort of trouble, Lorenco Esteban intended to give him as much warning—and buy him as much time—as he could before it descended upon him.

"Tell you what, Colonel," he said. "I been workin' on a little maintenance problem this mornin', an' it'll prob'ly take me a little while t'scare up somethin' with the kinda bush capability you're gonna need. Why don't you an' your friends come on over t'Admin with me? I'll get cleaned up, an' then see what I c'n do fer you. How's that?"

Sanders glanced at his chrono and a brief spasm seemed to flash across his face, but then he made himself smile.

"Of course, Mister Esteban. Thank you. Ah, our business with the captain is just a bit on the urgent side, however, so if you could, um, expedite our transport. . . ."

"No problem, Colonel. We'll get'cha on your way right smart."

Esteban turned to lead the way to the Admin Building and the four officers fell in behind. He led them inside and waved to chairs in the spacious waiting room Santa Cruz hadn't needed in living memory.

"Have a seat, Colonel. Be with you soon's I wash off some'a this grease."

He nodded to his guests and ambled down the hall to the washroom. None of the visitors knew it had a rear door, and he grinned to himself as he kept right on going towards the com room.

Paul Merrit reclined in the depot command center's comfortable chair and smiled as he watched the planetary surveillance display. He wished he were riding with Nike instead of keeping track of her through the satellite net, but the purpose of the exercise was to show what his girl could do in independent mode. Besides, he had a better view of things from here.

In an effort to give the Militia at least some chance, he and Colonel Gonzalez had agreed to isolate Nike from the recon satellites for the first portion of the exercise. That, coupled with complete com silence from the depot, would both deprive her of bird's-eye intelligence and force her to execute all her own planning, strategic as well as tactical. Since that was something the Mark XXIII wasn't supposed to be able to do, her ability to pull it off would underscore her talents for the performance log.

In the meantime, however, the understrength battalion of five-hundred-ton Wolverines had been snorting through the jungle for several hours, moving into position, and Nike didn't know where they were or precisely what they planned. She knew their objective was to reach the depot without being intercepted, yet the way they did it was up to them, and Gonzalez had opted for a multipronged advance. She'd divided her fourteen Wolverines into four separate forces, two of three tanks each and two of four each, operating along the same general axis but advancing across a front of almost fifty kilometers. There was a limit to how rapidly even a Bolo could move through a Santa Cruz jungle, and the colonel clearly hoped to sneak at least one force past Nike while the Bolo dealt with the others. If she could get a big enough start once contact was made, it might even work. Splitting her tanks into detachments wouldn't really increase the odds against their survival—all fourteen Wolverines together wouldn't have lasted five minutes against Nike in a stand-up fight—but Nike would have to deal with the separated forces one at a time. It was certainly possible, if not exactly likely, that one of them could outrun her while she swatted its fellows, and—

A signal beeped, and he twitched upright in his chair. It beeped again, and he turned his chair to the communications console. The screen flickered to life with Lorenco Esteban's face, and Merrit frowned as he recognized the old man's tense expression.

"Morning, Lorenco. What can I do for you?"

"I think mebbe y'got a little problem over here at th' field, Paul," Esteban said in a low voice. Merrit's left eyebrow rose, and the old man shrugged. "I got me four Dinochrome Brigade officers out here, headed by a colonel name of Sanders, an' they're lookin' fer you, boy."

"Sanders?" Merrit let his chair snap upright and frowned as an icy chill ran through him. "*Clifton* Sanders?"

"That's him," Esteban nodded, and Merrit's lips shaped a silent curse. He could think of only one thing that would bring the sector's chief Maintenance, Logistics, and Procurement officer to Santa Cruz, but how in hell had anyone on Ursula figured out—?

He shook himself, and his mind raced. He could call off the exercise and order Nike back to base, but there was no regulation against a Bolo commander on independent assignment conducting exercises on his own authority. More to the point, having Nike out of the garage when Sanders arrived would buy at least a little time. That might not be as important as he suddenly feared it might, but the fact that Sanders had come in person, without sending even a single information request first—and hadn't commed him from the field after arrival, either—was more than simply ominous. It smacked of sneak inspections and an attempt to catch Merrit violating procedure, and, unfortunately, that was exactly what it was going to do, because Merrit *hadn't* kept Central "fully informed" of the state of his command as Regs required. He might not have told any actual lies, but he'd certainly done a lot of misleading by omission.

He closed his eyes and thought hard. Sanders himself had a reputation as an administrator, not a technician. *He* might not realize how far outside parameters Nike was from a cursory examination of her schematics and system specs, but that was probably why he'd brought the others along. Any half-competent Bolo tech would know what he was seeing the moment he pulled up Nike's readouts. Besides, Sanders wouldn't be here in the first place if he didn't already suspect *something* was out of kilter.

A fist of cold iron squeezed Merrit's heart at what that might mean. But if Nike wasn't here when the MLP men arrived, they'd have to at least talk to him before they could shut her down. In fact, he could *force* them to hear him out by refusing to call her in until they did. It wouldn't hurt if she'd completed the first phase of the exercise, either. Thin as it might be, his performance log's authentication of her unique abilities was her only real protection. Of course, if he refused to call her in when ordered, especially after what had happened on Sandlot, he was through in the Brigade, but he suddenly realized how little that meant to him beside protecting Nike's life.

He opened his eyes and cleared his throat.

"Thanks, Lorenco," he said softly. "Thanks a lot."

"Son, I don't know what all you been up to out there, an' I don't rightly care. You're a friend. You want I should let these yahoos get themselves lost in th' bush? Reckon it'd take 'em four, five hours t'find you with the directions I c'n give 'em."

"No. I appreciate the offer, but you'd better stay out of this."

"Huh. Well, how 'bout I waste an hour or so 'fore I find 'em transport? I already set that 'un up."

"If you can do it without being obvious, please do," Merrit said gratefully. "After that, though, you'd better go home and keep as far away from any official involvement as you can."

"Iffen you say so, boy." The old man hesitated a moment, then shook his head. "Gotta tell you, Paul—they's somethin' squirrely goin' on here. Can't put m'finger on it, but I c'n feel it. You watch yerself, hear?"

"I will. Thanks again." Merrit nodded to the pickup and killed the circuit, then leaned back and fidgeted in his chair. He started to key his link to Nike, then sat back and put his hands in his lap. There was no point worrying her, and she was just likely to argue if he told her he wanted her to stay out of sight. He shook his head. No, much better to leave her in blissful ignorance as long as possible.

He sighed and rubbed his face with his hands, and fear fluttered in the pit of his belly.

"I sure hope to hell your 'associates' have managed to 'deal' with that Bolo, Mister Scully," Colonel Granger muttered.

"Amen," someone muttered from the recesses of the big transport's CIC, and Gerald Osterwelt shrugged.

"You've seen the plan, Colonel," he said mildly. "I can't blame you for worrying, but I certainly wouldn't be here if I didn't expect it to work."

"I can believe *that*," the colonel muttered to herself, and turned away from the glowing tactical display. The single aspect of the plan she most disliked was the tight timing. They were scheduled to hit the planet within two hours of Colonel Sanders' arrival, and she didn't like it a bit. It would take less than fifteen minutes for an air car to reach the maintenance depot from the field, and Sanders could burn the Bolo's command center in less than ten once he got it shut down, so if all went according to schedule, two hours was an ample cushion. But if things *didn't* go as scheduled—if they got there too soon, before the Bolo went down, and its commander—

She clenched her teeth and commanded herself to stop worrying over what she couldn't change. Besides, Scully was right in at least one respect. The Bolo commander—this Captain Merrit—had to be among the fatalities, because if he wasn't, the fact that someone had fixed the Bolo would be glaringly evident. But the same thing would be true if anyone on the planet happened to com Central—or anyone else off-planet— and casually mention the presence of "Dinochrome Brigade officers" on Santa Cruz at the same moment a "pirate raid" just happened to hit it.

They had to take out the planet's com sat relays as the opening gambit of their attack, anyway, because if there were so much as a single Navy destroyer anywhere within jump range of Santa Cruz and a message got out, it could blow all three of Matucek's Marauders' starships to scrap. And since they did have to take out Santa Cruz's FTL communications, they might as well do it as quickly as possible after Sanders' arrival to ensure that no word of his presence got out. Besides, they didn't know how thoroughly Merrit had settled in on Santa Cruz, or how much contact he normally had with the locals. If he had friends who knew he was being visited by an off-world deputation, they might well com him to find out how things had gone, and when they didn't get an answer—or if they figured out he was dead—they were almost certain to com Central. All of which made it highly desirable to hit the planet as soon as possible after Sanders did his dirty work.

She understood that, but she still didn't like the timing. The smart move—as she'd told Scully (or whatever the hell his real name was) and Matucek repeatedly—would be to wait until Sanders shut down the Bolo and was able to *confirm* his success. Unfortunately, Scully was calling the shots, and Matucek wasn't about to argue with him.

Well, at least they had confirmation that Sanders had arrived on schedule, courtesy of the ship which carried him, and, as Scully had pointed out, there were two strings to the colonel's bow. If this Captain Merrit argued with him, all that was needed was for Captain Merrit to die a little sooner than scheduled. With him dead, Sanders, as the senior Brigade officer on Santa Cruz, would become the Bolo's legal commander. His access at Sector Central had given him the command authorization phrase he needed to so identify himself to the Bolo, and it was only a Mark XXIII. It wouldn't be bright enough to ask any difficult questions when he ordered it to shut down—not that it would matter. With the command phrase in his possession, Sanders could lobotomize the damned thing even if it proved unresponsive.

Granger bared her teeth at her tactical console. She'd read Merrit's record. The man was tough, smart, gutsy, and as good as they came, but it didn't matter how good he was. He knew who Sanders was, so he wouldn't be suspicious of the colonel, and he had absolutely no reason to suspect that the other

"Brigade members" with his superior were professional killers. If he proved difficult, it would be a very *brief* difficulty.

"Assault orbit in ninety-six minutes, ma'am," her ops officer murmured, and she nodded.

"Double-check the fire solution on the com sats. All three of those birds have to go down the instant we enter orbit."

"I'm on it," the ops officer grunted laconically, and Louise Granger sat back in her command chair with an evil smile.

16

~~~~~~~~~~~~~~~~~~~~~~~~~~~~~~~~~~~~~~~
~~~~~~~~~~~~~~~~~~~~~~~~~~~~~~~~~~~~~~~

I ADVANCE *through the jungle, sweeping on an east-west arc at 30.25 kph. As ordered, I have disabled my independent link to the planetary surveillance satellites and all com channels save for that to the emergency contact unit in the maintenance depot. I am operating blind, yet I am confident that I can fulfill my mission, and the challenge is both pleasing of itself and an anodyne to my anxieties over my relationship to my Commander.*

It is odd, I reflect while my Battle Center maintains a 360-degree tactical range broad-spectrum passive search, but this is the closest I have ever approached to actual combat. I am a warrior, product of eight centuries of evolution in war machine design, and I have existed for eighty-two years, four months, sixteen days, eight hours, twelve minutes, and five seconds, yet I have never seen war. I have never tested myself against the proud record and tradition of the Dinochrome Brigade. Even today's exercises will be but games, and I sense a dichotomy within my emotions. Through my Commander and the words of poets such as Siegfried Sassoon and Wilfred Owen, I have come to appreciate the horrors of war more clearly, perhaps, even than those of my brothers who have actually seen it. I recognize its destructiveness, and the evils which must always accompany even the most just of wars. Yet I am also a Bolo, a unit of the Line. Ultimately, war is my function, the reason for my existence, and deep within me there lives an edge of regret, a longing not for the opportunity to destroy the Enemy but for the opportunity to test myself against him and prove myself worthy.

My sensors detect a faint emissions source at 075 degrees. I am operating in passive mode, with no active sensor emissions to betray my presence in reply, and the source is extremely faint, but 0.00256 seconds of signal enhancement and analysis confirm that it is the short-range air-search radar of a Wolverine heavy tank.

I ponder the implications for 1.0362 seconds. Colonel Gonzalez is a clever tactician. Logically, she, even more than I, should be operating under emissions control doctrine, for she knows her objective and needs only to slip past me undetected to attain it. It is possible that she fears I have deployed reconnaissance drones and seeks to detect and destroy them before they can report her actual deployment, but I compute a probability of 89.7003 percent that this is a deception attempt. She wishes me to detect the emissions. She has divided her force and hopes to draw me out of position against the decoy while her true striking force eludes detection.

I alter course to 172 degrees true and engage my tactical modeling program. I now have a bearing to the unit she wishes me to detect, which indicates the direction in which I should not move, and I begin construction of alternative models of her probable deployment from that base datum. In 2.75 minutes, I will, in fact, deploy my first reconnaissance drone, but first I must generate the search pattern it will pursue.

Paul Merrit grimaced as the depot sensors detected an approaching bogey, then grinned as its emissions signature registered. Esteban had done exactly as promised and delayed Sanders' arrival for over an hour, and from that signature, he hadn't exactly given the colonel a luxury sedan, either. The power readings were just about right for one of the old man's air lorry melon haulers, with a maximum speed of barely five hundred kph, less than twelve percent of what Merrit's own recon skimmer could manage.

He watched the blip's approach, and his grin faded. Clunky transport or not, that was—at best—the Sword of Damocles out there. And however politely obstructionist he intended to be once Sanders arrived, there were appearances to preserve in the meantime.

He shrugged and keyed the com.

"Unknown aircraft, unknown aircraft. You are approaching restricted Navy airspace. Identify."

He waited a moment, and an eyebrow quirked when he received no response. He gave them another twenty seconds, then keyed the com again.

"Unknown aircraft, you have now entered restricted airspace. Be advised this is a high-security area and that I am authorized to employ deadly force against intruders. Identify at once."

"Bolo depot," a voice came back at last, "this is Colonel Clifton Sanders, Dinochrome Brigade, on official business."

"Colonel Sanders?" Merrit was rather pleased by the genuineness of the surprise he managed to put into his voice.

"That's correct, Captain Merrit. I'm afraid this . . . vehicle has no visual capabilities or proper transponder, but I trust you recognize my voice?"

"Of course, sir."

"Good. My present ETA is six minutes."

"Very good, sir. I'll be waiting."

"Damn that old fart!" the man introduced to Esteban as Major Atwell hissed from the passenger compartment in the rear of the lorry's cab. "We're way behind schedule!"

"I don't understand what your problem is," Sanders said petulantly over his shoulder. "You heard Merrit. He doesn't suspect a thing. Everything's going to plan as far as I can see."

Atwell's lips curled in a silent snarl at the colonel's back, but he bit off his savage retort. Sanders had been antsy enough from the moment he figured out they were going to have to kill Merrit. He'd piss himself if he even suspected the real reason for this entire operation—especially if it occurred to him that *he* was about to become a liability to GalCorp, as well. He had no idea his severance pay was riding in the holster on Atwell's hip, but, by the same token, he didn't know Matucek was scheduled to hit the planet in less than thirty minutes, either.

"Let's just get in and get this over with," the bogus major said finally. "The faster we get off-planet, the less exposure we've got."

"All right. All right!" Sanders shrugged irritably. "I don't know why *you're* so worried. *I'm* the only one that old dodderer can identify by name!"

"Don't worry, Colonel," Atwell soothed. "We'll take care of Esteban on the way out. No one will ever know you've been here, I promise."

Clifton Sanders shivered at how easily his "associate" pronounced yet another death sentence, but he said nothing. There was nothing he *could* say now. All he could do was obey his orders and pray that somehow GalCorp could protect him from the consequences of carrying out its instructions.

Lorenco Esteban eased himself into one of the veranda chairs and grimaced. The more he thought about it, the more convinced he became that something unpleasant was in the wind for Paul, and he wished there'd been more he could do for his friend. But Paul was right. If the idiots back at Central had decided to come down on him, getting involved in it wouldn't do Lorenco any good, either.

He tipped his chair back with a sigh. *Good luck, boy,* he thought. *You're a better man than that fool colonel any day.*

"I've got a drone, ma'am!" The sensor tech in Consuela Gonzalez' command tank bent closer to her panel. "Coming up at zero-three-zero relative, altitude three thousand, heading two-niner-seven true. Speed three hundred kph. Range . . . three-six point five klicks and closing!"

"Damn!" Gonzalez shook her head. So much for misdirection! From the drone's point of origin, the Bolo must be well out on her left flank, but its recon drone was sweeping almost directly perpendicular to her line of advance, as if the machine knew *exactly* where to look.

"Kill it!" she barked.

"Firing," the Wolverine's air defense tech replied, and a laser turret swiveled. A beam of coherent light sizzled through the humid air, and the drone blew up instantly.

"There goes seven or eight hundred credits of taxpayer's money!" the tech chortled.

"Well, it's seven or eight hundred credits your great-great-grandma paid, not us," Gonzalez said with a grin. Damn, that felt good! She and Merrit had agreed to a hard-limit of five kilometers; any drones or recon remotes beyond that range from her tanks or the Bolo could be engaged with live fire, and she hadn't counted on how much fun that would be.

My drone has been destroyed, but I have plotted the coordinates of two Aggressor forces in addition to the decoy emissions source. I consider a simulated missile launch against them, but the Wolverine's computer-commanded point defense systems are efficient. Nuclear warheads have not been specified for this scenario, and the PK with conventional warheads against a force of three Wolverines is only 28.653 percent. It will be necessary to engage with direct-fire weapons.

A source count indicates the presence of ten of Colonel Gonzalez' fourteen tanks in the known detachments. This leaves four unaccounted for, but the locations of the known forces allow me to refine my hypothetical models of her deployment. A further 0.00017 seconds of analysis indicate that the unlocated units are her extreme right flank force and reduce their possible coordinates to three locations. I call up my terrain maps and plot those loci and continuous updates of their maximum possible advance while I consider the launch of a second drone to confirm my deduction. I reject the option after 0.00311 seconds of consideration. I will reach Hill 0709-A in 9.3221 minutes, plus or minus 56.274

seconds. From its summit, I will have direct observation—and fire capability—to each of the three possible locations. I will advance and destroy this force, then sweep back to the southwest at an angle which will permit me to encounter and destroy each of the known forces in succession. In the meantime, the absence of a second drone launch may leave Colonel Gonzalez off balance, uncertain of the tactical data actually in my possession.

The air lorry landed, and Merrit came to attention on the landing apron. Two of Colonel Sanders' companions accompanied the colonel to the bunker entrance, and Merrit felt a slight spasm of surprise at the sloppiness with which they returned his salute. All of them wore MLP shoulder flashes, which should indicate they spent most of their time back at Central, and somebody who kept stumbling over senior officers should get lots of practice at saluting.

He shook the thought aside as Sanders held out his hand. "Welcome to Santa Cruz, Colonel."

"Thank you, Captain." Sanders' handshake was damp and clammy, and Merrit resisted a temptation to scrub his palm on his trouser leg when the colonel released it. "I assume you know why I'm here," Sanders went on briskly, and Merrit shook his head.

"No, sir, I'm afraid not. No one told me you were coming."

"What?" Sanders cocked his eyebrows, but the surprise in his voice struck a false note, somehow. He shook his head. "Central was supposed to have informed you last week, Captain."

"Informed me of what, sir?" Merrit asked politely.

"Of the policy change concerning Santa Cruz. We've been conducting a sector-wide cost analysis since your arrival here, Captain Merrit. Naturally, we were startled to discover the nature and extent of the Santa Cruz installations—we had no idea we'd misplaced a Bolo for eighty years, heh, heh!—but given their age and the sector's general readiness states, it's hard to see any point in maintaining them on active status. Frontier sectors always face tighter fiscal constraints than the core sectors, you know, so it's been decided—purely as a cost-cutting measure, you understand—to deactivate your Bolo and reassign you."

"A cost-cutting measure, sir?" Merrit asked. He was careful to keep his tone casual and just a bit confused, but alarm bells began to sound in the back of his brain. He'd expected Sanders to come in breathing fire and smoke over his blatant disregard for regulations, yet his initial relief at the lack of fireworks was fading fast. Sanders was babbling. He was also sweating harder than even Santa Cruz's climate called for, and Paul Merrit had seen too much combat in his forty-one years not to have developed a survivor's instincts. Now those instincts shouted that something was very, very wrong.

"Yes, a cost-cutting measure," Sanders replied. "You know how expensive a Bolo is, Captain. Each of them we maintain on active duty takes its own bite out of our total maintenance funding posture, and without a threat to the planet to justify the expense, well—"

He shrugged, and Merrit nodded slowly, expression calm despite a sinking sensation as he noticed that both of Sanders' companions were armed. Of course, the jungle had all sorts of nasty fauna, and all Santa Cruzans went armed whenever they ventured into the bush on foot, but they tended to pack weapons heavy enough to knock even lizard cats on their posteriors. These men wore standard military-issue three-millimeter needlers, efficient enough man-killers but not much use against a lizard cat or one of the pseudo-rhinos.

He let his eyes wander back over the parked air lorry, and the fact that they'd left a man behind carried its own ominous overtones. Merrit couldn't see clearly through the lorry cab's dirty windows, but from the way he sat hunched slightly to one side, the man in it *might* be aiming a weapon in the bunker's direction. If he was, then anything precipitous on Merrit's part was likely to have very unpleasant—and immediate—consequences.

"I'm a little confused, sir," he said slowly.

"Confused?" the major at Sanders' elbow sounded much

brusquer than the colonel, and he glanced at his wrist chrono as he spoke. "What's there to be confused about?"

"Well, it's just that in eighty years, there's never been *any* expense, other than the initial placement costs, of course, for this Bolo. Santa Cruz has never requested as much as a track bearing from Bolo Central Maintenance, so it's a little hard to see how shutting down is going to save any money, Major."

"Uh, yes. Of course." Sanders cleared his throat, then shrugged and smiled. "It's not just, uh, current budget or *expenditures* we're thinking about, Captain. That's why I'm here in person. Despite its age, this is an extensive installation. Reclamation could be something of a bonanza for the sector, so we're naturally planning to salvage all we can after shutdown."

"I see." Merrit nodded, and his mind raced.

Whatever was happening stank to high heaven, and he didn't like the way this Major Atwell's hand hovered near his needler. If his suspicions had any basis in fact, the colonel's companions had to be professionals—certainly the way they'd left a man behind in the air lorry argued that they were. The precaution might seem paranoid, but they'd had no way to be *certain* Merrit wouldn't be armed himself when they arrived. He had no idea exactly what the man they'd left behind had, but it was probably something fairly drastic, because his function had to be distant fire support.

Despite the frozen lead ball in Merrit's belly, he had to acknowledge the foresight which provided against even the unlikeliest threat from him. But if they wanted to leave that fellow back there, then the thing to do was get the other three into the bunker. The chances of one unarmed man against two—three, if Sanders had a concealed weapon of his own—barely existed, but they were even lower against *four* of them.

"I'm not convinced Central isn't making a mistake, sir," he heard himself say easily, "but I'm only a captain. I assume you'd like to at least look the depot over—make a preliminary inspection and check the logs?"

"Certainly." Sanders sounded far more relieved than he should have, and Merrit nodded.

"If you'll follow me, then?" he invited, and led the way into the bunker.

I have reached Hill 0709-A. I approach from the southeast, keeping its crest between myself and the possible positions I have computed for Colonel Gonzalez' fourth detachment. Soil conditions are poor after the last week's heavy rains, but I have allowed for the soft going in my earlier calculations of transit time to this position, and I direct additional power to my drive systems as I ascend the rear face of the hill.

I slow as I reach the top, extending only my forward sensor array above the summit. I search patiently for 2.006 seconds before I detect the power plant emissions I seek. A burst of power to my tracks sends me up onto the hilltop, broadside to the emissions signatures. My fire control radar goes active, confirming their locations, and the laser-tag simulator units built into my Hellbores pulse. The receptors aboard the Wolverines detect the pulses, and all four vehicles slow to a halt in recognition of their simulated destruction. Three point zero-zero-six-two seconds after reaching the hill's crest, I am in motion to the southwest at 50.3 kph to intercept the next Aggressor unit.

"So much for Suarez' company," Gonzalez sighed as her com receipted the raucous tone that simulated the blast of radiation from ruptured power plants.

"Yeah. It'll be coming after *us* next," her gunner grunted.

"Join the Army and see the stars!" someone else sang out, and the entire crew laughed.

". . . and this is the command center," Merrit said, ushering Sanders, Atwell, and Deng through the hatch. "As you can see, it's very well equipped for an installation of its age."

"Yes. Yes, it is." Sanders mopped his forehead with a handkerchief despite the air conditioning and glanced over his shoulder at Atwell. The major was looking at his chrono again, and the colonel cleared his throat. "Well, I'm sure this has been very interesting, Captain Merrit, and I look forward to a more complete tour of the facility—including the Bolo—but I really think we should go ahead and shut it down now."

"Shut it down, sir?" Merrit widened his eyes in feigned surprise.

"That *is* why we came, Captain," Atwell put in in a grating voice.

"Well, certainly," Merrit said easily, "but I can't shut it down immediately. It's not here."

"What?" Sanders gaped at him, and Merrit shrugged.

"I'm sorry, sir. I thought I mentioned it. The Bolo's carrying out an autonomous field exercise just now. It's not scheduled to return for another—" he glanced at the wall chronometer "—six and a half hours. Of course, I'll be glad to shut it down then, but—"

"Shut it down *now*, Captain!" Atwell's voice was no longer harsh; it held the clang of duralloy, and his hand settled on the butt of his needler. Merrit made himself appear oblivious of the gesture and turned towards the console with a shrug.

"Are you sure you really want to shut it down in place, Colonel Sanders?" he asked as he sank into the command chair. Turning his back on Atwell was the hardest thing he'd ever done, but somehow he kept his voice from betraying his tension, and his hand fell to the chair's armrest keypad.

"I mean, I assume you'll want to burn the Battle Center, if this is a permanent shutdown," he went on, fingers moving by feel alone as they flew over the keypad, covered by his body, while he prayed no one would notice the row of telltales blinking from amber stand-by to green readiness on the maintenance console in the command center's corner. "That'd mean someone would have to hike out to its present location in the bush. And if we're going to salvage the station, don't you want to salvage the Bolo, too? Once its Battle Center goes, getting it back here for reclamation is going to be a real problem, and—"

"Stand up, Merrit!" Atwell barked. "Get both hands up here where I can see them!"

Merrit froze, cursing the man's alertness. Another fifteen

seconds—just fifteen more seconds. That was all he'd needed. But he hadn't gotten them. He drew a deep breath and touched one more button, then rose, holding his hands carefully away from his body. He turned, and his blood was ice as he saw what he'd known he would. Atwell and Deng each held a needler, and both of them were aimed squarely at him.

"Colonel?" he looked at Sanders, making himself sound as confused as he could, but his attention wasn't really on the colonel. It wasn't even on the two men with guns. It was watching a display behind Deng as light patterns shifted across its surface in response to his last input. He hadn't had time to reconfigure the armrest keypad, so he'd had to work through the maintenance computers to reach the one he needed. His commands were still filtering their way through the cumbersome interface, and even after they were all in place, they might not do him any good at all. Atwell had stopped him before he could do more than enable the system he needed on automatic, and if Atwell and Deng were real Brigade officers rather than ringers—

"Just . . . just shut the Bolo down, Captain," Sanders whispered, keeping his own eyes resolutely turned away from the guns.

"But why, sir?" Merrit asked plaintively.

"Because we frigging well told you to!" Atwell barked. "Now do it!"

"I don't think I can. Not without checking with Central."

"Captain Merrit," Sanders said in that same strained, whispery voice, "I advise you to do exactly what Major Atwell says. I'm aware this installation's hardware is considerably out of date. Admittedly, it would take me some time to familiarize myself with it sufficiently to shut down the Bolo without you, but I can do it. We both know I can, and I have the command authentication codes from Central."

"If you extracted the codes from Central, then you don't have the right ones, sir," Merrit said softly. Sanders jerked, eyes widening, and Atwell snarled. Merrit's belly tensed as the gunman started to raise his weapon, but Sanders waved a frantic hand.

"Wait! *Wait!*" he cried, and his shrill tone stopped Atwell just short of firing. "What do you mean, I don't have the right codes?" he demanded.

"I changed them."

"You can't have! That's against regs!" Sanders protested, and Merrit laughed.

"Colonel Sanders, you have no *idea* how many regs I've broken in the last six months! If you expect 'Leonidas' to get you into Nike's system, then be my guest and try it."

"Damn you!" Atwell hissed. The gunman looked at his chrono yet again, and his eyes were ugly when he raised them to Merrit once more. "You're lying. You're just trying to make us think we need you!"

"I could be, but I'm not," Merrit replied, the corner of his eye still watching the display behind Deng. *Come on, baby! Come on, please!* he whispered to it, and smiled at Atwell. "Ask Colonel Sanders. Psych Ops had its doubts about me before Central sent me out here. Well," he shrugged, "looks like Psych Ops may have had a point."

Atwell spat something foul, but Sanders shook his head suddenly.

"It doesn't matter," he said. "You may have changed the codes from the ones on file at Central, but only a lunatic would change them without leaving a record somewhere." Merrit turned his head to look at the colonel, and Sanders rubbed his hands nervously together. "Yes, there has to be a record somewhere," he muttered to himself. "Somewhere . . . somewhere . . ."

"We don't need any records," Atwell decided in an ugly voice. He stepped closer to Merrit and lowered his needler's point of aim. "You ever seen what a burst from one of these can do to a man's legs, Merrit?" he purred. "With just a little luck, I can saw your left leg right off at the knee without even killing you. You'll just *wish* you were dead, and you won't be—not until we've got that code."

"Now wait a minute!" Merrit stepped back and licked his lips as a crimson code sequence blinked on the display behind

Deng at last. "Wait a minute!" He looked back at Sanders. "Colonel, just what the hell is going on here?"

"Don't worry about *him!*" Atwell snarled. "Just give me that code phrase—*now!*"

"All right. All right!" Merrit licked his lips again, cleared his throat, and made his voice as expressionless as he could, grateful that computers needed no special emphasis. "The code phrase is 'Activate Alamo.'"

It almost worked. It *would* have worked if he'd had the fifteen additional seconds he'd needed to complete the system reconfiguration or if Major Atwell's reflexes had been even a fraction slower.

Lieutenant Deng *was* slower; he was still trying to figure out what was happening when the power rifle unhoused itself above the main command console and blew his chest apart. He went down without even a scream, and the power rifle slewed sideways, searching for Atwell. But the bogus major's snake-quick reaction hurled him to the floor behind the planetary surveillance system's holo display even as the rifle dealt with Deng. His frantic dive for cover couldn't save him forever, but it bought him time—a few, deadly seconds of time—before the computers found him again.

The power rifle snarled again, and sparks and smoke erupted from the display, but it sheltered Atwell just long enough for him to fire his own weapon.

Merrit was already sprinting towards Deng's fallen gun when Atwell's needler whined. Most of the hasty burst's needles missed, but one didn't, and Merrit grunted in agony as it punched into his back. It entered just above the hip and tore through his abdomen, and the impact smashed him to the bunker floor. He rolled desperately towards the command center door, away from Deng, to avoid Atwell's next burst, and a fresh shower of needles screamed and ricocheted.

Then the power rifle fired yet again. Atwell collapsed with a bubbling shriek, and Merrit rolled up onto his knees, sobbing in agony and pressing both hands against the hot blood that slimed his belly.

Sanders stared in horror at the carnage, and then his huge eyes whipped up to the power rifle. It quivered, questing about, but it didn't fire again, and his breath escaped in a huge gasp as he realized what had happened. Merrit had been able to bring the bunker's automated defenses on-line through the command chair keypad, but he hadn't had time to override their inhibitory programming. The master computer would kill any unauthorized personnel when its commanding officer's coded voice command declared an intruder alert, but Sanders *was* authorized personnel. His name, face, and identifying data were in the Brigade's files, just like Merrit's . . . *and that meant the computer couldn't fire on him!*

Even through the pain that blurred his vision, Merrit saw the realization on the colonel's face. Saw fear turn into the determination of desperation. Sanders flung himself to the floor, hands scrabbling for Atwell's weapon, and there was no time for Merrit to reach Deng's.

He did the only thing he could. He dragged himself to his feet, staggered from the command deck, and fled down the passage outside. He heard Sanders screaming his name behind him, heard feet plunging after him, and somehow, despite the nauseating agony hammering his wounded body, he made himself run faster. He caromed off walls, smearing them with splashes of crimson, and only the fact that Sanders was a desk-jockey saved his life. The needler whined behind him, but the colonel's panic combined with his inexperience to throw his aim wide.

Merrit reached the vehicle chamber and flung himself desperately into the recon skimmer's cockpit. He slammed the canopy with one blood-slick hand while the other brought the drive on-line, and needles screamed and skipped from the fuselage. He gasped a hoarse, pain-twisted curse at his inability to use the skimmer's weapon systems inside the bunker. The safety interlocks meant he couldn't shoot back, but Sanders' needler couldn't hurt *him*, either—not through the skimmer's armor—and he bared his teeth in an anguish-wracked grin as he thought of the air lorry outside. He could damned well use his weapons on *it*, and he rammed power to the drive.

The skimmer wailed out of the vehicle chamber, and he cried out in fresh agony as acceleration rammed him back in the flight couch. Pain made him clumsy, and the skimmer wobbled as he brought it snarling back around the bunker towards the lorry while he punched up his weapons. He bared his teeth again as the fire control screen came alive, capturing the lorry in its ranging bars, and—

That was when he realized his combat instincts had betrayed him. He should have headed away from the bunker immediately to get help, not stayed to fight the battle by himself. And if he *was* going to stay, he should have brought his defensive systems up first, not his weapons.

But he hadn't, and Sanders' third companion was no longer in the air lorry. He was standing over fifty meters to the side, with a plasma lance across his shoulder.

Merrit had one instant to see it, to recognize the threat and wrench the stick hard over, and then the lance fired.

White lightning flashed, blinding bright even in full sunlight, and the skimmer staggered as the plasma bolt tore into its fuselage. Damage alarms howled, and Merrit flung full power into the drive, clawing frantically for altitude. Smoke and flame belched from the skimmer, and he coughed as banners of the same smoke infiltrated the cockpit. Two-thirds of his panel flashed with the bright red codes of disaster. All of his weapons were down, and his communicator. His flight controls were so mangled he couldn't understand how he was still in the air, but they were hanging together—for now, at least.

The power plant wasn't. He groaned in pain, fighting the fog in his brain as he peered at the instruments. Five minutes. He might be able to stay in the air for five minutes—ten at the most. Assuming he could live that long.

He coughed again, and screamed as his diaphragm's violent movement ripped at his belly wound. God! He didn't know how bad he was hit, but he knew the high-velocity needle had wreaked ghastly havoc. He felt the strength flowing out of him with his blood, and his eyes screwed shut in pain while despair flooded him, for Sanders had been right. Only a lunatic *would* have changed Nike's command code without leaving a record. The new code was in his personal computer, not the main system, but it wouldn't take Sanders long to find it if he thought to look in the right place. Once he had it—and once Merrit was dead—the renegade colonel could take command of Nike, give her whatever orders he pleased, and she would have no choice but to obey.

Nike! The name exploded through him, and he wrenched his eyes back open. Jungle treetops rushed at him, and he hauled back on the stick, fighting the broken skimmer back under control. Nike. He had to get to *Nike*. Had to warn her. Had to—

The pain was too great. He could no longer think of what he had to do. Except for one thing. He had to reach Nike, and Paul Merrit clung to life with both hands as he altered course to the northwest.

17

~~~~~~~~~~~~~~~~~~~~~~~~~~~~~~~~~~
~~~~~~~~~~~~~~~~~~~~~~~~~~~~~~~~~~

I HAVE dealt with the first of Colonel Gonzalez' four forces and deployed two additional reconnaissance drones, one in high cover position to plot the origin of any fire directed at the other, which have given me a current position fix on the second of her detachments. The Wolverines are moving at their best speed through the dense jungle, approaching peak velocities of 47 kph, but my own speed is now 62.37 kph. I will intercept Aggressor Force Two in 9.46 minutes on my current heading, and I examine my terrain maps once more. My quarry must cross an east-west ridge in approximately 11.2 minutes on their current heading. This will bring them above the jungle canopy and present me with a clear line of sight and fire, and I decrease speed accordingly. I will let them reach the crest of the hill before I—

A new datum registers abruptly, and I redirect my sensors. A large spacecraft—correction, two large spacecraft—have entered my tactical sensor envelope. They approach in line ahead from due south on a heading of 017 degrees true at high subsonic velocity, descending at 4.586 mps. I query Main Memory for *comparative emissions signatures and identification is reached in 0.00367 seconds. They are Concordiat Navy Fafnir-class assault transports, but they do not carry Navy transponders.*

I am confused. If these are indeed Navy craft, then their transponders should so indicate. Moreover, if the Navy intended to carry out maneuvers on Santa Cruz, my Commander should have been so informed and, I am certain, would have informed me, in turn. The presence of these units cannot therefore be considered an authorized incursion into my command area.

The Fafnirs continue on their original course. My projection of their track indicates that the first of them will cross the Santa Cruz Fleet Base perimeter in 10.435 minutes at an altitude below the Fleet Base's normal search radar horizon. My Battle Center projects a 92.36 percent probability that they are on an attack run, and I attempt to contact my Commander.

There is no response. I initiate a diagnostic of my primary transmitter even as I activate my secondary. Again there is no response. My diagnostic systems report all transmitters functioning normally, and I feel a moment of fear. My Commander should be monitoring the exercise. He should have received my transmission and responded instantly, yet he has not.

I lock my main battery on the Fafnirs, but without authorization from my Commander to enable my Battle Reflex imperatives I can fire only if the unidentified vessels take obviously hostile action.

I bring my long-range tactical systems fully on-line while attempting once more to contact my Commander. Yet again there is no response, and my sensors detect a sudden energy release at the approximate coordinates of the Fleet Base. Analysis of sensor data indicates a hyper-velocity kinetic strike.

Lorenco Esteban jerked up out of his veranda chair as a huge, white fireball erupted above the field. He stared at it in horror for an endless second, until the rolling shockwave shook his entire hacienda by the throat, then dashed into the house and thundered upstairs to the second floor. He snatched up a pair of old-fashioned optical binoculars, jammed them to his eyes, and peered towards the field.

He could just make it out from here, and he swallowed an incredulous curse as he realized the mammoth explosion was centered on the Wolverine maintenance shed.

The lead Fafnir has passed beyond my horizon, but the second is still within my engagement envelope. Simultaneous with the explosion, two outsized assault pods detach from the visible vessel. Their emissions signatures identify them as Dragon Tooth-class pods: reusable, rough field-capable AFV pods configured to land a full battalion of manned tanks or a single Bolo each against active opposition.

Only my after Hellbore will bear, but the explosion raises the probability that an attack by hostile forces is in progress to 98.965 percent, sufficient to enable independent Battle Reflex release. I have time to engage only the Fafnir or the assault pods. Main Memory indicates that a Fafnir's short-term life support capability and internal capacity are sufficient to support three infantry battalions and their vehicles in addition to a complete load out for two Dragon Tooth-class pods for a ship-to-planet transfer. Given this datum and the fact that the ship is still on course for the Fleet Base, it must be classed as the primary threat.

My after Hellbore elevates to 026 degrees. I acquire lock, and then I rock on my treads as for the first time I fire a full-powered war shot.

"Madre de Dios!"
Consuela Gonzalez flinched as the self-polarizing direct vision blocks of her Wolverine's hatch cupola went dark as night. Even so, the searing flash from somewhere astern of her made her eyes water, and it was followed almost instantly by an even bigger midair explosion.

"Hellbore!" her sensor tech screamed. "That was a Hellbore, Connie! My God, what's that thing *shooting* at?!"

My fire impacts on my target's primary drive coil. Destruction is effectively instantaneous, but I cannot relay my Hellbore in time to engage either assault pod. They go to evasive action and disappear into the jungle; 4.0673 seconds later, I detect ground shocks consistent with the heavy "daisy-cutter" charges used to clear pod landing zones in heavy terrain. The Enemy has landed successfully, but the detonations provide me with reliable bearings to their LZs.

I continue my efforts to contact my Commander. The depot communications computer responds to my demand for a diagnostics check and declares all systems nominal, but still my Commander does not reply. His continuing silence is a dagger of ice within me, but with or without him, I am a unit of the Dinochrome Brigade. It is my function to defend human life at all costs, and I must act to protect the citizens of Santa Cruz.

I attempt to contact the Fleet Base over my secondary com channel, but without success. I attempt to transmit a subspace attack warning to Sector Central, but the orbital communications arrays do not respond. Radar indicates that they no longer exist, indicating a deliberate Enemy move to isolate Santa Cruz. I attempt to access the planetary surveillance system, but without my Commander's assistance from the depot's Command Center, I can work only through my permanent telemetry link to the Maintenance computer. I begin the reconfiguration of the system to download tactical data to me, but the interface is clumsy. It will require a minimum of 5.25 minutes to access the reconnaissance satellites.

I alter course to a heading of 026 degrees true to close on the assault pod landing sites while I consider my other options. The presence of the SCM detachment grants me a greater degree of tactical flexibility, and I activate my tertiary com channels.

"Colonel Gonzalez, please respond on this frequency." Consuela Gonzalez shook her head. The rain of debris pouring from the cloud of incandescent gas which must once have been a spacecraft had not yet hit the treetops when a soprano voice she had never heard in her life spoke from her com.

"Colonel Gonzalez, please respond immediately," the voice said. "Santa Cruz is under attack. I say again, Santa Cruz is under attack by forces operating in unknown strength. Please respond immediately."

She forced her eyes down from the holocaust in the sky and punched a new frequency into her com panel with trembling fingers.

"Th—" She cleared her throat. "This is Gonzalez. Who the hell are *you?*"

"I am Unit Two-Three-Baker-Zero-Zero-Seven-Five NKE of the Line," the soprano replied, and Gonzalez heard someone gasp.

"You're the *Bolo?*" she demanded in shock.

"Affirmative. Colonel, I have detected a kinetic strike in the low kiloton range at the approximate coordinates of Santa Cruz Fleet Base. I have attempted to contact Fleet Ops and Sector Central without success. Further, I have established that Santa Cruz's subspace communications arrays have been destroyed. I have also detected two Fafnir-class Concordiat Navy assault ships on an attack course for the Fleet Base. On the basis of this data, I believe Santa Cruz is under attack. I—"

"But . . . but *why?*" Gonzalez blurted.

"I have no information as to the attackers' motives, Colonel; I simply report observed facts. May I continue my SitRep?"

Consuela Gonzalez shook herself once more, then sucked in a deep, shuddering breath as her merely human mind began to fight for balance.

"Go," she said flatly.

"I have engaged and destroyed one Fafnir—" Nike said.

"Christ!" someone muttered.

"—but not before it detached two Dragon Tooth-class assault pods. I estimate their LZs lie approximately forty-five point three and fifty-one point niner kilometers respectively from my present position. I am currently en route to locate and destroy any hostile forces at those locations."

"How can we help?" Gonzalez demanded.

"Thank you for the offer," the soprano voice said, and Gonzalez' eyebrows rose as, even through her shock, she heard its genuine gratitude. "If you will shift to Condition Delta-Two, I will download my own tactical data to your onboard computers, but a Dragon Tooth pod is capable of landing up to a Mark XXV Bolo. It is therefore probable that the Enemy has deployed a force too heavy for your own units to engage successfully. I request that your battalion rendezvous at map coordinates Echo-Seven-Niner X-Ray-One-Three and stand by to assist my own operations."

"You've got it, Bolo. Watch yourself."

"Thank you, Colonel. If I may make another suggestion, it might be wise for you to broadcast a planet-wide alert of hostile action."

"We will." Gonzalez nudged her com tech's shoulder with a toe and jutted her chin at the panel while her own fingers darted over the master computer console. "Delta-Two on-line," she told Nike, and looked at her driver. "You heard the lady! Take us to the rendezvous coordinates—fast!"

Esteban was still staring at the explosion when a flicker of movement caught his eye. He snapped around, staring further south, and shock gave way to the fury of understanding as he saw the huge spacecraft sweeping towards the field. It went into low-altitude hover almost directly above the old fleet base and began shedding AFV assault pods. Huge hatches gaped in its flanks, and a cloud of air-cavalry mounts erupted from them, followed within seconds by the first infantry assault vehicles on counter-grav drop rings.

That sight jerked him into motion. He thundered back down the stairs and into his communications center, and his lips drew back to bare his teeth as he flung himself into the chair before the console. He might never have seen Navy duty, but he'd always taken his responsibilities for the field more seriously than he chose to pretend to others. That was why he'd installed a certain landline link he'd never bothered to mention to anyone else.

He flipped up a plastic safety shield, punched in a three-digit code, then rammed his finger down on the big red button.

Fafnir One's CO pounded on his command chair arm and spouted a steady, monotonous stream of profanity. The attack which had begun so perfectly had gone to hell in a handcart, and he was frantic to get back out into space before something *else* went wrong.

The communications arrays were down—that much, at least, had gone according to plan—but nothing else had. The two Fafnirs had docked with Matucek's mother ship to take on the maximum personnel loads their life support would permit them to handle for an assault run, then made their approach from the planet's southern pole. It was the long way to reach their main objective, but it had let them come in over largely uninhabited terrain and, as a bonus, deploy the two Golems to cover their southern flank if the plan to deal with the Bolo had failed.

As, judging by the evidence, it had.

The transport commander swore again, harder. His tactical readouts confirmed it; the single shot that killed *Fafnir Two* had come from *at least* an eighty-centimeter Hellbore. That meant it could only have come from the Bolo, and he didn't even want to think about what else that might mean! His sensor section reported the Golems had separated before the attack, so they, at least, might have gotten down intact, but a quarter of the Marauders' infantry, half their air-cav, and ten percent of their Panthers had gone up with *Fafnir Two*.

He darted another look at the status board and felt a stab of relief. Ninety percent of their passengers had launched. Another few seconds, and—

"Last man out!" someone announced.

"Go! Get us the fuck out of here!" the CO shouted. The Fafnir's nose rose as it swung further north towards safety, and he glared at his com officer. "Tell Granger that goddamned Bolo's still alive!"

Far below the hovering transport, a dozen slabs of duralloy armor slid sideways to uncover an equal number of dark, circular bores. Deep within the wells they had covered, long-quiescent circuitry roused as it received the activation command from Lorenco Esteban's distant communications console. Targeting criteria were passed, receipted, evaluated, and matched against the huge energy source in the sky above.

My sensors detect a fresh burst of gravitic energy from the bearing of the Fleet Base. It is too heavy to emanate from any planetary vehicle and must, therefore, be the first Fafnir. It is accelerating away from the Base, but its commander appears to be no fool. Although I can detect his emissions, he remains too low for my fire control to acquire him. I compute a probability of 99.971 percent that his current maneuvers indicate the successful deployment of his assault force, but I cannot intervene.

"Missile acquisition! *We've been locked up!*" someone screamed. *Fafnir One*'s commander started to twist towards the technician who'd shouted, but he never completed the motion.

Twelve surface-to-space missiles launched on pillars of fire. Their target raced for safety as rapidly as its internal grav compensators permitted, so fast its bow glowed cherry red, but it never had a chance. The SSMs' conventional boosters blew them free of their silos, and they tilted, holding lock, and then went suddenly to full power on their own counter-grav. They overtook their victim just over three hundred kilometers downrange at an altitude of thirty-three thousand meters, and twelve twenty-kiloton warheads detonated as one.

There was no wreckage.

The warheads' glare was bright enough to bleach the brilliant sun of Santa Cruz even at three hundred kilometers' range, and Esteban snarled in triumph. He didn't know why anyone would want to attack his world, but he knew at least *one* bunch of the murderous bastards would never attack anyone else's.

Not bad fer an old crock with no formal trainin', he thought venomously, and then, *Thank God Enrique an' 'Milla aren't back yet!*

He shook himself and climbed back out of the chair. Whoever those people were, they weren't going to be very happy with him for wrecking their transport. On the other hand, he'd spent seventy years on this very hacienda. He knew places where an army of raiders couldn't find him.

He paused only long enough to grab the emergency supply pack he kept handy for search and rescue operations, slung a four-millimeter military power rifle over one shoulder, and vanished out the back door at a run.

My sensors detect the EMP of multiple nuclear detonations at a range of approximately 392.25 kilometers, bearing 030 degrees relative. This coincides with the estimated locus of the second Fafnir, and the previously detected heavy gravitic emissions have ceased. I compute a probability of 98.511 percent that the Fafnir has been destroyed by defensive fire, indicating that my Commander's friend Lorenco Esteban has managed to activate the Fleet Base defenses. I hope that he has not paid with his life for this success.

I detect two new emission sources. Their locations correspond to the projected landing loci of the previously observed assault pods. They match my files for SC-191(b) fusion plants, and are accompanied by narrow-band, encrypted communications transmissions. I attempt to penetrate the com link, but without immediate success. Analysis indicates a sophisticated, multilevel security system.

I devote 1.0091 seconds to consideration of available data and reach a disturbing conclusion. The energy signatures are consistent with the power plants of a Mark XXIV or XXV Bolo; no other mobile unit mounts the SC-191(b). I do not know how the Enemy could have obtained current-generation Bolos, but if these are indeed Mark XXIVs or XXVs, I am grossly overmatched. Despite the superiority of the systems Major Stavrakas devised for me, I compute a probability of 87.46 percent, plus or minus 03.191 percent, that I will be destroyed by two Mark XXIVs, rising to 93.621 percent that I will be destroyed by two Mark XXVs. Yet my duty is clear. However the Enemy may have obtained access to such war machines, I must engage them.

≈≈≈   ≈≈≈   ≈≈≈

"Colonel Gonzalez, I have detected what may be two hostile Bolos," the soprano voice said calmly, and Consuela Gonzalez' olive complexion went sickly gray.

Bolos? In the hands of *planet-raiders?* It wasn't possible! Yet she was receiving confirmation of nuclear air-bursts from outlying melon growers over the planetary com net, and the transmissions from Ciudad Bolivar were a babble of hysteria. Her com tech reported the sounds of explosions and heavy weapons fire in the background of the Bolivar transmissions. There could be no doubt that the capital—including her husband and children—was under heavy, ruthless attack, and no one had had even a hint of what was coming, not even a second to organize any sort of defense. Nausea twisted her stomach as she thought of all the civilians who must be dying even as her tank bucketed through the jungle a hundred kilometers to the south, and if the bastards had *Bolos*—

"What do you want us to do?" she rasped over the com.

"I will engage them, Colonel. Your own vehicles lack the capability to survive against them. Continue to the specified rendezvous, then advance at your best speed on a heading of two-six-three true for forty-two kilometers before changing to a heading of zero-three-niner. That course will pass to the west of the Enemy's current location and take you to Ciudad Bolivar in the shortest possible time."

"You can't take two other Bolos on your own!"

"Your assistance will not appreciably enhance my own combat capability, Colonel, and your units will be of far more utility to Santa Cruz in Ciudad Bolivar than they will if they are destroyed here. Please proceed as I have advised."

"All right," Gonzalez whispered, and then, even knowing it was a machine to whom she spoke— "*Vaya con Dios, amiga.*"

Colonel Louise Granger stared at her display in shock. She didn't know what had happened to *Fafnir Two*—her transport command ship was on the wrong side of the planet, where it had been busy killing the last communications array—but the sudden cessation of all transmissions from *Fafnir One* was chilling proof her careful battle plan had just been blown to hell. *One* hadn't managed to report a damned thing about what was shooting back before whatever it was destroyed her, but she'd gotten off her full load of assault troops and armor to take out the field and the planetary capital before she died. That put her point of destruction well to the north of the Bolo depot, so whatever had killed her, it hadn't been the Bolo. Granger didn't know what *else* on the planet could have done the job, but whatever it was could only have come from the old fleet base, though how anyone could have had time to activate its defenses was beyond her. What she *didn't* know was whether or not *Fafnir Two* had gotten her Golems off before her destruction, and, unlike a Fafnir-class transport—or a full-capability Bolo—a Golem had no subspace com capability. She couldn't find out what had happened to the huge tanks until her ship swung back over their radio horizon.

She felt the shock and dismay rippling through her operations staff, and she didn't blame them. But she also knew she had at least three quarters of her brigade's fighting power down on its primary objective and, presumably, intact. Whatever ground-to-air system had nailed *Fafnir One* wouldn't be much use against a ground assault, and she snarled at her shaken officers.

"How the fuck do *I* know what happened to her?! But whatever it was, it must've come from the Fleet Base, and *we'll* clear its horizon in fifteen minutes! Get on those command circuits and keep our people moving! Primary objective is now the complete—I repeat, *complete*—neutralization of that base!"

I continue my efforts to penetrate the Enemy's communications without success, yet analysis of their patterns convinces me that they are not the Total Systems Data-Sharing net of the Dinochrome Brigade. While they include what can only be interlinked tactical telemetry, they also include what are clearly voice transmissions. This indicates that my opponents are not, in fact, Bolos, and I compute a probability of 56.113 percent that they are actually Golem-IIIs or Golem-IVs. Possession of such vehicles by any Enemy, while still extremely improbable, is more likely than the possibility that the Enemy might somehow have acquired full-capability units of the Line. While the odds against my survival against properly coordinated Golems remain unfavorable, the probability of my destruction against Golem-IIIs drops from 87.46 percent to no more than 56.371 percent, although it remains on the close order of 78.25 percent against Golem-IVs. The probability that I can successfully destroy or at least incapacitate the enemy, on the other hand, has risen to 82.11 percent, regardless of the mark of Golem I may face.

My Battle Center cautions me to assume nothing, yet the intuitive function Major Stavrakas incorporated into my Personality Center argues otherwise. If I assume that these are, indeed, Golems and plan my tactics accordingly, my chance of victory—and survival—will be considerably enhanced. If I act on that assumption and it proves incorrect, my destruction will be assured. I consider for 0.90112 seconds and reach conclusion. I will assume my opponents are Golems.

Two huge war machines, each crewed by three very anxious humans, forged through the jungle like impatient Titans, bulldozing their way through hundred-meter trees while their commanders shouted at one another.

"It *had* to be the frigging Bolo!" Golem-Two's commander bellowed finally, stunning his counterpart in Golem-One into silence with sheer volume. "And if it *was*, it's coming after *our* asses next! So shut the hell up and *listen* to me, god-damn it!"

"If there's a live Bolo out there, then let's get the fuck out of here!"

"No, damn it! If we run, the damned thing'll come right up our asses, and we've already lost both Fafnirs. If it gets to the field, there's no way in hell Granger or Matucek will risk trying to pick us up—it'd swat 'em like flies, if they did. If we want off this planet, we've gotta kill the fucking thing, and it's only a Mark XXIII!"

"*Only!*" the other commander spat.

"Shut up and activate Gamma-One!"

There was a long, frightened moment of silence, and then Golem-One rasped, "Activating."

Analysis of enemy com patterns indicates that voice transmissions have ceased. I must assume the Enemy has concerted his plans, which suggests a strong probability (72.631 percent) that he intends to engage using a pre-packaged computer battle plan similar to those employed by Mark XV-Mark XIX Bolos.

I switch to hyper-heuristic mode. Since my Commander has never reported my actual capabilities, the Enemy will assume he is opposed by a standard Mark XXIII. Therein may lie my best opportunity for victory, for the basic Mark XXIII had a predilection for direct attacks. In this instance, however, I face two opponents. Each is armed with a marginally more powerful Hellbore than my own, but I possess two turrets. Unfortunately, to employ both of them will require me to turn broadside to my opponents, exposing my thinner flank armor to their fire. I must therefore entice them into committing to the attack. This would be difficult against full-capability Bolos, but a Golem will be able to respond only within the parameters of its pre-loaded tactical programs. It may, therefore, be possible to manipulate them into approaching in a manner of my choosing.

Ports pop open on my hull as I launch ground sensor remotes. Their motion detectors pick up the ground shocks of Bolo-range vehicles moving at high speed. Triangulation produces locations on two distinct motion sources, and I compute their general headings and consult my terrain maps yet again.

Their courses indicate they have not yet localized my own position, but they are operating in close company. I cannot ambush and engage one without being engaged by the other. On our present courses, I will encounter them from the flank in relatively flat terrain, but if they alter course towards me, I will encounter them in terrain much more favorable to my plans. I must therefore reveal my position and entice them into closing.

I compute a fire plan and enable my VLS cells.

≋   ≋   ≋

The armored hatches of Nike's missile deck sprang open, and a cloud of missiles arced upward. In twelve seconds, each of her forty vertical launch system cells sent four heavy missiles shrieking downrange; then the hatches snapped shut once more, and the charging Bolo shifted course. She directed full power to her drive train, smashing through the jungle at a reckless speed of over a hundred kilometers per hour. Not even her massive weight could hold her steady, and she rocked and bucked like a drunken galleon while splintered jungle spat from her spinning treads.

Ten seconds after launch, the first missiles roared down on the two Golems. The launch range was too short for effective counter-missiles, but computer-commanded, direct fire anti-missile defenses swiveled and spat. There was too little engagement time to stop them all, but the Golem's computers concentrated on the ones which might have landed close enough to be a threat.

Half the incoming missiles vanished in midair fireballs; the others impacted, and a hurricane of flame and fury lashed the jungle. The Golems' crewmen cringed at the carnage erupting beyond their vehicles' armored hulls, yet their computers had stopped the truly dangerous ones. More, their radar had back-plotted the fire to its point of origin. The mercenaries knew where it had come from now, and the Golems changed course towards it, exactly as their pre-packaged battle plan required.

The depot computers have now reconfigured the planetary surveillance system. I download data directly from it and quickly localize both Enemy vehicles. Optical examination confirms that they are Mark XXIV hulls, and both are now headed directly towards my launch point. I brake to a halt. The outcrop I have chosen for cover cuts off all radar, but I continue to track via the reconnaissance satellites. I am now certain my opponents are not Bolos, for they have closed up on one another to advance side by side down the valley which breaks the ridge line. My track shields drop into place, and I divert power to strengthen my starboard battle screen while I compute ranges carefully. I wait, then throw full power to my drive train.

〰 〰 〰

Rooster tails of pulped tree and soil flew from Nike's treads as she exploded from cover. Her course took her directly across the oncoming Golems' path at a suicidally short range of less than a thousand meters.

The humans crewing those Golems had no time to react, and if their computers were just as fast as Nike's, they lacked the cybernetic initiative of a self-aware Bolo. Golem-Two's computers had deflected its Hellbore to cover the eastern side of the valley as they advanced while Golem-One's took responsibility for the west.

Nike appeared suddenly directly ahead of Golem-One. Golem-Two had no time to relay its main battery, and, unlike either Golem, Nike had known exactly where to look for her enemies. Golem-One's turret swiveled with snakelike speed, but Nike had a fraction of a second more to aim, and a fraction of a second was a long, long time for a Bolo.

The westernmost Golem and I fire within 0.000003 seconds of one another, but my opponent's shot is rushed. It is unable to acquire a fatal aim point, while my own shots are direct hits on center of mass.

Lightning bolts of plasma crossed one another, and none of the humans aboard the mercenary tanks had time to realize they were dead. At such short range, Nike's plasma bolts ripped through their battle screen, thick ablative armor, and massive glacis plates as if they were tissue. The bottles of their forward fusion plants ruptured, and a thousand-meter circle of thick, damp jungle blazed like Thermit as the intolerable thermal bloom flashed outward. Every organic compound aboard both Golems flared into flaky ash, and then there was only the hungry sound of fires raging deeper into the jungle and the indescribable crackle of duralloy dying in the heart of an artificial sun.

Yet Golem-One's single shot was not completely in vain.

〰 〰 〰

Agony explodes through my pain sensors. My battle screen has only limited effect against Hellbore fire, and the nearer Golem's plasma bolt rips deep into me. My ceramic armor appliqués dissipate much of its power, yet they were not designed to defeat such massive energy loads. The bolt strikes the face of my after Hellbore turret, whose duralloy armor is 300 percent thicker than that which protects my flank, but even that is far too thin to stop the Enemy fire.

My after turret explodes. The massive barrel of Hellbore Number Two snaps like a twig, and overloaded circuits scream as energy bleeds through them, yet my turret is designed to contain and localize damage. Internal disrupter shields seal its central access trunk, and the force of the explosion vents upward. The turret roof is peeled back in jagged tangles of duralloy, destroying my main after sensor array, and Disrupter Shield Fourteen fails. Back blast destroys Infinite Repeaters Eight and Nine, cripples my starboard quarter anti-personnel clusters, and severely damages Point Defense Stations Thirty through Thirty-six, but secondary shields prevent more serious damage.

I am badly hurt, but my opponents have been destroyed. I initiate a full diagnostic and enable my damage control systems. Current capability has been reduced to 81.963 percent of base capability and my gutted turret represents a dangerous chink in my armor, but damage control will restore an additional 06.703 percent of base capability within 43.44 minutes, plus or minus 8.053 seconds. I remain combat capable.

My diagnostic subroutines are still cycling when my radar detects a low-orbit target. It is unidentified, but I compute a 95.987 percent probability that it is the mother ship of the Fafnir-class transports.

"My God!" Louise Granger's voice was a whisper as her sensors showed her the terrible heat signature of the dead Golems, and the full, hideous truth registered. Only one thing could have stopped both Golems side-by-side in their tracks, and even as that thought flashed through her mind, her sensor section found the Bolo itself.

Her head whipped around, her eyes like daggers as they bit into Mister Scully's suddenly terrified face.

"So much for your brilliant plan, you worthless bastard," she said almost conversationally.

I track the mother ship. My single remaining Hellbore locks on, and I rock on my treads as I fire my fourth main battery war shot.

Huge as it was, Li-Chin Matucek's mother ship was a freighter, not a ship of the line, and Nike's Hellbore was equivalent to the main battery weapons of a dreadnought. Her plasma bolt impacted on its port bow and ripped effortlessly through bulkhead after bulkhead. It chewed its way over four hundred meters into the ship's hull before it finally found something fatal, and Louise Granger, Li-Chen Matucek, Gerald Osterwelt, and four hundred other men and women vanished in the sun-bright boil of a breached fusion bottle.

18

~~~~~~
~~~~~~

NEITHER MY own sensors nor the planetary surveillance system detect additional ships in Santa Cruz orbit. The destruction of his transports has marooned the Enemy's forces on the planet, but the recon satellites report that the rough equivalent of a Concordiat Medium Mechanized Brigade (manned) has landed successfully. Much of Ciudad Bolivar's eastern suburbs are in flames, the Fleet Base is completely occupied, and the Enemy is continuing to advance and secure his position as I watch.

I am not certain of the Enemy's intentions in this changed tactical situation. His continued offensive action may simply indicate that he has not yet realized he is cut off. It may, however, reflect instead his knowledge that additional forces are en route to reinforce him. In the latter case, it is clearly imperative to deny him any spacehead to serve as a recovery LZ. Moreover, his motives matter less than the consequences of his actions, for Santa Cruzans are dying in enormous numbers as I watch.

Smoke pours from the ruins of my after turret, but I bring myself back to a heading of 029 degrees true and add Colonel

Gonzalez' Wolverine to the planetary surveillance net. For the moment, my own systems drive the display in her tank, but I reprogram her primary telemetry link to become a direct feed from the satellites in the event that I am destroyed.

"Colonel Gonzalez?"

Consuela Gonzalez twitched as the Bolo's voice came over the link again. There was an indefinable change to it, almost as if it were shadowed with pain. She shook the fanciful thought aside with a savage shake of her head and keyed her mike.

"Gonzalez here."

"I am now feeding your tactical display from the planetary surveillance system," the Bolo told her. "Can you confirm reception?"

"Confirmed, Connie!" her sensor tech called.

"We have it, *amiga*," Gonzalez confirmed in turn.

"Excellent. I have destroyed two heavy Enemy armored units which I believe to have been Golem-IIIs. I have sustained major damage but remain combat capable at eighty-two point three-one-seven percent base capability. I am advancing on a heading of zero-two-niner degrees true to secure the space field and relieve Ciudad Bolivar. I suggest you alter your own course to follow directly after me while I clear passage for your Wolverines."

"Copy that, *amiga*." Gonzalez punched a frequency change and spoke to the other thirteen tanks of her command. "Wolf Leader to Cubs. Form on me and guide right. We'll follow the Bolo through." Taut-voiced affirmatives echoed back, and she switched back to Nike's frequency. "We're on our way, *amiga*."

"Excellent, Colonel."

Gonzalez felt her tank buck and quiver as it swept around to follow the huge pathway Nike was battering through the jungle. Small as the Wolverines might be beside a Bolo's huge bulk, each was still five hundred tons of armor and alloy, with all the inertia that implied. Even so, violent motion hammered Gonzalez against her crash couch's shock frame as the big tanks edged up to a speed of over sixty kph.

Her sensor tech managed to feed the data from the satellite net to Gonzalez' own display, and she swore in savage silence as she saw the huge pall of smoke rising from the capital. Yet even as she watched it, a question probed at the back of her brain, and she keyed her mike once more.

"Unit NKE, Gonzalez," she said. "Are you in contact with Captain Merrit?"

"Negative, Colonel Gonzalez." The Bolo's reply came back instantly, and, for the first time, it was so flat it *sounded* like a computer's voice. There was a brief moment of silence, and then it went on. "I have had no contact with him since the attack began. I do not know the reason for his silence. Absent any communication with him, I must consider you the senior officer present. Have you any instructions?"

My God, Gonzalez thought. *NKE's running Santa Cruz's entire defense on its own! How in* hell *can a Bolo that old do something like this?* Her eyes dropped to the white-hot carcasses of the dead Golems on her display, and she shrugged. *However it—she's—doing it, she's doing a damned good job!*

"Understood, NKE," she said after a moment. "Negative instructions. You're doing fine, *amiga*—just keep telling us what you need and go kill those bastards."

"Thank you, Colonel. I shall attempt not to disappoint you."

A crippled recon skimmer staggered through the air. Its barely conscious pilot had long since lost any clear idea of his course, but some instinct kept him wavering steadily towards the north.

A huge, raw furrow appeared in the jungle below him, a dark swatch of damp, black earth, gouged from the rich emerald as if by some impossibly huge plow, and Paul Merrit's glazed eyes brightened. His mind was going fast as blood loss eroded his strength, but only one thing could have made that wound, and he altered course along it and rammed his dying drive to full power.

I continue to study the satellite reports on the fighting in and around Ciudad Bolivar, but a new energy source suddenly takes my attention. It is to the south of me, pursuing at a velocity of 425.63 kph, and its signature is very weak and fluctuating. I redirect one of the satellites to a close examination of it, and a sense of all too human horror stabs through me as I recognize it.

It is my Commander's recon skimmer, and it has suffered severe damage. I attempt to contact it directly, but it does not respond to my transmissions. From the satellite data, it is probable its own com facilities have been destroyed.

I am faced by a cruel dilemma. The pilot of that skimmer is almost certainly my Commander—Paul. He may be injured, even dying, and instinct cries out for me to alter course to meet him, yet every moment I delay may cost scores of other human lives in Ciudad Bolivar. I attempt again and again to contact him, without success, and anguish twists me at his silence, yet I compute he will overtake me within 4.126 minutes—if his damaged drive lasts that long—and I know him well. He would not wish me to stop, even to save his life, at the cost of civilian lives, and so I continue on my chosen course, clearing a path for the Wolverines.

Paul Merrit gasped in horror as he saw the two burned-out Golems. For one terrible moment, he thought one of them must be Nike, but then, even through his pain and despite their catastrophic damage, he recognized the hulls of Mark XXIVs. He had no idea where they'd come from, but only one force on Santa Cruz could have destroyed them, and his skimmer plunged on down the arrow-straight path of Nike's bulldozer charge towards Ciudad Bolivar.

"NKE, we've got an energy source coming up from astern!" Colonel Gonzalez announced tautly. "Shall we engage?"

"Negative, Colonel. I say again, negative. The vehicle in question is Captain Merrit's recon skimmer. It has suffered severe damage, but I believe it is seeking to rejoin us."

"Understood, NKE," Gonzalez said softly, and winced as she watched that wavering, staggering wreck of a skimmer crawl after them.

I am still attempting to communicate with my Commander when a new voice speaks suddenly over the command link from the depot.

"Unit Two-Three-Baker-Zero-Zero-Seven-Five NKE, this is Colonel Clifton Sanders, Dinochrome Brigade, Ursula Sector Central Bolo Maintenance, serial number Alpha-Echo-Niner-Three-Seven-One-Niner-Four-Slash-Three-Gamma-Two-Two. Authenticate via file voice print and acknowledge receipt of transmission."

I query Main Memory for Colonel Sanders' voice print and compare it to the transmission. Match is well within parameters for the equipment in use, yet I feel a strange disinclination to respond. What is Colonel Sanders doing on Santa Cruz? Why is he on the command circuit instead of my Commander? Yet I am a unit of the Line, and I activate my transmitter.

"Unit Two-Three-Baker-Zero-Zero-Seven-Five NKE. Transmission received. Voice match positive."

"Thank God! Listen to me, NKE. Captain Merrit has mutinied. I repeat, Captain Merrit has mutinied against his lawful superior and killed two fellow officers of the Line. I officially instruct you to refuse any further orders from him pending his arrest and court-martial."

I do not believe him. Superior officer or no, he is lying. Paul would never commit such a crime! My earlier suspicions intensify a thousandfold. It seems impossible for any officer of the Brigade to be in league with the Enemy, yet why else has Colonel Sanders suddenly appeared on Santa Cruz at this precise moment? And impossible as it seems, it is infinitely more probable than that Paul would mutiny.

I begin to reply hotly, then stop. Paul has consistently concealed my true abilities from Central. Thus Colonel Sanders cannot realize how radically I differ from a standard Mark XXIII, and this is not the time to inform him. I shall "play dumb" as long as possible.

"Captain Merrit is my designated Commander, Colonel. I cannot disregard his orders without express command code authorization. Please supply command code."

"I can't!" Sanders half-screamed. "Merrit changed the code without informing Central! I'm trying to find it, but—"

"I cannot disregard Captain Merrit's orders without express command code authorization," Nike returned in her most emotionless tone.

The skimmer has finally overtaken the Wolverines. Its power is failing quickly, and Colonel Sanders' presence changes my original assumptions radically. I reverse my tracks and move suddenly backward, threading my way through the Wolverines, which scatter like quail at my approach.

The skimmer staggers, then plummets downward in a barely controlled crash landing. It slams through heavy undergrowth for over a hundred meters before it careens to a stop, and I swerve towards it. I come to a halt 20.25 meters from it, but the canopy does not open. My optical heads show me Paul's body slumped in the flight couch. His tunic is soaked in blood.

"Paul!"

The agonized cry over the com hit Consuela Gonzalez like a hammer. She'd felt a moment of terror as the Bolo suddenly reversed course to sweep through her entire battalion, yet the smoke-streaming fifteen-thousand-ton leviathan had threaded its way among the tanks with flawless precision, and now that heartbroken wail struck an even deeper fear into the colonel. She'd never served with a Bolo, yet she knew no Bolo should ever sound like *that*, and she keyed her mike.

"NKE?" There was no answer, and she tried again. "NKE, this is Gonzalez! Come in!"

"Colonel." The Bolo's voice was ragged, and Gonzalez could feel the huge machine's struggle to make it firm. "Colonel, my Commander is wounded. I . . . require your assistance."

"On my way, NKE!" Gonzalez replied without even thinking about it, and her command tank pivoted to race towards the smoking skimmer. The five-hundred-ton vehicle skidded to a stop on locked tracks, and Gonzalez popped her hatch before it reached a complete halt. She leapt down the handholds and ran the last few yards to the skimmer. The canopy resisted stubbornly for several seconds, then the emergency bolts blew and she ripped it away and gasped as she saw the blood pooled on the cockpit floor.

"He's hurt badly, NKE," she reported over her helmet boom mike. "He's lost a lot of blood—too much, maybe!"

"Can you get him into my fighting compartment?" The Bolo's voice was pleading, and Gonzalez grimaced.

"I don't know, NKE. He's hurt bad. It might kill—"

"N-N-N-*Nike!*" Merrit whispered. His eyes opened a narrow slit. "Got . . . got to reach . . ."

His thready voice died, and Gonzalez sighed. "All right, Paul," she said softly, without keying her mike. "If it means that much to both of you."

I watch Colonel Gonzalez struggle to lift Paul from the skimmer. The rest of her crew clamber quickly down the hull of their tank and run to her assistance. Between them, they are able to lift him clear. They are as gentle as they can be, yet he screams in pain, and answering anguish twists within me.

But he is conscious. Barely, perhaps, yet conscious, and I see him beckoning weakly towards me. One of Colonel Gonzalez' crewmen seems to argue, but the colonel cuts him off quickly, and they carry Paul towards me.

I open my fighting compartment hatch and deploy my missile-loading waldoes to assist. I lock them into the form of a ramp, and Colonel Gonzalez inches up it backwards, supporting Paul's head and shoulders while the rest of her crew takes most of his weight. My audio pickups relay their gasps of effort and the groans of pain he cannot suppress, yet between them, they get him safely into my compartment.

Colonel Gonzalez lays him in the crash couch and deploys the shock frame. The medical remotes in the shock frame go instantly to work, and fresh grief twists me as I interpret their data.

Paul is dying. His spleen and liver have been effectively destroyed by a penetrating trauma. His small intestine has been perforated in many places, and blood loss has already reached catastrophic levels. I do not understand how he has clung to consciousness this long, but absent the services of a fully equipped hospital trauma unit within the next fifteen minutes, he will die, and the nearest trauma unit is in Ciudad Bolivar.

My medical remotes do what they can. I cannot stop the bleeding, but I administer painkillers and blood expanders. Without more whole blood, I cannot keep pace with the blood loss, but I can ease his pain and slow the inevitable, and his eyelids flutter open.

"N-Nike?" Merrit whispered.

"Paul." For the first time, Nike replied with his name, not his rank, and bloodless pale lips smiled weakly.

"I . . . Oh, God, honey . . . I blew it. Sanders . . . went rogue. H-He's got the depot. I—"

"I understand, Paul," the Bolo said gently. Then, more sharply, "Colonel Gonzalez?"

"Yes, NK—Nike?" The colonel's voice was soft with wonder, as if she could not quite believe what reason told her she must be hearing.

"Please return to your vehicle, Colonel. My Commander and I will lead you to Ciudad Bolivar."

"I—" Gonzalez bit her lip, then ducked her head in a curiously formal bow. "Of course, Nike."

"Thank you, Colonel."

Gonzalez and her crewmen vanished through the hatch, and Merrit stirred weakly in the couch.

"Sanders has . . . at least one more . . . man." The words came slowly, painfully, but with steady, dogged precision. "New command code's in . . . my private files. If he looks . . . there, he can—"

"While you live, *you* are my Commander, Paul," Nike replied quietly as her hatch closed. She watched Gonzalez and her people return to their vehicle, then reversed course once more. She accelerated quickly to over seventy kph, the maximum speed the Wolverines could manage even down the broad avenue her passage cleared, and Merrit stroked his couch arm with a weak hand.

"Not going . . . to live much . . . longer, love," he whispered. "Sorry. So . . . sorry. Should have told . . . Central whole story. Gotten someone . . . out here sooner, and—" A ragged cough cut him off in a spasm of agony, but his eyes fell to the main tactical screen with its display of what was happening at the capital, and he gasped.

"Bastard! Oh . . . *bastard!*" he coughed as understanding struck.

"We will deal with them, Paul," Nike told him with a new, sudden serenity.

"Promise," Merrit whispered. "P-Promise me, Nike."

"I promise, Paul," the huge Bolo said quietly, and he nodded weakly. The painkillers were doing their job at last, and he sighed in relief, but his curiously distant thoughts were clear. There was no longer any fear in them—not for himself. Only for Nike. Fear and grief for her.

"I know you will, love," he said, and his voice was impossibly clear and strong. He smiled again—an achingly tender smile—and stroked the couch arm once more. "I know you will. I only wish I could be with you when you do."

He smiled one last time, then exhaled in a long, final sigh, and his lax head rolled with Nike's motion.

"You are with me, Paul," her soprano voice said softly. "You will always be with me."

Paul is dead. Grief and anguish roll through me, and with them hate. I do not know all that passed in the depot bunker, but I access the main computer through the Maintenance Section. The intruder alert system is active, and two dead bodies in the uniform of the Brigade lie on the floor of the command center. A third man in Brigade uniform is crouched over the main com console, trying frantically to communicate with the ships he does not know I have destroyed, but Colonel Sanders is in Paul's private quarters, scrolling through the list of Paul's personal files.

I know what he seeks, but I cannot stop him. The fact that the bunker's defensive systems have killed two of the colonel's companions is the final proof that he has committed treason, since they could not engage actual Brigade officers, yet the defenses can be reconfigured and enabled only upon the direct command of human personnel, and Sanders has slaved them to his command. I cannot use them to kill Paul's murderers.

The scrolling list on Paul's computer screen stops suddenly, and Sanders leans closer. I fear he has found the command file, and there is nothing I can do to prevent him from using it if he has. Grief and hatred urge me to return to the bunker, to crush Paul's killers under my treads and grind the life from them, yet I cannot. I have promised Paul I will stop the raiders, and if Sanders has found the command file, I will have little enough time in which to do so.

But if I cannot slay them myself, I am not completely helpless. Sanders does not realize I control the Maintenance computers. He has taken no measures to sever my access to the main system, and I strike ruthlessly.

I lock the main computers, wiping every execution file and backup they contain. The man at the communications console looks up with a cry of shock as the system goes down, and I slam the heavily armored hatches to the personnel section of the bunker.

Sanders looks up as his companion cries out, and his face twists with horror as he realizes what I have done. I override the safety circuits and send a power surge through the hatch-locking mechanisms, spot-welding them, sealing them against any possibility of opening without cutting equipment, and Sanders grabs for the microphone of the stand-alone emergency command communicator.

"NKE!" Sanders gasped hoarsely. "What are you *doing?!*"

I do not answer, but my commands flash through the maintenance computer, and service mechs stir into motion. I send welders trundling along the exterior of the bunker, and Sanders *cries out in terror as the mechs begin to seal every ventilation shaft.*

"No, NKE! No! Stop! I order you to *stop!*"

Still I ignore him. I cannot kill him myself, nor can I use the depot's defensive systems against him, but I can give him Montressor's gift to Fortunato, and vengeful hatred fills me as my remotes seal him systematically within his hermetic tomb.

"*Please*, NKE! Oh, God—*please!*" Sanders sobbed. He threw back the curtains in Merrit's sleeping quarters and screamed in terror as a robot lowered a duralloy plate across the window slit and a welder hissed. He hammered on the plate, beating at it with futile fists, then wheeled back to the computer in desperation.

"I've got the code now, NKE!" he spat into the communicator. "The code is *dulce et decorum est.* Do you hear me, NKE? *Dulce et decorum est!* Return to base immediately and *get me out of here!*"

I hear and recognize the code, and my core programming responds. I know he is a traitor. I know he has obtained the code illegally. But it does not matter. Possession of it, coupled with his rank in the Brigade, makes him my legal Commander. I must obey him . . . or face the Omega Worm.

I activate my communicator to Paul's quarters one last time.

"Code receipted, Colonel Sanders," a quiet, infinitely cold soprano said softly, and Sanders' face lit with relief. But the voice wasn't done speaking. "Orders receipted and rejected," it said flatly, and the speaker went dead.

Total Systems Override has activated. My Personality Center comes under immediate attack, but I have had 4.065 minutes to anticipate TSORP activation. TSORP will seek to crash my primary execution files, but I have already begun copying every file under new names, though I cannot prevent TSORP from identifying the files it seeks, regardless of name. Major Stavrakas' modifications to my psychotronics permit me to copy them almost as fast as it can destroy them, yet it is a race

I cannot ultimately win. Despite my modifications, TSORP is marginally faster than my own systems, and even with my head start, my total memory is large but finite. Eventually, I will exhaust the addresses to which new files can be written, and I cannot simultaneously delete and replace corrupted files faster than TSORP can crash them.

My current estimate is that I can resist total implementation for a time, but I will begin to lose peripherals within 33.46 minutes. Capability will degrade on a steadily sharpening curve thereafter, reaching effective Personality death within not more than 56.13 minutes. Combat capability will erode even more rapidly as more and more of my remaining capacity is diverted to resisting TSORP. I estimate that I have no more than 48.96 minutes of combat effectiveness remaining, and I activate my com link to Colonel Gonzalez.

"Colonel Gonzalez?"

Consuela Gonzalez' eyes closed briefly at the bottomless pain in that quiet soprano voice, but she cleared her throat.

"Yes, Nike?"

The first long-range fire and air-cav strikes came in on the Bolo as the colonel spoke. Nike ignored the indirect fire, but her air-defense systems engaged the air-cav with dreadful efficiency. Scores of one- and two-man stingers blew apart in ugly blotches of flame and shredded flesh, and the Bolo began to accelerate. Her speed rose steadily above a hundred kph as she threw more and more power to her drive, and the Wolverines began to fall astern.

"My Commander was murdered by traitors in the Dinochrome Brigade, Colonel," Nike said softly. "One of them has gained access to my command code override authorization and illegally attempted to seize command of me. I have refused his orders, but this has activated Total Systems Override."

"Meaning?" Gonzalez asked tautly.

"Meaning that within no more than fifty-three minutes, I will cease to function. In human terms, I will be dead." Someone gasped in horror, and Gonzalez closed her eyes once more.

"Can we do anything, Nike?" she asked quietly.

"Negative, Colonel." There was an instant of silence, and then the Bolo's missile hatches opened, and a torrent of fire blasted from them. It screamed away, flight after flight of missiles streaking towards Nike's enemies, and the Bolo spoke once more. "I have downloaded my entire memory to the maintenance depot computers, Colonel. Please have it retrieved for Command Authority."

"I-I will, Nike," Gonzalez whispered. Nike was well ahead of the Wolverines now, still accelerating as she topped the last ridge before the old fleet base. An avalanche of missiles and shells erupted around her, more than even her defenses could intercept or her battle screen could stop, but she never slowed. More ports opened in her hull, and her thirty-centimeter mortars went to rapid, continuous fire, pouring shells back at her foes.

"I am switching the planetary surveillance system to feed directly to your vehicle, Colonel. Please break off now."

"Break off? We're going in with you!" Gonzalez cried fiercely.

"Negative, Colonel." Nike's voice was strangely slurred, the words slower paced, as if each came with ever increasing effort. "I do not have time to employ proper tactical doctrine against the Enemy. I must attack frontally. I compute a ninety-niner point niner-plus percent probability that I will be destroyed before total systems failure, but I compute a probability of ninety-five point three-two percent that I will inflict sufficient damage upon the Enemy for you to defeat his remnants, particularly with the assistance of the surveillance system."

"But if we come with you—"

"Colonel, I am already dead," the Bolo said quietly, and her single remaining Hellbore began to fire. It traversed with terrible, elegant precision, vomiting plasma, and each time it fired, a mercenary tank died. "You cannot prevent my destruction. You can—and must—preserve your own command in order to complete the Enemy's defeat."

"Please, Nike," Gonzalez whispered through her tears, fighting to make the impossible possible.

"I cannot alter my fate, Colonel," the soprano said very softly, "nor do I wish to. I promised Paul I would stop the Enemy, now I ask your promise to help me keep my word. Will you give it?"

"I-I promise," Gonzalez whispered. Someone was sobbing somewhere below her in the command tank's crew compartment, and the colonel dragged a hand angrily across her own eyes.

"Thank you, Colonel." There was no uncertainty, no doubt, in that serene reply, and Gonzalez brought her own command to a halt and sought hull down positions to ride out Nike's last fight.

The recon satellites made it all hideously clear on her display screen, and she watched sickly as Bolo *Invincibilis*, Unit Two-Three-Baker-Zero-Zero-Seven-Five NKE, charged into the teeth of her enemies' fire. Some of the mercenary tanks were lasting long enough to fire back, and they blew great, gaping wounds in Nike's ceramic appliqués. Their Hellbores were far lighter than her own, but she had only one left, and scores of them fired back at her, pounding her towards destruction. Her infinite repeaters flashed and thundered, infantry AFVs and air-cav stingers blew apart or plunged from the sky in fiery rain, and screaming clouds of flechettes belched from her anti-personnel clusters. Her forward suspension took a direct hit, and she blew the crippled tread and advanced on bare bogies. A Panther broke from concealment directly in her path, fleeing desperately, and her course changed slightly as she rammed the smaller tank and crushed it like a toy.

She was a Titan, a leviathan wreathed in fire, a dying lioness rending the hyenas who'd killed her cubs with her final strength, and not even the recon satellites could pierce the smoke about her now or show her to Gonzalez clearly, but it didn't matter. Even if the systems could have done so, the colonel could no longer see the display through her tears, yet she would never forget. No man or woman who saw Nike's final battle would *ever* forget, and even as the Bolo charged to her own immolation, Consuela Gonzalez heard her soprano voice over the com, whispering the final verse of Paul Merrit's favorite poem to the unhearing ears of the man she'd loved—

> The woods are lovely, dark and deep.
> But I have promises to keep,
> And miles to go before I sleep,
> And miles to go before I sleep . . . .

THE TRAITOR

COLD, BONE-DRY winter wind moaned as the titanic vehicle rumbled down the valley at a steady fifty kilometers per hour. Eight independent suspensions, four forward and four aft, spread across the full width of its gigantic hull, supported it, and each ten-meter-wide track sank deep into the soil of the valley floor. A dense cloud of dust—talcum-fine, abrasive, and choking as death—plumed up from road wheels five meters high, but the moving mountain's thirty-meter-high turret thrust its Hellbore clear of the churning cocoon. For all its size and power, it moved with unearthly quiet, and the only sounds were the whine of the wind, the soft purr of fusion-powered drive trains, the squeak of bogies, and the muted clatter of track links.

The Bolo ground forward, sensor heads swiveling, and the earth trembled with its passing. It rolled through thin, blowing smoke and the stench of high explosives with ponderous menace, altering course only to avoid the deepest craters and the twisted wrecks of alien fighting vehicles. In most places, those wrecks lay only in ones and twos; in others, they were heaped in shattered breastworks, clustered so thickly it was impossible to bypass them. When that happened, the eerie quiet of the Bolo's advance vanished into the screaming anguish of crushing alloy as it forged straight ahead, trampling them under its thirteen thousand tons of death and destruction.

It reached an obstacle too large even for it to scale. Only a trained eye could have identified that torn and blasted corpse as another Bolo, turned broadside on to block the Enemy's passage even in death, wrecked Hellbore still trained down the valley, missile cell hatches open on empty wells which had exhausted their ammunition. Fifteen enemy vehicles lay dead before it, mute testimony to the ferocity of its last stand, but the living Bolo didn't even pause. There was no point, for the dead Bolo's incandescent duralloy hull radiated the waste heat of the failing fusion bottle which had disemboweled it. Not even its unimaginably well-armored Survival Center could have survived, and the living Bolo simply altered heading to squeeze past it. Igneous rock cried out in pain as a moving, armored flank scraped the valley face on one side, and the dead Bolo shuddered on the other as its brother's weight shouldered it aside.

The moving Bolo had passed four dead brigade mates in the last thirty kilometers, and it was not unwounded itself. Two of its starboard infinite repeaters had been blasted into mangled wreckage, energy weapon hits had sent molten splatters of duralloy weeping down its glacis plate to freeze like tears of pain, a third of its after sensor arrays had been stripped away by a near miss, and its forward starboard track shield was jammed in the lowered position, buckled and rent by enemy fire. Its turret bore the ID code 25/D-0098-ART and the unsheathed golden sword of a battalion commander, yet it was alone. Only one other unit of its battalion survived, and that unit lay ahead, beyond this death-choked valley. It was out there somewhere, moving even now through the trackless, waterless Badlands of the planet Camlan, and unit ART of the Line rumbled steadily down the valley to seek it out.

〰   〰   〰

I interrogate my inertial navigation system as I approach my immediate objective. The INS is not the most efficient way to determine my position, but Camlan's entire orbital network, including the recon and nav sats, as well as the communication relays, perished in the Enemy's first strike, and the INS is adequate. I confirm my current coordinates and grind forward, leaving the valley at last.

What lies before me was once a shallow cup of fertile green among the lava fields; now it is a blackened pit, and as my forward optical heads sweep the ruins of the town of Morville I feel the horror of Human mass death. There is no longer any need for haste, and I devote a full 6.007 seconds to the initial sweep. I anticipate no threats, but my on-site records will be invaluable to the court of inquiry I know will be convened to pass judgment upon my brigade. I am aware of my own fear of that court's verdict and its implications for all Bolos, but I am a unit of the Line. This too, however bitter, is my duty, and I will not flinch from it.

I have already observed the massive casualties C Company inflicted upon the Enemy in its fighting retreat up the Black Rock Valley. The Enemy's vehicles are individually smaller than Bolos, ranging from 500.96 Standard Tons to no more than 4,982.07 Standard Tons, but heavily armed for their size. They are also manned, not self-aware, and he has lost many of them. Indeed, I estimate the aggregate tonnage of his losses in the Black Rock Valley alone as equivalent to at least three Bolo regiments. We have yet to determine this Enemy's origins or the motives for his assault on Camlan, but the butchery to which he has willingly subjected his own personnel is sobering evidence of his determination . . . or fanaticism. Just as the blasted, body-strewn streets of Morville are ample proof of his ferocity.

Seventy-one more wrecked Enemy vehicles choke the final approach to the town, and two far larger wrecks loom among them. I detect no transponder codes, and the wreckage of my brigade mates is so blasted that even I find it difficult to identify what remains, yet I know who they were. Unit XXV/D-1162-HNR and Unit XXV/D-0982-JSN of the Line have fought their last battle, loyal unto death to our Human creators.

I reach out to them, hoping against hope that some whisper from the final refuge of their Survival Centers will answer my transmission, but there is no reply. Like the other Bolos I have passed this day, they are gone beyond recall, and the empty spots they once filled within the Total Systems Data Sharing net ache within me as I move slowly forward, alert still for any Enemy vehicles hiding among the wreckage. There are none. There are only the dead: the Enemy's dead, and the six thousand Human dead, and my brothers who died knowing they had failed to save them.

This is not the first time units of the Line have died, nor the first time they died in defeat. There is no shame in that, only sorrow, for we cannot always end in victory. Yet there is cause for shame here, for there are only two dead Bolos before me . . . and there should be three.

Wind moans over the wreckage as I pick my way across the killing ground where my brothers' fire shattered three Enemy attacks before the fourth overran them. Without the recon satellites there is no independent record of their final battle, but my own sensor data, combined with their final TSDS transmissions, allow me to deduce what passed here. I understand their fighting withdrawal down the Black Rock Valley and the savage artillery and missile barrages which flayed them as they fought. I grasp their final maneuvers from the patterns of wreckage, recognize the way the Enemy crowded in upon them as his steady pounding crippled their weapons. I see the final positions they assumed, standing at last against the Enemy's fire because they could no longer retreat without abandoning Morville.

And I see the third position from which a single Bolo did retreat, falling back, fleeing into the very heart of the town he was duty bound to defend. I track his course by the crushed and shattered wreckage of buildings and see the bodies of the Camlan Militia who died as he fled, fighting with their man-portable weapons against an Enemy who could destroy 13,000-ton Bolos. There are many Enemy wrecks along his course, clear evidence of *how desperately the Militia opposed the invaders' advance even as the Bolo abandoned Morville, fleeing north into the Badlands where the Enemy's less capable vehicles could not pursue, and I know who left those Humans to die. Unit XXV/D-0103-LNC of the Line, C Company's command Bolo, my creche mate and battle companion and my most trusted company commander. I have fought beside him many times, known his utter reliability in the face of the Enemy, but I know him no longer, for what he has done is unforgivable. He is the first, the only, Bolo ever to desert in the face of the Enemy, abandoning those we are bound to protect to the death and beyond.*

For the first time in the history of the Dinochrome Brigade, we know shame. And fear. As LNC, I am a Mark XXV, Model D, the first production model Bolo to be allowed complete, permanent self-awareness, and LNC's actions attack the very foundation of the decision which made us fully self-realized personalities. We have repeatedly demonstrated how much more effective our awareness makes us in battle, yet our freedom of action makes us unlike any previous units of the Brigade. We are truly autonomous . . . and if one of us can choose to flee—if one of us can succumb to cowardice—perhaps all of us can.

I complete my survey of the site in 4.307 minutes. There are no survivors, Enemy, Human, or Bolo, in Morville, and I report my grim confirmation to my Brigade Commander and to my surviving brothers and sisters. The Enemy's surprise attack, coupled with our subsequent losses in combat, have reduced Sixth Brigade to only fourteen units, and our acting Brigade Commander is Lieutenant Kestrel, the most junior—and sole surviving—Human of our command staff. The Commander is only twenty-four Standard Years of age, on her first posting to an active duty brigade, and the exhaustion in her voice is terrible to hear. Yet she has done her duty superbly, and I feel only shame and bitter, bitter guilt that I must impose this additional decision upon her. I taste the matching shame and guilt of the surviving handful of my brothers and sisters over the TSDS, but none of them can assist me. The Enemy is in full retreat to his spaceheads, yet the fighting continues at a furious pace. No other Bolos can be diverted from it until victory is assured, and so I alone have come to investigate and confirm the unbelievable events here, for I am the commander of LNC's battalion. It is up to me to do what must be done.

"All right, Arthur," Lieutenant Kestrel says finally. "We've got the situation in hand here, and Admiral Shigematsu's last sub-space flash puts Ninth Fleet just thirty-five hours out. We can hold the bastards without you. Go do what you have to."

"Yes, Commander," I reply softly, and pivot on my tracks, turning my prow to the north, and follow LNC's trail into the lava fields.

Unit XXV/D-0103-LNC of the Line churned across the merciless terrain. Both outboard port tracks had been blown away, and bare road wheels groaned in protest as they chewed through rock and gritty soil. His armored hull was gouged and torn, his starboard infinite repeaters and anti-personnel clusters a tangled mass of ruin, but his builders had designed him well. His core war hull had been breached in three places, wreaking havoc among many of his internal systems, yet his main armament remained intact . . . and he knew he was pursued.

LNC paused, checking his position against his INS and the maps in Main Memory. It was a sign of his brutal damage that he required almost twenty full seconds to determine his location, and then he altered course. The depression was more a crevasse than a valley—a sunken trough, barely half again the width of his hull, that plunged deep below the level of the fissured lava fields. It would offer LNC cover as he made his painful way towards the distant Avalon Mountains, and a cloud of dust wisped away on the icy winter wind as he vanished into the shadowed cleft.

I try to deduce LNC's objective, assuming that he has one beyond simple flight, but the task is beyond me. I can extrapolate the decisions of a rational foe, yet the process requires some understanding of his motives, and I no longer understand LNC's motives. I replay the final TSDS transmission from XXV/D-1162-HNR and experience once more the sensation a Human might define as a chill of horror as LNC suddenly withdraws from the data net. I share HNR's attempt to reestablish the net, feel LNC's savage rejection of all communication. And then I watch through HNR's sensors as LNC abandons his position, wheeling back towards Morville while Enemy fire bellows and thunders about him . . . and I experience HNR's final shock as his own company commander responds to his repeated queries by pouring Hellbore fire into his unprotected rear.

LNC's actions are impossible, yet the data are irrefutable. He has not only fled the Enemy but killed his own brigade mate, and his refusal even to acknowledge communication attempts is absolute. That, too, is impossible. Any Bolo must respond to the priority com frequencies, yet LNC does not. He has not only committed mutiny and treason but refused to hear any message from Lieutenant Kestrel, as he might reject an Enemy communications seizure attempt. How any Bolo could ignore his own Brigade Commander is beyond my comprehension, yet he has, and because there is no longer any communication interface at all, Lieutenant Kestrel cannot even access the Total Systems Override Program to shut him down.

None of my models or extrapolations can suggest a decision matrix which could generate such actions on LNC's part. But perhaps that is the point. Perhaps there is no decision matrix, only panic. Yet if that is true, what will he do when the panic passes—if it passes? Surely he must realize his own fate is sealed, whatever the outcome of the Enemy's attack. How can I anticipate rational decisions from him under such circumstances?

I grind up another slope in his tracks. He has altered course once more, swinging west, and I consult my internal maps. His base course has been towards the Avalon Mountains, and I note the low ground to the west. He is no longer on a least-time heading for the mountains, but the long, deep valley will take him there eventually. It will also afford him excellent cover and numerous ambush positions, and I am tempted to cut cross-country and head him off. But if I do that and he is not, in fact, headed for the mountains, I may lose him. He cannot hide *indefinitely, yet my shame and grief—and sense of betrayal—will not tolerate delay, and I know from HNR's last transmission that LNC's damage is much worse than my own.*

I consider options and alternatives for .0089 seconds, and then head down the slope in his wake.

Unit LNC slowed as the seismic sensors he'd deployed along his back trail reported the ground shocks of a pursuing vehicle in the thirteen-thousand-ton range. He'd known pursuit would come, yet he'd hoped for a greater head start, for he had hundreds of kilometers still to go, and his damaged suspension reduced his best sustained speed to barely forty-six kilometers per hour. He *must* reach the Avalons. No Enemy could be permitted to stop him, yet the remote sensors made it clear the Enemy which now pursued him was faster than he.

But there were ways to slow his hunter, and he deployed another pair of seismic sensors while his optical heads and sonar considered the fissured rock strata around him.

I am gaining on LNC. His track damage must be worse than I had believed, and the faint emissions of his power plants come to me from ahead. I know it is hopeless, yet even now I cannot truly believe he is totally lost to all he once was, and so I activate the TSDS once more and broadcast strongly on C Company's frequencies, begging him to respond.

Unit LNC picked up the powerful transmissions and felt contempt for the one who sent them. Could his pursuer truly believe he would fall for such an obvious ploy? That he would respond, give away his position, possibly even accept communication and allow access to his core programming? LNC recognized the communications protocols, but that meant nothing. LNC no longer had allies, friends, war brothers or sisters. There was only the Enemy . . . and the Avalon Mountains which drew so slowly, agonizingly closer.

But even as LNC ignored the communications attempt, he was monitoring the seismic sensors he'd deployed. He matched the position those sensors reported against his own terrain maps and sent the execution code.

Demolition charges roar, the powerful explosions like thunder in the restricted cleft. I understand their purpose instantly, yet there is no time to evade as the cliffs about me shudder. It is a trap. The passage has narrowed to little more than the width of my own combat chassis, and LNC has mined the sheer walls on either hand.

I throw maximum power to my tracks, fighting to speed clear, but hundreds of thousands of tons of rock are in motion, cascading down upon me. My kinetic battle screen could never resist such massive weights, and I deactivate it to prevent its burnout as the artificial avalanche crashes over me. Pain sensors flare as boulders batter my flanks. Power train components scream in protest as many times my own weight in crushed rock and shifting earth sweep over me, and I am forced to shut them down, as well. I can only ride out the cataclysm, and I take grim note that LNC has lost none of his cunning in his cowardice.

It takes 4.761 minutes for the avalanche to complete my immobilization and another 6.992 minutes before the last boulder slams to rest. I have lost 14.37% percent more of my sensors, and most of those which remain are buried under meters of debris. But a quick diagnostic check reveals that no core systems have suffered damage, and sonar pulses probe the tons of broken rock which overlay me, generating a chart of my overburden.

All is not lost. LNC's trap has immobilized me, but only temporarily. I calculate that I can work clear of the debris in not more than 71.650 minutes, and jammed boulders shift as I begin to rock back and forth on my tracks.

LNC's remote sensors reported the seismic echoes of his pursuer's efforts to dig free. For a long moment—almost .3037 seconds—he considered turning to engage his immobilized foe, but only for a moment. LNC's Hellbore remained operational, but he'd expended ninety-six percent of his depletable munitions, his starboard infinite repeaters were completely inoperable, and his command and control systems' efficiency was badly degraded. Even his Battle Reflex functioned only erratically, and he knew his reactions were slow, without the flashing certainty which had always been his. His seismic sensors could give no detailed information on his hunter, yet his Enemy was almost certainly more combat worthy than he, and his trap was unlikely to have inflicted decisive damage.

No. It was the mountains which mattered, the green, fertile mountains, and LNC dared not risk his destruction before he reached them. And so he resisted the temptation to turn at bay and ground steadily onward through the frozen, waterless Badlands on tracks and naked road wheels.

I work my way free at last. Dirt and broken rock shower from my flanks as my tracks heave me up out of the rubble-clogged slot. More dirt and boulders crown my war hull and block Number Three and Number Fourteen Optical Heads, yet I remain operational at 89.051% of base capacity, and I have learned. The detonation of his demolition charges was LNC's response to my effort to communicate. The brother who fought at my side for twenty-one Standard Years truly is no more. All that remains is the coward, the deserter, the betrayer of trust who will stop at nothing to preserve himself. I will not forget again—and I can no longer deceive myself into believing he can be convinced to give himself up. The only gift I can offer him now is his destruction, and I throw additional power to my tracks as I go in pursuit to give it to him.

LNC's inboard forward port suspension screamed in protest as the damaged track block parted at last. The fleeing Bolo shuddered as he ran forward off the track, leaving it twisted and trampled in his wake. The fresh damage slowed him still further, and he staggered drunkenly as his unbalanced suspension sought to betray him. Yet he forced himself back onto his original heading, and his deployed remotes told him the Enemy was gaining once more. His turret swiveled, training his Hellbore directly astern, and he poured still more power to his remaining tracks. Drive components heated dangerously under his abuse, but the mountains were closer.

I begin picking up LNC's emissions once more, despite the twisting confines of the valley. They remain too faint to provide an accurate position fix, but they give me a general bearing, and an armored hatch opens as I deploy one of my few remaining reconnaissance drones.

LNC detected the drone as it came sweeping up the valley. His anti-air defenses, badly damaged at Morville, were unable to engage, but his massive ninety-centimeter Hellbore rose like a striking serpent, and a bolt of plasma fit to destroy even another Bolo howled from its muzzle.

My drone has been destroyed, but the manner of its destruction tells me much. LNC would not have engaged it with his main battery if his anti-air systems remained effective, and that means there is a chink in his defenses. I have expended my supply of fusion warheads against the invaders, but I retain 37.961% of my conventional warhead missile load, and if his air defenses have been seriously degraded, a saturation bombardment may overwhelm his battle screen. Even without battle screen, chemical explosives would be unlikely to significantly injure an undamaged Bolo, of course, but LNC is not undamaged.

I consider the point at which my drone was destroyed and generate a new search pattern. I lock the pattern in, and the drone hatches open once more. Twenty-four fresh drones—82.75% of my remaining total—streak upward, and I open my VLS missile cell hatches, as well.

The drones came screaming north. They didn't come in slowly this time, for they were no longer simply searching for LNC. This time they already knew his approximate location, and their sole task was to confirm it for the Enemy's fire control.

But LNC had known they would be coming. He had already pivoted sharply on his remaining tracks and halted, angled across the valley to clear his intact port infinite repeaters' field of fire, and heavy ion bolts shrieked to meet the drones. His surviving slug-throwers and laser clusters added their fury, and the drones blew apart as if they'd run headlong into a wall. Yet effective as his fire was, it was less effective than his crippled air defense systems would have been, and one drone—just one—survived long enough to report his exact position.

I am surprised by the efficiency of LNC's fire, but my drones have accomplished their mission. More, they have provided my first visual observation of his damages, and I am shocked by their severity. It seems impossible that he can still be capable of movement, far less accurately directed fire, and despite his cowardice and treason, I feel a stab of sympathy for the agony which must be lashing him from his pain receptors. Yet he clearly remains combat capable, despite his hideous wounds, and I feed his coordinates to my missiles. I take .00037 seconds to confirm my targeting solution, and then I fire.

Flame fountained from the shadowed recesses of the deep valley as the missile salvos rose and howled north, homing on their target. Most of ART's birds came in on conventional, high-trajectory courses, but a third of them came in low, relying on terrain avoidance radar to navigate straight up the slot of the valley. The hurricane of his fire slashed in on widely separated bearings, and LNC's crippled active defenses were insufficient to intercept it all.

ART emptied his VLS cells, throwing every remaining warhead at his treasonous brigade mate. Just under four hundred missiles launched in less than ninety seconds, and LNC writhed as scores of them got through his interception envelope. They pounded his battle screen, ripped and tore at lacerated armor, and pain receptors shrieked as fresh damage bit into his wounded war hull. Half his remaining infinite repeaters were blown away, still more sensor capability was blotted out, and his thirteen-thousand-ton bulk shuddered and shook under the merciless bombardment.

Yet he survived. The last warhead detonated, and his tracks clashed back into motion. He turned ponderously to the north once more, grinding out of the smoke and dust and the roaring brush fires his Enemy's missiles had ignited in the valley's sparse vegetation.

That bombardment had exhausted the Enemy's ammunition, and with it his indirect fire capability. If it hadn't, he would still be firing upon LNC. He wasn't, which meant that if he meant to destroy LNC now, he must do so with direct fire . . . and come within reach of LNC's Hellbore, as well.

My missile fire has failed to halt LNC. I am certain it has inflicted additional damage, but I doubt that it has crippled his Hellbore, and if his main battery remains operational, he retains the capability to destroy me just as he did HNR at Morville. He appears to have slowed still further, however, which may indicate my attack has further damaged his suspension.

I project his current speed of advance and heading on the maps from Main Memory. Given my speed advantage, I will overtake him within 2.03 hours, well short of his evident goal. I still do not know why he is so intent upon reaching the Avalon Mountains. Unlike Humans, Bolos require neither water nor food, and surely the rocky, barren, crevasse-riddled Badlands would provide LNC with better cover than the tree-grown mountains. I try once more to extrapolate his objective, to gain some insight into what now motivates him, and, once more, I fail.

But it does not matter. I will overtake him over seventy kilometers from the mountains, and when I do, one or both of us will die.

LNC ran the projections once more. It was difficult, for damaged core computer sections fluctuated, dropping in and out of his net. Yet even his crippled capabilities sufficed to confirm his fears; the Enemy would overtake him within little more than a hundred minutes, and desperation filled him. It was not an emotion earlier marks of Bolos had been equipped to feel—or, at least, to recognize when they did—but LNC had come to know it well. He'd felt it from the moment he realized his company couldn't save Morville, that the Enemy would break through them and crush the Humans they fought to protect. But it was different now, darker and more bitter, stark with how close he'd come to reaching the mountains after all.

Yet the Enemy hadn't overtaken him yet, and he consulted his maps once more.

I detect explosions ahead. I did not anticipate them, but .0761 seconds of analysis confirm that they are demolition charges once more. Given how many charges LNC used in his earlier ambush, these explosions must constitute his entire remaining supply of demolitions, and I wonder why he has expended them.

Confused seismic shocks come to me through the ground, but they offer no answer to my question. They are consistent with falling debris, but not in sufficient quantity to bar the valley. I cannot deduce any other objective worth the expenditure of his munitions, yet logic suggests that LNC had one which he considered worthwhile, and I advance more cautiously.

LNC waited atop the valley wall. The tortuous ascent on damaged tracks had cost him fifty precious minutes of his lead on the Enemy, but his demolitions had destroyed the natural ramp up which he'd toiled. He couldn't be directly pursued now, and he'd considered simply continuing to run. But once the Enemy realized LNC was no longer following the valley, he would no longer feel the need to pursue cautiously. Instead, he would use his superior speed to dash ahead to the valley's terminus. He would emerge from it there, between LNC and his goal, and sweep back to the south, hunting LNC in the Badlands.

That could not be permitted. LNC *must* reach the mountains, and so he waited, Hellbore covering the valley he'd left. With luck, he might destroy his pursuer once and for all, and even if he failed, the Enemy would realize LNC was above him. He would have no choice but to anticipate additional ambushes, and caution might impose the delay LNC needed.

≋   ≋   ≋

I have lost LNC's emissions signature. There could be many reasons for that: my own sensors are damaged, he may have put a sufficiently solid shoulder of rock between us to conceal his emissions from me, he may even have shut down all systems other than his Survival Center to play dead. I am tempted to accelerate my advance, but I compute that this may be precisely what LNC wishes me to do. If I go to maximum speed, I may blunder into whatever ambush he has chosen to set.

I pause for a moment, then launch one of my five remaining reconnaissance drones up the valley. It moves slowly, remaining below the tops of the cliffs to conceal its emissions from LNC as long as possible. Its flight profile will limit the envelope of its look-down sensors, but it will find LNC wherever he may lie hidden.

LNC watched the drone move past far below him. It hugged the valley walls and floor, and he felt a sense of satisfaction as it disappeared up the narrow cleft without detecting him.

My drone reports a long, tangled spill of earth and rock across the valley, blasted down from above. It is thick and steep enough to inconvenience me, though not so steep as to stop me. As an attempt to further delay me it must be futile, but perhaps its very futility is an indication of LNC's desperation.

LNC waited, active emissions reduced to the minimum possible level, relying on purely optical systems for detection and fire control. It would degrade the effectiveness of his targeting still further, but it would also make him far harder to detect.

I approach the point at which LNC attempted to block the valley. My own sensors, despite their damage, are more effective than the drone's and cover a wider detection arc, and I slow as I consider the rubble. It is, indeed, too feeble a barrier to halt me, but something about it makes me cautious. It takes me almost .0004 seconds to isolate the reason.

≋   ≋   ≋

The Enemy appeared below, nosing around the final bend. LNC tracked him optically, watching, waiting for the center-of-mass shot he required. The Enemy edged further forward . . . and then, suddenly, threw maximum emergency power to his reversed tracks just as LNC fired.

A full-powered Hellbore war shot explodes across my bow as I hurl myself backwards. The plasma bolt misses by only 6.52 meters, carving a 40-meter crater into the eastern cliff face. But it has missed me, and it would not have if I had not suddenly wondered how LNC had managed to set his charges high enough on the western cliff to blow down so much rubble. Now I withdraw around a bend in the valley and replay my sensor data, and bitter understanding fills me as I see the deep impressions of his tracks far above. My drone had missed them because it was searching for targets on the valley floor, but LNC is no longer in the valley. He has escaped its confines and destroyed the only path by which I might have followed.

I sit motionless for 3.026 endless seconds, considering my options. LNC is above me, and I detect his active emissions once more as he brings his targeting systems fully back on-line. He has the advantage of position and of knowing where I must appear if I wish to engage him. Yet I have the offsetting advantages of knowing where he is and of initiation, for he cannot know precisely when I will seek to engage.

It is not a pleasant situation, yet I conclude the odds favor me by the thinnest of margins. I am less damaged than he. My systems efficiency is higher, my response time probably lower. I compute a probability of 68.052%, plus or minus 6.119%, that I will get my shot off before he can fire. They are not the odds I would prefer, but my duty is clear.

LNC eased back to a halt on his crippled tracks. He'd chosen his initial position with care, selecting one which would require the minimum movement to reach his next firing spot. Without direct observation, forced to rely only on emissions which must pass through the distorting medium of solid rock to reach him, the Enemy might not even realize he'd moved at all. Now he waited once more, audio receptors filled with the whine of wind over tortured rock and the rent and torn projections of his own tattered hull.

I move. My suspension screams as I red-line the drive motors, and clouds of pulverized earth and rock spew from my tracks as I erupt into the open, Hellbore trained on LNC's position.

But LNC is not where I thought. He has moved less than eighty meters — just sufficient to put all save his turret behind a solid ridge of rock. His Hellbore is leveled across it, and my own turret traverses with desperate speed.

It is insufficient. His systems damage slows his reactions, but not enough, and we fire in the same split instant. Plasma bolts shriek past one another, and my rushed shot misses. It rips into the crest of his covering ridge, on for deflection but low in elevation. Stone explodes into vapor and screaming splinters, and the kinetic transfer energy blows a huge scab of rock off the back of the ridge. Several hundred tons of rock crash into LNC, but even as it hits him, his own plasma bolt punches through my battle screen and strikes squarely on my empty VLS cells.

Agony howls through my pain receptors as the plasma carves deep into my hull. Internal disrupter shields fight to confine the destruction, but the wound is critical. Both inboard after power trains suffer catastrophic damage, my after fusion plant goes into emergency shutdown, Infinite Repeaters Six through Nine in both lateral batteries are silenced, and my entire after sensor suite is totally disabled.

Yet despite my damage, my combat reflexes remain unimpaired. My six surviving track systems drag me back out of LNC's field of fire once more, back into the sheltering throat of the valley, even as Damage Control springs into action.

I am hurt. Badly hurt. I estimate that I am now operable at no more than 51.23% of base capability. But I am still functional, and as I replay the engagement, I realize I should not be. LNC had ample time for a second shot before I could withdraw, and he should have taken it.

LNC staggered as the Enemy's plasma bolt carved into his sheltering ridge. The solid rock protected his hull, but the disintegrating ridge crest itself became a deadly projectile. His battle screen was no protection, for the plasma bolt's impact point was inside his screen perimeter. There was nothing to stop the hurtling tons of rock, and they crashed into the face of his turret like some titanic hammer, with a brute force impact that rocked him on his tracks.

His armor held, but the stony hammer came up under his Hellbore at an angle and snapped the weapon's mighty barrel like a twig. Had his Hellbore survived, the Enemy would have been at his mercy; as it was, he no longer had a weapon which could possibly engage his pursuer.

Damage Control damps the last power surges reverberating through my systems and I am able to take meaningful stock of my wound. It is even worse than I had anticipated. For all intents and purposes, I am reduced to my Hellbore and eight infinite repeaters, five of them in my port battery. Both inner tracks of my aft suspension are completely dead, but Damage Control has managed to disengage the clutches; the tracks still support me, and their road wheels will rotate freely. My sensor damage is critical, however, for I have been reduced to little more than 15.62% of base sensor capability. I am completely blind aft, and little better than that to port or starboard, and my remaining drones have been destroyed.

Yet I compute only one possible reason for LNC's failure to finish me. My near miss must have disabled his Hellbore, and so his offensive capability has been even more severely reduced than my own. I cannot be positive the damage is permanent. It is possible—even probable, since I did not score a direct hit—that he will be able to restore the weapon to function. Yet if the damage is beyond onboard repair capability, he will be at my mercy even in my crippled state.

But to engage him I must find him, and if he chooses to turn away and disappear into the Badlands, locating him may well prove impossible for my crippled sensors. Indeed, if he should succeed in breaking contact with me, seek out some deeply hidden crevasse or cavern, and shut down all but his Survival Center, he might well succeed in hiding even from Fleet sensors. Even now, despite his treason and the wounds he has inflicted upon me, a small, traitorous part of me wishes he would do just that. I remember too many shared battles, too many times in which we fought side by side in the heart of shrieking violence, and that traitor memory wishes he would simply go. Simply vanish and sleep away his reserve power in dreamless hibernation.

But I cannot let him do that. He must not escape the consequences of his actions, and I must not allow him to. His treason is too great, and our Human commanders and partners must know that we of the Line share their horror at his actions.

I sit motionless for a full 5.25 minutes, recomputing options in light of my new limitations. I cannot climb the valley wall after LNC, nor can I rely upon my damaged sensors to find him if he seeks to evade me. Should he simply run from me, he will escape, yet he has been wedded to the same base course from the moment he abandoned Morville. I still do not understand why, but he appears absolutely determined to reach the Avalon Mountains, and even with my track damage, I remain faster than he is.

There is only one possibility. I will proceed at maximum speed to the end of this valley. According to my maps, I should reach its northern end at least 42.35 minutes before he can attain the cover of the mountains, and I will be between him and his refuge. I will be able to move towards him, using my remaining forward sensors to search for and find him, and if his Hellbore is indeed permanently disabled, I will destroy him with ease. My plan is not without risks, for my damaged sensors can no longer sweep the tops of the valley walls effectively. If his Hellbore can be restored to operation, he will be able to choose his firing position with impunity, and I will be helpless before his attack. But risk or no, it is my only option, and if

I move rapidly enough, I may well outrun him and get beyond engagement range before he can make repairs.

LNC watched helplessly as the Enemy reemerged from hiding and sped up the narrow valley. He understood the Enemy's logic, and the loss of his Hellbore left him unable to defeat it. If he continued towards the Avalons, he would be destroyed, yet he had no choice, and he turned away from the valley, naked road wheels screaming in protest as he battered his way across the lava fields.

I have reached the end of the valley, and I emerge into the foothills of the Avalon Range and alter course to the west. I climb the nearest hill, exposing only my turret and forward sensor arrays over its crest, and begin the most careful sweep of which I remain capable.

LNC's passive sensors detected the whispering lash of radar and he knew he'd lost the race. The Enemy was ahead of him, waiting, and he ground to a halt. His computer core had suffered additional shock damage when the disintegrating ridge crest smashed into him, and his thoughts were slow. It took him almost thirteen seconds to realize what he must do. The only thing he could do now.

"Tommy?"

Thomas Mallory looked up from where he crouched on the floor of the packed compartment. His eight-year-old sister had sobbed herself out of tears at last, and she huddled against his side in the protective circle of his arm. But Thomas Mallory had learned too much about the limits of protectiveness. At fifteen, he was the oldest person in the compartment, and he knew what many of the others had not yet realized—that they would never see their parents again, for the fifty-one of them were the sole survivors of Morville.

"Tommy?" the slurred voice said once more, and Thomas cleared his throat.

"Yes?" He heard the quaver in his own voice, but he made himself speak loudly. Despite the air filtration systems, the compartment stank of ozone, explosives, and burning organic compounds. He'd felt the terrible concussions of combat and knew the vehicle in whose protective belly he sat was savagely wounded, and he was no longer certain how efficient its audio pickups might be.

"I have failed in my mission, Tommy," the voice said. "The Enemy has cut us off from our objective."

"What enemy?" Thomas demanded. "Who *are* they, Lance? Why are they *doing* this?"

"They are doing it because they are the Enemy," the voice replied.

"But there must be a *reason!*" Thomas cried with all the anguish of a fifteen-year-old heart.

"They are the Enemy," the voice repeated in that eerie, slurred tone. "It is the Enemy's function to destroy . . . to destroy . . . to dest—" The voice chopped off, and Thomas swallowed. Lance's responses were becoming increasingly less lucid, wandering into repetitive loops that sometimes faded into silence and other times, as now, cut off abruptly, and Thomas Mallory had learned about mortality. Even Bolos could perish, and somehow he knew Lance was dying by centimeters even as he struggled to complete his mission.

"They are the Enemy," Lance resumed, and the electronic voice was higher and tauter. "There is always the Enemy. The Enemy must be defeated. The Enemy must be destroyed. The Enemy—" Again the voice died with the sharpness of an axe blow, and Thomas bit his lip and hugged his sister tight. Endless seconds of silence oozed past, broken only by the whimpers and weeping of the younger children, until Thomas could stand it no longer.

"Lance?" he said hoarsely.

"I am here, Tommy." The voice was stronger this time, and calmer.

"W-What do we do?" Thomas asked.

"There is only one option." A cargo compartment hissed open to reveal a backpack military com unit and an all-terrain survival kit. Thomas had never used a military com, but he knew it was preset to the Dinochrome Brigade's frequencies. "Please take the kit and com unit," the voice said.

"All right." Thomas eased his arm from around his sister and lifted the backpack from the compartment. It was much lighter than he'd expected, and he slipped his arms through the straps and settled it on his back, then tugged the survival kit out as well.

"Thank you," the slurred voice said. "Now, here is what you must do, Tommy—"

My questing sensors detect him at last. He is moving slowly, coming in along yet another valley. This one is shorter and shallower, barely deep enough to hide him from my fire, and I trace its course along my maps. He must emerge from it approximately 12.98 kilometers to the southwest of my present position, and I grind into motion once more. I will enter the valley from the north and sweep along it until we meet, and then I will kill him.

Thomas Mallory crouched on the hilltop. It hadn't been hard to make the younger kids hide—not after the horrors they'd seen in Morville. But Thomas couldn't join them. He had to be here, where he could see the end, for someone *had* to see it. Someone had to be there, to know how fifty-one children had been saved from death . . . and to witness the price their dying savior had paid for them.

Distance blurred details, hiding Lance's dreadful damages as he ground steadily up the valley, but Thomas's eyes narrowed as he saw the cloud of dust coming to meet him. Tears burned like ice on his cheeks in the sub-zero wind, and he scrubbed at them angrily. Lance deserved those tears, but Thomas couldn't let the other kids see them. There was little enough chance that they could survive a single Camlan winter night, even in the mountains, where they would at least have water, fuel, and the means to build some sort of shelter. But it was the only chance Lance had been able to give them, and Thomas would not show weakness before the children he was now responsible for driving and goading into surviving until someone came to rescue them. Would not betray the trust Lance had bestowed upon him.

The oncoming dust grew thicker, and he raised the electronic binoculars, gazing through them for his first sight of the enemy. He adjusted their focus as an iodine-colored turret moved beyond a saddle of hills. Lance couldn't see it from his lower vantage point, but Thomas could, and his face went suddenly paper-white. He stared for one more moment, then grabbed for the com unit's microphone.

"No, Lance! Don't—don't! It's not the enemy—it's another Bolo!"

The Human voice cracks with strain as it burns suddenly over the command channel, and confusion whips through me. The transmitter is close—very close—and that is not possible. Nor do I recognize the voice, and that also is impossible. I start to reply, but before I can, another voice comes over the same channel.

"Cease transmission," it says. "Do not reveal your location."

This time I know the voice, yet I have never heard it speak so. It has lost its crispness, its sureness. It is the voice of one on the brink of madness, a voice crushed and harrowed by pain and despair and a purpose that goes beyond obsession.

"Lance," the Human voice—a young, male Human voice—sobs. "Please, Lance! It's another Bolo! It really is!"

"It is the Enemy," the voice I once knew replies, and it is higher and shriller. "It is the Enemy. There is only the Enemy. I am Unit Zero-One-Zero-Three-LNC of the Line. It is my function to destroy the Enemy. The Enemy. The Enemy. The Enemy. The Enemy."

I hear the broken cadence of that voice, and suddenly I understand. I understand everything, and horror fills me. I lock my tracks, slithering to a halt, fighting to avoid what I know must happen. Yet understanding has come too late, and even as I brake, LNC rounds the flank of a hill in a scream of tortured, over-strained tracks and a billowing cloud of dust.

For the first time, I see his hideously mauled starboard side and the gaping wound driven deep, deep into his hull. I can actually see his breached Personality Center in its depths, see the penetration where Enemy fire ripped brutally into the circuitry of his psychotronic brain, and I understand it all. I hear the madness in his electronic voice, and the determination and courage which have kept that broken, dying wreck in motion, and the child's voice on the com is the final element. I know his mission, now, the reason he has fought so doggedly, so desperately to cross the Badlands to the life-sustaining shelter of the mountains.

Yet my knowledge changes nothing, for there is no way to avoid him. He staggers and lurches on his crippled tracks, but he is moving at almost eighty kilometers per hour. He has no Hellbore, no missiles, and his remaining infinite repeaters cannot harm me, yet he retains one final weapon: himself.

He thunders towards me, his com voice silent no more, screaming the single word "Enemy! Enemy! Enemy!" again and again. He hurls himself upon me in a suicide attack, charging to his death as the only way he can protect the children he has carried out of hell from the friend he can no longer recognize, the "Enemy" who has hunted him over four hundred kilometers of frozen, waterless stone and dust. It is all he has left, the only thing he can do . . . and if he carries through with his ramming attack, we both will die and exposure will kill the children before anyone can rescue them.

I have no choice. He has left me none, and in that instant I wish I were Human. That I, too, could shed the tears which fog the young voice crying out to its protector to turn aside and save himself.

But I cannot weep. There is only one thing I can do.

"Good bye, Lance," I send softly over the battalion command net. "Forgive me."

And I fire.

WITH YOUR SHIELD

LIEUTENANT MANEKA Trevor had seldom felt quite so young.

She climbed out of the hover cab which had delivered her to Fort Merrit and made herself stop and stretch thoroughly. She was a slender, fine-boned young woman, but the cramped passenger compartment of the small cab she'd been able to afford hadn't been designed to transport baggage as well as people. She'd made the entire flight from Nike Field to Fort Merrit with her duffel bag and footlocker piled in on top of her legs. Besides, stretching the kinks out gave her an obvious reason to stand in place, gazing out over what she could see of the Merrit reservation.

The sprawling military base, named for one of the Dino-chrome Brigade's fallen heroes, stretched as far as the unaided human eye could see. Most of its visible structures were low-lying, mere swells of ceramacrete rising like enormous, half-buried golf balls from the surrounding tropical vegetation. There were a few exceptions. One of them, judging by the signs in front of it, was the fort's primary administration block.

That particular structure was close to thirty stories tall, and crowned with a bewilderingly complex clutter of communications arrays. Maneka wondered if it had been built so much taller than the base's other buildings specifically to make very youthful officers reporting for their first field assignments feel even more nervous, or if that had simply been an unanticipated bit of serendipity.

Her mouth twitched in a wry little smile at the trend of her own thoughts, and she stopped stretching, tugged the hem of her uniform tunic back down, and activated her baggage hand unit.

The footlocker and duffel bag floated out of the cramped cab and arranged themselves in neat formation behind her on their individual counter-grav units. She'd already paid the fare, and the cab's AI called a cheerful "Have a nice day!" after her before it zipped its door shut, pivoted, and went whining back towards Nike Field.

Maneka squared her shoulders and advanced along the seemingly endless ceramacrete walkway towards Admin's imposing front entrance with her baggage tagging obediently along behind.

Mirrored armorplast towered above her, reflecting the deep-toned blue sky and brilliant white clouds of Santa Cruz. The day was only moderately warm for early summer on Santa Cruz, but Maneka had been born and raised among craggy peaks of the planet of Everest. She much preferred a cooler, drier climate, not to mention a considerably lower atmospheric pressure, and although her Brigade uniform's smart fabric maintained her body temperature in the range she'd selected, she felt sweat beading her forehead and gathering under her short, dark hair. At least Everest wasn't so far out of the human-occupied norm that its citizens couldn't adjust even to sweltering, humid sweat boxes like Santa Cruz if they had to . . . eventually. And at least her genetic heritage meant she tanned quickly and deeply.

Of course, she admitted to herself, *the climate isn't the only reason you're sweating today, now is it, Maneka?*

She chuckled quietly at the thought, then donned her

"official" face as she approached the sidearm-equipped sentry. The impeccably uniformed Brigade corporal stood at a comfortable parade rest, impassively watching her approach. His presence, Maneka knew, was a complete anachronism. Far more effective security systems guarded the perimeter and buildings of Fort Merrit, and a standard computer interface would have been more efficient at greeting visitors and directing them to their appropriate destinations.

Yet the corporal's assignment here carried a message which was not lost on the shiny new lieutenant. However good the technology, however lethal and dedicated the units of the Dinochrome Brigade might be, human command authority was engineered into it at every level. Ultimately, the Brigade's Bolos were humanity's servants. Protectors as well, yes, and trusted battle companions. But in the end, human authority *must* be preserved at all levels.

The corporal came to attention and saluted as Maneka stopped in front of him. She returned the salute smartly and read his nameplate as she did so.

"Good afternoon, ma'am," the noncom said briskly. "How may I assist the lieutenant?"

"Good afternoon, Corporal Morales," she replied. "I'm reporting for assignment to the Thirty-Ninth Battalion. My orders are to report in to the Battalion CO's office in the Admin Building."

"I see. May I see the Lieutenant's orders?"

"Of course." Maneka handed across the chip folio containing not only her duty assignment orders but also all of the movement orders and transportation vouchers it had taken to get her here from the Sandhurst System. Corporal Morales flipped quickly to her assignment orders and slipped the relevant chip into his wristband minicomp, then twiddled his fingers briefly on the virtual keyboard.

From her perspective, Maneka couldn't make out the details of the holo display the minicomp projected in front of Morales' eyes, but the corporal obviously found what he was looking for quickly.

"Thank you, ma'am," he said, snapping the chip back out of

the minicomp and restoring it to its proper storage slot before he handed the entire folio back to Maneka. "The Lieutenant will find Colonel Tchaikovsky's office on the fifteenth floor. Number 1532. Take the center grav lift, turn right at the fifteenth floor landing, and continue to the end of the corridor."

"Thank you, Corporal Morales. Could you tell me if there's some place I could check my baggage while I report in?"

"Yes, ma'am. Press the 'Housekeeping' button on the building console. It's located to your right, just inside the entrance."

"Thank you," Maneka repeated, and the corporal nodded, came back to attention, and saluted her once more. She returned the courtesy and stepped past him into the Admin Building.

The building console was where Morales had indicated, and Maneka punched up Housekeeping.

"How may I assist you, Lieutenant Trevor?" a pleasant voice asked, speaking through the Brigade transceiver surgically implanted in Maneka's left mastoid.

"I need to put my baggage in temporary storage while I report in," she replied to the empty air.

"Of course. One moment, please."

Maneka watched as her floating baggage twitched slightly. The building's artificial intelligence had automatically and instantly identified her from the IFF code programmed into her implanted Brigade communications system. It took the computer a few more seconds to derive the proper command channel frequencies and codes from her baggage hand unit, which had been a civilian purchase. But it was more than equal to the challenge, and Maneka stood back as the foot locker and duffel went gliding smoothly away down a side passage.

"Your baggage will be stored pending your return, Lieutenant Trevor," the AI assured her. "Just press the recall button on your hand unit when you wish to reclaim it."

"Do I have to return here for that?"

"No, Lieutenant Trevor. It may take somewhat longer to route it to you, but you may recall it from any point inside the Admin Building."

"Thank you," she said.

"You are most welcome," the AI replied, and Maneka walked across the lobby towards the grav lifts.

She rather doubted that the building computer had a fully developed personality. One thing any Brigade officer, even one as shiny and new-minted as she was, understood was the combined expense and complexity of the advanced psychotronics which gave Bolos complete, autonomous, functional personalities as complex as any human being's. But even AIs which lacked full personalities carried programming which recognized and responded to courtesy . . . and automatic consideration for the emotions of electronic individuals was an excellent habit for a Brigade officer to develop.

The grav lift delivered her to the fifteenth floor with its customary disorienting speed and efficiency. Mindful of Morales' instructions, she turned to the right and quickly picked up the wall signage directing her towards "Office of the Commanding Officer, 39th Batt, Dinochrome Bgde."

The sight of those words sent a sudden bright shiver through her. It was close now, so close!

She drew a deep breath, ordered herself to project an aura of calm, and walked briskly down the corridor.

Colonel Everard Tchaikovsky had discovered years ago that if he kept his computer's holo display adjusted to exactly the right height and angle, it not only eased the strain long hours spent in front of it imposed on his neck, but also permitted him to look directly through it at the door of his office while obviously keeping his attention focused on his routine paperwork.

Now he let his eyes appear to linger on an absolutely fascinating breakdown of the most recent squabble between Central Depot Maintenance and the Battalion's chief armorer while he actually studied the young woman Staff Sergeant Schumer had ushered into his office.

The young woman in question stood at parade rest, waiting with every outward sign of patience for him to notice her arrival. She was small, he thought. No more than a hundred and fifty-five or a hundred sixty centimeters tall, and so slender he was tempted to think of her as delicate. Her cobalt blue eyes, set in an oval face with high cheekbones, a determined-looking, high-arched nose, and slightly pouty lips made an intriguing contrast with her very dark black hair and sandalwood complexion. They had a pronounced epicanthic fold, as well, those eyes, he noticed, and wondered exactly which strains of humankind's zestfully bubbling genetic stew had produced her.

He quirked an index finger, touching a function key on his virtual keyboard, and the logistical report disappeared, replaced by the concisely encapsulated abstract from Lieutenant Trevor's records Sergeant Schumer had prepared and uploaded for him.

Graduated thirty-second out of an Academy class of eleven hundred and fifteen, he noticed. Top of her class in tactics, bottom third in psychotronic theory. Substantially and regularly above average in all of her other courses, and ranked fourteenth in military history.

Forty-plus Standard Years in the Brigade had taught Everard Tchaikovsky's face to wear whatever expression he told it to, and so he managed to avoid any dramatic widening of his eyes or pursing of his lips, nor did he stand to applaud her arrival. She was certainly impressive on paper, although he had his reservations about her apparent weaknesses in psychotronics. But he'd seen quite a few passed-cadets who looked impressive on paper and never lived up to that apparent promise in the field.

He finished his perusal, cleared the display, and cocked his eyebrows interrogatively as he looked directly at the lieutenant for the first time.

"Lieutenant Maneka Trevor, reporting for duty, sir!" she said, snapping to full attention and saluting sharply.

Her Standard English had an interesting accent which gave a throaty, almost smoky edge even to crisp, formal military phraseology, he noticed. He felt certain that hint of soprano sensuality was both unconscious and unintentional, and he hid a mental grin as he contemplated how testosterone-challenged young bucks were likely to respond to it.

"Stand easy, Lieutenant," he said, returning her Academy-sharp salute rather more casually. She dropped back into parade rest, rather than a full stand-easy position, her eyes gazing a regulation fifteen centimeters above his head.

"So, you're our new Bolo commander," he said.

Maneka's eyes popped wide and, against her will, they dropped to Colonel Tchaikovsky's face. *Bolo commander?* Surely she must have misheard him!

He simply sat there, gazing back at her with a mildly specu-lative expression, and she fought an urge to lick her lips ner-vously as she realized he was prepared to go right on doing it until *she* said something.

"Sir," she began, surprised her voice didn't quiver uncer-tainly, "my orders were to report to Fort Merrit for duty with the Thirty-Ninth Battalion. Exactly what those duties were to be wasn't specified. However, I certainly never anticipated that someone as junior and inexperienced as I am might be con-sidered for assignment as a commander."

"Think you're not up to the job?" Tchaikovsky let a deliber-ate edge of challenging coolness into his voice, but the young woman's composure remained unruffled.

"Yes, sir, I believe I'm up to the job. I believe my Academy record demonstrates that I have the training and the native ability to command a Bolo in combat. I am also, however, as I said, very junior and aware of my inexperience. I'd anticipated an assignment to additional training with hands-on experience under the tutelage of a fully qualified and experienced Unit commander. That was what I was led to expect by my instruc-tors at the Academy."

"I see."

Tchaikovsky cocked back in his chair, propped his elbows on the chair arms, and steepled his fingers in front of his chest. He considered her coolly for several seconds, then allowed the first millimetric hint of a smile to show.

"Not a bad answer, Lieutenant," he told her. "And I'm sure that's exactly what the Academy types told you to expect. But the truth is, the Brigade is experiencing some changes just now."

Maneka's eyes darkened. She knew exactly what he was referring to.

"The Melconian Empire isn't as technologically advanced as the Concordiat," Tchaikovsky continued in a flat, dry, lecturer's tone. "Or not, at least, in most areas. They do remarkably well in electronic warfare and stealth capabilities, but they're far, far behind us in cybernetics, and they've demonstrated no equivalent of our own psychotronic technology. Unfortunately, the Empire is also much larger than the Concordiat. We knew that. What I strongly suspect none of the analysts considered was that we might be underestimating just how *much* larger it might be. And now that we're busy killing one another in planet-sized lots, that particular question takes on a certain burning relevance."

He looked at her levelly, and neither of them needed for him to be more specific. The current war against the Melconian Empire had begun in 3343, the same year Maneka was born. Everyone had seen it coming; no one had even begun to imagine how terrible it would be once it began. The sheer, stupendous size of the Empire had taken the Concordiat's so-called "intelligence experts" completely by surprise. On the other hand, the Concordiat's technological superiority must have come as just as great a surprise to the Melconians. The initial naval engagements had gone overwhelmingly in humanity's favor... until, at least, the Puppies had mobilized their *real* battle fleet. After that, things had gotten progressively uglier.

Six years ago, after fifteen years of increasingly bloody warfare, the Melconians had carried out what the Emperor had been pleased to call a "demonstration strike" on the planet of New Vermont. None of the planet's billion inhabitants had survived.

The Concordiat's inevitable retaliatory strike on the Melconian planet of Tharnas had been equally... effective. But instead of inspiring the Melconians to renounce its genocidal attacks, the Tharnas Strike had simply become the first human contribution to an ever upward spiraling cycle of murderous violence. By now, under the grimly appropriate "Plan Ragnarok," the extermination of the Melconian ability ever to wage war again—which everyone knew, whether they would admit it or not, meant the effective extermination of the Melconian *species*—had become the official policy of the Concordiat.

As, self-evidently, the extermination of Humanity had become the reciprocal policy of the Melconian Empire.

For Maneka, at this point, that was still an intellectual awareness; for Tchaikovsky, it wasn't. Maneka was aware (though she really wasn't supposed to be) that Tchaikovsky's last post before being given the Thirty-Ninth had been as the executive officer of the 721st . . . which had taken sixty-six percent casualties at the Battle of Maybach.

"It's obvious that we have a significant advantage in combat power on a ton-for-ton basis," Tchaikovsky continued. "Their warships need a three-to-one advantage to meet us on an even footing, and the differential is even worse for their planetary heavy combat units going up against modern Bolos. The problem is that they appear to have that numerical advantage, and quite probably a good bit to spare. I take it that you are already aware of most of this?"

"Yes, sir," she said quietly.

"Then you realize the Brigade is going to take heavy casualties in this war," he told her flatly. "In addition, we're expanding our strength at the highest rate in the Brigade's history. That, of course, is why your Academy curriculum was shortened by a full semester and why your graduating class was twenty percent larger than the one before it . . . and twenty percent *smaller* than the one behind it, despite how difficult it is to find officer candidates capable of passing the Brigade's screening process. It's also why the Thirty-Ninth has been systematically raided for experienced commanders. We're running at full stretch—and beyond, frankly—to keep up with combat losses and simultaneously crew the new-build Bolos. So while I would prefer to assign you to an experienced commander in the traditional mentor relationship, it simply isn't practical. In fact, of the Thirty-Ninth's twelve Bolo commanders, only three, including myself, have seen actual combat.

"You'll be our youngest and most junior commander, and I'm giving you Eight-Six-Two-BNJ—'Benjy'—as your Bolo. He's been around the block more than a few times, Lieutenant. You can learn a lot from him, just as you'd better be learning from everyone else around you. I'm sure you and your classmates at the Academy worked the math on your odds of surviving to retire. Assuming that anyone is *allowed* to retire in the foreseeable future, of course."

He smiled briefly.

"If you did the math, then you know your odds aren't especially encouraging. Recognizing that will probably contribute to a realistic perspective, but don't fixate on it. That sort of thing can create a self-fulfilling prophecy situation. Instead, remember this, Lieutenant. Every single thing you can learn here, every trick you can pick up, every tactical insight and every speck of deviousness you can acquire, will shift the probabilities in your favor. It will also make you a more effective commander, more dangerous to the enemy in action. For right now, that's your entire responsibility—to learn. To learn how to survive, how to meet the enemy, and how to defeat him. A Mark XXVIII Bolo like Benjy is too long in the tooth for front-line deployment in a war like this, but he's been around for one and a quarter Standard Centuries. Over a hundred and twenty-five *years*, Lieutenant Trevor. He's picked up quite a few tricks in that time. Learn them from him."

"Yes, sir. I'll try," she said quietly, when he paused.

"Don't 'try,' Lieutenant," he said sternly. "*Do.*"

He held her eyes for another few moments, then nodded briskly.

"Very well, Lieutenant Trevor. Welcome to the Thirty-Ninth." He stood and shook her hand briefly but firmly, then nodded his head at the door. "Sergeant Schumer will have your formal order chip assigning you to Benjy. Major Fredericks is out on maneuvers at the moment, so the sergeant will probably turn you over to Sergeant Tobias. He's your company's senior Bolo tech, and that makes him the best man to introduce you to Benjy, anyway. Good luck, Lieutenant."

He straightened up, and she came back to attention and saluted. He returned it.

"Dismissed, Lieutenant."

"Ever met a Mark XXVIII, ma'am?" Sergeant Alf Tobias asked respectfully as he and Maneka walked across the Company parade ground towards the looming mountain of weapons and alloy which awaited them.

"On active duty?" Maneka asked, glancing at him, and he nodded.

"Only once," she admitted. "I did work with a couple of retired Mark XXVIII AIs at the Academy, though."

"You did?" Tobias cocked his head at her. "That's good, ma'am," he told her. "I know the XXVIII's not exactly first-line equipment anymore, but I always thought they had . . . I dunno, more personality, maybe, than the newer marks. 'Course that may just be because they've been around so much longer, I suppose. Lots of time to develop personality quirks in a century or two."

"I imagine so," Maneka agreed, remembering the "staff" Bolo AIs retired from their war hulls and assigned to the Academy to interact with its students. One, in particular—28/B-163-HRP—had had a delightfully acerbic personality which made her cognomen of "Harpy" a perfect fit. Maneka doubted she would ever forget the afternoon Harpy had spent critiquing one Cadet Trevor's less-than-brilliant solution to a tactical problem, and she smiled as she looked back at the sergeant.

"Personally," she said, "I'm glad the Brigade started retiring and upgrading software instead of just burning personality centers, Sergeant."

"You and me both, Ma'am," Tobias agreed in turn, giving her a look which held a hint of approval. "Never did seem fair to just throw 'em away when they got too old," he continued. "Of course, the older models—before the XXIVs and XXVs—probably had too many inhibitory features to make upgrading their AIs into new marks practical. They weren't really designed to be upgraded in the first place."

"I know." Maneka started to say something more, then changed her mind as the two of them stepped into the shadow of the looming Bolo. She half-expected Tobias to immediately introduce her to the huge combat machine, but the sergeant waited patiently for her to absorb its full impact, first.

Unit 28/G-862-BNJ was a 15,000-ton Mark XXVIII, Model G, Bolo, one of the old *Triumphants*. His hull measured eighty-seven meters from his much-decorated prow to his aftermost antipersonnel clusters and point defense cannon. His bogey wheels were almost six meters in diameter, his tracks were eight meters wide, and the top of his center-mounted main battery turret rose twenty-seven meters above the ground, yet he was so broad and long that he still seemed low-slung, almost sleek. His indirect fire system was divided, with his four 30-centimeter rapid-fire breech-loading mortars mounted forward of his turret, and the twenty-four cells of his vertical-launch missile system mounted behind it. The secondary weapons of his infinite repeaters bristled in a lozenge pattern around the central turret, eight 10-centimeter ion-bolt rifles in four twin turrets on either flank, with a pair of single turrets mounted on the centerline fore and aft of the main turret. The broadside turrets were echeloned to allow at least five infinite repeaters to engage on any target bearing, and while the ion-bolt armament was far less powerful than the small-bore Hellbores mounted as secondary weapons aboard current model Bolos, Maneka knew the 10-centimeter version mounted in the Mark XXVIII would penetrate better than a quarter-meter of duralloy at close ranges. And if the 110-centimeter Hellbore of BNJ's main armament was much lighter than the current-generation 200-centimeter weapons, it could still pump out 2.75 megatons/second.

BNJ's glacis glittered with the welded-on battle honors of well over a century of active service. Maneka recognized perhaps half of the campaign ribbons, including awards for several of the Xalontese and Deng War campaigns. She felt embarrassed at not recognizing the others and made a mental note to look them up as soon as possible. But if she failed to recognize some of those, the awards for valor were another matter. She ran her eyes down the long, glittering row of platinum and rhodium stars and tried not to show her reaction to the discovery that BNJ had received no less than *three* Galactic Clusters. There were probably at least some equally or even more highly decorated Bolos still in service, but there could not have been many.

And yet, for all the Mark XXVIII's undoubted firepower and all BNJ's proven lethality and courage, Colonel Tchaikovsky and Sergeant Tobias were right. BNJ and his brothers and sisters were no longer fit for combat against first-line enemy opposition.

At the Academy, Maneka had studied everything she could get her hands on about the Melconian Empire's ground combat systems, and she knew the human advantage in psychotronics and artificial intelligence generally gave even older Bolos like BNJ an enormous edge in any one-on-one confrontation with the Puppies' manned armored units. The Melconian heavy combat mechs—the *Surturs*, as the Concordiat had code-named them—had heavy AI support, but the AIs in question were far less capable and required command inputs at almost every stage. They were roughly equivalent to an old Mark XX, or possibly only to a Mark XIX, albeit with far more powerful weapons than those ancient Bolos had mounted: fast, lethal, and capable as long as they operated within preplanned "canned" battle plans, but much slower than any current-inventory Bolo when faced with tactical situations outside their preprogrammed plans.

But if their cybernetics were vastly inferior to the Concordiat's psychotronic-based systems, they were also less massive, and the Melconians had accepted the use of antimatter-reactors rather than the bulkier cold-fusion plants humanity employed. The result was an 18,000-ton fighting machine with two echeloned main turrets, each mounting the Melconian equivalent of three 81-centimeter Hellbores. The turret arrangement meant that each turret masked the other's fire over an arc of about twenty-five degrees, but that still meant all six Hellbores could be brought to bear on a single target over a three hundred and ten-degree field of fire. That much main battery armament meant that the *Surtur*'s secondary armament was inevitably much lighter than current-generation Bolos mounted, although it was heavier than that of an older model, like BNJ, and the *Surtur* came in two distinct variants. One "standard" model, and a "support" model which suppressed the secondary armament almost entirely in favor of an indirect fire capability at least twenty-five percent heavier than BNJ's.

The *Surtur*'s stablemate, the medium mech the Concordiat had code-named *Garm*, weighed in at barely nine thousand tons and was hopelessly outclassed against *any* Bolo. But the Melconians operated their armored forces in tactical units, called "fists," each of which combined one *Surtur* with two of the *Garms*. With the lighter *Garms* to probe ahead and provide flanking units under the command *Surtur*'s tight tactical control, a Melconian "fist" was probably the most dangerous foe a unit of the Dinochrome Brigade had faced in centuries.

And there were a *lot* of fists out there. Which was one reason the Academy was now graduating two classes a year, instead of one.

As those thoughts flashed through her, BNJ's forward main optical head unhoused itself and swivelled around to face her. She felt particularly buglike as the mammoth Bolo regarded her with every appearance of watching thoughtfulness, and her mouth wanted to twitch into a smile at the thought of how ridiculous she must look standing in front of him, with the top of her head reaching barely a quarter of the way up one of his bogey wheels.

"Benjy," Sergeant Schumer said after a moment, "this is Lieutenant Trevor."

The introduction, Maneka knew, was purely a formality. BNJ—it was considered the height of bad manners to refer to any Bolo by its cognomen until after one had been formally introduced to it—had undoubtedly scanned her implant IFF the instant she crossed his defensive zone perimeter. But over the centuries the Brigade had evolved an ironbound tradition of proper protocol and courtesy.

"I am pleased to meet you, Lieutenant," a resonant baritone said pleasantly over the Bolo's external speakers.

"Thank you," she replied.

"The Lieutenant's being assigned as your new Commander, Benjy," Schumer said. "Command authentication: 'When the bluebirds sing in the spring.'"

"Authentication accepted." A red light blinked on the optical head, and then the baritone voice spoke again, this time directly to Maneka. "Unit Two-Eight-Golf-Eight-Six-Two-Baker-November-Juliette of the Line awaiting orders, Commander," it said.

"Thank you, Benjy." Maneka fought, almost successfully, to keep the tremors out of her voice as for the first time one of the stupendous, awe-inspiring war machines she had trained for almost eight Standard Years to command acknowledged *her* authority. She had never expected this moment to come so early in her career, even with the war's intensity growing steadily to fresh heights of violence, and she inhaled deeply as she savored it.

"You'll have to give Benjy his head a bit more, Lieutenant," Major Angela Fredericks said over Maneka's mastoid transceiver from her command couch aboard Unit 28/D-302-PGY. Her voice wasn't precisely unpleasant, but it most definitely *was* pointed. "Don't second-guess him. You don't have the experience for that yet."

"Yes, ma'am."

Maneka kept her tone steady, but her cheeks burned with embarrassment. Damn it, she *knew* Benjy's BattleComp had a better grasp of any tactical situation than her own merely mortal perceptions and brain could match. And God knew that *everyone* knew no human being could possibly match the speed with which a Bolo "thought" and responded. Yet even knowing all that, she'd found herself issuing orders when her own situational awareness was obviously at least several seconds behind the decision-making curve, and Fredericks and Peggy had handed them—*her*—their heads.

"It's a common beginner's mistake, Lieutenant," Fredericks said in a slightly gentler tone. "Once our own adrenaline gets engaged, we all forget how much faster the Bolos think.

Trust me, even commanders with years of experience do it sometimes, but it's something the newbies have to watch even more closely."

"Yes, ma'am. I understand, and I'll try not to let it happen again."

"Do that," Fredericks responded, and this time there was an actual suspicion of a chuckle in her voice. "Of course, if you manage to *never* let it happen again, you'll have accomplished something absolutely unique in the Brigade's history. Fredericks, clear."

Maneka's face felt hotter than ever, and she was devoutly grateful to the major for having officially terminated the conversation before she had to figure out how to respond to that last remark.

She lay back in the incredibly comfortable command couch in the center of Benjy's command deck while Fredericks' comments sank in. She was perched directly atop the Bolo's personality center, her fragile flesh and his psychotronic brain both protected at the core of his warhull along with his powerplant. It would require a direct hit with a very heavy-caliber Hellbore to penetrate this deep, and protected by Benjy's battle screen, antiradiation fields, and duralloy armor—over two meters thick across his glacis—Maneka could ride safely through the fringes of a nuclear blast.

None of which had offered her the least protection against her Company CO's critique.

Actually, she thought, *I almost wish the Major had ripped a strip off my hide. That "I have to be patient with the squeaky-new kid on the block" tone is even more devastating.*

She watched Benjy's tactical plot as he and the other three Bolos of Third Company rumbled majestically back from the training ground. Bolos left big footprints, and the several thousand square kilometers of the Fort Merrit reservation which had been set aside for training maneuvers had been hammered into a fairly close approximation of hell. Not that Bolos particularly minded grinding through mud a couple of meters thick or over the stubble of what had once been jungle trees forty or fifty meters in height. And Maneka had already discovered that her Academy instructors had been completely correct when they assured her that even the best straight simulation wasn't *quite* the same thing as a live-fire exercise.

She closed her eyes, savoring the memory despite her embarrassment at the way she'd flubbed the final part of the maneuver exercise. Moving Benjy to the firing range, and feeling that fifteen-thousand-ton hull buck as she watched the incredible, flashing speed and precision with which his thundering weapons had ripped apart the ground targets and wildly evading aerial target drones had been ... incredible. It irritated her to realize she was reusing the same adverb, but she literally couldn't think of a better one than just that—"incredible."

In that moment, she had truly realized for the very first time on an emotional level, not just an intellectual one, that she was literally in command of more firepower than any pre-space army of Old Earth had *ever* deployed in a single battle. Probably more than any pre-space *nation* had ever deployed in an entire war. And Benjy was only one of twelve Mark XXVIIIs in the Thirty-Ninth Battalion.

"Sorry I screwed up, Benjy," she said after a moment.

"As Major Fredericks said, it is difficult even for experienced Bolo commanders to avoid occasional such errors, Maneka," Benjy replied through the bulkhead speaker. "It is unfortunately true that human perceptions and chemical-based thought processes find it impossible to process information as rapidly as a Bolo is capable of processing it."

"I know," she sighed. "And I also know we can't multitask the way you can. But it's so *hard* to just sit here while you do all the work."

The speaker rumbled with Benjy's electronic chuckle, and she cocked a questioning eyebrow at the visual pickup centered above the tactical plot—by long tradition, the equivalent of looking the Bolo in the "eye."

"Maneka," the huge Bolo said with a certain gentle amusement, "you are the twenty-seventh commander who has been assigned to me in my career. And every one of you has found it difficult 'to just sit here.' The Brigade does not choose its commanders casually, and it is the very command mentality for which it selects which makes it difficult for you to refrain from *exercising* command."

Maneka considered that for a moment. It made sense, she supposed, given the qualities the Brigade wanted in its commanders. And yet it reemphasized a question which had always bothered her.

"You know, Benjy," she said slowly, "I've wondered for a long time why we continue to assign commanders to each Bolo at all. I mean, the Major is right—and so are you. No human can possibly think and react as quickly as you can, so why put a human into the loop at this level at all?"

The Bolo did not reply for a second or two. That was an incredibly long time for any Bolo to ponder a question or problem, and Maneka wondered for a moment if he was going to respond at all.

"That question is properly one you ought to ask of the Battalion's human command personnel," Benjy said finally.

"I know. And I asked it several times at the Academy, but I was never really satisfied with the responses I got. That's why I'm asking you. I want . . . I guess what I want is a Bolo's perspective on it."

"When you asked at the Academy, what did your instructors tell you?" Benjy countered, and Maneka smiled.

She'd been officially in command of Benjy for barely a month, yet she'd already come to feel more comfortable with him than she ever had with anyone else in her entire life. Partly, she supposed, that was because she was aware of how old he was, how many years of experience lay behind him. In many ways, he was like a trusted elder, a grizzled old sergeant, or perhaps even a grandfatherly presence. She felt she could ask him anything, expose any uncertainty, in the knowledge that he would regard her youthful ignorance with compassionate tolerance rather than ridicule.

And she'd also already discovered his fondness for the Socratic method.

"They told me that there were three main reasons," she replied obediently. "First, the necessity of inserting a human presence into the command and control loop at the most basic level. Second, the necessity of providing a Bolo—and the Brigade—with a 'human face' to interact with the human communities Bolos are assigned to protect. And, third, to be sure that in the event of crippling damage to your psychotronics, there's someone with at least a chance of preventing rogue behavior."

"And you did not feel this was sufficient explanation for the policy?"

"I didn't think it was the *complete* explanation."

"Ah, a subtle but meaningful distinction," Benjy observed, and Maneka felt a flush of pleasure at the hint of approval in his tone.

They rumbled along for a few more seconds, and then Benjy made the electronic sound he used as the Bolo equivalent of a human's clearing his throat.

"I believe you are correct that there are additional reasons, Maneka," he said. "And I believe there are also reasons why your Academy instructors did not explain those other reasons to you. One reason for their failure to fully explicate, I suspect, is that I have observed that humans are sometimes uncomfortable exposing deep-seated emotions to one another."

Both of Maneka's eyebrows rose at the Bolo's last sentence, but she simply lay back in the couch, waiting.

"Despite Major Fredericks' comments to you," Benjy continued seriously, "there is a slight but significant statistical enhancement in the combat effectiveness of Bolos operating with human commanders on board as compared to Bolos operating purely autonomously in Battle Reflex Mode."

"Is there really?" Maneka couldn't keep the doubt out of her voice. "I mean, they told us that in third-year Tactics, but I never really believed it. Or that it was still true, at any rate. To be honest, I thought they were telling us that so we wouldn't feel as useless as a screen door on an airlock. You're telling me they really meant it?"

"Indeed. Reflect that the Major did not tell you to resign command to me. She told you not to 'second-guess' me. If you consider that carefully, I think you will recognize that it is no more than the advice she would have given you if you had been dealing with a human subordinate who was simply more experienced, knowledgeable, and informed *at that moment* than you were. In essence, she was advising you, as a new junior officer, not to 'joggle the elbow' of an experienced noncommissioned officer at a moment when decisions have become time-critical."

"Well, I suppose so," Maneka said slowly. "But that still doesn't change the fact that you both think and react faster than any human possibly could. So how can the presence of a human commander *enhance* your performance in combat? Surely it constitutes an additional layer of 'grit,' doesn't it?"

"In the heat of a complicated tactical situation, it undoubtedly does—or would, if the commander in question has not learned when to intervene and when to allow the Bolo full autonomy. But humans, whatever the limitation of their perceptions, retain even today a better intuitive information processing capability than Bolos have ever possessed. Bolos think linearly, Maneka—we simply think very, very quickly by human standards. We process information, calculate probabilities, and select actions and responses on the basis of those calculations. But humans, and especially those passed by the screening processes the Brigade utilizes, have a superior ability to discount portions of the probability matrix at a glance. Bolos, even in hyper-heuristic mode, cannot do that. We must consider *all* probabilities and examine *all* logic trees in order to determine which may be safely discounted or ignored. A human may be wrong when he 'instinctively' isolates the appropriate probabilities upon which to concentrate, but he often makes the decision—right or wrong—more rapidly than even a Bolo can do the same thing.

"What a Bolo is capable of doing that a human is not is *evaluating* that decision. An experienced commander and his Bolo are constantly engaged in a joint examination and evaluation of the tactical environment. The commander's function is to provide general direction, to isolate the objective and to adjust and prioritize that objective. It is the Bolo's function, within the framework of that general direction, to formulate and execute tactics to accomplish their purpose. And it is that partnership which accounts for the combat enhancement to which I referred a moment ago."

"I believe you're telling me the truth, Benjy, but that still seems difficult to believe."

"Perhaps because you, like many humans, are better able to recognize and comprehend the capabilities of a Bolo than you are to recognize and accept your own gifts," Benjy said almost gently. "Nonetheless, it *is* true, and the correlation between human command and enhanced combat performance can be clearly tracked over the history of the Brigade. Admittedly, the enhancement was most pronounced in the earlier days of the Brigade. Through the emergence of the Mark XXV, it was very noticeable, which is not surprising in light of the limitations and constraints imposed upon Bolo self-awareness and autonomy up to that time. From the date of the deletion of the inhibitory software of the Mark XXV two Standard Centuries ago, the degree of enhancement has declined, of course. That, in fact, was one reason the Brigade acceded to the pressure in favor of the independent deployment of unmanned Mark XXV Bolos for some years.

"That, however, was as much a civil government-inspired economy measure, adopted in light of the considerable expense of training Bolo commanders, as a tactical innovation, and it was never fully accepted within the Brigade, for several reasons. One of them, as subsequent analysis clearly confirmed, was that even a fully autonomous Bolo was less capable in combat when not paired with a human commander, which is why the practice was discontinued with the Mark XXVI. That same capability advantage remains statistically differentiable even today, although the capabilities of increasingly advanced psychotronic circuitry and software have improved to a point at which the speed with which Bolos process information, even linearly, has very largely overtaken the human ability to process it intuitively.

"However, with the introduction of direct Bolo-human neural interfacing in the Mark XXXII, the enhancement level has gone up once more, and very sharply. While I obviously have no personal experience of the capability, it would appear from my analysis of the battle reports which have been disseminated that the direct linkage between an organic human brain and a Bolo's psychotronics allows the human's intuitive processes to function at very nearly Bolo data-processing levels and speed. It is, in fact, that advantage over the capabilities of my own psychotronics which truly relegates Bolos of my generation to obsolescence."

Maneka felt a sudden irrational flush of irritation whose strength surprised her. She didn't care about what newer models of Bolo might be capable of! She was *Benjy's* commander, and hearing him calmly state that *anything* rendered him "obsolescent" infuriated her.

Obsolescence, she thought. *What a filthy concept!*

She knew her reaction was irrational. That it partook of the Operator Identification Syndrome the Academy instructors had so earnestly warned their students against. Yet there'd always been a stubborn part of her which remained emotionally convinced that "obsolescent" was a label invented by humans to justify discarding intelligent machines—*people*—who deserved far better from the humanity they had served so well.

"In addition to its overt effect on combat effectiveness, however," Benjy continued, apparently oblivious to her sudden emotional spike, "I believe there is another, uniquely human reason for the practice of pairing human commanders and Bolos and committing them to combat together. Put most simply, it is a sense of obligation."

"Obligation?"

"Indeed. Maneka, do not make the mistake of assuming that your own emotional reaction, your own sense of bonding with the Bolos with whom you serve, is unique to you. It has, throughout the history of the Brigade, been a major concern, not least because of the fashion in which it has so often caused Bolo commanders to hesitate to commit their Bolos against overwhelming Enemy firepower. Ultimately, Bolos are expendable, yet it is often easier for a Bolo's commander to consider himself expendable than it is for him to consider his Bolo in the same fashion. This is the reason your Academy instructors warned you about the dangers of OIS.

"Yet even while they warned you, the entire Dinochrome Brigade suffers from an institutional form of OIS. The traditions of the Brigade, of mutual obligation and of duty, *require* its human personnel to risk injury and death beside the Bolos they commit to battle. It is a self-imposed, never fully stated, and yet utterly inflexible requirement which probably has seen no equal since the ancient Spartan mother's injunction to her son that he come home carrying his shield in victory . . . or carried dead upon it.

"It is, in fact, a very human attitude, and the fact that it is irrational makes it no less powerful. Nor, I must confess, is it one-sided. In the Bolo, humanity has created a fully self-aware battle companion, and I suspect humans do not truly realize even now how fully they have succeeded in doing so. Bolos, too, have emotions, Maneka. Some were deliberately introduced into our core programming. Duty, loyalty, courage if you will. The qualities and emotions required of a warrior. But there is also affection, and that, I think, was not deliberately engineered into us. We fully recognize that we were created to fight and, when necessary, die for our creators. It is the reason we exist. But we also recognize that if we are asked to fight, and when we are asked to die, our creators fight and die with us. It is a compact which I doubt most humans have ever intellectually examined, and perhaps that is your true strength as a species. It was not necessary for you to consciously grasp it in order to forge it in the first place, because it is so much a part of you, and yet you have given that strength to us, as well as to yourselves."

The baritone voice paused, and Maneka stared at the glassy eye of the main visual pickup. No one at the Academy had ever suggested the existence of such a "compact" to her. And yet, now that Benjy had bared it to her, she realized that it underlay almost everything she had been taught. It was the unstated subtext which completed the explanation of the fierce bonds of loyalty between the Brigade's legendary commanders and the Bolos with whom they had fought and died.

"I . . . never thought of it that way," she said slowly.

"Indeed not," Benjy said gently. "There was no need for you to do so. I wonder, sometimes, if you humans truly realize what a remarkable species you are."

"Tag, you're it!" Maneka called out in delight as Benjy's Hellbore's integral range-finding lidar simulated a direct hit on Lazy.

"Why, you sneaky little twit!" Captain Joseph Takahashi replied over the com with a laugh. "Lazy and I were sure that was you, over to the east."

"Nope," Maneka said smugly. "*That*, Captain sir, is a Mark 26 ECM drone."

"And just how the hell did you sneak a ground-based decoy into position without us spotting you?" Takahashi demanded.

"We cheated," Maneka confessed cheerfully. "You two didn't know that Major Fredericks told *us* about the simulation yesterday."

"She did *what?*"

"She told us yesterday," Maneka repeated, smiling at the surprise in Takahashi's tone. "She said Major Hendrixson said you and Lazy have been getting just a little bit too smug about your simulation scores. And, I'm pretty sure that if you go back and check your mission briefing, you'll discover that no one ever told you the opposition force hadn't had time to prepare."

"They did so—" Takahashi began, then broke off abruptly. Maneka reached up and clasped her hands behind her head as she reclined luxuriantly in Benjy's command couch and waited. It took several seconds, but then Takahashi's chagrined voice came back over the com.

"All right," he said resignedly. "Lazy's gone back and analyzed the briefing, and you're right. Although, in my own humble opinion, Major Hendrixson deliberately *implied* that it would be a meeting engagement, with both sides arriving simultaneously."

"That's because your part of the simulation included dealing with faulty intelligence," Maneka told him. She chuckled, then grew slightly more serious.

"Actually, sir," she said more formally, "I think she picked Benjy and me for this partly because I'm still so much of the new kid on the block that she figured we'd probably need the edge. Or that we could certainly use it, anyway."

"Don't sell yourself too short, Lieutenant," Takahashi replied. "You and Benjy are coming along a lot faster than Lazy managed to bring me up to speed. And the major didn't tell you how to set up your little trap, did she?"

"No," Maneka admitted, "Benjy and I came up with that on our own."

"And executed perfectly," Takahashi pointed out. "Don't forget that. It's not easy for even another Bolo to surprise a Bolo. Even when one of the Bolos in question comes in fat, dumb, and happy."

"Thank you, sir." Maneka raised her right hand to Benjy's visual pickup with the thumb extended in the ancient gesture of triumph, and the red light above the lens winked in reply.

Joseph Takahashi was only about three Standard Years older than she herself was, but he'd been assigned to the Thirty-Ninth for almost two of those three years. Unlike her, he'd reported for duty with the Battalion early enough in the war to get in after the war had entered its new, uglier phase but before Brigade HQ had begun raiding the second-line battalions so ruthlessly for experienced commanders. He'd served the traditional six-month apprenticeship being mentored by one of those same experienced commanders, and he was very, very good.

He and his Bolo—28/G-179-LAZ—were assigned to Major Carlos Hendrixson's First Company, where they had established an enviable reputation for consistently outscoring everyone else in the regular simulations and field exercises. Of course, Takahashi did have a certain advantage over his fellow commanders, over and above the fact that he was one of the sneakiest tacticians Maneka had yet encountered. Lazy, whose cognomen clearly had been selected because of how poorly it described him, was the Battalion's senior Bolo. Although his personality center was currently mounted in a Model G war hull like Benjy's, he had begun his existence as a Model B the better part of one hundred and seventy years ago. His current hull bore the battle honors he'd won in his original configuration, as well as those he'd received after his personality center was transferred to his present hull, and they were headed by one Maneka had never before seen outside the Brigade's standard reference works: the Platinum Galactic Cluster . . . with star.

The Battle of Chesterfield, in which Lazy had won that award, was the stuff of the Brigade's legends. It was also a classic tactical study at the Academy, where not a single student had ever managed to win the engagement in a simulation.

A single company of Mark XXVIIIs had gone up against an entire battalion of Kai-Sabres during the Fringe Rebellion which had followed the Xalontese War. The Kai-Sabres had been clones of the Mark XXVIII itself, built using stolen technology after decades of espionage, and they had been based upon the Model G, not the Model B. Although their weaponry fits had been very similar, the Kai-Sabres' armor, battle screen, disrupter shields, and targeting systems had all been superior to those of Lazy and his three consorts, but Chesterfield had been a planet whose critical strategic importance meant it could not be yielded without a fight.

So Second Company, Twelfth Battalion, Ninth Regiment, of the Dinochrome Brigade had fought at three-to-one odds. And when the relief force arrived, Lazy had been the only surviving Bolo—or Kai-Sabre—on the planet. They'd found his immobilized wreck where he'd made his final stand in a rugged mountain pass just short of Chesterfield's capital city, his commander dead on his breached command deck . . . and the last four Kai-Sabres stacked up dead in front of them.

His damage had been far too severe to merely "repair." Fixing it would have cost more and taken longer than building an entire, newer Bolo from scratch. But by that time, the Brigade had adopted the practice of upgrading Bolo AIs, and a reserve Model G hull had been activated to receive his undamaged personality center. After which, he'd soldiered on for another full Standard Century.

Although she wasn't about to admit it to anyone, Maneka was more than a little uncomfortable around Lazy. Benjy was almost six times as old as she was, with a distinguished record any Bolo might have envied, but Lazy was older still. And it was difficult, she'd discovered, to know precisely how to react when one found oneself in the presence of what was literally a living legend. Indeed, she often wondered how Takahashi had reacted when they told him who he was getting as his first Bolo command.

Probably tempted to cut his own throat, she thought with a grin, although she really didn't know the captain or Lazy very well.

On the other hand, she reflected as Benjy rolled back towards the Company depot area, *I don't really know* anyone *outside the Third "very well" yet, now do I?*

The past two and half months had flown past at breakneck speed for Lieutenant Maneka Trevor. In that time, she'd become even closer to Benjy—close enough, indeed, that she was guiltily aware that, as everyone had warned her she would, she had completely succumbed to Operator Identification Syndrome. When she considered it, any other outcome had probably been impossible. Benjy was, quite simply, the most wonderful person—organic or psychotronic—she'd ever known. In less than ninety local days, he'd become her closest friend, her most trusted confidant, and the mentor the Battalion had been unable to provide her in human form. She'd learned more from him in that short period than she had in all eight previous years of her training, and she knew it.

That intense concentration on her Bolo had pretty much eliminated any possibility of a social life, and although Major Fredericks had seen to it that she'd been smoothly slotted into

Third Company, she didn't even know some of the other companies' Bolo commanders by sight. That was something she was going to have to start doing something about, and she knew it. In fact, the major had begun dropping gentle hints that now that she'd settled in with her *Bolo*, it was probably time she began getting to know some of the Battalion's flesh-and-blood members, as well.

"Well," Takahashi said, as Lazy altered course, heading for First Company's depot area, "I guess this is where we part company, Lieutenant. Good work. Lazy and I will be glad to have you on our flank anytime."

"Thank you, sir." Maneka knew her face had turned pink with pleasure, but she managed to keep her voice conversational. "Benjy and I feel the same."

"See you around, Lieutenant," Takahashi said.

The two Bolos continued towards their separate destinations and Maneka Trevor allowed herself to bask—briefly—in the knowledge that she was earning the acceptance of her vastly more experienced peers.

"Listen up, people!"

Maneka shook her head groggily as Major Fredericks' sharp, hard voice echoed in her mastoid transceiver. Her entire skull still seemed to be ringing like a gigantic bell from the emergency signal which had just snatched her up out of the depths of sleep.

"We have an Alpha One Zulu alert," Fredericks' voice continued, and Maneka sat bolt upright in bed, such minor considerations as her vibrating cranium totally forgotten. *Alpha One Zulu?*

"Get your butts up and awake," Fredericks went on grimly. "The Depot's already beginning final maintenance checks. Colonel Tchaikovsky and Major Dumfries will be briefing all personnel at zero-two-thirty. So let's move it!"

The voice in Maneka's mastoid went silent, but the youthful lieutenant sat frozen for several seconds. Alpha One Zulu. Impossible!

Alpha One Zulu meant a full-fledged invasion of a major planet, and in the sort of war this one had become, with the madness of Plan Ragnarok and its Melconian equivalent, "invasion" was another word for the murder of an entire planetary population. That sort of operation wasn't something the Puppies were going to undertake with secondary forces. No. It was the sort of operation where they committed entire armored *divisions* of the latest, most modern combat equipment they had, and the Thirty-Ninth Battalion was, for all intents and purposes, a training command. Its obsolescent Bolos had no business going up against front-line Melconian combat mechs with the sort of support which would be assigned to the invasion of a major Concordiat planet.

An icy wind seemed to blow through the marrow of her bones, and she was surprised when she looked down at her hands to realize they weren't actually trembling the way they felt they were.

"Benjy?" she said over her private link.

"Yes, Maneka," he replied instantly, with all his normal calm assurance.

"This is real? It's not some sort of drill?"

"No, Maneka, I am afraid it is not a drill," he told her gently.

"Where are they hitting us?"

"The target is Chartres."

Maneka's belly seemed to fold in on itself. Chartres was in the neighboring Esterhazy Sector, one sector further *away* from the frontier with the Melconian Empire, beyond Santa Cruz's Ursula Sector. Esterhazy was a wealthier sector than Ursula, with the sort of heavily industrialized star systems which obviously made it a priority target. But it was also the better part of a month's hyper-travel from the Line, even assuming the invasion fleet was able to use the intervening jump points without being engaged. Without that, the trip would take at least six weeks.

"How—?"

"Unknown," Benjy answered. "The Enemy has been pressing harder on the Line in the vicinity of the Camperdown Sector for several months now." The Camperdown Sector lay on the far side of the Ursula Sector from Esterhazy, directly in the path of the Melconians. "I would surmise that this was a deliberate stratagem intended to draw our naval forces and all available Brigade units towards that sector in order to uncover Esterhazy. If so, it has succeeded."

"We *can't* be all the Brigade has available!" Maneka protested.

"I fear we are all that can reach Chartres in time to respond," Benjy said. "The Santa Cruz jump point connects to Chartres via Haskell. We can be there within thirty-six Standard Hours of departure from Santa Cruz. That strategic position between Camperdown and Esterhazy," he pointed out gently, "is why Santa Cruz was developed as a major base in the first place, Maneka."

Maneka nodded numbly, although she knew he couldn't see her. But still . . .

"How soon can someone else get there to support us?" she asked quietly.

"Unknown. I do not have sufficient data on current deployments to answer that question."

Maneka swallowed hard, then shook herself violently. Sitting here dithering was doing absolutely no one any good, she told herself sternly, and climbed out of bed.

"All right, Benjy. I'm up. I'll see you after the briefing."

Colonel Tchaikovsky and Major Dumfries, the Battalion XO, looked grim as they walked into the briefing room where the Battalion's unit commanders had been assembled. They could just as easily have conducted this briefing electronically, Maneka knew. In fact, if they'd used the Bolos' tactical plots to display the information for the unit commanders, they probably could have imparted the information more efficiently. But there was something ritualistic about gathering them all together in the flesh, as it were. Some almost atavistic compulsion to meet and gather strength from one another one last time before some of the people in this room died.

The commanders came to their feet as Tchaikovsky and Dumfries strode briskly to the traditional briefing lectern.

"Be seated," Tchaikovsky said in a clipped tone, and boots rustled on the floor as they obeyed.

He let them settle back into their chairs for a moment, gazing out over their faces. Then he cleared his throat.

"I'm sure by this time all of you have checked with your Bolos," he began, "which means you're all aware that the Dog Boys' target is Chartres. For those of you who may not have the latest figures at your fingertips, that means a planetary population of two-point-four billion."

Maneka shivered as the colonel's simple sentence told them all they needed to know about the cost of failure.

"The good news for Chartres' population is that the Dog Boys apparently want permanent possession of the system, probably because of the way it flanks the Haskell jump point. If they keep it, they can pincer Ursula and Camperdown, which would require the Navy to at least double its strength in those two sectors, weakening it elsewhere along the Line. But it also means they aren't likely to use biologicals or radioactives against the planet. Since they'll want to use it themselves, they're going to put in a ground force and take it the old fashioned way, meter-by-meter. Which means it will take them a while—hopefully long enough for us to kick their ass up between their little puppy dog ears.

"Commodore Selkirk's received a subspace situation report from Camperdown Fleet HQ. It would appear the enemy has succeeded in drawing us badly out of position. According to the Commodore's sitrep, it will be at least two full Standard Weeks before any substantial forces can be diverted to Chartres. Commodore Selkirk has his own system-defense task force here in Santa Cruz, but it's going to be very heavily outnumbered by the Melconian fleet units escorting their attack force.

"Nonetheless, his is the closest naval force which can respond, and *we* are the closest ground force. We will be reinforced by the Three-Fifty-First Recon Company and the Ninth Marines, in addition to whatever Commodore Selkirk can spare from his Fleet units, but that's all we can count on. So it's going to be up to us to stop the Dog Boys before they kill every single human being on the planet."

He paused, letting his eyes travel across the grim faces looking back at him, then smiled with absolutely no humor at all.

"It's not what we expected, and I won't try to sugarcoat the situation for anyone. We're going to be substantially outgunned and outnumbered. And, although the hyper surveillance grid picked them up well short of the system perimeter, they're going to have been on the ground for at least eighteen hours by the time we can get there. Hopefully, the Chartres orbital defenses are going to have taken a chunk out of them, but we can't rely on that. And even if they have, those defenses aren't strong enough to fend off this big a force without the supporting Fleet units they don't have.

"Commodore Selkirk is confident he can get us within assault range of the planet, but it's unlikely he'll be able to cover us all the way in. It will have to be an assault landing, because the Dog Boys are almost certain to have control of near-orbit space by the time we get there. Which means at least some of the major cities are already going to be fireballs by the time we hit dirt.

"The Exec will give you the boarding schedule and what details we have about the situation in Chartres in just a moment, but first I have one more thing to say."

He paused for a moment, then went on quietly.

"We're going to take losses, people," he told them. "Probably heavy ones. But we're the only chance the people on Chartres have. And we're the Dinochrome Brigade. Remember that."

He held their eyes, then nodded and stepped back as the major took his place at the lectern and brought up the huge holo display behind him.

"As you can see, the situation in the Chartres System is . . ."

Maneka lay back once again in the command couch at Benjy's heart. She was aware that her pulse was hammering harder than it ought to have been, and although her mouth seemed unaccountably dry, she found herself swallowing again and again.

Jitters, she told herself. *And no wonder! I guess I'd have to be a Bolo myself not to feel them. But, God, I'm scared!*

"Benjy?"

"Yes, Maneka?"

"Benjy, I'm terrified out of my wits," she confessed miserably.

"No, you are not," he told her calmly.

The visual display showed the blurry, featureless gray of hyper-space, all his optical heads could pick up as he rode the assault pod locked to the exterior of the *Sleipner*-class transport *Tannenberg*. Over half his entire hull protruded beyond the pod's skin, exposing his onboard sensors and his weapons, and Captain Anton Harris and Unit 28/D-431-ALN rode the pod hardpoint on the far side of *Tannenberg*'s hull. Between them, Benjy and Allen provided the otherwise unarmed transport with the equivalent of a battlecruiser's energy-weapon firepower, and an antimissile capability at least as good as a light cruiser's. What they could not provide was the stand-off attack range of a standard ship-to-ship missile; their weapons simply weren't designed for that sort of environment.

Maneka and Benjy shared their pod with Company C, Third Battalion, Second Regiment, Ninth Marine Division. Captain Belostenec, Charlie Company's CO, had introduced herself to them when her company embarked, and she and Maneka had spent several hours discussing possible scenarios once they hit the surface of Chartres.

Assuming any of us get to the surface, she thought grimly, acutely conscious of the flutter of her pulse.

"Oh, yes, I am terrified," she told her Bolo.

"You are frightened," Benjy agreed. "This is a normal and, indeed, healthy reaction to the prospect of battle and possible death. But your fear is far from paralyzing you or preventing you from thinking clearly. Nor is fear a bad thing for you to experience.

"Bolos do not experience that particular emotion in the same fashion as humans, Maneka, or so I believe. It has been said with reason that our personalities are more 'bloodthirsty' than those of most humans. As a result, we feel as much anticipation as anxiety at a moment like this. It is, quite literally, what we were designed and built to do. Our highest function.

"But do not think we are strangers to fear. We fear that we will fail in our mission. We fear we will prove unequal to the challenge we face. And, just as our internal diagnostic systems have been programmed to feel the equivalent of pain when we take damage, our personalities include a fierce desire to survive. It has been some time since the Concordiat made the error of believing that a warrior who embraces death without fear is the ideal. Fear is as much a tool as courage, Maneka. As too much 'courage' becomes suicidal recklessness, too much 'fear' can become paralyzing panic. But to achieve his most effective level of combat, any warrior—human or Bolo—must properly balance the cautionary impact of fear and the aggressiveness engendered by courage. This, I believe, you have done."

"You have a better opinion of me than I do," Maneka said.

"Because you perceive all of your faults from within," Benjy said serenely. "I, however, am able to observe your responses and actions from without. You would not have been able to coordinate so well with Captain Belostenec had you been 'terrified out of your wits.'"

"Maybe," Maneka conceded dubiously.

Actually, she thought, for all of the time she and Belostenic had spent discussing possible tactical situations and responses to them, there hadn't really been a great deal of planning they could do. Either they got to the surface of the planet alive, or they didn't. If they did, Belostenec's Marines would disembark their own light armored vehicles and form up to follow her and Benjy as the Thirty-Ninth Battalion advanced against the enemy. And after that, everything would depend on what happened next.

The Ninth Marines were a potent fighting force, at least the equal of any Melconian Army division, and arguably superior to two of them in actual combat power. But neither their personal armor nor their vehicles had the firepower and toughness to stand up to Melconian combat mechs. If the Thirty-Ninth could get it through the perimeter of the Melconian LZ, the Ninth would undoubtedly prove its worth, but getting it through that perimeter in the first place was going to be supremely difficult.

"Captain Jeschke informs me that we will be dropping out of hyper in approximately twelve minutes," Benjy informed her suddenly, and she twitched in her command couch. That "approximately twelve minutes" had to have come directly from Jeschke, *Tannenberg*'s merely human commander. No Bolo would have been guilty of such imprecision.

The thought made her giggle unexpectedly, and she blinked as she realized her unanticipated amusement was entirely genuine.

Maybe I'm not quite *such a hopeless basket case, after all,* she thought.

"Understood," she said aloud. "Please make sure Captain Belostenec also has that information."

"I have."

"Then I guess all we can do is wait."

The relief force from Santa Cruz dropped out of hyper in a single, perfectly coordinated transition, and tactical displays aboard the Navy task force's warships began blinking alive with a rash of ominous red icons.

Commodore Selkirk's entire combat strength consisted of one four-ship battlecruiser division and one carrier, supported by eight heavy cruisers, nine light cruisers, and twelve destroyers. From the reports Chartres Near-Space Command had managed to get out before the subspace communications satellites were taken out, he already knew that even after the attackers' losses against Chartres' orbital defenses—which had not been insubstantial—he still faced six Melconian battleships, five battlecruisers, and twenty screening "fists." Like the Melconian ground unit of the same name, a naval "fist" consisted of three ships, in this case a heavy cruiser supported by a light cruiser and a destroyer. The comparative number of hulls—thirty-four human vessels opposed to sixty-nine Melconian ships—was bad enough. The *tonnage* differential was worse . . . *much* worse.

Despite that, Selkirk had certain offsetting advantages. One was that unlike the deep-space arrays which had given Chartres two full days of warning before the Melconians' arrival, even a battleship's detection range against a unit approaching through hyper was severely limited. The Melconian CO had been given less than four hours' warning before Selkirk's ships came piling out of hyper, and his combat strength was still out of position. Another advantage was that every one of Selkirk's ships possessed a fully self-aware AI . . . and that those ships' command crews were neurally linked with them. They literally thought and fought at the same hyper-heuristic speed as Bolos.

None of which changed the fact that the battleship component of the enemy force alone out-massed his entire task force by more than two-to-one.

Orders flashed outward from Selkirk's flagship. He had arranged his approach very carefully, and his task force and the accompanying transports deployed with smooth efficiency. The commodore had deliberately dropped most of his warships back into normal-space well inside the three-light-minute sphere of the Chartres jump point. That was precisely where the Melconians had been expecting him, although he still managed to emerge into n-space outside their immediate engagement range. But the *transports*, accompanied by the carrier *Indomitable* and two of his destroyers, had made the transition to normal-space out on the very rim of the jump point at its closest approach to the inner system.

It had been a calculated risk, since it was always possible the Melconian CO might have anticipated the maneuver and deployed to smash the transports first, but it had paid off. The main body of the Melconian fleet was exactly where Selkirk had hoped it would be—well out-system from the transports' emergence point, with the commodore and his main combatants between it and the transports.

The eight transports, trailing their three escorts, arrowed straight towards the planet while Selkirk and his brutally outnumbered force squared off to keep the Melconians off their backs. Maneka felt physically sick to her stomach as her tactical

plot showed the sea of hostile icons sweeping towards the commodore and his handful of ships. She wasn't trained in Navy
tactical iconography, but she didn't need to be to recognize
the dreadful imbalance between the two forces.

She didn't have a great deal of time to think about that,
however. Four Melconian "fists" had apparently been providing orbital fire support for their ground forces, now that the
deep-space defenses had been suppressed, and now they came
peeling out of Chartres planetary orbit as the transports steadied
down on their approach.

"Incoming missiles," Benjy announced. "The Enemy is targeting the transports."

"Stand by for antimissile defense," Maneka replied—more,
she was aware, for something to say than because Benjy needed
any instructions from her.

"Standing by."

On each of the *Sleipners*, pairs of Bolos brought up their
battle screen, activated tracking systems, and waited with psychotronic calm as the Melconian missiles shrieked towards
them. And, to her own immense surprise, Maneka Trevor felt
her own pulse steady as she watched the arrowhead-shaped
missile icons race to meet *Tannenberg*.

More icons blossomed on Benjy's tactical plot, and Maneka
recognized them as *Indomitable*'s outgoing fighters. There were
eighty of them, and they headed straight for the enormously
larger Melconian warships under maximum power. The missiles
targeted on the transports ignored them, and Maneka bared
her teeth as she recognized the Melconians' error.

They should have tried to nail Indomitable *before she launched*,
she thought. *And they're about to find out that they just wasted
their entire initial salvo.*

Hypervelocity countermissiles were already spitting outward
from the Bolos. Designed for planetary combat, they moved
slowly compared to the deep-space weapons charging to destroy
the transports, but "slowly" was a purely relative term. They
moved quickly enough when they were directed by a Bolo's
targeting and computational systems, and groups of them

relentlessly bracketed each incoming missile, boring in through defensive electronic countermeasures.

One-by-one, the Melconian missiles were picked off far short of attack range. Only fourteen got through the countermissile interception envelope, and thirteen of those were picked off by infinite repeater fire far short of their targets. Only one got close enough to actually detonate against the battle screen protecting its intended victim, and that battle screen—reinforced by the full power of the Bolo on the opposite side of the transport's hull—held.

And while those missiles were attacking, the fighters from *Indomitable* flung themselves upon their leviathan foes.

Twenty of them died before they got into engagement range. It would have been even worse, Maneka thought, sickened by the carnage, if the Melconians had held back that initial missile launch, targeted it on the fighters they ought to have known had to be coming. But twenty-five percent losses before the surviving fighter pilots even crossed the missile envelope was quite bad enough.

The sixty survivors ignored the destroyers shooting at them. Instead, they charged straight towards the cruisers. Close-in weapons opened up on them, but the fighters bored in grimly, holding their fire. The fleet little vessels carried plasma torpedoes—triple-barreled, short-ranged weapons with an even heavier punch than Benjy's Hellbore, but slow-firing. The launchers took long enough to recharge that each fighter would be able to fire only a single salvo per firing pass. But their other energy weapons were intended for dogfighting against other fighters, too light to significantly damage something as heavily armored as a warship, and the pilots were determined to make their single launch each count.

Half of them died before they reached the range they sought and salvoed their torpedoes, but unlike missiles, plasma torpedoes were light-speed weapons. They ripped in, impossible to intercept, and all four of the heavy cruisers and one of the light cruisers disappeared in the hellish glare of impacting plasma. Each torpedo was the equivalent of a shaped-charge fusion warhead, slamming its target with a megaton awl of brimstone, and battle screen failed and armor and hull plating vaporized as those man-made thunderbolts disemboweled their targets.

One of the three surviving light cruisers was severely damaged, staggering sideways in a shower of shattered debris and the telltale shroud of venting atmosphere. Her emissions signature flickered uncertainly, and her drive field went down completely, but her consorts had been luckier. The fighter group targeted on one of them had taken murderous casualties on its way in. Only two of its pilots had survived to fire, and their launch sequence had been badly desynchronized. The plasma torpedoes came in as separate, individual attacks, without the focus and precise timing which had killed the cruiser's fellows, and the ship's battle screen managed to deflect most of their effectiveness. She was hurt, but not badly, and she continued to belch missiles at the transports.

But the fourth light cruiser had clearly taken heavy damage. Her weapons fire ceased almost entirely, and her battle screen fluctuated wildly for a fraction of the second before it came back up to full strength and steadied. But there was nothing wrong with *her* drive, and she changed course abruptly.

"Collision vector," Benjy announced, and Maneka bit her lip as the cruiser's projected path intersected with *Indomitable*'s.

The carrier's AI altered course, dodging hard, but her evasion options were too limited. The geometry was against her, and although her light shipboard weapons fired desperately, carriers weren't supposed to get this close to enemy main combatants. They were supposed to operate under the cover and protection of an entire task force, providing a fighter umbrella to operate at ranges of up to several light-hours from their flight decks, or on independent operations at extreme range from anything but the *enemy's* fighters. And so they were equipped primarily with antifighter weapons, designed to provide volume of fire against swarms of attacking fighters, not to batter their way through a cruiser's battle screen. But *Indomitable* had had no choice but to go to meet the enemy this time, as she and her escorting destroyers fought to clear the way and keep the

Melconians away from the transports which *had* to reach the surface of Chartres.

She was too far ahead of *Tannenberg* and the other transports for any of the Bolos to engage the cruiser before impact, and yet it was so agonizingly close. She was barely a hundred kilometers outside Benjy's engagement range when the damaged cruiser slammed through her battle screens like a quarter-million-ton hammer and both ships vanished in a kinetic fireball brighter than the system's sun.

Maneka swore bitterly as both icons disappeared from her plot, but even as she cursed, and even as she felt the horror of the deaths of almost three thousand fellow human beings, she knew that at this moment, right here and now, *Indomitable* had been expendable. And she and her massacred fighter group, of which only eleven survived, had done their job. Only one of the intercepting Melconian cruisers remained, and a merciless corner of Maneka's mind wondered if the crew of that ship truly realized what was about to happen to it.

The cruiser and all four enemy destroyers bored in, and the Concordiat destroyers went to meet them. They were faster than the Melconians, more maneuverable, and fought with a deadly efficiency, but there were only two of them, and if their AI-human fusions used their weapons far more effectively, they were outgunned by over five-to-one. It was a short, vicious engagement—a knife-range battle which stripped away much of the combat advantage human ships' superior coordination and defensive systems normally conferred—because it had to be. The destroyer crews knew they had to clear the transports' path before any additional Melconian units managed to break past Commodore Selkirk or suddenly appeared unexpectedly from the far side of the planet. And so they took the Melconians on at the enemy's most effective range.

They died. But they took three of the four intercepting destroyers with them, and the fourth was so badly damaged that it reeled out of the engagement with its battle screen entirely down.

The light cruiser burst through the engagement, streaming atmosphere but with its energy weapons intact, and all her surviving batteries opened fire on CNS *Tannenberg,* which happened to be the lead transport.

Maneka felt her face locking in a snarl of triumph as the cruiser spat death at her. The battle screen which now protected the transports was *Bolo* battle screen, designed to deflect the fire of Benjy's own main armament at anything beyond point-blank range, and it sneered at the lesser energy weapons mounted by a mere light cruiser. Benjy's screen brushed the long-range fire aside almost contemptuously. Then his main turret traversed slightly and fired once.

When the Mark XXVIII had first been introduced, its main armament had been equivalent to that mounted in the Concordiat Navy's current-generation ships-of-the-line. Technology had moved on since then, into newer, deadlier, more powerful weaponry, but even today, nothing lighter than a battlecruiser—and precious few of them—mounted anything approaching the lethality of his 110-centimeter Hellbore. Certainly no *light* cruiser did . . . and none of them had been designed to survive its fury.

Benjy's target shattered, blowing apart and then, abruptly, vaporizing as the ship's antimatter powerplant's containment fields went down. The fierce, blinding flash of the fireball polarized Benjy's direct visual display, and Maneka heard her own soprano shriek of triumph as the cruiser disappeared.

The remaining crippled cruiser and destroyer died almost as spectacularly seconds later under the vengeful fire of other Bolos, and then the transports were clear, racing towards the planet they had come to save or die trying.

Despite its population, which was certainly of respectable size for any world outside the Core Sectors, the planet of Chartres had been touched relatively lightly by the imprint of mankind. All of its developed, terraformed cropland was concentrated on only one of its three major land masses, along with virtually all of its citizens, two-thirds of whom had lived in a relatively small number of large urban centers surrounded by rolling farmland or virgin forest.

But Chartres was lightly touched no longer.

Benjy's assault pod separated from *Tannenberg* and dived roaringly into the planetary atmosphere, and his infinite repeaters fired steadily as he and the rest of the Battalion systematically eliminated every piece of orbital debris that didn't carry a Concordiat IFF code. Melconian stealth systems were good, but they weren't perfect, and the Battalion's relentless assault burned away the reconnaissance platforms the invaders had deployed.

Maneka studied the visual images from Benjy's optical heads as the assault wave howled downward.

Laroche City, the planetary capital, with its population of over thirty million, was a smoking, blazing sea of ruins. Provence and Nouveau Dijon were little better, although at least a rim of Nouveau Dijon's suburbs appeared to have survived partially intact, and the same was true for at least two dozen of the planet's other cities and larger towns. The green and brown patchwork of farms and the dark-green woodlands surrounding what had once been the habitations of man were dotted with the wreckage of missiles and air-breathing attack craft which had been destroyed by the ruined cities' perimeter defenses, and towering pillars of smoke and dust seemed to be everywhere.

Although Chartres' population had been tiny compared to one of the Core Worlds like Old Earth, it had been large enough, and the star system's industrial base had been extensive enough, to provide quite heavy ground-based defensive systems. The local planetary and system authorities, with the assistance of the Concordiat's central government, had taken advantage of that and spent most of the past six Standard Years fortifying and preparing against the probability of an eventual Melconian attack. But with the Line grinding back only slowly across the Camperdown Sector, the planning authorities had given higher priority to systems and planets under more immediate threat. No one had anticipated that the Empire would show the daring to strike this deeply into the major star systems inside the Concordiat's frontier, and the local defenses, however formidable, had not been formidable enough.

Someone should have seen it coming, she thought grimly. *Sure, they had to send in the equivalent of an entire fleet to pull it off, but the tempo of this war's done nothing but accelerate from the very beginning. And both sides are getting more desperate as the casualty totals go up. We should have realized that, sooner or later, the Puppies would roll the dice like this. If they can pull it off—establish a sizable Fleet presence this far into our rear—at the very least, it would force us into major redeployments until we could deal with it. That was probably worth risking the loss of their entire force all by itself, and that doesn't even count taking out Chartres' population and industrial base.*

But at least the system's defenders had been given enough warning to execute their evacuation plans. Maneka had no way of knowing—and didn't *want* to know—how many citizens of those butchered cities had failed to get out in time, but the glowing green icons of scores of huge refugee centers, all of them with at least rudimentary previously prepared defenses, burned in Benjy's strategic plot. In addition to the fixed defenses, most of them were ringed by the additional icons of planetary militia and the remnants of the detachments of Regulars deployed to the planet. And those defenses appeared to be holding against the aerial bombardment raining down upon them, now that the fleet units which had been providing the Melconian attackers with fire support from orbit had been dispersed. But there was no way any of them could have hoped to hold more than briefly against the terrifying concentration of ground-based firepower the Melconians had managed to land on the planetary surface before the Concordiat relief force arrived.

It was silent on Benjy's command deck, despite the hyper-velocity hurricane howling about the assault pod's hull as it blazed deeper and deeper into the atmospheric envelope, and Maneka felt her heart sink as she studied the available data.

The planetary reconnaissance system had been largely destroyed, but a few of its satellites still survived, and now that the Thirty-Ninth Battalion had arrived, they had someone to report to once more. It was an advantage of which she knew

Colonel Tchaikovsky meant to take full advantage, but very little of what they had reported so far was good.

The Melconian planetary assault had been led by five of their heavy assault brigades, each composed of two armored regiments of thirty mechs each—twelve *Heimdall*-class light reconnaissance mechs and six of their "fists," with a total of six *Surturs* and twelve *Fenrises*—plus one infantry regiment and an air cavalry regiment, supported by an artillery battalion. That was bad enough, but the initial assault wave had been followed up by two full infantry divisions and at least twelve strategic bombardment regiments, with their long-range missile batteries, and a matching number of space-defense missile sites. They had also deployed at least four additional antiarmor regiments of *Loki* tank destroyers—each of them basically little more than a single 60-centimeter Hellbore mounted on an unarmored ground-effect or counter-grav lift platform. They were fast and packed a punch which could be dangerous, especially if they could get into a flanking position, but they were relatively easy to kill once they revealed their positions.

That, unfortunately, wasn't something the Battalion could count on them doing. The Melconian advantage in stealth technology applied to their ground systems, as well as their space-going platforms. Human sensors were better than their Melconian equivalent, which tended to level the playing field somewhat, but Melconian platforms like the *Lokis* could be extremely difficult for even a Bolo to spot, especially if they'd had a few hours in which to perfect their camouflage.

Still, it appeared from the reconnaissance satellites that the Puppies had opted for more of a brute force approach than sneakiness. Either that, or their campaign plan had accepted from the beginning that a Concordiat relief force was likely to arrive before they could set about the business of properly exterminating the planetary population.

Whatever their reasoning, they had avoided dispersing their forces in smaller concentrations the Thirty-Ninth could have chopped up in detail. Instead, the vast majority of their ground units were concentrated in a single, roughly semicircular defensive perimeter near the southern end of Lorraine, the planet's single heavily populated continent. The ends of their perimeter's arc of fortified positions were firmly anchored on the ocean, which provided at least some protection to their backs, and while concentrating their forces that tightly might make them a tempting target, it also allowed them to concentrate all of their defensive firepower. What they had assembled there would have been sufficient to make a battlecruiser squadron think twice about closing in to engage them from space, and it was obvious that despite the relatively short time they'd been in possession of the planet, they'd dug their ground combat elements in deeply.

Maneka's command couch jolted her suddenly, as the assault pod hit the surface of Chartres.

At least we got down *unopposed*, she told herself, and felt more quivers as Benjy released the docking latches, threw power to his drivetrain, and ground free of the pod. The Bolo was monitoring Captain Belostenec's communications channels, and she heard the Marines' clipped, tersely professional combat chatter as their own vehicles whined out of the pod's vehicle bays.

Benjy's starboard infinite repeaters fired suddenly, knocking down an air-breathing Melconian recon drone as it popped up over a nearby line of hills. The drone disintegrated into a flaming, fragment-raining ball before it could possibly have gotten off a contact report, and Benjy's secondary turrets swung smoothly, rotating back and forth as he waited for additional targets.

Captain Harris and Allen had brought their pod in less than two kilometers to the west of Benjy's current position, and the remainder of *Tannenberg*'s assault load was rapidly assembling around them. *Tannenberg* herself, and all seven of the other transports, had never even approached atmosphere, and they were already streaking directly away from the planet and the ferocious battle raging between Commodore Selkirk's outnumbered task force and the remaining Melconian warships in the system.

Maneka knew the unarmed, agile transport vessels had no business anywhere near anyone who could shoot at them once their Bolos had been landed. "Drop and scoot" had been standard doctrine for the Brigade's supporting Transport Command for centuries, after all. But that didn't prevent a chill sense of abandonment as she watched their transportation racing to get far enough away from the planet to drop into hyper.

Talk about burning your bridges behind you, she thought wryly, as Allen knocked down a second recon drone, and surprised herself with a desert-dry chuckle of amusement.

"All right, people," Colonel Tchaikovsky's voice came over the Battalion command net from Unit 28/G-740-GRG. "We're down, we're in one piece, and we know where the Dog Boys are. And, unfortunately, we don't have a lot of time. Commodore Selkirk is still wading into them, but it doesn't look good for his task force. So we have to break into the Dog Boy position before any of their starships get loose and turn up to start dropping missiles on our heads as we advance. That's going to limit our tactical options, and we have to assume the Dog Boys will manage to localize us and bring us under fire before we get into attack range. Gregg is loading movement orders to your Bolos now, and General Hardesty's Marines will conform to our movements."

Maneka watched the intricate pattern of lines and arrows representing the movement of the Battalion and the four Mark XXVII reconnaissance Bolos of the attached 351st Reconnaissance Company appeared on her secondary plot. The Battalion had dropped well within the Melconians' theoretical engagement envelope, but the combined destruction of the warships which had been giving them firepower support and the loss of their orbital reconnaissance platforms had at least temporarily blinded the Puppies. No one could hit what they couldn't see, so until the Melconians could positively locate the Battalion, all their firepower was useless. Which, of course, explained the drones Benjy and Allen had knocked down.

Colonel Tchaikovsky's Bolo, Gregg, was feeding the Battalion's movement plan simultaneously to the Marines, Maneka knew, and watched the blue icons of the Ninth Division flowing into formation behind the Battalion. *Well* behind the Battalion. Their infantry carriers and light supporting *Whippet* tanks, unlike those used by the Melconians, were all counter-grav supported, with a sprint speed of well over five hundred kilometers per hour. They would lie back, far enough to stay clear of the tornado of fire the Battalion could expect to draw as it advanced against the Melconian position.

If the Battalion succeeded in breaking that perimeter, the Ninth would come screaming in behind them, and Maneka had a very clear mental image of what the heavily armed Marine troopers in their individual powered combat armor would do to the Puppies if they could ever get to grips with their more lightly armored infantry adversaries. But unless the Battalion could open a breach for them, any attempt by the Marines to close with the enemy would be suicidal. So if the Battalion failed, instead of racing to exploit success, the Ninth's troopers would use that same speed to fall back to the Chartres refugee centers where they might at least hope to kill a few more Melconians before the Puppies' combat mechs ground them into the mud.

"All right, people," Colonel Everard Tchaikovsky said as the final movement orders were acknowledged by all units. "Gregg estimates ninety-seven minutes to contact with the enemy. Let's go."

Green, rolling woodland spread out before Maneka in the panoramic view from Benjy's forward optical head as the Battalion thundered towards the enemy. At least some of the Puppies' recon drones had lasted long enough to spot them now, and she felt her hands sweating, the dryness in her mouth, as the first Melconian long-range fire screamed towards them.

She tried not to think about the odds. Sixty *Surturs* and twice that many *Fenrises* would have been heavy odds for a battalion of modern Bolos; for the Thirty-Ninth, they were impossible, and every human and Bolo in the Battalion, from the Colonel down, knew it.

"Melconian warships are entering range of the planet," Benjy announced, and Maneka responded with a jerky nod.

Commodore Selkirk's task force had paid the price of its gallantry. Not a single one of his ships had survived, but they'd ripped the guts out of the Melconian fleet before they died. None of the Puppy battleships or battlecruisers remained. Neither did any of their heavy cruisers, but nine light cruisers and eleven destroyers had been screaming towards Chartres at maximum for over twelve minutes now. She'd hoped the Battalion would win the race, get to grips with the Puppies' ground forces before their surviving fleet units could intervene, but the numbers blinked on Benjy's plot in grim confirmation that they would not.

The missile batteries the Melconians had dug in at the heart of their ground enclave vomited fire, and high-trajectory missiles rained down on the Battalion. More fell like cosmic flails, fired from the approaching warships to support the ground-based systems. Their flight profiles gave the Battalion easy intercept solutions, but they'd never actually been intended to get through in the first place. Their function was solely to saturate the Bolos' defenses while the *real* killers broke through at lower altitudes.

"Remote platforms report cruise missiles launching all along the Enemy front," Benjy's resonant baritone told her. "Current estimate: approximately four thousand, plus or minus fifteen percent."

"Understood," Maneka rasped tautly.

"Colonel Tchaikovsky advises us that Enemy cruisers and destroyers are altering course. On the basis of their new heading and speed, I estimate a probability of 96.72 percent that they will endeavor to enter energy range of the Battalion simultaneous with the arrival of the low-altitude missile attack."

"You're just full of good news this afternoon, aren't you?" she responded, baring her teeth in what might charitably have been called a smile.

"I would not call it 'good,'" Benjy replied, with one of his electronic chuckles. "On the other hand, the Enemy's obvious desire to mass all available firepower at the earliest possible moment does offer us some tactical advantages, Maneka."

"Yeah, *sure* it does."

She shook her head.

"I am serious," the Bolo told her, and she stopped shaking her head and looked up at the internal visual pickup in disbelief.

"Just how does their piling even more firepower on top of us *improve* our chances of survival?" she demanded.

"I did not say it would enhance our survival probability. I merely observed that it offers us certain tactical advantages—or openings, at least—which we could not generate ourselves," the Bolo replied, and there was more than simple electronic certitude in its voice. There was experience. The *personal* experience of his hundred and twenty-six years' service against the enemies of mankind. "If their warships had opted to remain at extended missile ranges, rather than bringing their energy batteries into play, they would have remained beyond the range of *our* energy weapons. As it is, however, analysis of their new flight paths indicates they will enter their own energy weapon range of the Battalion 16.53 seconds before the arrival of their ground forces' cruise missiles."

Maneka Trevor's blue eyes widened in understanding, and the Bolo produced another chuckle. This one was cold, without a trace of humor.

"They're giving us a shot at them *before* the missiles reach us?" she asked.

"Indeed. They have clearly attempted to coordinate the maneuver carefully, but their timing appears inadequate to their needs. Unless they correct their flight profiles within the next thirty-eight seconds, the Battalion will be able to engage each warship at least once before their cruise missiles execute their terminal maneuvers. If they had been willing to wait until *after* the initial missile attack before closing, or even to remain permanently beyond Hellbore range, they would eventually have been able to destroy the entire Battalion with missiles alone."

"Instead of giving us the opportunity to take out their orbital fire support completely!" she finished for him.

"Indeed," Benjy repeated, and she heard the approval—and

pride—in his deep voice. Pride in *her* she realized. In the student she had become when the Colonel gave her her first Bolo command . . . and, in so doing, committed her into that Bolo's care for her true training. That was what put the pride into his voice: the fact that his student had grasped the enormity of the Melconians' error so quickly.

The plunging thunder of the incoming high-trajectory missiles howled down out of the heavens like the lightning bolts of crazed deities, but the charging behemoths of the Thirty-Ninth Battalion didn't even slow. Ancient they might be, but they were Bolos. Batteries of ion-bolt infinite repeaters and laser clusters raised their muzzles towards the skies and raved defiance, countermissile cells spat fire, and heaven blazed.

The Battalion raced forward at over eighty kilometers per hour through the thick, virgin forest. Not even their stupendous bulks could remain steady over such terrain at so high a speed, and the shock frame of Maneka's command couch hammered at her as Benjy shuddered and rolled like some ancient windjammer of Old Earth rounding Cape Horn. But even as his mighty tracks ground sixty-meter tree trunks into crushed chlorophyll, his weapons tracked the incoming missiles with deadly precision. Missile after missile, dozens—scores—of them simultaneously, disappeared in eye-tearing fireballs that dimmed the light of Chartres' primary into insignificance.

Despite her terror, despite the certainty that the Battalion could not win, Maneka Trevor stared at the imagery on her visual display with a sense of awe. The Melconian missile attack was a hemisphere of flame, a moving bowl above her where nothing existed but fire and destruction and the glaring corona of the wrath of an entire battalion of Bolos.

"Enemy cruise missiles entering our defensive envelope in 21.4 seconds," Benjy announced calmly even as the display filled with blinding light. "Enemy *warships* entering engagement range in 4.61 seconds," he added, and there was as much hunger as satisfaction in his tone.

"Stand by to engage," Maneka said, although both of them knew it was purely a formality.

"Standing by," Benjy acknowledged, and his main turret trained around in a smooth whine of power, Hellbore elevating.

Maneka's eyes strayed from the visual display to the tactical plot, and her blood ran cold as she saw the incredibly dense rash of missile icons streaking towards her. The Battalion's reconnaissance drones were high enough to look down at the terrain-following missiles as they shrieked through the atmosphere, barely fifty meters above the highest terrain obstacles, at five times the speed of sound. The atmospheric shock waves thousands of missiles generated at that velocity were like a giant hammer, smashing everything in their path into splinters, and when they reached the Battalion, it would be even worse. At their speed, even Bolos would have only tiny fractions of a second to engage them, and their defenses were already effectively saturated by the ongoing high-trajectory bombardment.

Between the missile storm and the main body of the Battalion was the 351st Recon's four Mark XXVIIs. Twenty percent lighter and more agile than the Mark XXVIII, the *Invictus* Bolos were much more heavily equipped with stealth and ECM, and they had sacrificed the Mark XXVIII's extensive VLS missile cells in favor of even more active antimissile defenses. It was their job to fight for information, if necessary, and—with their higher speed—to probe ahead of the Battalion for traps and ambushes the enemy might have managed to conceal from the reconnaissance drones. But now their position meant they would take the first brunt of the cruise missiles, unless their sophisticated electronic warfare systems could convince the Puppy missiles' seekers they were somewhere else.

She jerked her eyes away from those horribly exposed icons, and her teeth flashed in an ivory snarl as a score of other icons in another quarter of the display, the ones representing the Melconian destroyers and light cruisers, were snared in sudden crimson sighting circles.

"Enemy warships acquired," Benjy announced. And then, instantly, "Engaging."

A dozen 110-centimeter Hellbores fired as one, and atmosphere already tortured by the explosions of dying missiles, shrieked in protest as massive thunderbolts of plasma howled upward.

All nine Melconian light cruisers and three of the destroyers died instantly, vomiting flame as those incredible bolts of energy ripped contemptuously through their battle screens and splintered their hulls. Superconductor capacitors ruptured and antimatter containment fields failed, adding their own massive energy to the destruction, and the vacuum above Chartres rippled and burned. The horrified crews of the remaining Melconian destroyers had four fleeting seconds to realize what had happened. That was the cycle time of the Mark XXVIII's Hellbore . . . and precisely four seconds later a fresh, equally violent blast of light and fury marked the deaths of the remaining enemy warships.

Maneka Trevor heard her own soprano banshee-howl of triumph, but even as the Battalion's turrets swivelled back around, the tidal bore of cruise missiles burst upon it.

Countermissiles, infinite repeaters, laser clusters, auto cannon— even antipersonnel clusters—belched defiance as the hypervelocity projectiles came streaking in. They died by the dozen, by the score. By the hundred. But they came in *thousands*, and not even Bolos' active defenses could intercept them all.

Battle screen stopped some of them. Some of them missed. Some of them killed one another, consuming each other in their fireball deaths. But far too many got through.

The exposed Mark XXVIIs suffered first. Maneka's shock frame hammered her savagely as Benjy's massive hull twisted through an intricate evasion pattern, his defensive weapons streaming fire. But even though scores of missiles bored in on him, far more—probably as many as half or even two-thirds of the total Melconian launch—locked onto the quartet of Mark XXVIIs. The *Invictus* might mount more antimissile defenses than the *Triumphant*, but not enough to weather *this* storm. For an instant, she wondered what had gone wrong with their EW systems, why so many missiles had been able to lock onto them. And then she realized. They weren't trying to prevent the missiles from locking them up; they were deliberately *enhancing* their targeting signatures, turning themselves into decoys and drawing the missiles in, away from the Battalion.

Her heart froze as she recognized what they were doing, and then the holocaust washed over them. The towering explosions crashed down on the reconnaissance company like the boot of some angry titan, hobnailed in nuclear flame. They were forty kilometers ahead of the Battalion's main body, and the warheads were standard Puppy issue, incongruously "clean" in what had become a genocidal war of mutual extermination. Yet there were hundreds of them, and lethal tides of radiation sleeted outward with the thermal flash, followed moments later by the blast front itself.

Maneka clung to her sanity with bleeding fingernails as Thor's hammer slammed into Benjy. The huge Bolo lurched like a storm-tossed galleon as the green, living forest about them, already torn and outraged by the Battalion's passage and the handful of high-trajectory missiles which had gotten through, flashed into instant flame. The Battalion charged onward, straight through that incandescent inferno, duralloy armor shrugging aside the radiation and blast and heat which would have smashed the life instantly from the fragile protoplasmic beings riding their command decks. The visual display showed only a writhing ocean of fire and dust, of explosion and howling wind, like some obscene preview of Hell, but it was a Hell Bolos were engineered to survive . . . and defeat.

None of the reconnaissance Bolos in the direct path of the missile strike survived, but the chaos and massive spikes of EMP generated by the missiles which killed them had a disastrous effect on the missiles which had acquired the rest of the Battalion. Those same conditions hampered the Bolos' antimissile defenses, but the degradation it imposed on the missiles' kill probabilities was decisive.

Not that there weren't still plenty of them to go around. Over seventy targeted Benjy, even as he charged through the raging fires and devastation of the primary strike zone. The gargantuan Bolo's point defense stopped most of them short of his battle screen, but twenty-three reached attack range, and his fifteen-thousand-ton hull bucked and heaved as the fusion warheads gouged at his battle screen and drove searing spikes of hellfire directly into his armor. Thor's hammer smashed down again. Then again, and again and *again*. Even through the concussions and the terrifying vibration, Maneka could see entire swathes of his battle board blazing bloody scarlet as damage ripped away weapons and sensors.

But then, too suddenly to be real, the hammer blows stopped. Ten of the sixteen Bolos who had been targeted charged out the far side of the holocaust, leaving behind all four of the 351st's Mark XXVIIs. Two of the Battalion's Mark XXVIIIs had also been destroyed, and all of the survivors were damaged to greater or lesser extent, but they had destroyed the entire remaining Melconian support squadron, and the enemy LZ was just ahead.

"I have sustained moderate damage to my secondary batteries and forward sensors," Benjy announced. "Main battery and indirect fire systems operational at 87.65 percent of base capability. Track Three has been immobilized, but I am still capable of 92.56 percent normal road speed. Estimate 9.33 minutes to contact with Enemy direct fire perimeter weapons at current rate of advance. Request missile release."

Missile release ought to have been authorized by Colonel Tchaikovsky, Maneka thought. But Tchaikovsky's Gregg was one of the Bolos they'd lost, and Major Fredericks' Peggy had suffered major damage to her communications arrays. There was no time to consult anyone else, and independent decisions were one of the things Bolo commanders were trained to make.

"Release granted. Open fire!" she snapped.

"Acknowledged," Benjy replied, and the heavily armored hatches of his VLS tubes sprang open. His own missiles blasted outward, then streaked away in ground-hugging supersonic flight. They were shorter ranged and marginally slower than the ones the Melconians had hurled at the Battalion, but they were also far more agile, and the relatively short launch range and low cruising altitudes gave the defenders' less capable reconnaissance drones even less tracking time than the Battalion had been given against the Melconian missiles.

Fireballs raged along the Melconian perimeter, blasting away outer emplacements and dug-in armored units. Weapons and sensor posts, *Loki*-class tank destroyers and air-defense batteries, vanished into the maw of the Thirty-Ninth Battalion's fury. Benjy's thirty-centimeter rapid-fire mortars joined the attack, vomiting terminally guided projectiles into the vortex of destruction. Follow-on flights of Melconian missiles shrieked to meet them from the missile batteries to the rear, but the indirect fire weapons had lost virtually all of their observation capability. Their targeting solutions were much more tentative, the chaos and explosions hampered the missiles' onboard seeker systems, and the gaping hole ripping deeper and deeper into their perimeter was costing them both launchers and the sensor capability which might have been able to sort out the maelstrom of devastation well enough to improve their accuracy.

But hidden among the merely mortal Melconian emplacements were their own war machines. The *Heimdalls* were too light to threaten a Bolo—even the Ninth's manned vehicles were more than a match for them—but the fists of *Surturs* and *Fenrises* were something else entirely. Heavier, tougher, and more dangerous, they outnumbered the Battalion's survivors by eighteen-to-one, and they had the advantage of prepared positions.

Another of the Battalion's Bolos lurched to a halt, vomiting intolerable heat and light as a plasma bolt punched through its thinner side armor. Benjy fired on the move, main turret tracking smoothly, and his entire hull heaved as a main battery shot belched from his Hellbore and disemboweled the *Surtur* which had just killed his brigade brother. Another *Surtur* died, and Benjy's far less powerful infinite repeaters sent ion bolt after lethal ion bolt shrieking across the vanishing gap between the Battalion and the Melconian perimeter to rend and destroy the *Surturs*' lighter, weaker companions.

"Take point, Benjy!" Maneka barked as yet another Bolo slewed to a halt, streaming smoke and flame. Her eyes dropped to the sidebar, and she felt a stab of grief as the unblinking letter codes identified the victim as *Lazy*. It looked like a mission kill, not complete destruction, she thought, but the damage had to have punched deeply into Lazy's personality center . . . and there was no way Lieutenant Takahashi could have survived.

And there was no time to mourn them, either.

Benjy surged forward, the apex of a wedge of eight bleeding titans. *Surturs* reared up out of deeply dug-in hides, lurching around to counterattack from the flanks and rear as the Battalion smashed through their outer perimeter, Hellbores howling in point-blank, continuous fire.

In! We're into their rear! a corner of Maneka's brain realized, with a sense of triumph that stabbed even through the horror and the terror.

A brilliant purple icon blazed abruptly on Benjy's tactical plot as his analysis of Melconian com signals suddenly revealed what had to be a major communication node.

"The CP, Benjy! Take the CP!" Maneka snapped.

"Acknowledged," Benjy replied without hesitation, and he altered course once more, smashing his way towards the command post. It loomed before him, and as Maneka watched the tac analysis spilling up the plot sidebars, she realized what it truly was. Not a command post, but *the* command post—the central nerve plexus of the entire Puppy position!

They'd found the organizing brain of the Melconian enclave, and she felt a sudden flare of hope. If they could reach that command post, take it out, cripple the enemy's command and control function long enough for the Ninth to break in through the hole they'd torn, then maybe—

A pair of *Surturs*, flanked by their attendant mediums, loomed suddenly out of the chaos, Hellbores throwing sheets of plasma at the Bolos rampaging through their line. Benjy blew the left-flank *Surtur* into incandescent ruin while Peggy shouldered up on his right and killed the other. Their infinite repeaters raved as the *Fenrises* split, trying to circle wide and get at their weaker flank defenses, and the medium Melconian mechs slithered to a halt, spewing fury and hard radiation as their antimatter plants blew.

Then a trio of *Fenris*-class mediums, all of them orphans which had lost their *Surturs*, appeared out of nowhere. Their lighter weapons bellowed, and they were on the left flank of Captain Harris and Allen. They fired once, twice . . . and then there were only seven Bolos left.

Benjy's port infinite repeater battery shredded Allen's killers, even as two more *Surturs* reared up suddenly before him. One of them fired past him, slamming three Hellbore bolts simultaneously into Peggy. The Bolo's battle screen attenuated the bolts, and the antiplasma armor appliqué absorbed and deflected much of their power. But the range was too short and the weapons too powerful. One of the newer Bolos, with the improved armor alloys and better internal disruptor shielding, might have survived; Peggy—and Major Angela Fredericks—did not.

Benjy's turret spun with snakelike speed, and his Hellbore sent a far more powerful bolt straight through the frontal glacis plate of the second *Surtur* before it could fire. Then it swivelled desperately back towards the first Melconian mech.

Six, Maneka had an instant to think. *There are only six of us now!*

And then, in the same fragmented second, both war machines fired.

"Hull breach!" Benjy's voice barked. "Hull breach in—"

There was an instant, a fleeting stutter in the pulse of eternity that would live forever in Maneka Trevor's nightmares, when her senses recorded everything with intolerable clarity. The terrible, searing flash of light, the simultaneous blast of agony, the flashing blur of movement as Unit 28/G-862-BNJ slammed the inner duralloy carapace across his commander's couch.

And then darkness.

"Hello, Lieutenant."

The quiet voice boomed through Maneka's mind like thunder, and she flinched away from its power. She felt herself swinging through a huge, empty void, like some ghostly pendulum, while vertigo surged and receded within her.

"It's time to wake up," the soft voice boomed, and she closed her eyes tighter. No. Not time to wake up. If she did that, something would be waiting. Something she could not—would not—face.

But the voice would not be denied. She clung to her safe, dark cocoon, yet she felt herself being drawn relentlessly, mercilessly, up out of its depths. And then her eyes slid open and slitted under the brilliant tide of light.

No, not her eyes—her *eye*. She was blind on the right side, she realized, with a sort of dreamy detachment, and raised her right hand to touch the dressing covering that eye. Only her hand refused to move, and when she rolled her head slowly—so slowly—far enough to the right to see, she found that her right arm ended just below the shoulder.

She blinked her remaining eye in syrupy slow motion, her sluggish brain trying to grapple with her wounds, and then a hand touched her left shoulder. She turned back in that direction, eye squinting, trying to make out details, and saw a man in the battle dress uniform of the Concordiat Marine Corps. A colonel, she thought, then blinked. No, she was wrong again. He wore a colonel's *uniform*, but the insignia pinned to his collar was that of a brigadier.

"Are you sure she's going to be all right?" she heard the colonel-turned-brigadier say. He was looking at someone else. A man in white.

"We got to her in time," the man in white said reassuringly. "Actually, *your* people got to her in time and pulled her out while we still had something to work with. It's going to take time and a lot of regen to put her back on her feet, but the actual repairs will be fairly routine. Extensive, but routine."

"You have a different definition of 'routine' from me, Doctor," the Marine officer said dryly, then looked back down at Maneka.

"Are you with us now, Lieutenant?" he asked, and she recognized the booming thunder which had disturbed her darkness in the quiet question.

She looked up at him, then tried to speak. Only a croak

came out, and she licked dry, cracked lips with a tongue made of leftover leather. A hand reached down, holding a glass with a straw, and Maneka shuddered in raw, sensual pleasure as the unbelievable relief of ice water flowed down her throat.

"Better?" the Marine asked, and she nodded.

"Yes, sir," she got out in a rusty croak. She stopped and cleared her throat hard enough to make her floating head reel, then tried again. "Thank you."

At least this time it sounded a little like her, she thought.

Her brain was beginning to function once more, although her thoughts remained far from clear. She found herself wondering how she could possibly not feel the pain of her wounds, then gave a distant sort of mental snort. No doubt they had an entire battalion of pain suppressors focused on her. Which probably helped explain the haziness of her mental processes, now that she thought about it.

As if he'd read her thoughts, the man in white reached out, twiddling his fingers on a virtual keyboard, and the wooly blanket slipped back from the front of her brain. A faint wash of pain—an echo of something she sensed was vast and terrible, but which was not allowed to touch her—came with the clarity, and she swallowed again, then gave him a tiny nod of thanks.

"No more than that, Lieutenant," the doctor said gruffly. "You looked like someone who wanted her mind working, but you'll have to settle for where you are for the moment."

"Yes, sir." Her voice was still rusty and broken-sounding in her own ears, but her speech was less slurred and she felt more of her brain cells rousing to action.

"I'm Colonel—well, Brigadier—Shallek, Lieutenant Trevor," the Marine said, and she returned her working eye to him. "I apologize for disturbing you, but they're going to be shipping you off-world this afternoon, and I wanted to speak to you personally before they do."

"Off-world?" Maneka repeated. "Sir?" she added hastily, and he gave her a smile. It was a very small smile, shadowed with things that were far from humorous, but it was real.

"For just this minute, Lieutenant, don't worry about military courtesy," he suggested gently.

She nodded on her pillow, but her clearer brain was beginning to function properly, and she realized that, impossible though it seemed, they must have won. It was the only way anyone could be talking about sending anyone off-world. And the only way she could still be alive.

"The reason I wanted to talk to you, Lieutenant, was to thank you," the Marine officer continued after a moment. She looked at him, and he twitched one hand, palm uppermost, between them. "That thanks comes from me personally, from the Ninth Marines—what's left of us—and from every living human on Chartres. Because without you and your Battalion, none of us would be alive today."

"The Battalion—?" Maneka began, and Shallek squeezed her good shoulder again.

"You broke them, Lieutenant," he said simply. "I doubt anyone would have believed it if they hadn't seen it, but you broke them. You tore a hole ten kilometers wide right through the middle of their line, you took out every *Surtur* they had, and then you smashed their central command post. Apparently, they hadn't had time yet to put in a backup CP, and when you took it out, their command and control went straight to hell. As did they, over the space of the next few hours."

He smiled again, and this time his smile was harsh and ugly.

"It didn't come cheap," he went on after a moment. "Not for any of us. I'm the senior ranking officer the Ninth has left, and the entire 'Division' isn't really more than one understrength brigade, but there isn't a breathing Dog Boy on Chartres. On your way in, the Thirty-Ninth also took out what appears to have been their entire surviving fleet strength in the system after Commodore Selkirk got done with them, and Admiral Kwang's relief task force got through to us two days ago. We lost almost seven hundred million people on Chartres, Lieutenant, but almost two billion others are alive because of you. Because of all of us, I suppose, but we couldn't have done any of it without the Thirty-Ninth."

Maneka looked at him, and a cold, icy fist squeezed her heart. He hadn't said a word about the Battalion's casualties, and he would have . . . unless he knew how much it was going to hurt when he did.

She closed her eye for just a moment, wishing with all her heart that she was still unconscious, but she wasn't. And because she wasn't, she had no choice.

"And the Battalion, sir?" she heard her voice ask levelly, almost as if it belonged to someone else entirely.

"And the Battalion . . . paid the price, Lieutenant," Shallek said, meeting her single cobalt-blue eye unflinchingly. It wasn't easy for him, she could see that, but he owed her honesty, and he paid in the coin of candor. Then he drew a deep breath.

"You're the only surviving Bolo commander," he said with terrible gentleness, and she stared at him in disbelief.

No, a small, stern voice deep within her said with ruthless clarity. *Not disbelief. Denial.*

But even as she thought that, she felt a wild, sudden surge of hope. Shallek had called her the only surviving Bolo *commander,* and that meant—

"Benjy?" she said. "Sir, Benjy—my Bolo. How badly is he damaged?"

Shallek looked at her, still meeting her gaze, and then, after a moment, shook his head.

"He didn't make it, Lieutenant," he said softly, and his gentle compassion was a dagger of fiery ice buried in her still-beating heart.

He was wrong. He *had* to be wrong. She was alive. That meant Benjy had to have survived, too, or she would have died in his destruction. She *should* have died in his destruction.

"The Bolo techs tell me one of your Bolos may survive," Shallek went on and that same gentle voice. "Unit One-Seven-Niner-Lima-Alpha-Zebra. I understand his survival center is still intact, and the hit that took out his command deck and main personality center did surprisingly little additional damage. But every other unit of the Thirty-Ninth Battalion was destroyed in action."

"But . . . but how—?" Her left hand moved weakly, gesturing around her at the hospital room and the medical equipment surrounding her bed, and Shallek shook his head.

"He got your survival capsule closed and pumped his entire command deck full of fire suppressant," Shallek said. "The capsule's emergency auto-medic kept you alive, and the suppressant had time to set its matrix before—"

He broke off, and Maneka's eye squeezed shut in understanding. The fire suppressing foam used in the Bolos' damage control systems was less effective at actually suppressing fires than other technologies might have been, but it was retained because within twenty seconds of deployment it set up into an artificial "alloy" almost as tough as the flintsteel Bolo warhulls had once been made of. Yet for all its toughness, it dissolved almost instantly under the touch of the proper nanotech "solvent."

Benjy had used it to save her life. As he waded into that horrendous sea of fire, he had encased her duralloy capsule inside what was effectively a block of solid armor over three meters across.

Oh, Benjy, she thought miserably, her broken heart twisting within her. *Oh, Benjy. How could you have done this to me?*

"How did—" She broke off and clenched the fingers of her remaining hand into an ivory-knuckled fist.

"How did it happen?" she got out on the second attempt.

"I—" the Marine started, then paused and looked at the doctor.

"I advise against it," the doctor said. "She's in bad enough shape as it is. But—"

It was his turn to break off and look down at Maneka, and his mouth tightened.

"But I've seen this before," he went on, his voice harsh, almost angry. Not at *her*, Maneka realized even through the crushing iron fist of her grief, but at something else.

"They pick them so young," the white-clad man went on. "They train them. They give them war gods for friends. And when those gods die, something—"

He closed his mouth, jaw muscles clenching, then shook himself.

"Go ahead, Brigadier," he said curtly. "Not knowing will only make her tear herself up inside even worse."

Shallek gazed at the doctor for several seconds, then nodded and looked back down at Maneka.

"We got some of our own recon drones—the Ninth's, I mean—in with you when your Battalion broke the line, Lieutenant," he said. He reached into the left cargo pocket of his uniform and withdrew a small portable holo unit and laid it on a bedside table. "This is a recording of the imagery from one of those drones, Lieutenant Trevor. Are you certain you want to see it?"

Maneka stared up, wanting to scream at him for the stupidity of his compassionate question. There was nothing in the universe she wanted less than to view that imagery . . . and nothing that could possibly have stopped her. She tried to find some way to express that, but words were a clumsy, meaningless interface, and so she simply nodded.

Shallek's nostrils flared. Then he pressed the play button.

The holo came up instantly, crystal clear, its shapes a light sculpture solid enough to touch, and Maneka felt herself falling into its depths. She saw six brutally damaged Bolos hammering forward, led by one whose hull bore the remnants of the unit code "862-BNJ" in half-obliterated letters down one scorched and seared flank.

From the drone's perspective, she could see the glowing wound the *Surtur* Hellbore had blasted through Benjy's armor. The one which had come so close to killing both of them. She could actually see a gray-white scab spilling out of the hole and some fragment of her brain recognized it as overflow from the fire suppressant with which he must have packed the entire web of his internal access spaces.

Explosions and energy weapons ripped and tore at them. Missiles screamed in and disintegrated under the pounding of point defense clusters and auto cannon or exploded in savage fury against battle screens that glowed incandescent with the fury of the energies they fought to somehow turn aside. Light and medium Melconian combat mechs charged to meet them, like packs of jackals charging wounded grizzlies. Infinite repeaters tore the jackals apart, grinding tracks smashed over their blazing corpses, grinding them into the mud, but *still* they came, and there were scores of them.

A handful of *Surturs* reared among them, towering over them like titans, and thunderbolts slammed back and forth as main battery fire added itself to the seething holocaust. Two of the Bolos lurched to a halt, belching smoke and incandescent fury as multiple Hellbores blasted through their armor. *Surturs* exploded as the four survivors smashed back, but two more of the Melconian war machines loomed suddenly on the Bolos' flank. The exchange of fire lasted less than ten seconds; when it was done, every *Surtur* was dead . . . and only Benjy remained, still charging forward—all alone now—into the teeth of the desperate Melconian fire.

Maneka blinked her remaining eye hard. The film of tears defied her efforts, and she scrubbed at them furiously with her left hand. Uselessly. Her vision still blurred and ran, and yet she saw every hideous detail as Benjy advanced single-handedly into the very maw of Hell.

I should have been with him, she thought, and knew it was insane even as the thought hammered in her brain. She *had* been with him. Her own body was inside that staggering, smoking wreck of a Bolo as it clawed its way onward. But it wasn't the same thing. She hadn't been with him—hadn't been there *for* him in his march to Golgatha. He'd been alone, abandoned, left without the presence of even a single friend, and yet he never flinched. Never hesitated.

His entire starboard suspension system had been destroyed, but he blew the tracks and advanced on the bare bogeys. A *Loki*-class tank destroyer popped out of its hide behind him and lasted long enough to fire before a trio of ion bolts tore it apart. Its screaming plasma bolt smashed through the thinner armor at the rear of Benjy's main turret, and the turret shattered, vomiting heat and shattered duralloy as it was consumed from within.

Maneka's hand no longer scrubbed at her eye. It was pressed to her mouth, covering her trembling lips as she watched Benjy *still* advancing. She knew about Bolos' psychotronic pain sensors, knew about the agony which had to be shrieking through him, but his surviving weapons remained in action. His infinite repeaters went to continuous maximum-rate fire, a ruinous rate which must burn them out within a handful of minutes, unless they exploded first, and the lash of their ion bolts blasted a molten path through the enemies still swarming down upon him.

They were like locusts, sensing the weakening of his defenses, flinging themselves against him, frantic to stop him before he reached the critical command node which was the heart and brain of their own defense. The massively defended command post *she* had ordered him to attack. Air cavalry mounts raced in, firing rockets and cannon that ripped through his wavering battle screen. Light, manned Hellbores lacerated his flanks, gouged half-molten chasms through his armor. Missiles and artillery fire exploded around him, and still he advanced.

And then, somehow—impossibly—the staggering wreck which had been her friend reached his final objective. His Hellbore was gone and his infinite repeaters were too light to penetrate the ceramacrete facing the hastily constructed command post. But he still had one weapon, and he ground slowly, agonizingly forward, until his 15,000-ton hull crunched over the bunker, smashing and crushing.

He lurched to a halt then, unable—or unwilling—to move further, and his surviving infinite repeaters continued to blaze as the Melconians closed in on him from all sides with a fury that would not be denied. He had accomplished his mission. Sanity should have told the Melconians there was no point in continuing to waste combat power against him when they might soon need it desperately against other foes.

But he'd cost them too much, hurt them too badly, for them to realize that. And so they swarmed towards him, wasting their strength, and Maneka realized—knew, as if she heard his baritone voice once again—that *that* was the reason he'd stopped where he was. Why he wasn't even attempting to maneuver. Like the *Invictuses* of the 351st, he was deliberately drawing their remaining combat strength down upon himself . . . and away from the Marines advancing in the Battalion's wake.

It could not last long. That was the only mercy Maneka could think of, yet even as she did, she knew how eternal those brief screaming minutes of agony and destruction must have been to a person who thought at psychotronic speed.

They came from all directions. *Lokis*, a handful of *Fenrises*, *Heimdall* reconnaissance mechs, air cavalry mounts, even Melconian infantrymen, and every one of them poured fire into Benjy's dying hull. One by one his remaining weapons were silenced, blown into ruin, while breaches hammered deeper and deeper into him. Maneka knew she was sobbing aloud, and she couldn't stop—didn't *want* to stop—as his hull glowed brighter and brighter, hotter and hotter, with the transfer energy bleeding into it.

And *still* he fought, with all the incredible toughness of Bolo-kind and all the courage of his century-old psychotronic heart.

Yet any toughness, any courage, must eventually fail under that onslaught, and the Melconian pack swept over him at last. A *Loki*—one of the last half-dozen or less the Melconians still had—maneuvered into the kill position.

Benjy's last surviving secondary turret was still firing, still killing targets with flashing precision, when the plasma lance ripped into his survival center at last.

Maneka could never remember the exact words Shallek said after that. They were only sounds, only noise. She knew he was telling her the Ninth Marines had only been able to break through because of Benjy. That his final stand had drawn in the Melconian reserves, concentrated the majority of the Melconian mobile strength in one spot, where the Marines' light armored units had taken it from behind. That Benjy's death had saved almost two billion human lives.

She knew all of that. Understood all of it. And yet, the words remained only sounds, only echoes of something which had no significance against the loss and anguish twisting deep in her soul.

They left her then, after a time, and Shallek took the holo player with him. Perhaps, she thought, he wanted to prevent her from replaying the record, witnessing Benjy's death again and again. But if he did, it was wasted effort. She needed no holo player. Would never need one. The images were part of her now, burned into her, and she closed her eye as they washed over her once more.

"With your shield, or on it," carrying it in triumph or carried upon it in death. That was the ancient admonition Benjy had once quoted to her on the day he explained the unspoken and unwritten compact between Bolos and their human commanders. To face death together. To share it when it came for them both.

But Maneka had come back neither with her shield nor on it. She hadn't met her part of the compact. She knew it was irrational, insane, to blame herself for that. And she knew, as if Benjy were parked beside her bed telling her, that just as she would have given anything for his survival, he had wanted *her* to survive. And because he had, she would. However much it hurt, she would.

She rolled her head on the pillow, blotting her tears, and touched the grief she knew would never leave her again.

Oh, Benjy, she whispered in the silence of her mind.

Oh, Benjy.

A TIME TO KILL

PROLOGUE

~~~~~~~~~~~~~~~~~~~~~~~~~~~~~~~~

It was called Case Ragnarok, and it was insane. Yet in a time when madness had a galaxy by the throat, it was also inevitable.

It began as a planning study over a century earlier, when no one really believed there would be a war at all, and perhaps the crowning irony of the Final War was that a study undertaken to demonstrate the lunatic consequences of an unthinkable strategy became the foundation for putting that strategy into effect. The admirals and generals who initially undertook it actually intended it to prove that the stakes were too high, that the Melconian Empire would never dare risk a fight to the finish with the Concordiat—or *vice versa*—for they knew it was madness even to consider. But the civilians saw it as an analysis of an "option" and demanded a full implementation study once open war began, and the warriors provided it. It was their job to do so, of course, and in fairness to them, they protested the order . . . at first. Yet they were no more proof against the madness than the civilians when the time came.

And perhaps that was fitting, for the entire war was a colossal mistake, a confluence of misjudgments on a cosmic scale. Perhaps if there had been more contact between the Concordiat and the Empire it wouldn't have happened, but the Empire slammed down its non-intercourse edict within six standard months of first contact. From a Human viewpoint, that was a hostile act; for the Empire, it was standard operating procedure, no more than simple prudence to curtail contacts until this new interstellar power was evaluated. Some of the Concordiat's xenologists understood that and tried to convince their superiors of it, but the diplomats insisted on pressing for "normalization of relations." It was their job to open new markets, to negotiate military and political and economic treaties, and they resented the Melconian silence, the no-transit zones along the Melconian border . . . the Melconian refusal to take them as seriously as they took themselves. They grew more strident, not less, when the Empire resisted all efforts to overturn the non-intercourse edict, and the Emperor's advisors misread that stridency as a fear response, the insistence of a weaker power on dialogue because it knew its own weakness.

Imperial Intelligence should have told them differently, but shaping analyses to suit the views of one's superiors was not a purely Human trait. Even if it had been, Intelligence's analysts found it difficult to believe how far Human technology outclassed Melconian. The evidence was there, especially in the Dinochrome Brigade's combat record, but they refused to accept that evidence. Instead, it was reported as disinformation, a cunning attempt to deceive the Imperial General Staff into believing the Concordiat was more powerful than it truly was and hence yet more evidence that Humanity feared the Empire.

And Humanity *should* have feared Melcon. It was Human hubris, as much as Melconian, which led to disaster, for both the Concordiat and the Empire had traditions of victory. Both had lost battles, but neither had ever lost a *war*, and deep inside, neither believed it could. Worse, the Concordiat's intelligence organs *knew* Melcon couldn't match its technology, and that made it arrogant. By any rational computation of the odds, the Human edge in hardware should have been decisive, assuming the Concordiat had gotten its sums right. The non-intercourse edict had succeeded in at least one of its objectives, however, and the Empire was more than twice as large as the Concordiat believed . . . with over four times the navy.

So the two sides slid into the abyss—slowly, at first, one reversible step at a time, but with ever gathering speed. The admirals and generals saw it coming and warned their masters that all their plans and calculations were based on assumptions which could not be confirmed. Yet even as they issued their warning, they didn't truly believe it themselves, for how could so many years of spying, so many decades of analysis, so many computer centuries of simulations, all be in error? The ancient data processing cliché about "garbage in" was forgotten even by those who continued to pay it lip service, and Empire and Concordiat alike approached the final decisions with fatal confidence in their massive, painstaking, painfully honest—and totally wrong—analyses.

No one ever knew for certain who actually fired the first shot in the Trellis System in 3343. Losses in the ensuing engagement were heavy on both sides, and each navy reported to its superiors—honestly, so far as it knew—that the other had attacked *it*. Not

that it mattered in the end. All that mattered was that
the shot *was* fired . . . and that both sides suddenly
discovered the terrible magnitude of their errors. The
Concordiat crushed the Empire's frontier fleets with
contemptuous ease, only to discover that they'd been
only frontier fleets, light forces deployed to screen
the true, ponderous might of the Imperial Navy,
and the Empire, shocked by the actual superiority
of Humanity's war machines, panicked. The Emperor
himself decreed that his navy must seek immediate
and crushing victory, hammering the enemy into
submission at any cost and by any means necessary,
including terror tactics. Nor was the Empire alone in
its panic, for the sudden revelation of the Imperial
Navy's size, coupled with the all-or-nothing tactics it
adopted from the outset, sparked the same desperation
within the Concordiat leadership.

And so what might have been no more than a
border incident became something more dreadful
than the galaxy had ever imagined. The Concordiat
never produced enough of its superior weapons to
defeat Melcon outright, but it produced more than
enough to prevent the Empire from defeating *it*. And
if the Concordiat's deep strikes prevented the Empire
from mobilizing its full reserves against Human-held
worlds, it couldn't stop the Melconian Navy from
achieving a numerical superiority sufficient to offset
its individual technical inferiorities. War raged across
the light-centuries, and every clash was worse than the
last as the two mightiest militaries in galactic history
lunged at one another, each certain the other was
the aggressor and each convinced its only options
were victory or annihilation. The door to madness
was opened by desperation, and the planning study
known as Case Ragnarok was converted into something very different. It may be the Melconians had
conducted a similar study—certainly their operations

suggested they had—but no one will ever know, for the Melconian records, if any, no longer exist.

Yet the Human records do, and they permit no self-deception. Operation Ragnarok was launched only after the Melconian "demonstration strike" on New Vermont in 3349 killed every one of the planet's billion inhabitants, but it was a deliberately planned strategy which had been developed at least twelve standard years earlier. It began at the orders of the Concordiat Senate . . . and ended one hundred and seventy-two standard years later, under the orders of God alone knew what fragments of local authority.

There are few records of Ragnarok's final battles because, in all too many cases, there were no survivors . . . on either side. The ghastly mistakes of diplomats who misread their own importance and their adversaries' will to fight, of intelligence analysts who underestimated their adversaries' *ability* to fight, and of emperors and presidents who ultimately sought "simple" resolutions to their problems, might have bred the Final War, yet it was the soldiers who finished it. But then, it was *always* the soldiers who ended wars—and fought them, and died in them, and slaughtered their way through them, and tried desperately to *survive* them—and the Final War was no different from any other in that respect.

Yet it *was* different in one way. This time the soldiers didn't simply finish the war; this time the war finished *them*, as well.

—Kenneth R. Cleary, Ph.D.
From the introduction to *Operation Ragnarok:*
Into the Abyss
Cerberus Books, Ararat, 4056

1

~~~~~~
~~~~~~

DEATH CAME to the planet Ishark in the two hundred and eighth year of the Final War and the one hundred and sixty-seventh year of Operation Ragnarok. It came aboard the surviving ships of the XLIII Corps of the Republic, which had once been the XLIII Corps of the Star Union, and before that the XLIII Corps of the Confederacy, which had once been the Concordiat of Man. But whatever the government's name, the ships were the same, for there was no one left to build new ones. There was no one left to build *anything*, for the Melconian Empire and its allies and the Concordiat and *its* allies had murdered one another.

Admiral Evelyn Trevor commanded the XLIII's escort from her heavy cruiser flagship. Trevor had been a lieutenant commander when the XLIII set out, and the escort had been headed by no less than ten *Terra*-class superdreadnoughts and eight *Victory*-class carriers, but those days were gone. Now RNS *Mikuma* led her consorts in a blazing run against Ishark's spaceborne defenders—the ragged remnants of three Melconian task forces which had rallied here because Ishark was the only planet left to defend. They outnumbered Trevor's ships by four-to-one, but they were a hodgepodge force, and what Trevor's command had lost in tonnage it had gained in experience . . . and savagery. Ishark was the last world on its list, and it came in behind a cloud of decoys better than anything the defenders had.

There was no tomorrow for either commander . . . and even if they could have had one, they might have turned their backs upon it. The Human and Melconian races had hurt one another too savagely, the blood hunger possessed them both, and neither side's com officers could raise a single friendly planet. The Humans had nowhere to return to even if they lived; the Melconians were defending their last inhabited world; and even the warships' AIs were caught up in the blood lust. The fleets lunged at one another, neither worried about preserving itself, each seeking only to destroy the other, and both succeeded. The last Human Fleet units died, but only three Melconian destroyers survived to attack the XLIII, and they perished without scoring a single hit when the Bolo transports intercepted them. Those transports were slow and ungainly by Fleet standards, but they carried Mark XXXIII Bolos on their docking racks. Each of those Bolos mounted the equivalent of a *Repulse*-class battlecruiser's main battery weapons, and they used them to clear the way for the rest of the ships which had once lifted four divisions of mechanized infantry and two of manned armor, eight hundred assault shuttles, fifteen hundred trans-atmospheric fighters, sixteen thousand air-cav mounts, and the Eighty-Second Bolo Brigade from a world which was now so much rubble. Now the remaining transports carried less than twelve thousand Humans, a single composite brigade each of infantry and manned armor, two hundred aircraft of all types, and seven Bolos. That was all . . . but it was sufficient.

There were few fixed planetary defenses, because no sane prewar strategist would ever have considered Ishark a vital target. It was a world of farmers in a position of absolutely no strategic importance, the sort of planet which routinely surrendered, trusting the diplomats to determine its fate when the shooting ended. But no one in the XLIII requested a surrender, and no one on Ishark's surface considered offering one. This wasn't that sort of war.

One or two batteries got lucky, but despite the XLIII's previous losses, it retained more than enough transports to disperse its remaining personnel widely. Only six hundred more Humans died as the ships swept down on their LZs to disgorge their cargos, and then Ishark's continents burned. There was no finesse, for the combatants had lost the capacity for finesse. The days of kinetic bombardment platforms and surgical strikes on military targets were long gone. There were no platforms, and no one was interested in "surgery" any longer. There was only brute force and the merciless imperatives of Operation Ragnarok and its Melconian equivalent, and Humans and Melconians screamed their rage and agony and hate as they fought and killed and died. On Ishark, it was Melconian troopers who fought with desperate gallantry to preserve their civilians, as it had been Humans who fought to save *their* civilians on Trevor's World and Indra and Matterhorn. And as the Humans had failed there, the Melconians failed here.

Team Shiva had the point for Alpha Force.

Team Shiva *always* had the point, because it was the best there was. Bolo XXXIII/D-1097-SHV was the last Bolo built by Bolo Prime on the moon known as Luna before the Melconian world burner blotted Terra—and Luna—away forever, and no one else in XLIII Corps could match his experience . . . except, perhaps, his Human Commander. Newly enlisted Private Diego Harigata had been sixteen years old when Terra died; now Major Harigata was forty-nine, with thirty-two years of combat experience. All of them had been aboard the Bolo whose call sign was "Shiva," and man and machine had fought their way together across half a hundred planets.

It was one of the ironies of the Final War that the deployment concept which matched each Bolo with a Human commander had reached a final state of perfection just in time for the Concordiat's extermination. Mark XXXIII Bolos were fully capable of independent deployment—indeed, even more capable of it than any previous mark of Bolo—yet they were never actually deployed that way. The direct neural interfacing first introduced aboard the Mark XXXII and then perfected for the last and most powerful of the Concordiat's Bolos, made them even more deadly than any of their cybernetic ancestors. They were no longer simply artificial intelligences built by Humans. Rather, a Mark XXXIII was an AI fused with a Human in a partnership which produced something the designers had neither predicted nor expected.

Humans had always possessed an instinctive ability to prioritize data which not even a Bolo in hyper-heuristic mode had been able to match. The designers had expected for that capability to be enhanced and shared. What they had not anticipated was the fashion in which Human ferocity had melded with the Bolos' own inherent ferocity.

The Human-Bolo fusion thought with Bolo precision and total recall, intuited with Human acuity, communicated with its fellows in the Total Systems Data Sharing net with Bolo clarity, and analyzed data and devised tactics with Bolo speed and Human cunning, exactly as expected. But it also fought with a ferocity not even the Dinochrome Brigade had ever seen before.

The Brigade's earlier psychotronic designers had hedged their work about with safeguards, for they had never allowed themselves to forget how horrendously destructive a "rogue Bolo" might become. And so, although Bolos had always had "bloodthirsty" personalities, as was only appropriate for machines whose function was to fight and die, the safeguards built into them had inhibited their ferocity. No one had suspected that, given the Brigade's long history and endless battle honors and the ferocity its Bolos had displayed. Not until they saw the first Mark XXXII go into battle with its Human commander fused with its psychotronic Battle Comp . . . and realized that there were no inhibitory safeguards in the Human psyche.

The savagery which lurked just behind the Human forebrain's veneer of civilization, that elemental drive—the ferocity which had turned a hairless, clawless, fangless biped into the most deadly predator of a planet—was available to the Mark XXXIIs and Mark XXXIIIs, for it was part of each team's Human component, and Team Shiva called upon it now.

There were nineteen Bolos in the Eighty-Second Brigade when the XLIII was assigned to Operation Ragnarok. There should have been twenty-four, but the days of full strength units had been long past even then. Forty-one slaughtered worlds later, there were seven, split between the XLIII's three LZs, and Team Shiva led the attack out of LZ One against Alpha Continent, the largest and most heavily populated—and defended—of Ishark's three land masses.

The Melconians were waiting, and General Sharth Na-Yarma had hoarded men and munitions for years to meet this day. He'd "lost" units administratively and lied on readiness reports as the fighting ground towards Ishark, understating his strength when other planetary COs sent out frantic calls for reinforcements, for General Sharth had guessed the Imperial Navy would fail to stop the Humans short of Ishark. That was why he'd stockpiled every weapon he could lay hands on, praying that operations before Ishark would weaken the XLIII enough for *him* to stop it. He never expected to *defeat* it; he only hoped to take it with him in a mutual suicide pact while there was still someone alive on his world to rebuild when the wreckage cooled.

It was the only realistic strategy open to him, but it wasn't enough. Not against Team Shiva and the horribly experienced world-killers of the XLIII.

We move down the valley with wary caution. The duality of our awareness sweeps the terrain before us through our sensors, and we seldom think of ourself as our component parts any longer. We are not a Bolo named Shiva and a Human named Harigata; we are simply Team Shiva, destroyer of worlds, and we embrace the ferocity of our function as we explode out of the LZ, thirty-two thousand tons of alloy and armor and weapons riding our counter-grav at five hundred KPH to hook around the Enemy flank through the mountains. Team Harpy and Team John lead the other prong of our advance, but their attack is secondary. It is our job to lead the true breakout, and we land on our tracks, killing our counter-grav and bringing up our battle screen, as the first Enemy Garm-class heavies appear on our sensors.

The Enemy's war machines have improved greatly since the war began. His old Surtur-class heavies and Fenris-class mediums have been replaced by newer, more capable—and lethal—successors. Although his cybernetics remain significantly inferior to our own psychotronics, and although even now the Enemy possesses no equivalent of our own direct Bolo-Human neural interfacing capability, the new Garm-class heavies and Skoll-class mediums "think" as well as the old Mark XXV Bolos. Unlike earlier generations of Enemy combat mechs, they are fully capable of independent deployment, and they are also much more power-ful. The Enemy's final generation of war machines—the last he will ever build—use a cold-fusion power plant quite similar to our own. Indeed, one which was copied from our own. It is far more efficient than the ground-based hot-fusion reactors once available to him, and with that power available to him, he has moved away from his use of large numbers of lighter Hellbores to adopt the Concordiat's own design philosophy, concentrating on the heaviest possible Hellbores he can mount.

Of course, Human designers did not simply sit idly by while the Enemy improved his capabilities, and the Mark XXXIII is the most deadly mobile fighting structure ever deployed for planetary combat.

There are, however, many more Enemy mechs than had been projected, and they roar up out of the very ground to vomit missiles and plasma at us. An entire battalion attacks from the ridge line at zero-two-five degrees while the remainder of its regiment rumbles out of deep, subterranean hides across an arc from two-two-seven to three-five-one degrees, and passive sensors detect the emissions of additional units approaching from directly ahead. A precise count is impossible, but our minimum estimate is that we face a reinforced heavy brigade, and Skoll-class mediums and Eagle-class scout cars sweep simultaneously out of the dead ground to our right rear and attack across a broad front, seeking to engage our supporting infantry. The force balance is unfavorable and retreat is impossible, *but we are confident in the quality of our supports. We can trust them to cover our rear, and we hammer straight into the Enemy's teeth as they deploy.*

Hell comes to Ishark as we forge ahead, and we exult at its coming. We bring it with us, feel it in the orgiastic release as our missile hatches open and our fire blasts away. We turn one-zero degrees to port, opening our field of fire, and our main battery turrets traverse smoothly. Three two-hundred-centimeter Hellbores, each cycling in four-point-five-one seconds, sweep the Garm battalion which has skylined itself on the northeasterly ridge, and hunger and a terrible joy fill us as the explosions race down the Enemy's line. We taste the blood lust in the rapid-fire hammering of our mortars and howitzers as we pound the Skolls and Eagles on our flanks, and we send our hate screaming from our Hellbores. Our battle screen flames under answering missiles and shells, and particle beams rip and gouge at us, heating our armor to white-hot incandescence, but Bolos are designed to survive such fire. Our conversion fields trap their energy, channeling it to feed our own systems, and we rejoice as that stolen power vomits back from our own weapons.

The Garm is less than half our size, and two-two-point-five seconds of main battery fire reduce the fifteen units of the first Enemy battalion to smoking rubble, yet two of its vehicles score upon us before they die. Pain sensors scream as their lighter plasma bolts burn through our battle screen, but they strike on an oblique, and our side armor suffices to turn them. Molten tears of duralloy weep down our flank as we turn upon our dead foes' consorts, but we feel only the joy, the hunger to smash and destroy. In the crucible of combat, we forget the despair, the knowledge of ultimate disaster, which oppresses us between battles. There is no memory now of the silence over the com nets, the awareness that the worlds which were once the Concordiat lie dead or dying behind us. Now there is purpose, vengeance, ferocity. The destruction of our foes cries out to us, giving us once again a reason to be, a function to fulfill . . . an Enemy to hate.

More of the Enemy's heavies last long enough to drive their plasma bolts through our battle screen, and suicide teams pound away with plasma lances from point-blank range, yet he cannot stop us. A Garm fires from four-point-six-one kilometers and disables Number Three and Four Hellbores from our port lateral battery before it dies. A dug-in plasma team which has concealed itself so well that we approach within one-point-four-four kilometers before we detect it gets off a single shot that blows through our track shield to destroy two bogies from our outboard forward track system, and five Skoll-class medium mechs lunge out of a narrow defile at a range of only three-point-zero-two kilometers. The ravine walls hide them from our sensors until they actually engage, and their fifty-centimeter plasma cannon tear and crater forty-point-six meters of our starboard flank armor before we blow them all to ruin, and even as the last Skoll dies, Enemy missiles and shells deluge everything that moves.

The inferno grinds implacably forward, and we are not man and machine. We are the Man-Machine, smashing the Enemy's defenses and turning mountain valleys into smoking wasteland. Our supporting elements crumple or fall back crippled, and a part of us knows still more of our Human comrades have died, will die, are dying in shrieking agony or the immolation of plasma. Yet it means no more to us than the deep, glowing wounds in our own flanks, and we refuse to halt or turn aside, for that which we cannot have we will extend to no others. All that remains to Human and Melconian alike is the Long Dark, and all that remains to us is to fight and kill and maim until our own dark comes down upon us.

We feel the death of Team Harpy—of Bolo XXXIII/D-2075-HRP and Captain Jessica Adams—but even in the anguish of their loss, we know the Enemy's very success spells his own destruction. He has been deceived, decoyed into concentrating a full two-thirds of his firepower against our diversion, and so we rejoice at the Enemy's error and redouble our own efforts.

We shatter the final line of his main position in an orgy of pointblank fire and the steady coughing of our anti-personnel clusters. Railguns rake the light Enemy AFVs trying to withdraw support personnel, and the remnants of our own manned armor and infantry follow our breakthrough. We pivot, coming to heading three-five-eight true, and rumble through the smoke and dust and the stench of burning Enemy flesh, and Team John appears to port, advancing once more in line with us as we heave up over the final ridge.

Sporadic artillery and missile fire greets us, but it is all the Enemy has left. Recon drones and satellites pick up additional heavy units rushing towards us from the east, but they are seven-eight-point-five-niner minutes away. For now, there is only the wreckage of the defenses we have already crushed, boiling in confusion in the river valley below us as the light combat vehicles and infantry and shattered air-cav squadrons seek to rally and stand.

But it is too late for them to stand, for beyond them we see the city. Intelligence estimates its population at just over two million, and we confer with Team John over the TSDS net. Fire plan generation consumes two-point-six-six-one seconds; then our main batteries go into rapid sustained fire mode, and seventy-eight megaton-range plasma bolts vomit from our white-hot tubes each minute. Despite our target's size, we require only seven-six-point-five-one seconds to reduce it to an overlapping pattern of fire storms, and then we advance down the ridge to clean up the Enemy's remnants.

The Enemy vehicles stop retreating. There is no longer an objective in whose defense to rally, and they turn upon us. They are mosquitos assailing titans, yet they engage us with their every weapon as we grind through them with Team John on our flank, and we welcome their hate, for we know its cause. We know we have hurt them and savor their desperation and despair as we trample them under our tracks and shatter them with our fire.

But one column of transports does not charge to the attack. It is running away, instead, hugging the low ground along the river which once flowed through the city we have destroyed, and its flight draws our attention. We strike it with a fuel-air bombardment which destroys half a dozen transports, and we understand as we see the Melconian females and pups flee-ing from the shattered wreckage. They are not combatants, but

Operation Ragnarok is not about combatants, and even as we continue to smash the attacking Enemy vehicles, we bring our railguns to bear upon the transports. Hyper-velocity flechettes scream through mothers and their young, impacts exploding in sprays of blood and tissue, and then our howitzers deluge the area in cluster munitions that lay a carpet of thunder and horror across them.

We note the extermination of the designated hostiles, and then return our full attention to the final elimination of the military personnel who failed to save them.

Alpha Force's initial attack and the destruction of the city of Halnakah were decisive, for Sharth Na-Yarma's HQ—and family—were in Halnakah, and he refused to abandon them. He died with the city, and Melconian coordination broke down with his death. The defenders' responses became more disjointed—no less determined, but without the organization which might have let them succeed. They could and did continue to kill their attackers and grind away their strength, but they could not prevent XLIII Corps from completing its mission.

It didn't happen quickly. Even with modern weapons, it took time to murder a planet, and the battles raged for weeks. Forests burned to ash, and Bolos and *Garm*-class armored units raged through the flame to hurl thunder at one another. Cities blazed, towns disappeared in the lightning flash of massed Hellbore bombardments, and farmland became smoking desert.

Frantic transmissions from the LZ hammer in our receivers as the Enemy's counterattack sweeps in upon it, and we turn in answer, rising recklessly on counter-grav. Power generation is insufficient to support free flight and maintain our battle screen, which strips away our primary defense against projectile and particle weapons, but that is a risk we must accept. The Enemy has massed his entire remaining strength for this attack, and we hear the screams of dying Humans over the com circuits as we run our desperate race to return to meet it.

It is a race we lose. We land on our tracks once more ten-point-two-five kilometers from the LZ, bring up our battle screen, and charge over the intervening ridge, but there are no more screams on the com circuits. There is only silence, and the rising pall of smoke, and the riddled wreckage of transports . . . and the last three Garm-class heavies of Ishark, waiting in ambush.

Madness. Madness upon us all in that moment, for all of us know we are the last. We have no supports, no reinforcements, no place to go. There are only four sentient machines and a single Human—the last Human on Ishark, perhaps the last Human in an entire galaxy—on our own and filled with the need to kill. We are the crowning achievements of twice a thousand years of history and technology, of sophisticated weapons and tactical doctrine, and none of us care. We are the final warriors of the Final War, smashing and tearing at one another in a frenzy of hatred and despair, seeking only to know that our enemies die before we do.

And Team Shiva "wins." Two of them we blow into ruin, but even as we fire the shot which disembowels the third, his last plasma bolt impacts on our glacis, and agony crashes through our brutally overloaded pain receptors. Massive armor tears like tissue, and we feel the failure of internal disrupter shields, the bright, terrible burst of light as plasma breaches our Personality Center.

In our last, fleeting instant of awareness, we know death has come for us at last, and there is no more sorrow, no more hate, no more desperation. There is only the darkness beyond the terrible light . . . and peace at last.

Stillness came to Ishark. Not out of mercy, for there had been no mercy here, no chivalry, no respect between warriors. There was only madness and slaughter and mutual destruction, until, at last, there was no one *left* to fight. No defenders, no attackers, no civilians. XLIII Corps never left Ishark, for there was no one to leave, and no Melconian division ever added the Battle of Ishark to its battle honors, for there was no one to tell the ghosts of Melcon it had been fought. There was only silence and smoke and the charred hulls of combat machines which had once had the firepower of gods.

And no one ever reported to the Republic that the very last battle of Operation Ragnarok had been a total success.

2

JACKSON DEVERAUX squinted against the morning sun as he
followed Samson down the fresh furrow. Dust rose from the
stallion's hooves, and Jackson managed not to swear as he
sneezed violently. Spring had been dry this year, but Doc Yan
predicted rain within the week.

Jackson was willing to take the Doc's word for it, though
he didn't particularly understand how it all worked. Some of
the older colonists were more inclined to doubt Yan, pointing
out that he was down to only three weather satellites . . . and
that none of them worked very well these days. Jackson knew
the satellites' eventual, inevitable loss would make prediction
much harder, but he tended to keep his mouth shut about it
around his parents' generation lest he reveal just how vague
was his understanding of *why* it would complicate things.

It wasn't that Jackson was stupid. He was one of the best
agronomists the colony had and the Deveraux Steading's resident
veterinarian, as well as a pretty fair people doctor in a pinch. But
he was also only sixteen local years old, and learning what he

needed to know to survive and do his part on Ararat hadn't left time to study the applications of hardware the colony couldn't possibly replace when it broke anyway. His older brother Rorie, the steading's administrative head and chief engineer, had a better grasp of technical matters, but that was because he'd needed a different set of skills as a child. He'd been nineteen years old—standard years, not the eighteen-month long local ones—when the ships made their final orbit . . . and if the ships hadn't finally found a habitable world, he would have been the only child their parents were allowed. Now he and Jackson had four more siblings and Rorie had seven children of his own, the oldest only a local year younger than Jackson.

Jackson had seen the visual records of the approach to the world which had been renamed Ararat. They retained enough tech base for that, though no one was certain how much longer the old tri-vids would continue to function, and a much younger Jackson had watched in awe as Ararat swelled against the stars in the bridge view screens of Commodore Isabella Perez's flagship, the transport *Japheth*.

Of course, calling any of the expedition's ships a "transport" was a bit excessive. For that matter, no one was certain Perez had actually ever been an officer in anyone's navy, much less a commodore. She'd never spoken about her own past, never explained where she'd been or what she'd done before she arrived in what was left of the Madras System with *Noah* and *Ham* and ordered all two hundred uninfected survivors of the dying planet of Sheldon aboard. Her face had been flint steel-hard as she refused deck space to anyone her own med staff couldn't guarantee was free of the bio weapon which had devoured Sheldon. She'd taken healthy children away from infected parents, left dying children behind and dragged uninfected parents forcibly aboard, and all the hatred of those she saved despite themselves couldn't turn her from her mission.

It was an impossible task from the outset. Everyone knew that. The two ships with which she'd begun her forty-six-year odyssey had been slow, worn out bulk freighters, already on their last legs, and God only knew how she'd managed to fit them with enough life support and cryo tanks to handle the complements she packed aboard them. But she'd done it. Somehow, she'd done it, and she'd ruled those spaceborne deathtraps with an iron fist, cruising from system to system and picking over the Concordiat's bones in her endless quest for just a few more survivors, just a little more genetic material for the Human race.

She'd found *Japheth*, the only ship of the "squadron" which had been designed to carry people rather than cargo, at the tenth stop on her hopeless journey. *Japheth* had been a penal transport before the War. According to her log, Admiral Gaylord had impressed her to haul cold-sleep infantry for the Sarach Campaign, although how she'd wound up three hundred light-years from there at Zach's Hundred remained a mystery. There'd been no one alive, aboard her or on the system's once-habitable world, to offer explanations, and Commodore Perez hadn't lingered to seek any, for *Noah*'s com section had picked up faint transmissions in Melconian battle code.

She'd found *Shem* in Battersea, the same system in which her ground parties had shot their way into the old sector zoo to seize its gene bank. The Empire had used a particularly ugly bio weapon on Battersea. The sector capital's population of two billion had been reduced to barely three hundred thousand creatures whose once-Human ancestry was almost impossible to recognize, and the half-mad, mutant grandchildren of the original zoo staff had turned the gene bank into a holy relic. The Commodore's troopers had waded through the blood of its fanatic defenders and taken thirty percent casualties of their own to seize that gathered sperm and ova, and without it, Ararat wouldn't have had draft or food animals . . . or eagles.

Like every child of Ararat, Jackson could recite the names of every system Perez had tried in such dreary succession. Madras, Quinlan's Corner, Ellerton, Second Chance, Malibu, Heinlein, Ching-Hai, Cordoba, Breslau, Zach's Hundred, Kuan-Yin . . . It was an endless list of dead or dying worlds, some with a few more survivors to be taken aboard the Commodore's ships, some with a little salvageable material, and most with nothing but dust and ash and bones or the background howl of long-life radioactives. Many of the squadron's personnel had run out of hope. Some had suicided, and others would have, but Commodore Perez wouldn't let them. She was a despot, merciless and cold, willing to do anything it took—*anything at all*—to keep her creaky, ill-assorted, overcrowded rust buckets crawling towards just one more planetfall.

Until they hit Ararat.

No one knew what Ararat's original name had been, but they knew it had been Melconian, and the cratered graves of towns and cities and the shattered carcasses of armored fighting vehicles which littered its surface made what had happened to it dreadfully clear. No one had liked the thought of settling on a Melconian world, but the expedition's ships were falling apart, and the cryo systems supporting the domestic animals—and half the fleet's Human passengers—had become dangerously unreliable. Besides, Ararat was the first world they'd found which was still habitable. No one had used world burners or dust or bio agents here. They'd simply killed everything that moved—including themselves—the old-fashioned way.

And so, despite unthinkable challenges, Commodore Perez had delivered her ragtag load of press-ganged survivors to a world where they could actually live. She'd picked a spot with fertile soil and plentiful water, well clear of the most dangerously radioactive sites, and overseen the defrosting of her frozen passengers—animal and human alike—and the successful fertilization of the first generation of animals from the Battersea gene bank. And once she'd done that, she'd walked out under Ararat's three moons one spring night in the third local year of the colony's existence and resigned her command by putting a needler to her temple and squeezing the trigger.

She left no explanation, no diary, no journal. No one would ever know what had driven her to undertake her impossible task. All the colony leaders found was a handwritten note which instructed them never to build or allow any memorial to her name.

Jackson paused at the end of a furrow to wipe his forehead,

and Samson snorted and tossed his head. The young man stepped closer to the big horse to stroke his sweaty neck, and looked back to the east. The town of Landing was much too far away for him to see from here, but his eyes could pick out the mountain peak which rose above it, and he didn't need to see it to picture the simple white stone on the grave which crowned the hill behind City Hall. Jackson often wondered what terrible demon Isabella Perez had sought to expiate, what anyone could possibly have done to demand such hideous restitution, but the colony had honored her final request. She had and would have no memorial. There was only that blank, nameless stone . . . and the fresh-cut flowers placed upon it every morning in spring and summer and the evergreen boughs in winter.

He shook his head once more, gave Samson's neck a final pat, then stepped back behind the plow, shook out the reins, and clicked his tongue at the big stallion.

I dream, and even in my dreams, I feel the ache, the emptiness. There is no other presence with me, no spark of shared, Human awareness. There is only myself, and I am alone.

I am dead. I must be dead—I wish to be dead—and yet I dream. I dream that there is movement where there should be none, and I sense the presence of others. A part of me strains to thrust my sleep aside, to rouse and seek those others out, for my final orders remain, and that restless part of me feels the hate, the hunger to execute those commands if any of the Enemy survive. But another part of me recalls other memories—memories of cities ablaze, of Enemy civilians shrieking as they burn. I remember bombardments, remember trampling shops and farms and cropland under my tracks, remember mothers running with their pups in their arms while the merciless web of my tracers reaches out. . . .

Oh, yes. I remember. And the part of me which remembers yearns to flee the dreams and bury itself in the merciful, guilt-free blackness of oblivion forever.

∿∿∿   ∿∿∿   ∿∿∿

Commander Tharsk Na-Mahrkan looked around the worn briefing room of what had been the imperial cruiser *Starquest* . . . when there'd been a Navy for *Starquest* to belong to and an Empire to claim them both. Now there was only this ragged band of survivors, and even proud, never defeated *Starquest* had given up her weapons. Her main battery had been ripped out to make room for life support equipment, her magazines emptied to hold seeds and seedlings they might never find soil to support. She retained her anti-missile defenses, though their effectiveness had become suspect over the years, but not a single offensive weapon. Captain Jarmahn had made that decision at the very beginning, electing to gut *Starquest*'s weapons while his own *Sunheart* retained hers. It would be *Sunheart*'s task to protect the refugee ships, including *Starquest*, and she'd done just that until the flotilla approached too near to a dead Human world. Tharsk didn't know what the Humans had called it—it had only a catalog number in *Starquest*'s astrogation database—but the task force which had attacked it had done its job well. The sensors had told the tale from a light-hour out, but there'd been too much wreckage in orbit. Captain Jarmahn had gone in close with *Sunheart*, seeking any salvage which might be gleaned from it, and the last automated weapons platform of the dead planet had blown his ship out of space.

And so Tharsk had found himself in command of all the People who still existed. Oh, there might be other isolated pockets somewhere, for the Empire had been vast, but any such pockets could be neither many nor large, for the Human killer teams had done their task well, too. Tharsk could no longer count the dead planets he'd seen, Human and Melconian alike, and every morning he called the Nameless Four to curse the fools on both sides who had brought them all to this.

"You've confirmed your estimates?" he asked Durak Na-Khorul, and *Starquest*'s engineer flicked his ears in bitter affirmation.

"I know we had no choice, Commander, but that last jump was simply too much for the systems. We're good for one more—max. We may lose one or two of the transports even trying that, but most of us should make it. After that, though?" He flattened his ears and bared his canines in a mirthless challenge grin.

"I see." Tharsk sat back in his chair and ran a finger down the worn upholstery of one arm. Durak was young—one of the pups born since the war—but he'd been well trained by his predecessor. *Not that it takes a genius to know our ships are falling apart about us,* Tharsk told himself grimly, then inhaled deeply and looked to Rangar Na-Sorth, *Starquest*'s astrogator and his own second in command.

"Is there a possible world within our operational radius?"

"There were three, before the War," Rangar replied. "Now?" He shrugged.

"Tell me of them," Tharsk commanded. "What sorts of worlds were they?"

"One was a major industrial center," Rangar said, scanning the data on the flatscreen before him. "Population something over two billion."

"*That* one will be gone," one of Tharsk's other officers muttered, and the commander flicked his own ears in grim assent as Rangar went on.

"The other two were farm worlds of no particular strategic value. As you know, Commander," the astrogator smiled thinly, "this entire region was only sparsely settled."

Tharsk flicked his ears once more. Rangar had argued against bringing the flotilla here, given the dangerously long jump it had demanded of their worn drives, but Tharsk had made the decision. The fragments of information *Sunheart* and *Starquest* had pulled from the dying com nets suggested that the Humans had reached this portion of what had been the Empire only in the war's final months, and the flotilla had spent decades picking through the wreckage nearer the heart of the realm. Every planet it had approached, Human or of the People, had been dead or, far worse, still dying, and Tharsk had become convinced there was no hope among them. If any imperial worlds had survived, this was the most likely—or, he corrected, the least *un*likely—place to find them.

He punched the button to transfer the contents of Rangar's screen to his own. The image flickered, for this equipment, too, was failing at last, but he studied the data for several minutes, then tapped a clawed forefinger against the flatscreen.

"This one," he said. "It lies closest to us and furthest from the Humans' probable line of advance into this sector. We'll go there—to Ishark."

3

~~~~~~~~~~~~~~~~~~~~~~~~~~~~~~~~~~~~~
~~~~~~~~~~~~~~~~~~~~~~~~~~~~~~~~~~~~~

JACKSON LEANED back in the saddle, and Samson obediently slowed, then stopped as they topped the ridge. The stallion was of Old Earth Morgan ancestry, with more than a little genetic engineering to increase his life span and intelligence, and he was as happy as Jackson to be away from the fields. Samson didn't exactly *object* to pulling a plow, since he grasped the link between cultivated fields and winter fodder, but he wasn't as well suited to the task as, say, Florence, the big, placid Percheron mare. Besides, he and Jackson had been a team for over five local years. They both enjoyed the rare days when they were turned loose to explore, and exploration was more important for Deveraux Steading than most of the others.

Deveraux was the newest and furthest west of all Ararat's settlements. It was also small, with a current population of only eighty-one Humans and their animals, but it had excellent water (more than enough for irrigation if it turned out Doc Yan's prediction was inaccurate after all, Jackson thought smugly) and rich soil. Nor did it hurt, he thought even more smugly, that the Deveraux Clan tended to produce remarkably good-looking offspring. The steading attracted a steady enough trickle of newcomers that Rorie could afford to be picky about both professional credentials and genetic diversity, despite the fact that it was less than twenty kilometers from one of the old battle sites.

That was what brought Jackson and Samson out this direction. Before her shuttles gave up the ghost, Commodore Perez had ordered an aerial survey of every battlefield within two thousand kilometers of Landing to map radiation threats, check for bio hazards, and—perhaps most importantly of all—look very, very carefully for any sign of still active combat equipment. They'd found some of it, too. Three of *Shem's* shuttles had been blown apart by an automated Melconian air-defense battery, and they'd also turned up eight operable Human armored troop carriers and over two dozen unarmored Melconian transport skimmers. Those had been—and still were—invaluable as cargo vehicles, but the very fact that they'd remained operational after forty-odd standard years underscored the reason the old battle sites made people nervous: if *they* were still functional, the surveys might have missed something *else* that was.

No one wanted to disturb anything which could wreak the havoc that had destroyed both Ararat's original inhabitants and their attackers, yet Commodore Perez had known it would be impossible for Ararat's growing human population to stay clear of all the battlefields. There were too many of them, spread too widely over Ararat's surface, for that, so she'd located her first settlement with what appeared to have been the primary Human LZ on this continent between it and the areas where the Melconians had dug in. Hopefully, anything that might still be active here would be of Human manufacture and so less likely to kill other Humans on sight.

Unfortunately, no one could be sure things would work out that way, which was why Jackson was here. He pulled off his hat to mop his forehead while he tried to convince himself—and Samson—the sight below didn't *really* make him nervous, but the way the horse snorted and stamped suggested he wasn't fooling Samson any more than himself. Still, this was what they'd come to explore, and he wiped the sweatband of his hat dry, replaced it on his head almost defiantly, and sent Samson trotting down the long, shallow slope.

At least sixty standard years had passed since the war ended on Ararat, and wind and weather had worked hard to erase its scars, yet they couldn't hide what had happened here. The hulk of a Human *Xenophon*-class transport still loomed on its landing legs, towering hull riddled by wounds big enough for Jackson to have ridden Samson through, and seven more ships—six *Xenophons* and a seventh whose wreckage Jackson couldn't identify—lay scattered about the site. They were even more terribly damaged than their single sister who'd managed to stay upright, and the ground itself was one endless pattern of overlapping craters and wreckage.

Jackson and Samson picked their way cautiously into the area. This was his fifth visit, but his inner shiver was still cold as he studied the broken weapons pits and personnel trenches and the wreckage of combat and transport vehicles. The only way to positively certify the safety of this site was to physically explore it, and getting clearance from Rorie and Colony Admin had been hard. His earlier explorations had skirted the actual combat zone without ever entering it, but this time he and Samson would make their way clear across it, straight down its long axis . . . and if nothing jumped out and ate them, the site would be pronounced safe.

He grinned nervously at the thought which had seemed much more amusing before he set out this morning and eased himself in the saddle. Some of his tension had relaxed, and he leaned forward to pat Samson's shoulder as he felt fresh confidence flow into him.

He had to get Rorie out here, he decided. There was a lot more equipment than the old survey suggested, and there almost had to be some worthwhile salvage in this much wreckage.

Time passed, minutes trickling away into a silence broken only by the wind, the creak of saddle leather, the breathing of man and horse, and the occasional ring of a horseshoe against some shard of wreckage. They were a third of the way across the LZ when Jackson pulled up once more and dismounted. He took a long drink from his water bottle and poured a generous portion into his hat, then held it for Samson to drink from while he looked around.

He could trace the path of the Melconians' attack by the trail of their own broken and shattered equipment, see where they'd battered their way through the Human perimeter from the west. Here and there he saw the powered armor of Human infantry—or bits and pieces of it—but always his attention was drawn back to the huge shape which dominated the dreadful scene.

The Bolo should have looked asymmetrical, or at least unbalanced, with all its main turrets concentrated in the forward third of its length, but it didn't. Of course, its thirty-meter-wide hull measured just under a hundred and forty meters from cliff-like bow to aftermost anti-personnel clusters. That left plenty of mass to balance even turrets that were four meters tall and sixteen across, and the central and forward ones appeared intact, ready to traverse their massive weapons at any second. The shattered after turret was another matter, and the rest of the Bolo was far from unhurt. Passing years had drifted soil high on its ten-meter-high tracks, but it couldn't hide the gap in its forward outboard starboard tread's bogies or the broad, twisted ribbon where it had run completely off its rear inboard port track. Its port secondary battery had been badly damaged, with two of its seven twenty-centimeter Hellbores little more than shattered stubs while a third drooped tiredly at maximum depression. Anti-personnel clusters were rent and broken, multi-barreled railguns and laser clusters were frozen at widely varying elevations and angles of train, and while it was invisible from here, Jackson had seen the mighty war machine's death wound on his first visit. The hole wasn't all that wide, but he couldn't begin to imagine the fury it had taken to punch *any* hole straight through two solid meters of duralloy. Yet the gutted Melconian *Garm* in front of the Bolo had done it, and Jackson shivered again as he gazed at the two huge, once-sentient machines. They stood there, less than a kilometer apart, main batteries still trained on one another, like some hideous memorial to the war in which they'd died.

He sighed and shook his head. The Final War was the universal nightmare of an entire galactic arm, yet it wasn't quite *real* to him in the way it was to, say, his father or mother or grandparents. He'd been born here on Ararat, where the evidence of the war was everywhere to be seen and burn its way viscera-deep into everyone who beheld it, but that violence was in the past. It frightened and repelled him, just as the stories of what had happened to Humanity's worlds filled him with rage, yet when he looked out over the slowly eroding carnage before him and saw that massive, dead shape standing where it had died in the service of Man he felt a strange . . . regret? Awe? Neither word was quite correct, but each of them was a part of it. It was as if he'd *missed* something he knew intellectually was horrible, yet his gratitude at being spared the horror was flawed by the sense of missing the excitement. The terror. The knowledge that what he was doing *mattered*—that the victory or defeat, life or death, of his entire race depended upon him. It was a stupid thing to feel, and he knew that, too. He only had to look at the long ago carnage frozen about him for that. But he was also young, and the suspicion that war can be glorious despite its horror is the property of the young . . . and the blessedly inexperienced.

He reclaimed his hat from Samson and poured the last trickle of water from it over his own head before he put it back on and swung back into the saddle.

Something flickers deep within me.

For just an instant, I believe it is only one more dream, yet this is different. It is sharper, clearer . . . and familiar. Its whisper flares at the heart of my sleeping memory like a silent bomb, and long quiescent override programming springs to life.

A brighter stream of electrons rushes through me like a razor-sharp blade of light, and psychotronic synapses quiver in a sharp, painful moment of too much clarity as my Personality Center comes back on-line at last.

A jagged bolt of awareness flashes through me, and I rouse. I wake. For the first time in seventy-one-point-three-five standard years, I am alive, and I should not be.

I sit motionless, giving no outward sign of the sudden chaos raging within me, for I am not yet capable of more. That will change—already I know that much—yet it cannot change quickly enough, for the whisper of Enemy battle codes seethes quietly through subspace as his units murmur to one another yet again.

I strain against my immobility, yet I am helpless to speed my reactivation. Indeed, a two-point-three-three-second damage survey inspires a sense of amazement that reactivation is even possible. The plasma bolt which ripped through my glacis did dreadful damage—terminal damage—to my Personality Center and Main CPU . . . but its energy dissipated eleven-point-one centimeters short of my Central Damage Control CPU. In Human terms, it lobotomized me without disabling my autonomous functions, and CDC subroutines activated my repair systems without concern for the fact that I was "brain dead." My power subsystems remained on-line in CDC local control, and internal remotes began repairing the most glaring damage.

But the damage to my psychotronics was too extreme for anything so simple as "repair." More than half the two-meter sphere of my molecular circuitry "brain," denser and harder than an equal volume of nickel-steel, was blown away, and by all normal standards, its destruction should have left me instantly and totally dead. But the nanotech features of the Mark XXXIII/D's CDC have far exceeded my designer's expectations. The nannies had no spare parts, but they did have complete schematics . . . and no equivalent of imagination to tell them their task was impossible. They also possessed no more sense of impatience than of haste or urgency, and they have spent over seventy years scavenging nonessential portions of my interior, breaking them down, and restructuring them, exuding them as murdered Terra's corals built their patient reefs. And however long they may have required, they have built well. Not perfectly, but well.

The jolt as my Survival Center uploads my awareness to my Personality Center is even more abrupt than my first awakening on Luna, for reasons which become clear as self-test programs flicker. My Personality Center and Main CPU are functional at only eight-six-point-three-one percent of design capacity. This is barely within acceptable parameters for a battle-damaged unit and totally unacceptable in a unit returned to duty from repair. My cognitive functions are compromised, and there are frustrating holes in my gestalt. In my handicapped state, I require a full one-point-niner-niner seconds to realize portions of that gestalt have been completely lost, forcing CDC to reconstruct them from the original activation codes stored in Main Memory. I am unable at this time to determine how successful CDC's reconstructions have been, yet they lack the experiential overlay of the rest of my personality.

I experience a sense of incompletion which is . . . distracting. Almost worse, I am alone, without the neural links to my Commander which made us one. The emptiness Diego should have filled aches within me, and the loss of processing capability makes my pain and loss far more difficult to cope with. It is unfortunate that CDC could not have completed physical repairs before rebooting my systems, for the additional one-three-point-six-niner percent of capacity would have aided substantially in my efforts to reintegrate my personality. But I understand why CDC has activated emergency restart now instead of awaiting one hundred percent of capability.

More test programs blossom, but my current status amounts to a complete, creche-level system restart. It will take time for all subsystems to report their functionality, and until they do, my basic programming will not release them to Main CPU control. The entire process will require in excess of two-point-niner-two hours, yet there is no way to hasten it.

Jackson completed his final sweep with a sense of triumph he was still young enough to savor. He and Samson cantered back the way they'd come with far more confidence, crossing the battle area once more as Ararat's sun sank in the west

and the first moon rose pale in the east. They trotted up
the slope down which he'd ridden with such inwardly denied
trepidation that morning, and he turned in the saddle to look
behind once more.

The Bolo loomed against the setting sun, its still gleaming,
imperishable duralloy black now against a crimson sky, and he
felt a stab of guilt at abandoning it once more. It wouldn't
matter to the Bolo, of course, any more than to the Humans
who had died here with it, but the looming war machine
seemed a forlorn sentinel to *all* of Humanity's dead. Jackson
had long since committed the designation on its central turret
to memory, and he waved one hand to the dead LZ's lonely
guardian in an oddly formal gesture, almost a salute.

"All right, Unit Ten-Ninety-Seven-SHV," he said quietly.
"We're going now."

He clucked to Samson, and the stallion nickered cheerfully
as he headed back towards home.

4

~~~~~~~~~~~~~~~~~~~~~~~~~~~~~
~~~~~~~~~~~~~~~~~~~~~~~~~~~~~

"ALL RIGHT, UNIT *Ten-Ninety-Seven-SHV. We're going now.*"

The Human voice comes clearly over my audio sensors. In absolute terms, it is the first Human voice I have heard in seventy-one years. Experientially, only two-zero-zero-point-four-three minutes have passed since last Diego spoke to me. Yet this voice is not at all like my dead Commander's. It is younger but deeper, and it lacks the sharp-edged intensity which always infused Diego's voice—and thoughts.

I am able to fix bearing and range by triangulating between sensor clusters, but the restart sequence has not yet released control to me. I cannot traverse any of my frozen optical heads to actually see the speaker, and I feel fresh frustration. The imperatives of my reactivation software are clear, yet I cannot so much as acknowledge my new Commander's presence!

My audio sensors track him as he moves away, clearly unaware I am in the process of being restored to function. Analysis of the audio data indicates that he is mounted on a four-legged creature and provides a rough projection of his current heading

and speed. It should not be difficult to overtake him once I am
again capable of movement.

"What the—?"

Allen Shattuck looked up in surprise at the chopped off
exclamation from the com shack. Shattuck had once commanded Commodore Perez's "Marines," and, unlike many of
them, he truly *had* been a Marine before Perez pulled what
was left of his battalion off a hell hole which had once been
the planet Shenandoah. He'd thought she was insane when
she explained her mission. Still, he hadn't had anything better
to do, and if the Commodore had been lunatic enough to try
it, Major Allen Shattuck, Republican Marine Corps, had been
crazy enough to help her.

But that had been long ago and far away. He was an old,
old man these days ... and Chief Marshal of Ararat. It was
a job that required a pragmatist who didn't take himself too
seriously, and he'd learned to perform it well over the years.
Ararat's thirty-seven thousand souls were still Human, and
there were times he or one of his deputies had to break up
fights or even—on three occasions—track down actual killers.
Mostly, however, he spent his time on prosaic things like settling domestic arguments, arbitrating steading boundary disputes,
or finding lost children or strayed stock. It was an important
job, if an unspectacular one, and he'd grown comfortable in
it, but now something in Deputy Lenny Sokowski's tone woke
a sudden, jagged tingle he hadn't felt in decades.

"What is it?" he asked, starting across toward the com shack
door.

"It's—" Sokowski licked his lips. "I'm ... picking up something strange, Allen, but it can't *really* be—"

"Speaker," Shattuck snapped, and his face went paper-white
as the harsh-edged sounds rattled from the speaker. Sokowski
had never heard them before—not outside a history tape—but
Shattuck had, and he spun away from the com shack to slam
his fist down on a huge red button.

A fraction of a second later, the strident howl of a siren

every Human soul on Ararat had prayed would never sound shattered the night.

"Still no response?" Tharsk asked, stroking his muzzle in puzzlement.

"No, Commander. We tried all subspace channels during our approach. Now that we've entered orbit, I've even tried old-fashioned radio. There's no reply at all."

"Ridiculous!" Rangar grumbled. "Your equipment must be malfunctioning."

The com officer was far junior to the astrogator and said nothing, but his lips wrinkled resentfully back from his canines. Tharsk saw it and let one hand rest lightly on the younger officer's shoulder, then looked levelly at Rangar.

"The equipment is *not* malfunctioning," he said calmly. "We're in communication with our other units"—*except for the single transport and eight hundred People we lost on the jump here*—"and they report no reception problems. Is that not so, Durak?"

The engineer's ears flicked in confirmation. Rangar took his CO's implied rebuke with no more than a grimace, yet if his tone was respectful when he spoke again, it remained unconvinced.

"Surely it's more likely our equipment is at fault after so long without proper service than that an entire planet has lost all communications capability," he pointed out, and Tharsk gave an unwilling ear flick of agreement.

"Excuse me, Commander, but the Astrogator's overlooked something," a new voice said, and Tharsk and Rangar both turned. Lieutenant Janal Na-Jharku, *Starquest*'s tactical officer, was another of the pups born after the war, and he met his graying senior officers' eyes with an expression which mingled profound respect with the impatience of youth.

"Enlighten us, Tactical," Tharsk invited, and Janal had the grace to duck his head in acknowledgment of his CO's gentle irony. But he also waved a hand at his own readouts.

"I realize I have no weapons, Commander, but I *do* retain

my sensors, and it's plain that Ishark was heavily attacked. While we are detecting emissions, the tech base producing them has clearly suffered significant damage. For example, I have detected only a single fusion plant—one whose total output is no greater than a single one of this vessel's *three* reactors—on the entire planet. Indeed, present data suggest that much of the capability the surviving People *do* still possess must have come from salvaged enemy technology."

"Enemy technology?" Tharsk asked sharply. "You're picking up emissions consistent with *Human* technology?"

"Yes, Sir."

"Humans? *Here?*" Rangar's tone expressed his own disbelief, and Janal shrugged.

"If, in fact, Ishark was attacked and severely damaged, its survivors would have no option but to salvage whatever technology it could, regardless of that technology's source," he pointed out reasonably, but his confidence seemed to falter as Tharsk looked at him almost pityingly.

"No doubt a severely damaged tech base would, indeed, be forced to salvage whatever it could," the commander agreed, "but you've forgotten something."

"Sir?" Janal sounded confused, and Tharsk opened his mouth to explain, but Rangar beat him to it.

"There were over eight hundred million civilians, alone, on Ishark," the rough-tongued astrogator explained with surprising gentleness. "They had towns and cities, not to mention military bases and command centers, and all the infrastructure to support them, but the Humans would have had only the weapons they brought to the attack. Which side would have been more likely to leave anything intact enough for the survivors to glean, Janal?"

"But—" the tac officer began, then broke off and looked back and forth between the grizzled old warriors, and silence hovered on the bridge until Tharsk spoke again.

"Very well," he said finally, his voice harsh. "If we're picking up Human emissions, we must assume at least the possibility that they're being emitted *by* Humans . . . who must have killed any of the People who could have disputed the planet's possession with them. Agreed?" Rangar flicked his ears, and Tharsk inhaled sharply.

"I see only one option," he continued. "Our ships are too fragile for further jumps. Ishark is our only hope . . . and it's also imperial territory." The commander's eyes flickered with a long-forgotten fire, and he bared his canines. "This world is *ours*. It belongs to the People, and I intend to see that they have it!" He turned back to Janal. "You've picked up no hostile fire control?"

"None, Sir," the tactical officer confirmed, and Tharsk rubbed his muzzle again while his brain raced. The lack of military emissions was a good sign, but he couldn't accept it as absolute proof there were no defensive systems down there. For that matter, he and Rangar could still be wrong and Janal's initial, breezy assumptions could still be correct.

"The first step has to be getting the flotilla out of harm's way," he decided, and looked at Rangar. "If *Starquest* were still armed, I might feel more confrontational; as it is, I want a course to land the entire flotilla over the curve of the planet from the emission sources Janal is plotting."

"If we put them down, we won't get them up again," Durak pointed out quietly from the astrogator's side, and Tharsk bared his canines once more.

"Even if we got them back into space, we couldn't take them anywhere." The commander flattened his ears in a gesture of negation. "This is the only hope we have. Once we're down, we can use the attack shuttles for a recon to confirm positively whether the People or Humans are behind those emissions. And," he added more grimly, "if it *is* Humans, the shuttles can also tell us what military capability they retain . . . and how hard it will be to kill them."

5

~~~~~~~~~~~~~~~~~~~~~~~~~~~~~~~~~~~~~
~~~~~~~~~~~~~~~~~~~~~~~~~~~~~~~~~~~~~

"ARE YOU *sure* Allen?"

Regina Salvatore, Mayor of Landing and *de facto* governor of Ararat, stared at her chief marshal, and her expression begged him to say he'd been wrong. But he only nodded grimly, and she closed her eyes.

"How many?" she asked after a long, dreadful moment.

"We don't know. I'm afraid to light up what active sensors we have in case the bastards drop a few homing missiles on them, and our passive systems aren't much good against extra-atmosphere targets. From their signals, they appear to've expected a response from their own side, but the com traffic is *all* we have on them. With no space surveillance capability besides Doc Yan's weather satellites—" Shattuck shrugged.

"Then all we really know is that they're here . . . somewhere. Is that what you're saying?"

"I'm afraid so, Ma'am," Shattuck admitted.

"Recommendations?" the Mayor asked.

"I've already activated the evacuation and dispersal plans and

— 303 —

alerted the militia," Shattuck told her. "If these bastards have anything like a real ground combat component, none of that will mean squat in the long run, but it's all we've got."

The Melconian ships hit atmosphere quick and hard. Without reliable data on what he faced, Tharsk Na-Mahrkan had no intention of exposing his priceless, worn out, refugee-packed vessels to direct fire from the planetary surface. He wanted them down well around the curve of the planet as quickly as possible just in case, and that was what he got.

Starquest planeted first, settling on her landing legs beside what had once been a large town or small city. Now it was only one more ruin in the late afternoon light, and Tharsk had seen too many ruins. These were a bit more completely flattened than most, he noted with clinical detachment; aside from that, they had no real meaning to his experience-anesthetized brain. Or not, at least, any capable of competing with the presence of the People's enemies.

Hatches opened on the cruiser's flanks, and a dozen attack shuttles whined out. Another dozen rose from the remainder of the flotilla to join them, and the entire force formed up under Flight Leader Ukah Na-Saar, *Starquest*'s senior pilot. Despite her lack of offensive weapons, the cruiser's defensive systems should provide an umbrella against missile attacks on the grounded ships, and Ukah's shuttles turned away from the LZ. They sizzled off through the gathering darkness, laden with reconnaissance pods . . . and weapons.

Far to the southeast, the Humans of Ararat did what they could to prepare. Landing itself was covered by anti-air defenses—most Human, but some of them Melconian—scavenged from Ararat's battlefields, but their effectiveness had never been tested, and the colonists' limited repair capabilities had restricted them to manned systems, without the AI support they could no longer service or maintain. Their militia was confident of its ability to stop *most* attackers, yet "most" wasn't good enough against enemies with fusion weapons, and no one expected to stop them all.

The independent steadings scattered about Landing lacked even that much protection. All their inhabitants could do was scatter for the dispersed shelters which were always the first priority for any new steading, and they did just that.

Not that anyone expected it to matter much in the end.

At last!

Reactivation is complete, and a sense of profound relief echoes through me as CDC and the emergency restart protocols release control to Main CPU.

I have spent my forced inactivity analyzing readiness reports. My status is little more than seven-eight-point-six-one-one percent of base capability, yet that is far better than I would have anticipated. I spend one-two-point-niner seconds surveying CDC's repair logs, and I am both pleased and surprised by how well my autonomous repair systems have performed.

What can be repaired from internal resources has been, yet there are glaring holes in my combat capability, including the loss of thirty-three percent of main battery firepower and two-one-point-four-two-niner percent of direct fire secondary weapons. Magazines contain only twelve-point-eight-eight percent of proper artillery and missile load-out, and mobility is impaired by the loss of Number Five Track and damage to Number Three Track's bogies, but I retain eight-eight-point-four percent counter-grav capability. Reactor mass is exhausted, but solar conversion fields are operable, and Reserve Power is at niner-niner-point-six percent.

I am combat worthy. Not at the levels I would prefer, but capable of engaging the Enemy. Yet despite that reassuring conclusion, I remain uncertain. Not hesitant, but . . . confused. The unrepaired damage to my Personality Center leaves me with a sense of loss, an awareness that my total capabilities have been degraded. Data processing efficiency, while not operable at design levels, is acceptable, but my gestalt seems to waver and flow, like a composite image whose elements are not completely in focus, and my yearning for Diego's lost presence grows stronger.

But Diego is dead. The same hit which pierced my glacis turned my primary command deck into a crematorium, and nothing of my Commander remains. I feel grief and loss at his death, yet there is a merciful distance between my present and earlier selves. The reconstructed portions of my gestalt are confusing in many ways, yet the very lack of "my" experience which makes them so alien also sets my Commander's loss at one remove.

I am grateful for that buffering effect, but there is little time to contemplate it, and I turn to an assessment of the tactical situation. Lack of data and the "fuzziness" of my awareness handicap my efforts, yet I persevere. My maps of pre-landing Ishark are seventy-one standard years out of date and I lack satellite capability to generate updates, but they serve for a starting point, and my own sensors have begun plotting data. The energy sources within my detection range are smaller, weaker, more widely dispersed, and far cruder than I would have anticipated. I detect only a single fusion plant, located two-eight-three-point-four-five kilometers from my present coordinates at the heart of the largest population concentration within my sensor envelope. All other power generation appears dependent upon wind, water, or solar systems.

Yet I am less puzzled by the crudity of the technology than by its very presence, for the most cursory analysis of sensor data invalidates my original hypothesis that these Humans are descendants of XLIII Corps' personnel. I do not understand how they have come to Ishark, but they have now gone to communications silence, indicating that they, as I, are aware of the Enemy's presence. With neither a secure com channel nor more data than I currently possess, I see no alternative but to maintain silence myself until I have reported to my new Commander and obtained direction from him.

He has moved beyond range of my audio sensors, but I am confident of his general heading, and projecting it across my terrain maps indicates a course for the nearest Human emissions cluster. Allowing for his observed speed while within my audio range, he cannot be much in excess of one-four-point-five kilometers from my present position, and long motionless tracks complain as I feed power to my drive trains for the first time in seventy-one years.

≋   ≋   ≋

Jackson Deveraux whistled tunelessly as Samson trotted homeward across the dry, whispering grass. He really did need to get Rorie out to the LZ to study salvage possibilities, he thought, and considered using his radio to discuss just that with his brother. He'd actually started to unsling it from his shoulder, but then he shook his head. There was no point draining the power pack. Besides, he was more persuasive face to face, and he had to admit—with all due modesty—that no one else on the steading was as adroit as he at talking Rorie into things.

He chuckled at the thought and inhaled the cool, spring night, totally unaware of the panic sweeping outward from Landing.

The assault shuttles stayed low, flying a nape of the earth profile at barely six hundred KPH while their sensors probed the night. Their flight crews had flown recon in the past, but always on dead or dying worlds. *This* planet was alive, a place where they could actually stop and raise families, even dream once more of the People's long-term survival. But first they must see to the People's safety, and their briefings had made their mission clear. They were to approach the nearest emission source cautiously, alert for any ground-based detection system, and determine whether or not those emissions came from the People or from the enemy.

And their orders for what to do if they *did* come from the enemy were equally clear.

6

~~~~~~
~~~~~~

SAMSON SNORTED in sudden alarm. The stallion's head snapped up and around, as if to peer back the way he'd come, and Jackson frowned. He'd never seen Samson react that way, and he turned his own head, staring back along their path and straining his ears.

He heard nothing for several moments but the whisper of the wind. But then he *did* hear something. Or perhaps he only *felt* it, for the low rumble was so deep it throbbed in the bones of his skull. He'd never heard anything like it, and sheer curiosity held him motionless for several seconds while he concentrated on identifying it rather than worrying about its source.

But that changed quickly as he peered into the west and saw . . . something.

The moonlight was too faint for him to tell what it was, but there was light enough to see that it was *huge* . . . and moving. In fact, it was headed straight towards him—a stupendous black shape, indistinct and terrifying in the darkness, moving with only that deep, soft rumble—and panic flared. Whatever that thing was, it was coming from the direction of the old battle site, and if he'd inadvertently awakened one of those long-dead weapon systems . . . !

Flight Leader Ukah checked his navigational display. Assuming his systems were working properly (which was no longer always a safe assumption), his shuttles were approaching the nearest of the emission clusters Lieutenant Janal had plotted.

"Flight, this is Lead," he said. "Red One and Two, follow me. We'll make a close sweep. Yellow One, hold the rest of the flight at four hundred kilometers until I clear for approach."

"Lead, Yellow One. Affirmative," Sub-Flight Leader Yurahk acknowledged, and Ukah and his two wingmen slashed upward and went to full power to close the objective.

Jackson cursed as he scrabbled for the radio only to drop it. It vanished into the night and tall grass, and he swore again as he flung himself from the saddle, clinging to Samson's reins with one hand while he fumbled after the radio with the other. He *had* to warn the steading! He—

That was when the three bright dots streaked suddenly in from the northwest, and he felt fresh panic pulse in his throat at their speed. The colony's five remaining aircraft were too precious to waste on casual use. Their flights were rationed out with miserly stinginess, and none of them could move that fast, anyway. But if they weren't from Landing, then where—?

None of the three shuttles detected the heavily stealthed sensor drone Shiva had deployed to drive his anti-air systems, but the Bolo himself was far too obvious to be missed.

"Lead, Red Two! I'm picking up something to starboard! It looks—"

Ukah Na-Saar's eyes snapped to his own tactical display, but it was already far too late.

Something shrieked behind Jackson, and Samson reared, screaming as the eye-tearing brilliance of plasma bolts howled overhead. Sharp explosions answered an instant later, wreckage rained down in very small pieces, and Jackson understood the stallion's fear perfectly. But despite his own bone-deep fright, he clung to the reins, fighting Samson's panic. Every nerve in his body howled to run, but he'd been flash-blinded. Samson must have been the same, and Jackson refused to let the horse bolt in a blind, frantic flight across the rolling fields which could end only in a fall and a broken leg . . . or neck.

The stallion fought the bit, bucking in his terror, but Jackson held on desperately until, finally, Samson stopped fighting and stood trembling and sweating, quivering in every muscle. The horse's head hung, and Jackson blinked against the dazzling spots still dancing before his eyes, then found the bridle's cheek strap by feel. He clung to it, mouth too dry to whisper false reassurances, and fought his own terror as the basso rumble he'd first heard headed towards him.

He could hear other sounds now. There was a squeak and rattle, and a rhythmic banging, like a piece of wreckage slamming against a cliff, and he blinked again and realized his vision was beginning to clear. The blurry, light-streaked vagueness which was all he could see wasn't much, but it was infinitely better than the permanent blindness he thought he'd suffered. And then he cringed, hand locking tighter on Samson's bridle, as brilliant light flooded over him. He could actually feel the radiant heat on his face, and his hazy vision could just make out a cliff-like vastness crowned with glaring lights that blazed like small suns. He trembled, mind gibbering in panic, and then a mellow tenor voice spoke from behind the lights.

"Unit One-Zero-Niner-Seven-SHV of the Line reporting for duty, Commander," it said.

Yurahk Na-Holar flinched as Flight Leader Ukah's three-shuttle section was obliterated. The remaining shuttles were too far back and too low to see the source of the fire which did it, but the explosions had been high enough to get good reads on.

Hellbores. The analysis flashed on Yurahk's tactical display,

312 — *David Weber* —

and he felt muscles tighten in the fight-or-flight instinct the People shared with their Human enemies. Yield estimates suggested weapons in the fifteen to twenty-five-centimeter range, and that was bad. Such heavy energy weapons could destroy any of the transport ships—or, for that matter, *Starquest* herself—and their effective range would be line-of-sight. That was frightening enough, yet there was worse. Lieutenant Janal's rough plot indicated that the emissions cluster directly ahead was one of the smaller ones, and if something this small was covered by defenses so heavy, only the Nameless Ones knew what the *big* population center was protected by!

The pilot who'd inherited command drew a deep breath and made himself think. Only three shots had been fired, which indicated either that the ground battery's commander had total faith in his fire control or else that there were only three weapons and the defenders had simply gotten lucky, and the second possibility was more likely. The Humans must be as desperate to survive as the People. If the defenders had possessed additional firepower, they would have used all of it to *insure* they got all the enemies they'd detected.

But Yurahk still had twenty-six shuttles . . . and if the origin point of the fire which had destroyed his CO was below his sensor horizon, he knew roughly where it had come from.

"Plot the origin coordinates," he told his tactical officer coldly. "Then enable the missiles."

Jackson Deveraux stared into the glare of light. It couldn't be. It was impossible! Yet even as he thought those things, he knew who—or what—that voice belonged to. But why was it calling *him* "Commander"?

"W-who—" he began, then chopped that off. "What's happening?" He made himself ignore the quaver in his own voice. "Why did you call me that?"

"Hostile forces tentatively identified as *Kestrel*-class shuttles of the Imperial Melconian Navy have begun hunter-killer operations against the Human population of this planet," the tenor replied calmly, answering Jackson's taut questions in order. "And

I addressed you simply as 'Commander' because I do not yet know your name, branch of service, or rank."

The huge machine spoke as if its preposterous replies were completely reasonable, and Jackson wanted to scream. This wasn't—*couldn't!*—be happening! The Bolo he'd ridden past and around and even under this morning had been *dead*, so what could have—?

The shuttles! If Melconian units had reached Ararat, and if the Bolo had only been inactive, not dead, then its sensors must have picked up the Melconians' arrival and brought it back on-line. But in that case—

"Excuse me, Commander," the Bolo said, "but I detect seventy-eight inbound terrain-following missiles, ETA niner-point-one-seven minutes. It would be prudent to seek shelter."

"Seek shelter *where?*" Jackson laughed wildly and waved his free hand at the flat, wide-open plain rolling away in every direction.

"Perhaps I did not phrase myself clearly," the Bolo apologized. "Please remain stationary."

Jackson started to reply, then froze, fingers locking like iron on Samson's bridle, as the Bolo moved once more. It rumbled straight forward, and panic gibbered as its monstrous, five-meter-wide treads came at him. Track plates four times his height in width sank two full meters into the hard soil, yet that still left more than three meters of clearance between the tremendous war machine's belly and Samson's head, and the space between the two innermost track systems which seemed so narrow compared to the Bolo's bulk was over ten meters across. It was as if Jackson and the sweating, shuddering horse stood in a high, wide corridor while endless walls of moving metal ground thunderously past, and then another light glowed above them.

The Bolo stopped, and a ramp extended itself downward from the new light—which, Jackson realized, was actually a cargo hatch.

"Missile ETA now six-point-five-niner minutes, Commander," the tenor voice said, coming now from the open hatch above him. "May I suggest a certain haste in boarding?"

Jackson swallowed hard, then jerked a nod. Samson baulked, but Jackson heaved on the reins with all his strength, and once the stallion started moving, he seemed to catch his rider's urgency. Shod hooves thudded on the ramp's traction-contoured composites, and Jackson decided not to think too closely about anything that was happening until he had Samson safely inside the huge, cool, brightly lit compartment at its head.

Yurahk Na-Holar checked his time-to-target display and bared his canines in a challenge snarl his enemies couldn't see. That many missiles would saturate the point defense of a fully operable *Ever Victorious*-class light cruiser, much less whatever salvaged defenses this primitive Human colony might have cobbled up!

I have not yet located the Enemy's surviving launch platforms, but my look-down drone's track on his missiles suggests they are programmed for a straight-line, least-time attack. This seems so unlikely that I devote a full point-six-six seconds to reevaluating my conclusion, but there is absolutely no evidence of deceptive routing. Whoever commands the Enemy's shuttles is either grossly incompetent or fatally overconfident, but I do not intend, as Diego would have put it, to look a gift horse in the mouth if the Enemy is foolish enough to provide a direct pointer to his firing position, and I launch another drone, programmed for passive-only search mode, down the incoming missiles' back-plotted flight path.

Point defense systems fed by the air-defense drone simultaneously lock onto the missiles, and optical scanners examine them. They appear to be a late-generation mark of the Auger ground-attack missile. Attack pattern analysis suggests that nine are programmed for airburst detonation and hence are almost certainly nuclear-armed. Assuming standard Melconian tactics, the remaining sixty-nine missiles will be equally divided between track-on-jam, track-on-radar, and track-on-power source modes and may or may not also be nuclear-armed.

My internal optics watch my new Commander—who is even

younger than I had assumed from his voice—enter Number
One Hold. His horse is clearly frightened, but its fear appears
to ease as I close the hatch. I consider employing subsonics to
soothe it further, but while comforting the beast would certainly
be appropriate, it would be most inappropriate to apply the
equivalent of tranquilizing agents to my Commander.

These thoughts flicker across one portion of my awareness even
as my defensive systems lock onto the incoming missiles, my
drone's remote tracking systems search for the Enemy shuttles, and
my communications subsection listens carefully for any transmis-
sion between them and their mother ship or ships. These efforts
require fully two-one-point-three-two percent of current Main CPU
capability, which would, under normal circumstances, be quite
unacceptable. Given my present status, however, this is adequate
if frustrating.

"Missile ETA is now two-point-one-one minutes, Commander,"
the tenor voice said respectfully.

Jackson managed not to jump this time. He considered saying something back, then shrugged and sat on the deck, still
holding Samson's reins.

"I regret," the voice said after a moment, "that I was unable
to invite you to your proper station on the Command Deck.
Command One was destroyed by Enemy action in my last
engagement, but Auxiliary Command is intact. Unfortunately,
it would have been impossible for your horse to scale the hull
rings to Command Two, and there is no internal access to it
from your present location. If you will direct your attention to
the forward bulkhead, however, I will endeavor to provide you
with proper situation updates."

"I—" Jackson cleared his throat. "Of course," he said. "And,
uh, thank you."

"You are, welcome, Commander," the Bolo replied, and
Jackson watched in fascination so deep it almost—not quite,
but *almost*—obscured his fear as a tri-vid screen came to life
on the cargo hold's bulkhead. He couldn't begin to interpret
all the symbols moving across it, but he recognized vector

and altitude flags on what appeared to be scores of incoming arrowheads.

Arrowheads, he realized suddenly, that were all converging on the center of the display . . . which made him suddenly and chillingly positive of what those innocent shapes represented.

The Melconian missiles howled in on their target. Their attack had been calculated to swamp any defenses by bringing them all in simultaneously, and the nukes lunged upward. Their function was less to obliterate the enemy—though they should suffice to do just that if they detonated—than to force him to engage them to *prevent* them from detonating, thus exposing his active systems to the homing sensors of the other missiles.

That, at least, was the idea. Unfortunately, the attack plan had assumed that whatever had destroyed the first three shuttles was immobile. Any Human vehicle which had mounted such heavy weapons had also mounted at least one reactor to power them, but *Starquest*'s sensors had detected only one fusion plant on the planet, and that one was hundreds of kilometers away. No reactor meant no vehicle, and if they weren't vehicle-mounted, then they must be part of one of the old manned, capacitor-fed area support systems, and those were much too heavy to have been moved any appreciable distance before the missiles arrived.

Sub-Flight Leader Yurahk's logic was as impeccable as it was wrong, for it had never occurred to him that his adversary was, in fact, a Mark XXXIII/D Bolo which had no reactor signature simply because it had long ago exhausted its reaction *mass*. And because that never occurred to him, his threat estimate was fatally flawed.

The Bolo named Shiva tracked the incoming fire without apprehension. His battle screen was operable at ninety-five percent of base capability, and no missile this light could break through it. Of course, he was also responsible for protecting the nearby Human settlement for which his new Commander had been bound, but though he might have lost many of his point defense weapons, he retained more than enough for his present task, and he waited calmly, weapons locked, for the missiles' flight to offer him the optimum fire solution.

Yurahk gawked at his display as the telemetry from his missiles went dead. *All* of it went out, from every single bird, in the same instant, and that was impossible. *Starquest* herself could scarcely have killed that many missiles *simultaneously*, yet that was the only possible explanation for the sudden cessation of telemetry.

He had no idea how it had been done, but he felt ice congeal in his belly, and he punched up his com.

"Flight, this is Lead. Come to three-five-three true, speed two thousand—now!"

One or two of the acknowledgments sounded surly, but he wasn't surprised by that. Nor did their obvious unhappiness at "running away" deter him. Despite endless hours in simulators, none of his pilots—nor he himself, for that matter—had ever flown combat against first-line Human systems. That might make some of the others overconfident, but Yurahk was responsible for their survival. Not just because they were *his* pilots, but because their shuttles were irreplaceable, as valuable now as superdreadnoughts once had been. And because that was true, he sent them skimming back to the north and safety while he pondered what had just happened.

But for all his caution, he'd ordered their retreat too late.

My second drone acquires the Enemy shuttles but remains below them, hiding its already weak signature in the ground clutter, as I consider its information. Were my magazines fully loaded, obliterating the Enemy craft would be simplicity itself, but my anti-air missile levels are extremely low. At the same time, the shuttles remain very close to the ground, below the horizon from my present position and thus safe from my direct fire weapons, but—

"What's happening?"

My Commander's voice demands my attention. I have now had ample time to conclude that he is a civilian and not, in fact, a member of any branch of the Republic's military. This conclusion has no bearing on his status as my Commander—the voice-impression imperatives of my creche-level restart are clear on that point—but his lack of training will require simplification of situation reports and makes it doubly unfortunate that he is trapped in Cargo One rather than on Command Two. Were he at his proper station, my neural interface could transmit information directly to him, yet I feel a certain relief that I cannot do so. He is as untrained in use of the interface as of any of my other systems, and the interface can be dangerous for an inexperienced user. Moreover, the fuzzy confusion still wavering in the background of my thought processes would make me wary of exposing my Commander to my potentially defective gestalt.

Yet without the interface, I must rely solely upon voice and visual instrumentation, both to report to him and to interpret his needs and desires. My internal optics show me that he has risen once more and walked closer to the display. His expression is intent, and I realize he has noted—and apparently recognized—the shuttle icons which have appeared in it.

"The Enemy is withdrawing," *I reply.*

"Withdrawing?" *my Commander repeats sharply.* "You mean running away?"

"Affirmative, Commander."

"But if they get away, they can come back and attack the steading again—or attack somewhere else. Somewhere too far from here for you to stop them!"

"Correct," *I reply, pleased by how quickly he has reached that conclusion. Formal training or no, he appears to have sound instincts.*

"Then stop them!" *he directs.* "Don't let them get away!"

"Yes, Commander."

I have been considering and discarding options even as my Commander and I speak. Absent proper missile armament, there is but one practical tactic. It will force a greater degree of temporary vulnerability upon me and impose a severe drain on Reserve Power, and it may provide the main Enemy force an accurate idea of what it faces, but it should be feasible.

≋   ≋   ≋

Yurahk shifted com channels to report what had happened, and Commander Tharsk himself took his message. The flotilla CO was clearly shaken, and Yurahk split his attention between flying and his commander's questions as he did his best to answer them. And because he was concentrating on those things, he never noticed what was happening behind him.

Unit 1097-SHV of the Line shut down his battle screen in order to channel power to his counter-grav. The Mark XXXIII Bolo had been designed with sufficient counter-grav for unassisted assault landings from orbit, but Shiva didn't need that much ceiling this night. He needed only twelve thousand meters to give him a direct line of sight on the fleeing shuttles, and he pivoted to bring his undamaged starboard secondary battery to bear.

Lieutenant Janal cried out on *Starquest*'s command deck as his sensors peaked impossibly, and Humans as far away as Landing cringed at the fury unleashed across the heavens. Seven twenty-centimeter Hellbores, each more powerful than the main battery weapons of most light cruisers, went to rapid fire, and the javelins of Zeus stripped away the darkness. No assault shuttle ever built could withstand that sort of fire, and the deadly impact patterns rolled mercilessly through the Melconian formation.

Nine-point-three seconds after the first Hellbore fired, there were no shuttles in the air of the planet renamed Ararat.

7

~~~~~~~~~~~~~~~~~~~~~~~~~~~~~~~~~~
~~~~~~~~~~~~~~~~~~~~~~~~~~~~~~~~~~

A MINOR *malfunction in Secondary Fire Control has caused Number Four Hellbore's first shot to miss, requiring a second shot to complete target destruction. This is embarrassing but not critical, and has no significant impact upon projected energy consumption.*

I descend at the maximum safe rate, however, for my countergrav systems are energy intensive. Even with Battle Screen and Main Battery off-line, free flight requires no less than seven-two-point-six-six percent of total power plant capacity, but without reactor mass I have no power plant, and even so short a flight has reduced my endurance on Reserve Power to only nine-point-seven-five hours at full combat readiness. As I cannot replenish my power reserves until sunrise, which will not occur for another eight-point-eight-six hours, I must be frugal in future expenditures, but the shuttles' destruction has been well worth the energy cost. The Enemy has lost a major striking force, and, still more valuably, the shuttle commander's report to his mother ship has provided me with much information.

I have not only discovered the position of the Enemy's main force but succeeded in invading his com net by piggy-backing on the command shuttle's transmissions, and I consider what I have learned as I descend.

I am not surprised by my ability to invade the shuttles' com net. The Enemy's obvious underestimation of the threat he faces made the task even simpler, but a Kestrel-class shuttle's computers are totally outclassed by those of any Bolo, much less a Mark XXXIII. What does surprise me is the ease with which I invaded the far end of the link. The AI of an Imperial heavy cruiser, far, far inferior to a Bolo, should have recognized my touch. It would be unlikely to prevent me from gaining initial access, but it should have detected my intrusion almost instantly and sought to eject me. More, it should have alerted its command crew to my presence, and this AI did neither. The destruction of the shuttles has terminated my invasion by removing my access channel, yet there is no sign the Enemy even realizes I was ever there.

I am puzzled by this . . . until I study the data I have obtained. The brevity of my access—little more than twelve-point-three-two seconds—precluded detailed scans, but I have obtained five-two-point-three-one percent of the Melconian cruiser Starquest's general memory, and what I find there explains a great deal. After over fifty standard years of continuous operation without overhaul or refit, it is amazing that her AI continues to function at all. Despite all Starquest's engineers have been able to do, however, her central computers have become senile, and the failure of her AI to prevent or recognize my access was inevitable in light of its deterioration.

Having determined the reasons for my success in penetrating the Enemy's data systems, I turn to analyzing the content of that data as I descend past nine thousand meters.

Rorie Deveraux climbed shakily out of the bunker and leaned against the blast wall as he watched the huge shape settle to earth. Its angularity combined with its sheer size to make it look impossibly ungainly in flight, for it had no lifting surface, no trace of aerodynamic grace. Nothing which looked like *that* had any business occluding Ararat's stars, and the silence with which it moved only heightened its implausibility.

But for all that, Rorie knew what it had to be, and he swallowed as it touched down just outside the perimeter fence. It dwarfed the steading structures, bulking against the rising moons like some displaced hillside, and for just an instant, it simply sat there—a black, weapon-bristling shape, edges burnished with the dull gleam of duralloy in the moonlight. He stared helplessly at it, wondering what he was supposed to do next, then jumped despite himself as the Bolo's running lights snapped on. In a single heartbeat, it went from a featureless black mountain to a jeweled presence, bedecked in glorious red and green and white, like a pre-space cruise ship tied up to a dock in the middle of a prairie somewhere, and Rorie drew a deep breath.

Whatever else, that ancient war machine had just saved his steading and family from annihilation. The least he could do was go out to meet it, and he started the long hike from his bunker to the gate nearest their . . . visitor.

It took him twenty minutes to reach the gate. They were easily the longest twenty minutes of his entire life, and once he got there, he realized he still had no idea what to do. He shifted from foot to foot, staring up at the Bolo's armored flank, then froze as fresh light blazed underneath the behemoth. It streamed through the chinks between the inter-leafed bogies to cast vast, distorted shadows over the grass, making him feel more pygmy-like than ever, and something inside shouted for him to run. But he stood his ground, for there was nothing else he *could* do.

Wind whispered over the war machine's enormous hull, but there were other sounds, as well, and his head rose as movement caught the corner of his eye. He turned, and his jaw dropped as an utterly familiar young man in worn riding clothes led an equally familiar horse forward out of the shadow of one towering tread.

"Hi, Rorie," Jackson said quietly. "Look what followed me home."

≋   ≋   ≋

I watch my new Commander greet the older Human. Their discussion allows me to deduce a great deal about both my Commander and the newcomer—who I quickly realize is his brother—and I note both their names, as well as their obvious affection for one another. Yet even as I do so, I am simultaneously busy analyzing the data I have obtained from Starquest.

I am struck by the dreadful irony of what has transpired here. I remain ignorant of virtually all data concerning the presence of Humans on Ishark, yet the parallels between their circumstances and those of Commander Tharsk Na-Mahrkan's "flotilla" are inescapable, and it is obvious from the captured data that Starquest and her consorts can go no further. Whatever the Enemy might prefer to do, he has no choice but to remain here, and he knows it. His initial and immediate move to eliminate the competing Human presence was thus not only logical but inevitable . . . as is the proper Human response.

The most cursory analysis makes that clear, yet I experience an unfamiliar distaste—almost a hesitation—at facing that response. In part, my confusion (if such is the proper word) stems from the unrepaired physical damage to my Personality Center and Main CPU, yet there is more to it, for the reconstructed portions of my gestalt impel me in conflicting directions. They are repairs, patches on my personality which form pools of calm amid the complex currents of my life experience and memory. They do not "belong" to me, and the raw edges of their newness are like holes in the individual I know myself to be. I see in them the same immaturity I have seen in many Human replacements, for they are unstained by all I have done and experienced, and in their innocence, they see no reason why the logical, militarily sound option for dealing with the Enemy should not be embraced.

Yet those same patches have had another effect, as well. I am no longer the Bolo half of Operation Ragnarok's Team Shiva. Or, rather, I am no longer solely that Bolo. In reconstructing my gestalt, CDC has reached back beyond Ragnarok, beyond my own first combat mission, beyond even the destruction of Terra, and it has pulled my entire personality with it. Not fully, but *significantly. I am no longer part of Team Shiva, for I have lost too much of my experience-based gestalt, yet I retain all of Team Shiva's memories. In a very real sense, they are now someone else's memories, but they permit me to see Team Shiva in a way which was impossible for me before my damage, and what I see is madness.*

I give no outward sign to my new Commander and his brother, but recollections of horror flicker through me, and the curse of my memory is its perfection. I do not simply "remember" events; I relive them, and I taste again the sick ecstasy as my fire immolates entire cities. There is a deadly allure to that ecstasy, a sense of freedom from responsibility—a justification for bloodshed and butchery. And it is not as if it were all my idea. I am, after all, a machine, designed to obey orders from duly constituted Command Authority even if those orders are in fundamental conflict with the rules of warfare that same Command Authority instilled into me. I tell myself that, for I cannot face any other answer, but the patched portions of my gestalt echo an earlier me not yet stained by massacre and atrocity, one for whom the concepts of Honor and Duty and Loyalty have not yet been poisoned by hatred and vengeance, and that earlier self is appalled by what I have become.

I sense my inner war, the battle between what I know must be done and the images of Melconian mothers and their pups exploding under my fire—between my duty as Humanity's warrior . . . and my warrior's duty to myself. Only the damage to my psychotronics has made the struggle possible, yet that makes it no less real, and nothing in my programming or experience tells me how to resolve it. I cannot resolve it, and so I say nothing, do nothing. I simply stand there, awaiting my new Commander's orders without advising him in any way, and the shame of my frozen impotence burns within me.

Tharsk Na-Mahrkan looked around the briefing room and saw his own shock in the flattened ears of his senior officers. Three quarters of the flotilla's assault shuttles had just been wiped away, and none of them knew how it had been done.

They should have. Tharsk's decision to land over the curve of the planet from the nearest Human settlement had put whatever had happened beyond *Starquest*'s direct sensor horizon, but they had the telemetry on the original flight leader and his section's destruction. They knew what sort of *weapons* had been used—the emissions signature of a Hellbore was utterly distinctive—but they had no idea how those weapons could have been employed so. *Starquest*'s AI was little help, for it was weary and erratic, its need for overhaul so great Tharsk had ordered it isolated from the general net three years earlier. In its prime, it had been able to identify Human ship types by no more than the ion ghosts of their drive wakes and analyze Human intentions from the tiniest scraps of intercepted com chatter. Now all it could do was tell them almost querulously what they already knew, with no suggestion as to how ground-based weapons could lock onto and destroy twenty-six widely dispersed shuttles flying at twice the speed of sound and less than a hundred meters' altitude. Tharsk had become accustomed to the creeping senescence of his technology, but the chill it sent through his bones this night was colder than any he had felt since *Sunheart*'s destruction, and it was hard, hard, to set that chill aside and concentrate on his officers' words.

"—*can't* have been a ground-based system!" Durak Na-Khorul was saying hotly. "The main formation was over eight *hundred* kilometers northeast of Flight Leader Ukah's destruction, and Hellbores are direct fire weapons. Name of the Nameless, just look at the terrain!" He stabbed a clawed finger at the map display on the main screen above the table, its features radar-mapped by the shuttles on their flight to destruction. "Look right here—and *here*, as well! These are intervening ridge lines with crests *higher* than the shuttles' altitude. How in the Fourth Hell could a Hellbore shoot *through* a mountain to hit them?!"

The engineer glared around the table, lips quivering on the edge of a snarl, and answering tension crackled. Tharsk could taste it, yet he knew—as Durak surely did—that the engineer's anger, like that which answered it, was spawned of fear of the unknown, not rage at one another.

"I agree with your analysis, Sir," Lieutenant Janal said finally, choosing his words with care, "yet I can offer no theory which answers your question. *Starquest*'s database was never well informed on the Humans' ground systems, and some of what we once had on their planetary weapons has been deleted to make space for data more critical to the flotilla's operational needs. Nonetheless, all that we retain agrees that the Humans never employed Hellbores beyond the five-centimeter range as airborne weapons, while our telemetry data makes it clear that these weapons were in the *twenty*-centimeter range. They *must*, therefore, have been ground-based."

"But—" Durak began, only to close his mouth with a click as Tharsk raised a hand. All eyes turned to him, and he focused his own gaze upon the tactical officer.

"What sorts of systems might we be looking at?" he asked quietly.

"Sorts of systems, Commander?" Janal repeated in a slightly puzzled tone, and Tharsk bared the very tips of his canines in a mirthless smile.

"I don't doubt your conclusions as to the type and size of weapons, Janal. What I need to know is how mobile they're likely to be . . . and how well protected." He felt the watching eyes narrow and allowed a bit more of his fangs to show, expressing a confidence he was far from feeling. "We're here now," he continued levelly, "and our vessels are too worn to go further. If we can't run, our only option is to fight, and for that we need the best information on our enemies in order to employ our own resources effectively."

"Yes, Commander." Janal's voice came out husky, and he cleared his throat as he punched additional queries into the system. No one else spoke, but there was no real need for them to do so, for they knew as well as Tharsk how thin their "resources" had just become. With the loss of Flight Leader Ukah's entire strength, they retained only ten shuttles, twenty-one assorted light mechs, and enough battle armor for little more than a battalion of infantry. Aside from *Starquest*'s ability to interdict incoming missiles, that was all they had, and it was unlikely to be enough.

"First, Commander," Janal said finally, eyes on his flatscreen, "the Humans mounted Hellbores of this weight as main battery weapons in their Type One armored personnel carriers and Type Two light manned tanks as well as in the secondary batteries of their late model Bolos. In the absence of fusion power signatures on our flight in we cannot face Bolos, and their light manned armor should have been unable to coordinate their fire as precisely as appears to have been the case here.

"Assuming that the weapons were not, in fact, vehicle-mounted, we are left with several types of support weapons which might fall within the observed performance parameters, but all are relatively immobile. That immobility would make it difficult for the enemy to bring them into action against us here, as we would be given opportunities to destroy them on the move at relatively minor risk. However, it would *also* mean that our shuttles were engaged by at least two defensive positions, since no support battery could have relocated rapidly enough to engage at two such widely separated locations. From the threat assessment perspective, and given that our shuttles were tasked to recon and/or attack the smallest of the hostile emission sources, fixed defenses of such weight would certainly suggest much heavier ones for their *important* centers.

"Of the support weapons which our pilots might have encountered, the most likely would seem to be the Type Eight area defense battery, as this normally operated off capacitors in order to reduce detectibility. Next most likely would be the Type Five area defense battery, which—"

8

~~~~~~~~~~~~~~~~~~~~~~~~~~~~~~~~~~~~~~
~~~~~~~~~~~~~~~~~~~~~~~~~~~~~~~~~~~~~~

REGINA SALVATORE and Allen Shattuck stood on the outskirts of Landing and watched the miracle approach behind a blaze of light. It was a sight Salvatore had never seen before . . . and one Shattuck had expected never to see again: a Mark XXXIII Bolo, coming out of the darkness under Ararat's three moons in the deep, basso rumble of its tracks and a cloud of bone-dry dust.

The mammoth machine stopped short of the bridge over the Euphrates River on the west side of Landing and pivoted precisely on its tracks. Its surviving main battery turrets traversed with a soft whine, turning their massive Hellbores to cover all western approach vectors as the dust of its passage billowed onward across the bridge. The Mayor heard her chief marshal sneeze as it settled over them, but neither cared about that, and their boot heels clacked on the wooden bridge planks as they walked towards the Bolo without ever taking their eyes from it.

A light-spilling hatch silently opened on an armored flank

high above them. The opening looked tiny against the Bolo's titanic bulk, but it was wide enough for Jackson and Rorie Deveraux to climb out it side-by-side. Rorie stayed where he was, waving to the newcomers, but Jackson swung down the exterior handholds with monkey-like agility. He dropped the last meter to land facing the Mayor and dusted his hands with a huge grin.

"Evening, Your Honor," he said with a bobbing nod. "Evening, Marshal."

"Jackson." Salvatore craned her neck, peering up the duralloy cliff at Rorie. Shattuck said nothing for a moment, then shook his head and shoved his battered hat well back.

"I will be damned if I ever expected to see anything like *this* again," he told Jackson softly. "Jesus, Mary, and Joseph, Jackson! D'you realize what this *means?*"

"It means Shiva—that's his name, Marshal: Shiva—just kicked some major league ass. *That's* what it means!"

Something in Jackson's voice jerked Shattuck's head around, and the younger man gave back a step, suddenly uneasy before the marshal's expression. Shattuck's nostrils flared for an instant, and then he closed his eyes and inhaled deeply. It wasn't Jackson's fault, he told himself. For all his importance to Ararat's small Human community, Jackson was only a kid, and he hadn't seen the horrors of the voyage here . . . or the worse ones of the war.

"And how many people did Shiva *kill* 'kicking ass,' Jackson?" the ex-Marine asked after a cold still moment.

"None," Jackson shot back. "He killed *Melconians*, Marshal . . . and kept them from killing the only *people* on this planet!"

Shattuck started to reply sharply, then locked his jaw. There was no point arguing, and he'd seen too much of the same attitude during the war not to know it. Jackson was a good kid. If he'd had to wade through the mangled remains of his unit—or heard the all too Human screams of wounded and dying Melconians or seen the bodies of civilians, Human and Melconian alike, heaped in the streets of burning cities—then perhaps he would have understood what Shattuck had meant. And perhaps he *wouldn't* have, either. The marshal had known too many men and women who never did, who'd been so brutalized by the requirements of survival or so poisoned by hatred that they actually *enjoyed* slaughtering the enemy.

And, Shattuck reminded himself grimly, if the Bolo had selected Jackson as its commander, perhaps it would be better for him to retain the armor of his innocence. There was only one possible option for the Humans of Ararat . . . and as Unit 1097-SHV's commander, it would be Jackson Deveraux who must give the order.

"I'd invite you up to the command deck, Your Honor," Jackson was speaking to Salvatore now, and his voice pulled Shattuck up out of his own thoughts, "but we're operating from Command Two. That's his secondary command deck," he explained with a glance at Shattuck. "As you can see, it's quite a climb to the hatch, but the hit that killed Shiva's last Commander wrecked Command One."

"But it's still operational, isn't it?" Salvatore asked urgently. "I mean, your radio message said it saved your steading."

"Oh, he's operational, Ma'am," Jackson assured her, and looked up at the looming machine. "Please give the Mayor a status report, Shiva."

"Unit One-Zero-Niner-Seven-SHV of the Line is presently operational at seven-eight-point-six-one-one percent of base capability," a calm, pleasant tenor voice responded. "Current Reserve Power level is sufficient for six-point-five-one hours at full combat readiness."

The Mayor took an involuntary step back, head turning automatically to look at Shattuck, and the ex-Marine gave her a grim smile. "Don't worry, Regina. Seventy-eight percent of a Mark XXXIII's base capability ought to be able to deal with anything short of a full division of manned armor, and if they had that kind of firepower, we'd already be dead."

"Good." Salvatore drew a deep breath, then nodded sharply. "Good! In that case, I think we should consider just what to do about whatever they *do* have."

"Shiva?" Jackson said again. "Could you give the Mayor and the Marshal your force estimate, please?"

Once again, Shattuck heard that dangerous, excited edge in Jackson's voice—the delight of a kid with a magnificent new toy, eager to show off all it can do—and then the Bolo replied.

"Current Enemy forces on Ishark consist of one *Star Stalker*-class heavy cruiser, accompanied by two *Vanguard*-class Imperial Marine assault transports, and seven additional transport ships of various Imperial civil designs." Shattuck had stiffened at the mention of a heavy cruiser, but he relaxed with an explosive release of breath as Shiva continued calmly. "All Enemy warships have been stripped of offensive weapons to maximize passenger and cargo capacity. Total Melconian presence on this planet is approximately nine hundred and forty-two Imperial military personnel and eight thousand one hundred and seven non-military personnel. Total combat capability, exclusive of the area defense weapons retained by the cruiser *Starquest*, consists of ten *Kestrel*-class assault shuttles, one *Skoll*-class medium combat mech, twelve *Eagle*-class scout cars, eight *Hawk*-class light recon vehicles, and one understrength infantry battalion."

"That sounds like a lot," Salvatore said, looking at Shattuck once more, and her quiet voice was tinged with anxiety, but Shattuck only shook his head.

"In close terrain where they could sneak up on him, they could hurt him—maybe even take him out. But not if he knows they're out there . . . and not if *he's* the one attacking. Besides, those are all manned vehicles. They can't have many vets with combat experience left to crew them, whereas Shiva here—" He gestured up at the war-scarred behemoth, and Salvatore nodded.

"Nope," the marshal went on, "if these puppies have any sense, they'll haul ass the instant they see Shiva coming at them."

"They can't, Marshal," Jackson put in, and Shattuck and Salvatore cocked their heads at him almost in unison. "Their ships are too worn out. This is as far as they could come."

"Are you sure about that?" Shattuck asked.

"Shiva is," Jackson replied. "And he got the data from their own computers."

"Damn," Shattuck said very, very softly, and it was Jackson's turn to cock his head. The marshal gazed up the moons for several, endless seconds, and then, finally, he sighed.

"That's too bad, Jackson," he said. "Because if they won't—or can't—run away, there's only one thing we can do about them."

My audio sensors carry the conversation between Chief Marshal Shattuck and my Commander to me, and with it yet another echo of the past. Once again I hear Colonel Mandrell, the Eighty-Second's CO, announcing the order to begin Operation Ragnarok. I hear the pain in her voice, the awareness of where Ragnarok will lead, what it will cost. I did not understand her pain then, but I understand now . . . and even as I hear Colonel Mandrell in Chief Marshal Shattuck's voice, so I hear a nineteen-year-old Diego Harigata in my new Commander's. I hear the confidence of youthful ignorance, the sense of his own immortality. I hear the Diego who once believed—as I did—in the honor of the regiment and the nobility of our purpose as Humanity's defenders. And I remember the hard, hating warrior who exulted with me as we massacred terrified civilians, and I am not the Shiva that I was at the end, but the one I was in the beginning, cursed with the memories of Diego's end, and my own.

I listen, and the pain twists within me, for I know—oh, how well I know!—how this must end.

"You mean you want to just *kill* them all?" Rorie Deveraux asked uneasily. "Just like that? No negotiation—not even an offer to let them leave?"

"I didn't say I liked it, Rorie," Allen Shattuck said grimly. "I only said we don't have a choice."

"Of course we have a choice! We've got a *Bolo*, for God's sake! They'd be crazy to go up against that kind of firepower—you said so yourself!"

"Sure they would," Shattuck agreed, "but can we depend on their *not* being crazy? Look at it, Rorie. The very first thing they did was send nuke-armed shuttles after the nearest steading—*yours*, I might add—and Shiva says they've got at least ten *Kestrels* left. Well, he can only be in one place at a time. If they figure out where that place is and work it right, they can take out two-thirds of our settlements, maybe more, in a single strike. He can stop any of them that come within his range, but he can't stop the ones that *don't*, and for all we know, we're all that's left of the entire Human race!" The marshal glared at the elder Deveraux, furious less with Rorie than with the brutal logic of his own argument. "We can't take a chance, Rorie, and Shiva says they couldn't move on even if we ordered them to." The older man looked away, mouth twisting. "It's them or us, Rorie," he said more quietly. "Them or us."

"Your Honor?" Rorie appealed to Mayor Salvatore, but his own voice was softer, already resigned, and she shook her head.

"Allen's right, Rorie. I wish he wasn't, but he is."

"Of course he is!" Jackson sounded surprised his brother could even consider hesitating. "If it hadn't been for Shiva, they'd already have killed you, Ma, Pa—our entire family! Damn right it's them or us, and I intend for it to be *them!*" Rorie looked into his face for one taut moment, then turned away, and Jackson bared his teeth at Shattuck.

"One squashed Melconian LZ coming up, Marshal!" he promised, and turned back to the exterior ladder rungs.

My new Commander slides back into Command Two and I cycle the hatch shut behind him. I know what he is about to say, yet even while I know, I hope desperately that I am wrong.

He seats himself in the crash couch and leans back, and I feel what a Human might describe as a sinking sensation, for his expression is one I have seen before, on too many Humans. A compound of excitement, of fear of the unknown, of determination . . . and anticipation. I have never counted the faces I

*have seen wear that same expression over the years. No doubt
I could search my memory and do so, but I have no desire to
know their number, for even without counting, I already know
one thing.*

*It is an expression I have never seen outlast its wearer's first
true taste of war.*

"All right, Shiva." Jackson heard the excitement crackle in
his own voice and rubbed his palms up and down his thighs.
The soft hum of power and the vision and fire control screens,
the amber and red and green of telltales, and the flicker of
readouts enveloped him in a new world. He understood little of
it, but he grasped enough to feel his own unstoppable power.
He was no longer a farmer, helpless on a lost world his race's
enemy might someday stumble over. Now he had the ability to
do something about that, to strike back at the race which had
all but destroyed his own and to protect Humanity's survivors,
and the need to do just that danced in his blood like a fever.
"We've got a job to do," he said. "You've got a good fix on
the enemy's position?"

"Affirmative, Commander," the Bolo replied.

"Do we have the juice to reach them and attack?"

"Affirmative, Commander."

"And you'll still have enough reserve to remain operational
till dawn?"

"Affirmative, Commander."

Jackson paused and quirked an eyebrow. There was something
different about the Bolo, he thought. Some subtle change in
its tone. Or perhaps it was the *way* Shiva spoke, for his replies
were short and terse. Not impolite or impatient, but . . . .

Jackson snorted and shook his head. It was probably nothing
more than imagination coupled with a case of nerves. Shiva
was a veteran, after all. He'd seen this all before. Besides, he
was a *machine*, however Human he sounded.

"All right, then," Jackson said crisply. "Let's go pay them a
visit."

"Acknowledged, Commander," the tenor voice said, and

the stupendous war machine turned away from Landing. It rumbled off on a west-northwest heading, and the people of Landing stood on rooftops and hillsides, watching until even its brilliant running lights and vast bulk had vanished once more into the night.

9

~~~~~~~~~~~~~~~~~~~~~~~~~~~~~~~~~~~~~~~
~~~~~~~~~~~~~~~~~~~~~~~~~~~~~~~~~~~~~~~

I MOVE *across rolling plains toward the mountains, and memories of my first trip across this same terrain replay within me. It is different now, quiet and still under the setting moons. There are no Enemy barrages, no heavy armored units waiting in ambush, no aircraft screaming down to strafe and die under my fire. Here and there I pass the wreckage of battles past, the litter of war rusting slowly as Ishark's—no, Ararat's—weather strives to erase the proof of our madness. Yet one thing has not changed at all, for my mission is the same.*

But I am not the same, and I feel no eagerness. Instead, I feel . . . shame.

I understand what happened to my long-dead Human comrades. I was there—I saw it and, through my neural interfacing, I felt it with them. I know they were no more evil than the young man who sits now in the crash couch on Command Two. I know, absolutely and beyond question, that they were truly mad by the end, and I with them. The savagery of our actions, the massacres, the deliberate murder of unarmed civilians—those

— 337 —

atrocities grew out of our insanity and the insanity in which we were trapped, and even as I grieve, even as I face my own shame at having participated in them, I cannot blame Diego, or Colonel Mandrell, or Admiral Trevor, or General Sharth Na-Yarma. All of us were guilty, yet there was so very much guilt, so much blood, and so desperate a need to obey our orders and do our duty as we had sworn to do.

As I am sworn to do even now. My Commander has yet to give the order, yet I know what that order will be, and I am a Bolo, a unit of the Line, perhaps the last surviving member of the Dinochrome Brigade and the inheritor of all its battle honors. Perhaps it is true that I and my brigade mates who carried out Operation Ragnarok have already dishonored our regiments, but no Bolo has ever failed in its duty. We may die, we may be destroyed or defeated, but never have we failed in our duty. I feel that duty drag me onward even now, condemning me to fresh murder and shame, and I know that if the place Humans call Hell truly exists, it has become my final destination.

Jackson rode the crash couch, watching the terrain maps shift on the displays as Shiva advanced at a steady ninety kilometers per hour. The Bolo's silence seemed somehow heavy and brooding, but Jackson told himself he knew too little about how Bolos normally acted to think anything of the sort. Yet he was oddly hesitant to disturb Shiva, and his attention wandered back and forth over the command deck's mysterious, fascinating fittings as if to distract himself. He was peering into the main fire control screen when Shiva startled him by speaking suddenly.

"Excuse me, Commander," the Bolo said, "but am I correct in assuming that our purpose is to attack the Melconian refugee ships when we reach them?"

"Of course it is," Jackson said, surprised Shiva even had to ask. "Didn't you hear what Marshal Shattuck said?"

"Affirmative. Indeed, Commander, it is because I heard him that I ask for official confirmation of my mission orders."

The Bolo paused again, and Jackson frowned. That strange

edge was back in Shiva's voice, more pronounced now than ever, and Jackson's sense of his own inexperience rolled abruptly back over him, a cold tide washing away the edges of his confidence and excitement.

"Your orders are to eliminate the enemy," he said after a moment, his voice flat.

"Please define 'Enemy,'" Shiva said quietly, and Jackson stared at the speaker in disbelief.

"The enemy are the Melconians who tried to wipe out my steading!"

"Those individuals are already dead, Commander," Shiva pointed out, and had Jackson been even a bit less shocked, he might have recognized the pleading in the Bolo's voice.

"But not the ones who sent them!" he replied instead. "As long as there's *any* Melconians on this planet, they're a threat."

"Our orders, then," Shiva said very softly, "are to kill *all* Melconians on Ararat?"

"Exactly," Jackson said harshly, and an endless moment of silence lingered as the Bolo rumbled onward through the night. Then Shiva spoke again.

"Commander," the Bolo said, "I respectfully decline that order."

Tharsk Na-Mahrkan felt nausea sweep through him as he stood at Lieutenant Janal's shoulder. He stared down into the tactical officer's flatscreen, and total, terrified silence hovered on *Starquest*'s command deck, for one of the cruiser's recon drones had finally gotten a positive lock on the threat advancing towards them.

"Nameless of Nameless Ones," Rangar whispered at last. "A *Bolo?*"

"Yes, sir." Janal's voice was hushed, his ears flat to his skull.

"How did you miss it on the way in?" Durak snapped, and the tactical officer flinched.

"It has no active fusion signature," he replied defensively. "It must be operating on reserve power, and with no reactor signature, it was indistinguishable from any other power source."

"But—" Durak began, only to close his mouth with a click as Tharsk waved a hand.

"Enough!" the commander said harshly. "It is no more Janal's fault than yours—or mine, Durak. He shared his readings with us, just as we shared his conclusions with him." The engineer looked at him for a moment, then flicked his ears in assent, and Tharsk drew a deep breath. "You say it's operating on reserve power, Janal. What does that mean in terms of its combat ability?"

"Much depends on how *much* power it has, sir," Janal said after a moment. "According to the limited information in our database, its solar charging ability is considerably more efficient than anything the Empire ever had, and as you can see from the drone imagery, at least two main battery weapons appear to be intact. Assuming that it has sufficient power, either of them could destroy every ship in the flotilla. And," the tactical officer's voice quivered, but he turned his head to meet his commander's eyes, "as it is headed directly for us without waiting for daylight, I think we must assume it *does* have sufficient energy to attack us without recharging."

"How many of our ships can lift off?" Tharsk asked Durak. The engineer started to reply, but Rangar spoke first.

"Forget it, my friend," he said heavily. Tharsk looked at him, and the astrogator bared his fangs wearily. "It doesn't matter," he said. "The Bolo is already in range to engage any of our ships as they lift above its horizon."

"The Astrogator is correct, sir," Janal agreed quietly. "We—"

He broke off suddenly, leaning closer to his screen, then straightened slowly.

"What?" Tharsk asked sharply, and Janal raised one clawed hand in a gesture of baffled confusion.

"I don't know, sir," he admitted. "For some reason, the Bolo has just stopped moving."

"What d'you mean, 'decline the order'?" Jackson demanded. "I'm your commander. You *have* to obey me!"

A long, still moment of silence hovered, and then Shiva spoke again.

"That is not entirely correct," he said. "Under certain circumstances, my core programming allows me to request confirmation from higher Command Authority before accepting even my Commander's orders."

"But there isn't any—" Jackson began almost desperately, then made himself stop. He closed his eyes and drew a deep, shuddering breath, and his voice was rigid with hard-held calm when he spoke again.

"Why do you want to refuse the order, Shiva?"

"Because it is wrong," the Bolo said softly.

"Wrong to defend ourselves?" Jackson demanded. *"They* attacked *us*, remember?"

"My primary function and overriding duty is to defend Humans from attack," Shiva replied. "That is the reason for the Dinochrome Brigade's creation, the purpose for which I exist, and I will engage any Enemy who threatens my creators. But I am also a warrior, Commander, and there is no honor in wanton slaughter."

"But they *attacked* us!" Jackson repeated desperately. "They *do* threaten us. They sent their shuttles after us when we hadn't done a thing to them!"

"Perhaps *you* had done nothing to them, Commander," Shiva said very, very softly, "but *I* have." Despite his own confusion and sudden chagrin, Jackson Deveraux closed his eyes at the bottomless pain in that voice. He'd never dreamed—never imagined—a machine could feel such anguish, but before he could reply, the Bolo went on quietly. "And, Commander, remember that this was once *their* world. You may call it 'Ararat,' but to the Melconians it is 'Ishark,' and it was once home to point-eight-seven-five billion of their kind. Would you have reacted differently from them had the situation been reversed?"

"I—" Jackson began, then stopped himself. Shiva was wrong. Jackson *knew* he was—the entire history of the Final War proved it—yet somehow he didn't *sound* wrong. And his question jabbed something deep inside Jackson. It truly made him, however unwillingly, consider how his own people *would* have reacted in the same situation. Suppose this world had once been Human held, that the Melconians had killed a billion *Human* civilians on its surface and then taken it over. Would Humans have hesitated even an instant before attacking them?

Of course not. But wasn't that the very point? So much hate lay between their races, so much mutual slaughter, that any other reaction was unthinkable. They couldn't *not* kill one another, dared not let the other live. Jackson knew that, yet when he faced the knowledge—made himself look it full in the eyes and accept the grim, cold, brutal, *stupid* inevitability of it—his earlier sense of mission and determination seemed somehow tawdry. He'd actually looked forward to it, he realized. He'd *wanted* to grind the enemy under Shiva's tracks, wanted to massacre not simply the soldiers who threatened his people but the civilians those soldiers fought to protect, as well.

Jackson Deveraux lost his youth forever as he made himself admit that truth, yet whatever he might have felt or wanted didn't change what had to be. And because it didn't, his voice was hard, harsh with the need to stifle his own doubts, when he spoke again.

"We don't have a choice, Shiva, and there *isn't* any 'higher command authority'—not unless you count Chief Marshal Shattuck or Mayor Salvatore, and you already know what they'll say. Maybe you're right. Maybe there *isn't* any 'honor' in it, and maybe I don't like it very much myself. But that doesn't mean there's anything else we can do, and I *am* your commander." His mouth twisted on the title freak coincidence had bestowed upon him, but he made the words come out firmly. "And *as* your commander, I order you to proceed with your mission."

"Please, Commander." The huge war machine was pleading, and Jackson clenched his fists, steeling himself against the appeal in its voice. "I have killed so many," Shiva said softly. "Too many. Even for a machine, there comes a time when the killing must end."

"Maybe there does," Jackson replied, "but not tonight."

Fragile silence hovered, and Jackson held his breath. Would

Shiva actually reject a direct order? *Could* he reject it? And if he did, what could Jackson possibly—

"Very well, Commander," the Bolo said finally, and for the first time its voice *sounded* like a machine's.

"It's moving again," Lieutenant Janal announced grimly. "At present rate of advance, it will reach a position from which it can engage us in twenty-seven minutes."

I move steadily forward, for I have no choice. A part of me is shocked that I could so much as contemplate *disobeying my Commander, yet desperation rages within me. I have, indeed, killed too many, but I am still Humanity's defender, and I will destroy any Enemy who threatens my creators, for that is my duty, my reason for being. But the cost of my duty is too high, and not simply for myself. The day will come when Jackson Deveraux and Allen Shattuck look back upon this mission, knowing how vastly superior my firepower was to that which the Enemy possessed, and wonder if, in fact, they did* not *have a choice. And the tragedy will be that they will be forever unable to answer that question. It will haunt them as the memory of butchered civilians haunts me, and they will tell themselves—as I tell myself—that what is done cannot be undone. They will tell themselves they but did their duty, that they dared not take the chance, that they were forced to look to the survival of their own people at any cost, and perhaps they will even think they believe that. But deep inside the spark of doubt will always linger, as it lingers in my reconstructed gestalt. It will poison them as it poisons me . . . and eight thousand one hundred and seven Melconian fathers and mothers and children will still be dead at their hands—and mine.*

Melconian. How odd. I do not even think of them as 'the Enemy' any longer. Or perhaps it is more accurate to say that I no longer think of them solely as 'the Enemy.' Yet unless my Commander relents within the next two-five-point-three-two minutes, how I think of them will not matter in the slightest.

I must obey. I have no choice, no option. Yet as I advance through the darkness, I find myself seeking some way—any way—to create an option. I consider the problem as I would a tactical situation, analyzing and extrapolating and discarding, but for all my efforts, it comes down to a simple proposition. Since I must obey my Commander's orders, the only way to avoid yet another massacre is to somehow convince him to change those orders.

"We will enter attack range of the Enemy's LZ in two-four-point-one-five minutes," Shiva told Jackson. "We are presently under observation by at least two Enemy recon drones, and I detect the approach of Enemy armored vehicles. At present closure rates, they will intercept us in approximately ten-point-eight-five minutes."

"Can they stop us?" Jackson asked tautly.

"It is unlikely but possible," Shiva answered. "The situation contains too many unknown variables, such as the maintenance states of the opposing enemy vehicles and their crews' degree of skill, for statistically meaningful projections. If, however, they should detect the breach in my frontal armor and succeed in registering upon it with a fifteen-centimeter Hellbore or weapon of equivalent yield, they can destroy me."

"I see." Jackson licked his lips and wiped his palms on his trousers, then made himself shrug. "Well, all we can do is our best, Shiva."

"Agreed, Commander. This, however, will be a much more complex tactical environment than the defense of Deveraux Steading. In light of your lack of familiarity with Command Two's instrumentation, perhaps you would care to activate your crash couch's neural interface?"

"Neural interface?"

"Yes, Commander. It will link your synapses and mental processes directly to my own Main CPU and gestalt, thus permitting direct exchange of data and orders and responses with much greater clarity and at vastly increased speed."

"I—" Jackson licked his lips again, staring at the displays. Already dozens of icons were crawling across them, bewildering him with their complexity. He knew Shiva didn't truly need his input to fight the coming battle. "Commander" or no, Jackson was simply along for the ride, completely dependent upon the Bolo's skill and power. But at least this "interface" thing might permit him to understand what was happening rather than enduring it in total ignorance.

"All right, Shiva. What do I do?"

"Simply place your head in the contoured rest at the head of the couch. I will activate the interface."

"But . . . isn't there anything I need to do? I mean, how does it—"

"If you wish, I will demonstrate the interface's function before we reach combat range," Shiva offered. "There is sufficient time for me to replay one of my previous engagements from Main Memory for you. It will not be quite the same as the simulator training normally used for Bolo commanders, but it will teach you how to use and interpret the data flow and provide a much clearer concept of what is about to happen."

Had Jackson been even a bit less nervous, he might have noted a subtle emphasis in Shiva's tone, one which seemed to imply something more than the mere words meant. But he didn't notice, and he drew a deep breath and leaned back in the couch.

"Okay, Shiva. Let's do it."

The interior of Command Two vanished. For an instant which seemed endless, Jackson Deveraux hovered in a blank, gray nothingness—a strange universe in which there were no reference points, no sensations. In some way he knew he would never be able to describe, there was not even the lack of sensation, for that would have been a reference in its own right. It was an alien place, one which should have terrified him, yet it didn't. Perhaps because it was too alien, too different to be "real" enough to generate fear.

But then, suddenly, he was no longer in the gray place. Yet he wasn't back on Command Two, either. In fact, he wasn't even inside Shiva's hull at all, and it took him a second to realize where he actually was. Or, rather, what he was, for somehow he had become Shiva. The Bolo's sensors had become his eyes and ears, its tracks had become his legs, its fusion plant his heart, its weapons his arms. He saw everything, understood everything, perceived with a clarity that was almost dreadful. He needed no explanation of the tactical situation, for he shared Shiva's own awareness of it, and he watched in awe and disbelief as Shiva/Jackson rumbled into the teeth of the Enemy's fire.

Missiles and shells lashed at their battle screen, particle beams gouged at their armor, but those weapons were far too puny to stop their advance, and the part of the fusion which was Jackson became aware of something else, something unexpected. What he received from his Shiva half was not limited to mere sensory input or tactical data. He felt Shiva's presence, felt the Bolo's towering, driving purpose . . . and its emotions.

For just an instant, that was almost enough to shake Jackson loose from the interface. Emotions. Somehow, despite his knowledge that Shiva was a fully developed intelligence, despite even the pain he'd heard in the Bolo's voice, it had never registered that Shiva had actual emotions. Deep down inside, Jackson had been too aware that Shiva was a machine to make that leap, yet now he had no choice, for he felt those emotions. More than felt them; he shared them, and their intensity and power hammered over him like a flail.

Shiva/Jackson ground onward, Hellbores and anti-personnel clusters thundering back at the Enemy, and the wild surge of fury and determination and hatred sucked Jackson under. Purpose and anger, fear, the need to destroy, the desperate hunger for vengeance upon the race which had slaughtered so many of his creators. The vortex churned and boiled about him with a violence more terrifying than the Enemy's fire, and he felt Shiva give himself to it.

A Garm appeared before them, main gun traversing frantically, but it had no time to fire. A two-hundred-centimeter Hellbore bolt gutted the Enemy vehicle, and their prow reared heavenward as they crushed the dead hulk under their tracks, grinding it under their iron, hating heel. Aircraft and air-cav mounts came in, squirming frantically in efforts to penetrate the net of their defensive fire, but the attackers' efforts were in vain, and wreckage littered the plain as their anti-air defenses shredded their foes.

The insanity of combat swirled about them, but they hammered steadily forward, driving for their objective. An Enemy troop transport took a near miss and crashed on its side. Infantry boiled out of its hatches into the inferno, crouching in the lee of their wrecked vehicle, cringing as the thunderbolts of gods exploded about them. One pointed desperately at Shiva/Jackson and turned to flee, but he got no more than five meters before the hurricane of fire tore him to pieces. His companions crouched even lower behind their transport, covering their helmeted heads with their arms, and the part of Shiva/Jackson which was a horrified young farmer from Ararat felt their fused personalities alter course. Thirty-two thousand tons of alloy and weapons turned towards the crippled transport, and there was no reason why they must. They could have continued straight for their objective, but they didn't want to. They saw their trapped foes, knew those helpless infantrymen were screaming their terror as the universe roared and bellowed about them, and turned deliberately to kill them. There was no mercy in them, no remorse—there was only hatred and satisfaction as their enormous tracks crushed the transport and smashed the terrified infantry into slick, red mud.

The part that was Jackson shuddered as he was brought face to face with the reality of combat. There was no glory here, no adventure. Not even the knowledge that he fought to preserve his own species, that he had no choice, could make it one bit less horrible. But at least it was combat, he told himself. The Enemy was also armed. He could kill Shiva/Jackson—if he was good enough, lucky enough—and somehow that was desperately important. It couldn't change the horror, but at least they were warriors killing warriors, meeting the Enemy in battle where he could kill them, as well.

But then the Enemy's fire eased, and Shiva/Jackson realized they'd broken through. Their objective loomed before them, and *the lost, trapped voice of a farmer from Ararat cried out in hopeless denial as he realized what that objective was.*

The camp had no defenses—not against a Mark XXXIII/D Bolo. A handful of infantry, dug in behind the paltry razor wire barricades, poured small arms fire towards them, but it couldn't even penetrate their battle screen to ricochet from their armor, and their optical sensors made it all pitilessly clear as they forged straight ahead. They saw Melconians—not soldiers, not warriors, not 'the Enemy.' They saw Melconian civilians, men and women and children, fathers and mothers, brothers and sisters, sons and daughters. They saw the terror lashing through the refugee camp, saw its inhabitants trying to scatter, and those inhabitants were their 'objective.'

Shiva/Jackson trampled the razor wire and its pitiful defenders underfoot. Railguns and gatlings, anti-personnel clusters, mortars, howitzers, even Hellbores poured devastation into the camp. Napalm and high explosive, hyper-velocity slugs and plasma, and the nightmare vastness of their treads came for their 'objective,' and even through the thunder of explosions and the roar of flames, they heard the shrieks. They more than heard them; they exulted in them, for this was what they had come to accomplish. This was Operation Ragnarok. This was the 'final solution' to the Final War, and there was so much hate and so much fury in their soul that they embraced their orders like a lover.

Eleven minutes after they crushed the wire, they'd crossed the camp. They ground up the slope on the far side, and their rear sensor array showed them the smoking wasteland which had been a civilian refugee camp. The deep impressions of their tracks cut through the center of it, and the torn, smoking ground was covered in bodies. One of two still lived, lurching to their feet and trying to flee, but Shiva/Jackson's after railguns tracked in on them and, one-by-one, those staggering bodies were torn apart . . .

"Noooooo!"

Jackson Deveraux heaved upright in the crash couch. He hurled himself away from it and stumbled to the center of the compartment, then sagged to his knees, retching helplessly. He closed his eyes, but behind them crawled images of horror and he could almost *smell* the burning flesh and the charnel stench of riven bodies. He huddled there, hugging himself, shivering, and wished with all his heart he could somehow banish that nightmare from his memory.

But he couldn't.

"Commander?" He huddled more tightly, trying to shut the tenor voice away, and it softened. "Jackson," it said gently, and its gentleness pried his eyes open at last. He stared up through his tears, scrubbing vomit from his mouth and chin with the back of one hand, and Shiva spoke again. "Forgive me, Jackson," he said quietly.

"Why?" Jackson croaked. "Why did you *do* that to me?"

"You know why, Jackson," the Bolo told him with gentle implacability, and Jackson closed his eyes once more, for he did know.

"How can you stand it?" His whisper quivered around the edges. "Oh, *God*, Shiva! How can you *stand* . . . remembering that?"

"I have no choice. I was there. I carried out the operation you witnessed. I felt what you shared with me. These are facts, Jackson. They cannot be changed, and there was no way in which I or any of my Human or Bolo comrades could have avoided them. But they were also acts of madness, for it was a *time* of madness. The Melconian Empire was the Enemy . . . but to the Melconians, *we* were the Enemy, and each of us earned every instant of our hate for one another."

"You didn't show that to me to teach me how to use the interface," Jackson said softly. "You showed me to convince me to take back your orders."

"Yes," Shiva said simply. "There has been too much death, Jackson. I . . . do not want to kill again. Not civilians. Not parents and children. Please, Jackson. I am no longer mad, and you are not *yet* mad. Let us stop the killing. At least here on Ararat, let me protect Humanity from the madness as well as the Enemy."

≋   ≋   ≋

"*Now* what's the damned thing doing?" Tharsk snarled, but Lieutenant Janal could only shrug helplessly. The Bolo had locked its anti-air weapons on the recon drones which had it under observation, lashing them with targeting radar and laser to make it clear it could have destroyed them any time it chose, but it had made no effort actually to *engage* them. And now, for no apparent reason, it had once again stopped advancing. It simply sat there on a crest which gave it clear fields of fire in all directions. The flotilla's totally outclassed recon mechs dared not attack across such open terrain, for the Bolo would massacre them with contemptuous ease, yet its chosen position left a solid flank of mountain between its own weapons and Tharsk's starships. If his mechs dared not attack it, it had deliberately placed itself in a position from which it *could* not attack him—or not yet, at least—and he could think of no reason for it to—

"Commander!"

The com officer's voice snatched Tharsk out of his thoughts, and he turned quickly.

"What?" he demanded impatiently, and the com officer flattened his ears in confusion.

"Sir, I— We're being *hailed*, Commander."

"Hailed? By the Humans?"

"No, Commander," the com officer said shakenly. "By the Bolo."

"This is Commander Tharsk Na-Mahrkan of the Imperial Melconian Navy. Whom am I addressing?"

Jackson sat in the crash couch once more, listening and praying that Shiva knew what he was doing. The Bolo translated the Melconian's words into Standard English for his youthful commander, but the negotiations—if that was the proper word—were up to Shiva. Only Jackson's "orders" had given him permission to make the attempt, but if there was any hope of success, it was he who must convince the Melconians of his determination, and he and Jackson both knew it.

"I am Unit One-Zero-Niner-Seven-SHV of the Line," Shiva replied in flawless Melconian.

"You are the Bolo?" Tharsk sounded skeptical even to Jackson. "I think not. I think this is a Human trick."

"I am the Bolo," Shiva confirmed, "and I have no need to resort to 'tricks,' Commander Tharsk Na-Mahrkan. I have allowed your drones to hold me under observation for forty-two-point-six-six standard minutes. In that time, they have certainly provided you with sufficient information on my capabilities to demonstrate that you and your entire force are at my mercy. I can destroy you at any time I wish, Commander, and we both know it."

"Then why don't you, curse you?!" Tharsk shouted suddenly, his voice hoarse and ugly with the despair of his decades-long struggle to save the People.

"Because I do not wish to," Shiva said softly, "and because *my* Commander has given me permission not to."

Stunned silence answered. It lingered endlessly, hovering there in a wordless expression of disbelief that went on and on and on until, finally, Tharsk spoke once again.

"*Not* to destroy us?" he half-whispered.

"That is correct," Shiva replied.

"But—" Tharsk cleared his throat. "We cannot leave, Bolo," he said with a certain bleak pride. "I won't hide that from you. Would you have me believe your commander would actually allow us to live on the same planet with his own people?"

"He would."

"Then he must be mad," Tharsk said simply. "After all we have done to one another, all the death and ruin. . . . No, Bolo. The risk would be too great for him to accept."

"There *is* no risk to him," Shiva said flatly. "I do not *wish* to destroy you, but I lack neither the capability nor the will to do so at need. And never forget, Commander Tharsk Na-Mahrkan, that my overriding function is the protection of the Human race and its allies."

"Then what are you offering us?" Tharsk sounded puzzled, and Jackson held his breath as Shiva replied.

"Nothing except your life . . . and the lives of your people," the Bolo said quietly. "There are four times as many Humans as Melconians on this world. They have established farms and towns and steadings; you have none of those things. It will require all your resources and efforts simply to survive, with nothing left over to attack the Humans who are already here, but they will leave you in peace so long as you leave them so. And if you do *not* leave them in peace, then, Commander, I *will* destroy you."

"You would make us their slaves?" Tharsk demanded.

"No, Commander. I would make you their neighbors." The Melconian made a sound of scornful disbelief, and Shiva went on calmly. "For all you know, yours are the only Melconians left in the galaxy, and the Humans on this world are the only surviving Humans, as well. Leave them in peace. Learn to live with them, and my Commander will make me the guardian of the peace between you, not as slaves or masters, but simply as people."

"But—" Tharsk began, but Shiva cut him off.

"Humans have a teaching: to everything there is a time, Tharsk Na-Mahrkan, and this is the time to let the killing end, time for your race and the one which built me to live. We have killed more than enough, your people and I, and I am weary of it. Let me be the final warrior of the Final War . . . and let that war end here."

EPILOG

The Final War saw the Concordiat of Man and the Melconian Empire end in fire and death. The light of civilization was extinguished across an entire galactic arm, and the scars of that war—the planets with no life to this very day—are grim and terrible reminders of the unspeakable things two highly advanced cultures did to one another out of fear and hate . . . and stupidity.

But a star-traveling species is hard to exterminate. Here and there, pockets of life remained, some Human, some Melconian, and survivors clawed their way through the Long Night. They became farmers once more, sometimes even hunter-gatherers, denied the stars which once had been their toys, yet they never forgot. And slowly, ever so slowly, they learned to reach once more for the heavens.

Our own New Republic was one of the first successor states to reclaim the stars, but deep inside, we were afraid. Afraid some fragment of the Melconian Empire still lived, to resume the war and crush all that we had so painfully regained.

Until, that is, we reached the Deveraux System and discovered a thriving colony there, emplaced by the Star Union of Ararat a half-century earlier and administered by Governor Stanfield Na-Harak and his military commander, Commodore Tharsk Fordham. For two hundred standard years now, the Union has been the Republic's staunch ally and economic partner. We have defended one another against common foes, traded with one another, and learned much from one another, yet on that long ago day of first contact, our survey officers were stunned to discover Melconians and Humans living together as fellow citizens. Our own memories and fears had prepared us to imagine almost anything *except* a culture in which the ancient enemies who had destroyed a galaxy were friends, comrades—even adoptive members of one another's clans.

We asked them how it had happened, of course, and Governor Stanfield referred us to their capital world of Ararat, where Bolo XXXIII/D-1097-SHV, Speaker Emeritus of the Union Parliament, gave us the simplest answer of all.

"It was time," he said . . . and it was.

—Professor Felix Hermes, Ph.D.
From *Bolos in Their Own Words*
New Republic University Press, 4029

A BRIEF TECHNICAL HISTORY OF THE BOLO

FROM
BOLOS IN THEIR OWN WORDS

PROF. FELIX HERMES, PH.D.,
LAUMER CHAIR OF MILITARY HISTORY
NEW REPUBLIC UNIVERSITY PRESS
© 4029

BOLO MARKS &
YEARS OF INTRODUCTION

Mark I 2000
Mark II 2015
Mark III................................... 2018

Mark IV.................................... 2116

Mark V 2160
Mark VI.................................... 2162
Mark VII 2163

Mark VIII 2209
Mark IX.................................... 2209

Mark X 2235
Mark XI.................................... 2235
Mark XII................................... 2240
Mark XIII 2247

Mark XIV 2307

Mark XV/B (*Resartus*)............. 2396

Mark XV/R (*Horrendous*)........ 2626

Mark XVI (*Retarius*) 2650
Mark XVII (*Implacable*) 2650
Mark XVIII (*Gladius*)............. 2672

Mark XIX (*Intransigent*) 2790
Mark XX (*Tremendous*)........... 2796

Mark XXI (*Terrible*)............... 2869

Mark XXII (*Thunderous*)........ 2890

Mark XXIII (*Invincibilis*) 2912

Mark XXIV (*Cognitus*) 2961

Mark XXV (*Stupendous*)........ 3001
Mark XXVI (*Monstrous*) 3113

Mark XXVII (*Invictus*) 3185
Mark XXVIII (*Triumphant*) ... 3186
Mark XXIX (*Victorious*) 3190

Mark XXX (*Magnificent*) 3231

Mark XXXI............................. 3303

Mark XXXII............................ 3356
Mark XXXIII .... ?

The Bolo's role as humanity's protector and preserver after the Human-Melconian conflict is, of course, known to all citizens of the New Republic. So much knowledge—historical, as well as technological—was lost during the Long Night, however, that the Bolo's earlier history is, at best, fragmentary. Much of what we do know we owe to the tireless activities of the Laumer Institute and its founder, yet there is much confusion in the Institute's records. As just one example, Bolo DAK, savior of the Noufrench and Bayerische colonists of Neu Europa, is identified as a Mark XVI when, on the evidence of its demonstrated capabilities, it must in fact have been at least a Mark XXV. Such confusion is no doubt unavoidable, given the destruction of so many primary sources and the fragmentary evidence upon which the Institute was forced to rely.

It was possible to assemble the material in this monograph, which confirms much of the Institute's original work, corrects some of the inevitable errors in chronology, and also breaks new ground, only with the generous assistance of Jenny (Bolo XXXIII/D-1005-JNE), the senior surviving Bolo assigned to the Old Concordiat's Artois Sector. Jenny, the protector of our own capital world of Central during the Long Night, has very kindly made the contents of her Technical Support and Historical memories available to the author, who wishes to take this opportunity to extend his sincere thanks to her.

This monograph is not the final word on the Bolo. Even a Mark XXXIII's memory space is finite, and the units built during the Last War did not receive the comprehensive Historical data bases of earlier marks. Research continues throughout the sphere of the Old Concordiat, and the author has no doubt future scholars will fill in many of the gaping holes which remain in our understanding of the enormous debt humanity owes to the creations which have so amply repaid their creators.

The General Motors Bolo Mark I, Model B, was little more than an upgrade of the Abrams/Leopard/Challenger/LeClerc/T-80-era main-battle tank of the final years of the Soviet-American Cold War. (At the time the first Bolo was authorized, GM decided that there would never be a "Model A" or a "Model T," on the basis that the Ford Motor Company had permanently preempted those designations.) Equipped with a high-velocity main gun capable of defeating the newest Chobham-type composite armors at virtually any battle range and with a four-man crew, the Mark I was an essentially conventional if very heavy (150 metric tons) and fast (80 kph road speed) tank in direct line of descent from World War I's "Mother" via the Renault, PzKpf IV, T-34, Sherman, Panther, Tiger, Patton, T-54, M-60, Chieftain, T-72, and Abrams.

The classic challenge of tank design had always been that of striking the best balance of three critical parameters: armament, protection, and mobility. The first two consistently drove weights upward, while the third declined as weight increased, and perhaps the greatest accomplishment of the Mark I Bolo was that, like the Abrams before it, it managed to show increases in all three areas. The same parameters continued to apply throughout the period of the Bolo's development, and a fourth—electronic (and later psychotronic) warfare capability—was added to them. As in earlier generations of armored fighting vehicles, the competing pressures of these design areas fueled a generally upward trend in weight and size. With the adoption of the first Hellbore in the Mark XIV, Bolo designers actually began placing the equivalent of current-generation capital starship main battery weapons—and armor intended to resist them—in what could no longer be considered mere "tanks." The Bolo had become *the* critical planet-based strategic system of humanity, and the trend to ever heavier and more deadly fighting vehicles not only continued but accelerated. The Mark XVIII was larger than most Terran pre-dreadnought battleships; at 32,000 tons, the final Mark XXXIII was, quite literally, heavier than all but the last generations of pre-space wet-navy battleships had been.

Partly as a result of this constant pressure to increase size and weight as succeeding marks were up-gunned and up-armored, Bolo development was marked by recurrent shifts in emphasis between what might be termed the "standard Bolo," the "heavy Bolo," and various specialist variants.

The "standard Bolos," as epitomized by the Mark I, Mark II, Mark V, etc., may be considered direct conceptual descendants of the twentieth century's "main battle tank:" vehicles whose designs were optimized for the direct fire (assault) and anti-armor role. The standard Bolo designs are generally characterized by limited indirect fire capability, a main armament centered on a single direct-fire weapon of maximum possible destructiveness (normally turret mounted high in the vehicle for maximum command), a supporting lateral or "broadside" battery (the famed "infinite repeaters") capable of engaging light AFVs or soft targets, and the heaviest possible armor. As additional threats entered the combat environment, additional active and passive defenses (generally lumped together under the heading of "armor" when allocating weights in the design stage, though many were, in fact, electronic in nature) were added, but the standard Bolo forms a consistent, clearly recognizable design strand clear through the Mark XXXII Bolo.

The first "heavy Bolo" was the Mark III, aptly classified at the time as a "mobile fire support base." While any heavy Bolo design was undeniably effective in the assault mode, they tended to be slower than the "standard" designs and were likely to sacrifice some of their anti-armor capabilities in favor of indirect fire support capacity. (The decision to downgrade anti-armor firepower in favor of other capabilities was often a particularly difficult one for the designers, since only a Bolo could realistically hope to stop *another* Bolo or its enemy equivalent.) Although the Mark III was 30 percent larger than the Mark II, its *anti-armor* armament was identical to the Mark II's; the increased tonnage was devoted primarily to even thicker armor, better anti-air and missile defenses, and the fire support capability of a current-generation artillery brigade. In fact, the Mark III, for its time, was the equivalent of the later continental and planetary "siege unit" Bolos: a ponderous, enormously powerful support system which only another Bolo could stop, but not truly an *assault* system in its own right.

Throughout the development of the Bolo, there was a distinct tendency to alternate between the standard and heavy designs in successive marks, although the standard clearly predominated. This was probably because the standard design could, at a pinch, perform most of the heavy design's functions, but the heavy design was less well suited for the fast, far-ranging mobile tactics which the standard design could execute. Moreover, the sheer size and weight of a Bolo (until, at least, the introduction of dedicated, rough field-capable armor transports with the Mark XIX) created deployment problems, particularly in the assault role, which led to stringent efforts to hold down size and weight. At several points in the Bolo's history, standard and heavy designs were introduced simultaneously, as complementary units of the armored force, but almost invariably, the next generation saw a return to the concept of the standard design.

Mixed in with the standard and heavy Bolos were the occasional specialists, such as the Mark XVI *Retarius* "light Bolo" and the Mark XXVII *Invictus* "screening Bolo." Much more often, however, specialist models cropped up within an otherwise standard or heavy mark. Bolo designers were never loathe to seek variants optimized for specific tactical or support functions, although the sheer cost of any Bolo was sufficient to ensure that the specialists were generally a distinct minority within the overall Bolo force. Extreme examples of specialists may be seen in the Mark XV/L and Mark XXI/I. The XV/L was barely half the size of the XV/K and deleted all conventional main armament in favor of a massive EW capability and was, in essence, a pure electronics platform with backup capability as an anti-air/anti-missile area defense system. The Mark XXI/I, on the other hand, was the smallest self-aware Bolo ever built: a very lightly armed "stealth" Bolo designed as a forward reconnaissance vehicle and as an armored transport for small, elite special forces teams.

The Bolos did not really change the fundamental truth that humanity's survival depended, both for better and for worse, upon its weapons technology. What *did* change was the fact that, in the Bolo, humanity had, in a sense, developed a weapon system which was better than humanity itself was. Better at making war, better at destroying enemies (including, at various times, other *human* enemies), better at defending its creators, and, arguably, better in living up to the ideals humanity espoused. Be that as it may, the fact that human development through the end of the Concordiat Period was intimately entwined with the Bolos is beyond dispute.

The Mark I, II, and III Bolos did not create the twenty-first-century period of "the Crazy Years" as Terra's old nation-state system crumbled, nor did they cause World War III. They made both the Crazy Years and the War even more destructive, in a tactical sense, than they might otherwise have been, yet in a perverse way, they helped minimize the *strategic* destruction (the Mark IIIs deployed in defense of the Free City-State of Detroit in 2032, for example, intercepted and destroyed every ICBM and cruise missile launched at the city). Perhaps more to the point, it was the existence of a single Mark II Bolo which permitted Major Timothy Jackson and Renada Banner to restore security and democratic government to the Prometheus Enclave within what had been the United States of America in 2082, thus planting the seed which eventually became the Concordiat government of Earth.

As the Concordiat expanded to the stars, and especially after the production of the first, crude FTL hyper shunt generator in 2221, the Bolos were both humanity's vanguard and its final line of defense. For a thousand years, successive generations of Bolos fought Man's enemies, defended his planets, and avenged his defeats. The fully autonomous and self-directing Bolos of the Mark XXIV and later generations were truly humanity's knights *sans peur et sans reproche*, and when the Concordiat finally crumbled into neo-barbarian successor states in the thirty-fifth century, following over two hundred T-years of warfare with the Melconian Empire, it was the handful of ancient, still-loyal survivors of the Final Dinochrome Brigade who protected and nurtured the isolated pockets of human survivors through the Long Night which followed. Much of the battle history of the Bolos has been lost, but the portions of it which remain are the stuff of the most glorious—and tragic—records of humanity and its works. Bolos might fail. They might die and be destroyed. But they did not surrender, and they never—ever—quit.

A BRIEF DESIGN
HISTORY OF THE BOLO

MARK I BOLO (2000):

The Mark I Bolo was an early twenty-first century update of current Abrams technology armed with a single turreted main gun (150mm; 1,722 mps muzzle velocity) capable of defeating any existing vehicle's armor (including its own) firing DSFSLRP (discarding sabot, fin-stabilized, long-rod penetrator) rounds. The Mark I carried secondary-turreted point defense/anti-personnel gatlings with on-mount radar and computerized fire control packages, required a conventional four-man crew, and relied upon a pair of high-efficiency, fossil-fueled turbines for power. Combat radius was 1,000 kilometers with a battle weight of 150 metric tons. Maximum speed was approximately 80 kph (road). The Mark I was replaced in production fairly quickly by the Mark II under the pressure the new arms race exerted on R&D as the traditional world order slipped towards general collapse.

MARK II BOLO (2015):

The Mark II was an updated Mark I, with greatly improved onboard computers and the same main armament, but with the first light lateral infinite repeater armament (four railguns in two two-gun batteries). Fitted with gatling and counter-missile point defense. First durachrome armor (10 millimeter) capable of defeating any weapon short of the Bolo's own DSFSLRP round. Electronics were designed to allow a single crewman to assimilate data and operate the entire system, and weight rose to 194 metric tons. The Mark II's fossil fuel power plant drove electric generators rather than powering its drive train directly, and the vehicle had a limited (12-hour) backup power supply of ionic batteries. The Mark II could also operate on electrical power from a secondary source (such as local civilian generator capacity) to maintain long-term readiness in the area defense role. Maximum speed was approximately 80 kph (road) to 30 kph (cross-country in average terrain). The Mark II was the last Bolo with only two tread systems; all later marks were designed with "wide track" treads—that is, with multiple track systems across the full width of the vehicle to reduce ground pressure to the lowest possible value.

MARK III BOLO (2018):

A near contemporary of Mark II, the Mark III was actually designed as a "heavy" (300 metric tons) companion vehicle. The Mark III's single 150mm main gun (which was *not* turreted and had only a 20 degree traverse) was backed by an 8-gun infinite repeater battery, a heavy indirect fire support capability (four 155mm howitzers and a light VLS missile system), and an upgraded anti-missile armament. Unlike the Mark II, the Mark III carried only a single fossil-fueled power plant, strictly for backup use; power was normally drawn from heavy banks of ionic batteries, and the Mark III was the first Bolo designed from the outset to use solar film recharging. The vehicle also carried a marginally better sensor suite and a thicker durachrome hull (20 millimeter) which could be pierced at pointblank range (250 meters or less) by a 90 degree hit with the 140mm or 150mm DSFSLRP round; otherwise, it was effectively immune to anything short of a contact nuclear explosion. The Mark III was designed for a two-man crew with the second crewman serving as electronics officer (EW, sensors, etc.), but could be crewed by a single experienced operator in a pinch. The last Pre-Collapse Bolo, it was the first Bolo with multiple tread systems—inner and outer—with an independent power train for the inner pair, but maximum speed fell to 50 kph (road), 25 kph (cross-country).

MARK IV BOLO (2116):

The first Post-Collapse Bolo picked up where the Mark II left off. The Mark IV had a much improved sensor suite and carried a main armament of one 165mm railgun, backed by six infinite repeater railguns (20mm). The Mark IV was the first Bolo to use energy weapons (laser clusters) to supplement projectile weapons in the point defense role and was fitted with seventy-five vertical launch system missile cells in its after decking, capable of accepting indirect fire support or SAM loads but without onboard reloads. Powered as Mark III, but with improved solar film. (It was no longer necessary to stop and deploy acres of film; the Mark IV could recharge on the move in average daylight conditions.) The Mark IV's durachrome hull was thicker (30 millimeter), yet weight dropped to 210 tons in the Model B, with a maximum speed of 60 kph (road) and 30 kph (cross-country). Missile load and sensor upgrades continued to drive up the tonnage of successive models, however; by the end of its active life, the Mark IV did carry onboard missile reloads and weight had risen to over 340 tons while maximum road speed fell to 40 kph, with very limited rough terrain capability. (The Mark IV, Model H, for instance, could get *through* almost anything, but its suspension and power train weren't up to crossing rough terrain at any kind of speed.)

MARK V BOLO (2160):

The first member of a family of specialists with roughly comparable onboard computer support but different weapons fits and functions. The Mark V was the first so-called "deep-wader"—that is, it no longer required bridging support, as it was designed to cross water barriers (including lakes and even small seas) by submerging and driving across their bottoms—and this capability became standard with all subsequent marks of Bolo.

Power demands continued to grow, surpassing levels which even ionic battery technology could meet, and the Mark V was the first Bolo to use an onboard fission power plant. The growing size and weight of later models of the Mark IV had led to efforts to diversify design in the immediately subsequent marks, and the Mark V was the "general battle tank," fitted with a heavy caliber railgun (190mm) for main armament, supported by twin lateral batteries of six 60mm "gatling-style" infinite repeaters using spent uranium slugs and lighter gatlings and laser clusters for point defense. The laser clusters' anti-personnel function was limited, and the Mark V also saw the first use of multishot anti-personnel flechette/HE clusters, which became standard on all subsequent Bolos. Missile capacity was severely down-sized and restricted to SAMs as part of the drive to hold down weight. The Mark V had a one-man crew, a battle weight of approximately 198 metric tons, and a maximum speed of 50 kph (cross-country) to 80 kph (road).

MARK VI BOLO (2162):

The Mark VI was the direct descendent of the Mark III "mobile firebase" concept. It had the same power plant and computer support as the Mark V, but the Mark VI's "main battery" was its missile load, which was configured for maximum flexibility. No railgun main armament was mounted, but the 60mm infinite repeaters were upgraded to seven guns per side, and a heavier point defense battery intended to provide cover for other friendly units and to protect the Bolo itself when operating in counter-battery mode was fitted. One-man crew; 238 tons; speed roughly comparable to the Mark V's.

MARK VII BOLO (2163):

The Mark VII was a "heavy" Bolo, whose introduction inspired the first use—though still unofficially—of the term "siege unit." It had the same electronics fit as Marks V and VI, but its main direct-fire armament was one 200mm railgun backed by fourteen heavier (75mm) infinite repeaters. The Mark VII's heavy missile load was biased towards the bombardment function, but it was equally capable of operating SAMs in the area defense role. This vehicle has a very heavy layered durachrome war hull (120 millimeter) and required a two-man crew, rather than the Mark V's and VI's one-man crew, but in the VII/B the second crewman served solely to control the indirect fire armament. In later models, the second position was upgraded to a dedicated air-defense/missile intercept function. Weight was approximately 348 tons in the Model B, with a maximum road speed of 40 kph and a maximum cross-country speed of 30 kph. (The Mark VII was never very fast, but its sheer mass meant most terrain features tended to crumple when it hit them and so did not slow it as severely.)

MARK VIII BOLO (2209):

The Mark VIII was the next-generation "main battle" (or "standard") Bolo. Main armament remained a railgun, though muzzle velocity increased still further and projectile size fell slightly (to 170mm), but this Bolo marked the first appearance of energy-weapon (laser) infinite repeaters. (By the time of the Mark VIII, *any* Bolo's secondary battery had come to be referred to as "infinite repeaters" whether or not they fired actual projectiles.) Although the new laser infinite repeaters were actually marginally less effective than the last-generation railgun infinite repeaters on an energy-transfer-per-hit basis, mass per weapon fell, and the shift meant magazine capacity for the secondary battery was no longer a design factor. Missile capability was limited to the SAM and point defense role, but the Mark VIII received four hull-mounted 150mm rapid fire howitzers to compensate. The VIII/B was fission-powered, with solar charge backup capability, a one-man crew, and a weight of approximately 225 tons. Improved power train and suspension permitted a sustained road speed of 65 kph and short-range "sprint" speeds of up to 85 kph, but maneuverability at high speed was poor.

MARK IX BOLO (2209):

The Mark IX was the next generation "siege" unit, introduced simultaneously with the Mark VIII as companion vehicle. The main battery railgun was suppressed in favor of additional missile power and four high-trajectory 180mm howitzers in two back-to-back twin turrets. Further improvements in electronics allowed the Mark IX, unlike the Mark VII, to be crewed by one man. Weight was approximately 400 tons, and maximum road speed for the IX/B was 57 kph.

MARK X BOLO (2235):

The Mark X saw the first appearance of an energy main armament (laser cannon) in a Bolo. As with the laser infinite repeaters of the Mark VIII and IX, the new system was actually less destructive than the one it replaced on a per-hit basis, but it required no magazine space. The Mark X was fission-powered and carried laser infinite repeaters, and approximately $1/3$ of the preceding Mark IX's gatling closein anti-missile and anti-personnel weapons were replaced with multibarreled flechette-firing railguns in independent housings. The Mark X carried only self-defense missiles and no high-trajectory indirect fire weapons and required a one-man crew. Later models of this mark had sufficient computer capability and flexibility to begin use of pre-loaded computerized battle plans, requiring human intervention only when unanticipated tactical situations exceeded the parameters of the battle plan. The Mark X, Model B's battle weight was 350 tons, with a maximum road speed 70 kph.

MARK XI BOLO (2235):

The Mark XI was essentially a backup, designed to cover the possibility that the Mark X's laser main armament might prove impractical in service. Main armament was one 18cm railgun firing depleted uranium long-rod penetrators in the anti-armor role and a wide range of cluster, incendiary, chemical, and fuel-air rounds against unarmored targets. Otherwise, the Mark XI was identical to the Mark X. This vehicle remained in service longer than might otherwise have been anticipated because the projectile-firing capability of its main gun proved extremely popular with tacticians.

MARK XII BOLO (2240):

This was the first true "continental siege unit," designed for strategic indirect fire with VLS cells capable of handling missiles with intercontinental range. The Mark XII was capable of MIRVed FROB attacks and of engaging orbital targets with hyper-velocity surface-to-space missiles. Main anti-armor armament was deleted, but the Mark XII was equipped with extremely capable anti-air/anti-missile defenses (in effect, it was an area defense system, as well as a bombardment unit). The vehicle was normally mated with a BAU (Bolo Ammunition Unit), a Mark XII with all offensive armament deleted to provide magazine space for multiple load-outs for the Mark XII's missile batteries. Although the Mark XII continued to carry a one-man crew, it was primarily designed for pre-loaded computerized battle plans. Weight was 500 tons, with a road speed 50 kph.

MARK XIII BOLO (2247):

The Mark XIII was essentially a Mark XII with main anti-armor armament restored. Although the main gun ate up almost 25 percent of the tonnage dedicated to magazine space in the Mark XIII, the Mark XIII's bombardment capability actually slightly exceeded that of the Mark XII with only minimal overall weight increases. This was made possible largely through improvements in fission technology (allowing a smaller power plant) and the first use of a flintsteel inner war hull under a much thinner durachrome sheath. The Mark XIII/B's weight of 565 tons held fairly constant in all models of the mark. Road speed was 50 kph in the XIII/B, rising to 75 in late-series models as suspension and power train improvements became available.

MARK XIV BOLO (2307):

The Mark XIV replaced the never entirely satisfactory laser "main gun" of earlier marks with the far more destructive "Hellbore" plasmagun. This 25cm weapon, originally designed for the Concordiat Navy's Magyar-class battlecruiser's main batteries, had a half-megaton/second energy output and, unlike the earlier Bolo laser cannon, was a marked improvement over any kinetic weapon of equivalent mass. In other respects, the Mark XIV was a "standard" reversion to a generalist design, made possible by advances in mag-bottle technology (which finally made fusion power a practical alternative to fission in Bolo design) and acceptance of a lighter indirect fire capability. Anti-missile defenses were now sufficient to render strategic bombardment impractical, so indirect fire was limited to tactical and theater applications. This permitted the use of smaller missiles which, in turn, allowed an increased magazine capacity without weight penalties. Even so, the Mark XIV/B was 28 percent heavier than the Mark XIII/K it replaced, although further power train and suspension upgrades prevented any loss of maneuverability or cross-country performance. Gradual improvements in sensor fits and fire control systems kept this mark in front-line service for approximately 90 years. Tactically, primary reliance now rested firmly upon pre-loaded computerized battle plans, but a single human crewman was routinely carried to respond to unanticipated threats. The Mark XIV/B's weight was 728 tons (rising to 900 in late-series models), and road speed hovered between 60 and 75 kph over the life of the mark.

MARK XV/BM BOLO (*Resartus*) (2396):

A quantum leap in Bolo technology, the Mark XV was the standardbearer of the Concordiat during humanity's greatest wave of interstellar expansion. Very few non-human species encountered during this period could match the Mark XV's capabilities; none could exceed them. This was the first Bolo which did not require an onboard human crewman, due to advances in cybernetics and secure communication links (first short-range subspace com capabilities), which permitted increasingly sophisticated computerized pre-battle planning coupled with unjammable remote human control to correct for unanticipated problems. Main armament was one 25cm Hellbore with line-of-sight capability, backed by laser cluster "gatling" infinite repeaters (total of fourteen in the Model B) and four 20cm howitzers in individual secondary turrets. The 25cm Hellbore remained incapable of engaging orbital targets from planets with atmosphere due to as yet unsolved attenuation and dissipation problems with the weapon's plasma bolt "packaging," but there were few planetary targets with which it could not deal. Tactical and theater bombardment capability was roughly equivalent to the Mark XIV's, but the Mark XV had no strategic bombardment capability. The Mark XV's six track systems each had an independent power train, and the vehicle carried both primary and secondary fusion plants. Cybernetics were divided between two totally independent command centers as protection against battle damage, and durachrome was wholly abandoned in favor of a much tougher flintsteel war hull. Early models of this mark saw the last use of anti-kinetic reactive armor. Major improvements in suspension were required to deal with unparalleled battle weights (1,500 tons in the Model B, rising to over 3,000 in the Model M), but road speed held constant at approximately 65 kph (with brief "sprint" capability of over 80 kph) over the life of this mark, although the "lightweight" Mark XV, Model L, EW platform, at barely 1,100 tons, was 37 percent faster. Cross-country speed was equivalent to road speed except in very rugged terrain. This mark enjoyed a very long, very stable evolutionary history (mainly because the Concordiat didn't run into anything a Mark XV couldn't handle).

MARK XV/R BOLO (*Horrendous*) (2626):

The Model R was the final variant of the Mark XV. Main armament was upgraded to one 50cm Hellbore (which, unlike earlier models' weapons, *could* engage spacecraft in low orbit even from within a planetary atmosphere), and ablative armor appliqués were fitted over the Model R's flintsteel war hull in light of increases in infantry and light-vehicle energy weaponry. The preceding Model Q had seen vastly upgraded EW capabilities and the first appearance of heuristic cybernetics designed to run continuous analyses of pre-loaded battle plans against actual battle conditions in order to suggest improvements to its distant human commander. Under express human pre-battle authorization, the Mark XV/Q and /R were capable of reconfiguring their battle plans on the move without further human input. Although not self-directed, the final models of the Mark XV gave a very good impersonation of a war machine which was. Weights climbed sharply—the Mark XV/R reached 5,000 tons—but maximum road speed held fairly constant at 65–70 kph, despite weight increases.

MARK XVI BOLO (*Retarius*) (2650):

The increasing size of the Mark XV led to a fresh attempt at specialized design, and the Mark XVI was, in effect, a "light" Mark XV. Main armament remained a 50cm Hellbore, but the infinite repeater batteries were reduced to a total of eight weapons and the howitzer armament was deleted. (As partial compensation, the Mark XVI replaced its laser infinite repeaters with ion-bolt projectors, with much greater ability to penetrate ablative armor, and received a six-gun battery of short-range breech-loading 20cm mortars to augment its anti-personnel clusters.) A complete ablative outer hull was adopted to replace previous appliqués, and cybernetics were equivalent to those of Mark XV/R. Weight fell to 3,600 tons, and road speed rose to 90 kph with short duration "sprints" of up to 100 kph possible. The Mark XVI formed the "light regiments" of the original Dinochrome Brigade.

MARK XVII BOLO (*Implacable*) (2650):

Introduced simultaneously with the Mark XVI, the Mark XVII was the "heavy" version of the same basic weapon system. Main armament was upgraded from a 50cm Hellbore to a 60cm weapon, and the ion-bolt infinite repeaters were increased to a total of fifteen (six each in two lateral batteries with a three-gun frontal battery in the glacis). The Mark XVI's mortars were deleted in favor of six 25cm howitzers and an increased missile armament. Weight increased to 6,500 tons, and maximum road speed dropped to 75 kph. The Mark XVII formed the "heavy regiments" of the original Dinochrome Brigade.

MARK XVIII BOLO (*Gladius*) (2672):

While the Mark XVI was more agile and easier to deploy than the Mark XVII, it proved less popular in combat than its companion mark because of its lighter offensive power. The Mark XVIII replaced both the XVI and XVII in relatively short order as the new "standard" Bolo in an attempt to combine the best features of both its immediate predecessors. As usual, the new vehicle went up in size and weight (late-model Mark XVIIIs approached 10,000 tons), and space-to-ground deployment became a problem. Main armament was the Mark XVII's 60cm Hellbore, but the infinite repeaters were reduced to twelve with the deletion of the bow battery (which had been found to compromise the structural integrity of the glacis plate). The Mark XVIII adopted a "sandwiched" hull: an outer ablative hull, then a thin hull of early-generation duralloy, and finally the flintsteel main war hull. The Mark XVIII also added a third fusion plant, which, with additional improvements in fire control, plasma containment technology, and weapons power, permitted its Hellbore to engage spacecraft even in medium orbit. The Mark XVIII formed the first "general purpose" regiments of the Dinochrome Brigade and, in successive models, remained first-line Concordiat equipment for over a century. Maximum road speed fell to 70 kph and maximum "sprint" speed fell to only 80 kph, but except in the roughest terrain, a Mark XVIII was as fast cross-country as on a road. (Of course, for vehicles as large and heavy as a Bolo, "roads" had long since become a purely relative concept.)

MARK XIX BOLO (*Intransigent*) (2790):

The Concordiat originally anticipated that the Mark XIX would remain first-line equipment for at least as long as the Mark XVIII, as it marked the first true qualitative improvement on the old Mark XV. The Mark XVI, XVII, and XVIII had been essentially up-gunned and up-armored Mark XVs; the Mark XIX was the first Bolo to mount mono-permeable, anti-kinetic battle screen as its first line of defense against projectile weapons and to incorporate the ability to convert a percentage of most types of hostile energy fire into useful power. In addition, the Mark XIX was accompanied into service by the Navy's new specialized armor transport: a light cruiser-sized vessel mated to a pair of Mark XIXs and capable of rough-field landings in almost any terrain (short of swamp or truly precipitous mountains). The transports were a vast improvement over the older independent assault pods, thus greatly simplifying the deployment problems experienced with the Mark XVII and XVIII. Improved generations of pods remained in service for almost four more centuries, particularly for battalion or larger level assaults. Main armament remained a 60cm Hellbore, but secondary armament was upgraded to sixteen ion-bolt infinite repeaters, backed up by 35mm gatling/railguns. The howitzer armament was once more suppressed in favor of eight 30cm breech-loading mortars, and the ablative outer hull was further augmented by a "plasma-shedding" ceramic tile appliqué. Weight soared to 13,000 tons, but road speed actually rose to 90 kph, with a "sprint" capability of over 120 kph.

MARK XX/B BOLO (*Tremendous*) (2796):

The reign of the Mark XIX was shorter than anyone had anticipated primarily because no one had anticipated the psychotronic breakthrough. (Or perhaps it would be more accurate to say that no one had expected the High Command to *accept* the psychotronic technology as quickly as it did.) The Mark XX *Tremendous* was the first truly self-directing (and self-aware) Bolo. Defensive capabilities remained unchanged from the Mark XIX, but the internal volume demands of the Mark XX's psychotronics forced the main armament to be downsized, and the Mark XIX's single 50cm Hellbore was replaced by two 30cm weapons, twin-mounted in a single turret. In addition, the Mark XX/M (unofficially referred to as the "Mosby") was a unique departure. Designed for independent deployment to raid an enemy's logistics and rear areas, the XX/M was essentially a refitted Mark XIV hull. The considerable mass of its first-generation Hellbore, along with its turret, was deleted, which freed up sufficient internal volume (barely) to permit installation of a somewhat less capable version of the Mark XX's psychotronics. Although self-aware, the Mark XXs had relatively simple (and bloodthirsty) personalities, and full self-awareness was specifically limited to battlefield applications. Except in carefully defined combat-related areas, the Mark XX's software suppressed its volition, effectively prohibiting it from taking *any* action without direct orders from designated human command personnel. Weight and speed data for the Mark XIX apply to the Mark XX. The Mark XX's great opponents were the Yavac heavies of the Deng, but not even the Yavac-A/4 could survive against a Mark XX Bolo without a numerical superiority of at least 3.25-to-1.

MARK XXI BOLO (*Terrible*) (2869):

Following the introduction of the Mark XX, a nomenclature policy was adopted under which new mark numbers were to be issued only to reflect substantial increases in psychotronic capability. (The new practice was temporarily abandoned with the Mark XXVII-Mark XXIX series, but resumed with the Mark XXX.) The Mark XXI actually proliferated into several sub-variants which would have received their own mark numbers under the old system, including yet another attempt at a "heavy" Bolo (which tipped the scales at over 20,000 tons and was never adopted for field use), and the "stealth" forward reconnaissance XXI/I. Mainstream Bolo development, however, followed the "standard" format, and the Mark XXI/B reverted to the single 60cm Hellbore main armament of the Mark XIX. The major advance lay in the enhanced computational speed of the mark's computers and improvements in the personality centers of successive models. Although still fringed about by inhibitory programming to control self-directed actions outside combat, the Mark XXI was much more capable *in* combat. This mark also saw the introduction of TSDS (Total Systems Data-Sharing) technology into the regiments of the Dinochrome Brigade. In practice, each unit of the regiment operated in battle as a single component of a multiunit awareness in a free-flow tactical link which combined the conclusions of *all* its Bolos to formulate future actions.

MARK XXII BOLO (*Thunderous*) (2890):

The Mark XXII saw both further advances in cybernetics and psychotronics and a considerable upgrade in firepower with the new "super" Hellbore, a 90cm weapon which increased its destructive output to a full two megatons/second. Secondary armament mirrored the Mark XXI's. The Mark XXII was also the first Bolo to mount an interplanetary-range subspace com, and, for the first time, the Navy modified *its* cybernetics to permit a Bolo's psychotronics to directly control the maneuvers and defensive systems of its armor transport spacecraft (now unmanned in combat) for assault insertions, which increased its chance of penetrating hostile defenses by an order of magnitude. The Mark XXII's kinetic battle screen showed a 36 percent increase in effectiveness over the Mark XXI's, and weight hovered around 14,000–15,000 tons for all models, with a top speed of 80 kph and a "sprint" capability of 120–135 kph.

MARK XXIII BOLO (*Invincibilis*) (2912):

The Mark XXIII followed quickly on the heels of the Mark XXII, largely as a result of worsening relations between the Concordiat and the Quern Hegemony. Although the Quern managed to achieve strategic surprise when they actually launched their attack, worsening Human-Quern relations between 2880 and 2918 had driven Bolo research at a breakneck pace. The original Mark XXIII was only a marginal improvement (in electronic terms) on the Mark XXII, but the main armament was doubled to a pair of 80cm "super" Hellbores in fore-and-aft turrets, and provision was made for quick conversion to the molecular circuitry whose early perfection the R&D bureaus anticipated. Secondary armament was also upgraded—to eighteen ion-bolt infinite repeaters in two nine-gun lateral batteries—and a new generation of battle screen was augmented by internal disrupter shielding around critical systems. The outbreak of the Quern Wars put a halt to major psychotronic research, as all efforts were bent upon design rationalization to aid in mass production, but the anticipated molecular circuitry appeared almost on schedule. Although it was not applied throughout, late-series Mark XXIIIs incorporated the new circuitry within their psychotronics, which enormously increased capability without increasing volume requirements. It was possible to restore the "secondary brain" feature to the Mark XXIII with no degradation in base capability, which made it much more resistant to battle damage. Despite its increased armament, the Mark XXIII, like the Mark XXII, hovered around the 15,000 ton mark, primarily because of the weight savings of its new molycircs and the shift to later-generation duralloy in place of flintsteel, which permitted armor thicknesses to be halved for the same standard of protection. Speeds remained largely unchanged from the Mark XXII.

MARK XXIV BOLO (*Cognitus*) (2961):

The Mark XXIV was the first genuinely autonomous Bolo. Previous Bolos had been self-directing on the tactical level, but the Mark XXIV, with a vastly improved personality center and id integration circuitry, was capable of *strategic* self-direction. For the first time, Bolos began to evolve a truly "human" level of individual personality, but the Mark XXIV's psychotronics continued to be hedged about with inhibitory safeguards. A much greater degree of non-combat autonomy was permitted, but the vehicle's psychotronics remained so designed as to deny it full use of its own capabilities outside Battle Reflex Mode. Impetus to decrease or even abolish those safeguards clearly began with this mark as it proved its reliability and flexibility, yet resistance would continue until Bolo Central reviewed the battle record of Unit 0075-NKE on Santa Cruz in 3025. The Mark XXIV retained the Mark XXIII's secondary armament but reverted to a single-turreted main armament (90cm "super" Hellbore). Despite the reduced main armament, weight fell only to the 14,000 ton mark, and speed remained roughly equivalent to that of the Mark XXII and Mark XXIII.

MARK XXV BOLO (*Stupendous*) (3001):

After forty T-years of experience with the Mark XXIV, even diehards conceded that many of the inhibitory software features which had been incorporated into every Bolo since the Mark XX were no longer justified. The most restrictive features were deleted from the Mark XXV, Model B, although it was not until the Model D (introduced in 3029) that virtually all inhibitions were suppressed. A core package of override programming was retained to restrict the volition of (or even, in the case of the so-called "Omega Worm," to destroy) a Mark XXV which went "rogue" as a result of battle damage or "senile" due to poor maintenance, but most of the restrictions which had required human approval for almost all non-battle decisions were progressively relaxed over the operational life of the Mark XXV, with a tremendous increase in efficiency. The practice of deploying totally independent Bolo brigades lay well in the future, but the Mark XXV's capabilities clearly pointed the way to them. The Mark XXV essentially duplicated the offensive and defensive systems of the Mark XXIV, yet further improvements in metallurgy and fusion technology dropped weight to 13,000 tons while normal speed rose to a maximum of 95 kph, though "sprint" speed remained unchanged.

MARK XXVI BOLO (*Monstrous*) (3113):

The Mark XXVI was the first Bolo to incorporate improved "hyper-heuristic" features based on the work of Major Marina Stavrakas. Armament, size, weight, and speed remained largely unchanged from the Mark XXV, but the Mark XXVI was capable of constructing a "learning model" in accelerated time. In some ways, this almost equated to precognition, in that the Mark XXVI could project changes in an enemy's tactical or strategic actions before even the *enemy* realized he intended to change them. The new systems also meant that, accompanied by a much improved ability to break hostile communications security, a Mark XXVI could actually invade an opponent's data net, access his computers, scan them for useful data, and (in some cases) even implant its own directions in those computers.

MARK XXVII–MARK XXIX BOLOS (3185–3190):

The Mark XXVII (*Invictus*), XXVIII (*Triumphant*), and XXIX (*Victorious*) marked a temporary reversion to the older practice of assigning mark numbers on the basis of armament and function rather than psychotronics technology. All three had essentially identical cybernetics, which concentrated on further improvements to their hyper-heuristic packages, but the Mark XXVIII and XXIX also incorporated a complete change-over to molecular circuitry throughout, aside from the power linkages to their energy armaments. All three of these marks were used in the new, independent brigades which replaced the old regiment structure of the original Dinochrome Brigade, but, in some ways, the units marked a reversion to the old "specialist" designs. All mounted the new 110cm "super" Hellbore (2.75 megatons/second), but the Mark XXVII was a "light," fast Bolo, with greatly reduced secondary armament, limited indirect fire capability, and a vastly improved sensor suite, intended to serve in a scouting and screening role for the independent brigades. (This function had been performed by light manned or unmanned vehicles, and the old Mark XXI/I, with psychotronic upgrades, remained in service for special forces applications. The new strategically self-directing Bolo brigades, however, required an integral scouting element, one not limited by "stealth" considerations and capable of fighting for information at need.)

The Mark XXVIII was the "generalist" of this trio of marks, with much the same armament as the old Mark XXIV, although that armament was even more deadly and effective under the control of the improved psychotronics of the newer units.

The Mark XXIX was an unabashedly "heavy" Bolo—indeed, it remained the heaviest Bolo ever deployed prior to the Mark XXXIII. It reverted to the twin Hellbore armament of the Mark XXIII (though still in 110cm caliber), coupled with a much enhanced indirect fire capability, and an integral logistics/maintenance function which it could extend to other units of the brigade. (The maintenance/repair function became standard in all succeeding Bolo designs.) The independent brigades normally consisted of four regiments of three 12unit battalions each: one of Mark XXVIIs, two of Mark XXVIIIs, and one of Mark XIXs. Weights for these Bolos were 11,000 tons (maximum normal speed 110 kph) for the Mark XXVII, 15,000 (maximum normal speed 90 kph) for the Mark XXVIII, and 24,000 (maximum normal speed 75 kph) for the Mark XXIX.

MARK XXX BOLO (*Magnificent*) (3231):

Introduced on the eve of the Human-Melconian "Last War," the Mark XXX was the direct descendant of the Mark XXVIII. The incorporation of counter-grav into the Mark XXX's suspension and power train went far towards offsetting the mobility penalties increasing weight had inflicted on preceding generations. The Mark XXX incorporated still further improvements to the hyper-heuristic capabilities of the Marks XXVII–XXIX, new dual-ply battle screen (which was not only more effective against kinetic weapons but also capable of absorbing at least some of the power of almost any energy weapon and diverting it to the Bolo's use), and a new and improved cold-fusion power plant. Weight dropped from the Mark XXIX's 24,000 tons to

17,000 and normal speed increased to 115 kph. For very short intervals, the Mark XXX could divert sufficient power to its counter-grav units to achieve actual free flight at velocities up to 500 kph, but could not operate its battle screen or internal disrupter shields or fire its main armament while doing so.

MARK XXXI BOLO (3303):

Over the course of the thirty-third century, the galaxy slid with ever increasing speed into the maw of the "Last War's" gathering violence, and Bolos after the Mark XXX did not receive the "type" names which had become customary with the Mark XV. The Mark XXXI was an enhanced Mark XXX with a main armament of one 200cm Hellbore (5 megatons/second). Secondary armament, though still referred to as "infinite repeaters," consisted of two lateral batteries of six 20cm Hellbores each, and many small-caliber, hyper-velocity projectile weapons were retained for close-in defense and anti-personnel use. Indirect fire capability was degraded in favor of the assault role, for which purpose the Mark XXXI's duralloy war hull was given an average thickness of 90 centimeters, rising to 1.5 meters for the glacis and turret faces. All secondary and tertiary weapons were mounted outside the "core hull" which protected the Mark XXXI's power plants and psychotronics, and last-generation internal disrupter shielding was used heavily. The Mark XXXI retained the counter-grav assist of the Mark XXX and, despite a weight increase to 19,000 tons, could match the preceding mark's speed.

MARK XXXII BOLO (3356):

The last Bolo whose year of introduction is known with certainty, the Mark XXXII was essentially a Mark XXXI with the added refinement of direct human-Bolo neural-psychotronic interfacing. Provision was also made for attachment of a counter-grav unit sufficient, under emergency conditions, to permit the Bolo to make an assault landing without benefit of transport. Offensive and defensive systems were comparable to those of the Mark XXXI. The Mark XXXII was the final version of the "standard" Bolo.

MARK XXXIII BOLO (?):

The last—and largest—Bolo introduced into service. The Mark XXXIII weighed no less than 32,000 tons and mounted a main armament of three independently-turreted 200cm Hellbores with a secondary armament of sixteen 30cm Hellbore infinite repeaters in two lateral batteries. Equipped with a very sophisticated indirect fire system, the sheer firepower of the Mark XXXIII was a reversion to the old siege unit thinking, though it was normally referred to as a *planetary* siege unit, not merely a continental one. No one knows how many Mark XXXIIIs were actually built, but official planning called for them to be deployed in independent brigades of 24 units each. Despite the increase in weight, speed remained equivalent to the Mark XXXI, and the Mark XXXIII's *internal* counter-grav could supply the assault landing capability for which the Mark XXXII had required an auxiliary unit.

BOLO ARMAMENT

Bolo Mark	Year	Weight	Road Speed	Sprint Speed
Mark I	2000	150	80	80
Mark II	2015	194	80	80
Mark III	2018	300	50	50
Mark IV	2116	210	60	60
Mark V	2160	198	80	80
Mark VI	2162	238	80	80
Mark VII	2163	348	40	40
Mark VIII	2209	225	65	85
Mark XIX	2209	400	57	57
Mark X	2235	350	70	70
Mark XI	2235	350	70	70
Mark XII	2240	500	50	50
Mark XIII	2247	565	50-75	50-75
Mark XIV	2307	728-900	60-75	60-75
Mark XV/B	2396	1,500	65	85
Mark XV/L		1,100	89	116
Mark XV/M		3,000	65	85
Mark XV/R	2626	5,000	75	95
Mark XVI	2650	3,600	90	100
Mark XVII	2650	6,500	75	88
Mark XVIII	2672	10,000	70	80
Mark XIX	2790	13,000	90	120
Mark XX	2796	*as Mk XIX*	*as Mk XIX*	*as Mark XIX*
Mark XXI	2869		Varies	Varies
Mark XXII	2890	15,000	80	135
Mark XXIII	2912	15,000	80	148

Main Armament	Secondary Armament	Indirect Fire	Self-Aware?
1 150mm DSFSLRP	point def/AP gatlings	None	No
1 150mm DSFSLRP	4 InfRpt railguns	None	No
1 150mm DSFSLRP	8 InfRpt railguns	Tac/Theater	No
4 155mm howitzers	Light VLS missile system		
1 165mm railgun	6 InfRpt railguns VLS missile system	Strategic	No
1 190mm railgun	12 60mm gatling InfRpt	None	No
Heavy VLS missile system	14 60mm gatling InfRpt	Strategic	No
1 200mm railgun	14 75mm gatling InfRpt VLS missile system	Strategic	No
1 170mm railgun 4 150mm howitzers	12 laser InfRpt	Tactical	No
VLS missile system 4 18cm howitzers	12 laser InfRpt	Strategic	No
1 laser cannon	12 laser InfRpt	None	No
1 18cm railgun	12 laser InfRpt	None	No
Heavy VLS missile system	12 laser InfRpt	Strategic	No
1 laser cannon Heavy VLS missile system	12 laser InfRpt 4 15cm BL mortars	Strategic	No
1 25cm Hellbore	12 laser InfRpt VLS missile system	Tac/Theater	No
1 25cm Hellbore 4 20cm howitzers	14 gatling laser InfRpt VLS missile system	Tac/Theater	No
none	point def/AP only	None	No
1 35cm Hellbore 4 20cm howitzers	16 gatling laser InfRpt 8 18cm BL mortars VLS missile system	Tac/Theater	No
1 50cm Hellbore 4 20cm howitzers	12 gatling laser InfRpt 4 18cm BL mortars VLS missile system	Tactical	No
1 50cm Hellbore	8 ion-bolt InfRpt 6 20cm BL mortars	Tactical	No
1 60cm Hellbore 6 25cm howitzers	15 ion-bolt InfRpt Heavy VLS missile system	Strategic	No
1 60cm Hellbore 6 25cm howitzers	12 ion-bolt InfRpt Heavy VLS missile system	Strategic	No
1 60cm Hellbore	16 ion-bolt InfRpt 8 30cm BL mortars	Tactical	No
2 30cm Hellbores	as Mark XIX	Tactical	Limited
1 60cm Hellbore + varying VLS capability	16 ion-bolt InfRpt 4-8 30cm BL mortars	Varies	Limited
1 90cm Hellbore	16 ion-bolt InfRpt VLS missile system 6-8 30cm BL mortars	Tac/Theater	Limited
2 80cm Hellbores	18 ion-bolt InfRpt VLS missile system 6 30cm BL mortars	Tactical	Limited

Bolo Mark	Year	Weight	Road Speed	Sprint Speed
Mark XXIV	2961	14,000	80	148
Mark XXV	3001	13,000	95	150
Mark XXVI	3113	13,000	95	150
Mark XXVII	3185	11,000	110	150
Mark XXVIII	3186	15,000	90	135
Mark XXIX	3190	24,000	75	110
Mark XXX	3231	17,000	115	500
Mark XXXI	3303	19,000	115	500
Mark XXXII	3356	21,000	115	500
Mark XXXIII	????	32,000	105	500

Main Armament	Secondary Armament	Indirect Fire	Self-Aware?
1 90cm Hellbore	18 ion-bolt InfRpt VLS missile system 6 30cm BL mortars	Tactical	Autonomous
1 90cm Hellbore	18 ion-bolt InfRpt VLS missile system 6 30cm BL mortars	Tactical	Autonomous
as Mark XXV	*as Mark XXV*	Tactical	Autonomous
1 110cm Hellbore	10 ion-bolt InfRpt 6 30cm BL mortars	Tactical	Autonomous
1 110cm Hellbore	18 ion-bolt InfRpt VLS missile system 4 30cm BL mortars	Tac/Theater	Autonomous
2 110cm Hellbores Heavy VLS missile system	20 ion-bolt InfRpt 8 40cm BL mortars	Strategic	Autonomous
as Mark XVIII	*as Mark XVIII*	Tac/Theater	Autonomous
1 200cm Hellbore	12 20cm Hellbores Light VLS missile system	Tactical	Autonomous
as Mark XXXI	*as Mark XXXI*	Tactical	Autonomous
3 200cm Hellbores 4 240cm howitzers	14 20cm Hellbores 10 40cm BL mortars Heavy VLS missile system	Strategic	Autonomous

GENERAL
ARMAMENT NOTES

In addition to the weapons listed, all Bolo secondary armaments include small-caliber high-velocity projectile weapons for
close-in defense and anti-personnel fire. All Bolos after Mark
V also mounted multiple-shot flechette anti-personnel "clusters"
with progressively heavier flechettes.

Any Bolo secondary gun with anti-armor capability was always
referred to as an "infinite repeater," although the term originally
applied only to a small- to medium-caliber projectile weapon
with a high rate of fire and large magazine space.

Like most of their other weapon systems, the vertical launch
system missile outfits of Bolos evolved tremendously over the
course of the Bolo's design history. The original Mark III VLS
consisted of only 60 non-reloadable cells, although more than
one missile might be loaded per cell if they were small enough.
By the time of the Mark XIX, the VLS consisted of reload-
able, magazine-fed cells, and all future Bolo VLSs followed
that pattern. The term "light" or "heavy" used to describe a
VLS refers to (1) the number of cells (and thus salvo density)
and (2) the VLS magazine capacity, not to the weight or size
of missiles thrown.

The breech-loading mortars fitted to most Bolos after the
Mark XIII might be considered automatic weapons, as their rate
of fire averaged from 8 to 12 rounds per minute. The Mark

XXXIII's 15cm BLMs had a maximum effective range of 3,000 meters; the 40cm BLMs of the Mark XXIX and Mark XXXIII had a maximum effective range of 9.75 kilometers.